Factory Girls

Also by Michelle Gallen

Big Girl, Small Town

Factory Girls

Michelle Gallen

JOHN MURRAY

First published in Great Britain in 2022 by John Murray (Publishers)
An Hachette UK company

1

Factory Girls receives financial assistance from the Arts Council

A CIP catalogue record for this title is available from the British Library

Hardback ISBN 9781529386264
Trade Paperback ISBN 9781529386271
eBook ISBN 9781529386295

Typeset in Sabon MT by Manipal Technologies Limited

Printed and bound in Great Britain by Clays Ltd, Elcograf S.p.A.

John Murray policy is to use papers that are natural, renewable and recyclable products and
made from wood grown in sustainable forests. The logging and manufacturing processes are
expected to conform to the environmental regulations of the country of origin.

John Murray (Publishers)
Carmelite House
50 Victoria Embankment
London EC4Y 0DZ

www.johnmurraypress.co.uk

For factory workers everywhere

'They let you dream just to watch 'em shatter
You're just a step on the boss man's ladder
But you got dreams he'll never take away'

Dolly Parton, 'Nine To Five'

'We are gods in the chrysalis'

Elbert Hubbard quoted in
How to Win Friends and Influence People

Thursday, 2 June 1994

74 days until results

Maeve Murray was just eighteen years old when she first met Andy Strawbridge but she knew he was a fucker the minute she laid eyes on him. In fairness, she'd expected it. He was an Englishman who drove into the town for work. Nobody knew him, but everyone knew of him. She'd heard the stories about him taking his pick of the factory girls, offering them lifts home where he'd park his Jag up some lonely lane so he could get a blowjob from whoever was belted into the front passenger seat. She'd tried to listen to the stories with only one ear, for she knew the people spouting that shite about Andy would've said the same of Father Goan, who wasn't fit to find his mickey for a pish.

But when Maeve stood face to face with Andy Strawbridge in his office in the factory, she knew every last word she'd heard about him was true – and was probably only half the story. She'd come prepared, slouching in like she already worked there, with her hair scraped into a ponytail and not a lick of make-up on her face. She'd dressed in baggy grey joggers and one of the fleeces her mam bought by the dozen in the Primark sales. She looked like a lump of dropped dough in that get-up.

But Andy still looked at her like he'd fuck her. Like he'd *already* fucked her.

Maeve stuck her hand out at him. 'Hi, Mr Strawbridge. I'm Maeve Murray.'

Andy leaned back in his chair, smirking, his crotch bulging in the fanciest pair of trousers Maeve'd ever laid eyes on. She dragged her gaze back up to his face. He'd clamped a pen between his teeth the way Hannibal off *The A-Team* clenched a cigar. Now Maeve understood why Maria McCanny, Dervla Daly and the rest of them talked shite about Andy Strawbridge. But she didn't get why nobody'd warned her that he was a ride. Then she realised her hand was still stuck out and Andy had no intention of shaking it. She took a massive reddener, feeling even the cheeks of her arse glow.

'Well, Maeve Murray. What can I do for you?'

The snotty English accent woke Maeve up. *Fuck you*, she thought – *fuck you and the horse you rode in on*. She sat down, took out her CV and tossed it on his desk. Then she took out a fag and lit up like she was the frigging boss.

'I'm looking into the factory for a summer job. My CV will tell you everything ye need to know. If you want a reference, ye can chat to the principal out in St Jude's.'

Andy didn't touch her CV. Instead, he sat licking her with his eyes.

Maeve was well used to bucks his age gawping at her down the town, eyeing her up in the pubs. But most fellas that deep into their thirties were fat and filthy. Andy was in great shape. And he knew it.

'Tell me. What's not in the CV?'

Maeve blew a tunnel of smoke at his desk, playing for time, mulling over what she thought she knew about herself. She'd a suspicion she had terrible taste in men. She hoped she was smarter than she looked and more sophisticated than she sounded. She'd a notion she was good at blowjobs – a performance she'd perfected early in order to distract fellas from the Holy Grail of her Blessed Virginity. She dreamed in secret of writing for a fancy magazine in a swanky office in London by day and living by night with a depressed, dark-eyed musician who'd only feel alive when he was alone with her. She couldn't wait to get out of the shitty wee town she'd grown up in and had learned everything she needed to know about burning bridges from her sister, Deirdre.

She knew it'd be a bad idea to share too much of this information with Andy Strawbridge. 'My A-level results aren't in my CV yet. When they come out in August, I'm getting the frig out of this place.'

Andy leaned his chair back to tipping point. His shirt was open at the neck. Maeve's eyes jumped from button to button, following them like stepping stones all the way down. He caught her looking. Of course he did.

'You're very sure of yourself, aren't you?'

Maeve realised there and then that Andy Strawbridge wasn't great at reading women.

'Sure that you'll get good results,' he said. 'That you'll get what you want.'

Maeve raised an eyebrow at him – a look she'd spent years practising in the mirror – and she lied. 'I usually do.'

Andy said nothing for what felt like a long time, then tossed his pen onto the table. 'So tell me. Why should I bother hiring and training you if you're going to walk out of my door as soon as you get your results?'

Maeve parroted what her mam'd said over breakfast. 'I'd say your labour doesn't come much cheaper than teenage girls still living with their mammies.'

Andy narrowed his eyes, then stretched into a yawn. The sound of the leather chair creaking under his arse did something funny to Maeve's lady garden. She crossed her legs and squeezed her thighs together to try and smother the feeling, which was a mistake.

'You can start Monday. Go down to Mary in the office. She'll fill you in on what to expect.'

Maeve mashed her fag out in the ashtray like she was used to smoking only half a cigarette instead of sucking it right down to the butt. Then she stood up and looked Andy dead in the eye. 'See you Monday.'

'If you're lucky, Ms Murray, you'll see me.'

Nobody had ever called Maeve 'Mizz Murray' before. Teachers used 'Miss Murray' when they were sneering at her. So did neighbours who knew she was a daughter of Seán Murray, but couldn't remember if she was *the poor dead one* or *that girl who needs manners put on her*. Maeve didn't know what 'Mizz Murray' meant, but she suspected Andy was being a dick. She grabbed her bag and walked out.

When the spring-hinged office door snapped shut behind her, she gulped for air the way you do after a low punch in the guts. But the fear that Andy was listening sent her clattering down the stairs towards the safety of Caroline and Aoife.

Maeve knocked on the office door and said, 'Hiyas.'

Mary growled, 'C'mon in,' without turning her head. She was hunched over a fag behind a desk piled high with folders and paperwork. Fabric samples, shirts and patterns lay in heaps on the chairs and floor. Mary's office, like her cardigan, had the whiff of being occupied by a woman who was long past caring.

Maeve sat down beside a row of mucky green filing cabinets that put her in mind of British soldiers – hulking awkwardly, no matter where they were stationed. Caroline sat opposite, tugging at her curly red hair and frowning at a form. Aoife held a clipboard on her lap and had her legs crossed, with one foot bobbing as if she was performing at a feis. Maeve had made Aoife go in to Andy first, because she was giving her the bokes with the way she was dressed in a beige skirt suit and a lacy cream blouse.

She was wearing a fucking *blouse*.

Maeve knew by the cut of Aoife that her mother had dressed her. But the awful thing was that the whole outfit suited her, from her blush-pink click-clack heels, all the way up to her naturally blonde chignon.

Aoife.

They'd learned in Irish class that 'Aoife' meant 'pleasant radiance' while 'Maeve' meant 'she who intoxicates' (which

4

betrayed just how much Irish Maeve's parents had understood at her christening back in 1976).

Mary eyed Maeve as though she was a suspicious package. 'Did he give ye a start?'

'Aye. He said to come down tae ye for the paperwork.'

Mary sighed and got to her feet. She was of that last generation where first-born girls were called Mary, and the girls who came after were Bridget, Kathleen, Margaret, Elizabeth or Anne. She'd had the same grey hair, brown NHS glasses, blue cardigan and sharp tongue for as long as Maeve had known her and had worked in fits and starts around the town: she'd done stints in the chemist, the school canteen, the solicitor's and a few shops. But Mary never lasted anywhere. Maeve's mam said it was because she'd missed her true calling when they'd shut the Magdalene laundries.

Mary picked up a form and glared at it as if it was filthy with sin. 'This is an equal opportunities form. Ye're required to fill it in but ye can rest assured it's anonymous and confidential. No one'll ever know what you've put down.' She grabbed another, longer form. 'These are the factory forms. They'll give us the measure of ye.' She pinioned the forms to a clipboard that she passed to Maeve. 'Ah'm away out fer a cuppa tay. Get them done before ah'm back.'

Maeve read the equal opportunities questions regarding sex, ethnicity, religion and sexual orientation and ticked the 'Male', 'Black', 'Jewish' and 'Lesbian' boxes. Then she wrote her name, address, age, marital status, number of kids and next of kin on the factory forms, creating the sort of dossier that she knew paramilitaries often battered office workers to get hold of. 'That's it!' she said, tossing her clipboard onto Mary's desk. 'That's me signed up as a factory girl.'

'Me, too,' Aoife said, gently placing her clipboard on top of Maeve's. 'Though it's just for the summer. We'll be university students by September, won't we?'

Maeve's breath caught in her chest. She wasn't sure that she'd become a proper student; that she'd swap the town for

London and escape the dole for a career as a journalist. Only the high grey factory walls felt real.

Mary slapped back into the room in her Scholls, clutching a mug of tea so strong Maeve could smell it over the reek of stale fags. 'Are yeez done?'

Caroline – 'Female', 'White', 'Roman Catholic' and 'Heterosexual' – placed her clipboard on the table.

'Right,' Mary said, collapsing into her seat. 'Yeez'll work a forty-hour week over four days.'

Maeve remembered her da working five-day weeks when he was in the pig factory. Great pay he'd got for that. But the fifty hours of work on top of ten hours sat packed into a smoky factory bus morning and evening eventually took its toll. She was glad she'd only be working over the road from home, doing a short week in a factory that didn't have enough work stacked up to sustain a full week.

'Clock in's on the dot of eight each morning,' Mary continued. 'Clock out's at half six. Ye'll get a fifteen-minute break morning and afternoon. Lunch's half an hour. Yer basic wage is seventy quid a week.'

All the chat of clocks and hours and breaks and bells did frig all for Maeve. But the mention of money put a firework up her arse. Seventy quid, week in, week out, for the thirteen weeks between now and the day she'd move to London. She pictured the CDs, clothes and books she'd be able to buy. She tried not to count how many days the same money'd buy her in London.

'Overtime's by arrangement only – ye'll get nothing extra for hanging your arse over the toilet after the last bell. I work out yer wages and bonus on Thursday evening. Youse come in Friday morning tae lift yer cheques. Any questions?'

Maeve waited for Aoife to pipe up. Aoife *always* piped up.

'What'll we be doing?'

'Well, ye were born yesterday if ye don't know we make shirts,' Mary said. 'Andy decides who does what. Anything else?' She glared, daring them to speak. 'Well, if youse are done ye can head on and let me finish my tay in peace.'

They chorused, 'Thanks a million,' and left.

As Maeve walked through the factory gates arm in arm with Caroline and Aoife, she got the feeling Andy was watching them from behind the blinds of his office window. And she liked that.

Maeve bagged the window seat in what had once been McHugh's Shoes – a dim, damp runt of a shop that'd been euthanised by a bomb. After the dust settled, the McHughs had boarded up the broken windows, painted BOMB SALE in red letters on the plywood and reduced the stock to next to nothing because the shoes were full of glass. Maeve's mam, being Maeve's mam, had said there wouldn't be a hate wrong with the shoes after she'd got at them with the hoover and a pair of tweezers, so she'd raided everyone's piggy banks and the Christmas savings biscuit tin and bought up as much footwear as she could carry home.

When the McHughs got their compensation, they reneged on the shoe selling and set up the town's first café. On opening day Maeve's mam had asked what type of an eejit would buy a cuppa tay for thirty pence when ye could make thirty cups at home for the same price? What fool'd pay fifty pence for a bun on a plate when ye could buy six in the shop for forty-nine pence? But after a few weeks, McHugh's Brews was bunged with wee women murmuring over an iced bun and tearing the arse out of a pot of tea. Caroline's mam'd eventually coaxed Maeve's mam in the door by telling her the café had all the good of a wake but without the weight of a corpse sitting under your nose.

It also had Philomena Maguire. 'What are youse having, cuddies?'

Philomena – who was no spring chicken – was wearing a gingham blouse, cut-off denim shorts, forty denier American Tan tights and a don't-fucken-try-me face. Philomena's 'uniform' wasn't what lured the town's middle-aged housewives

7

into the café, but it did give legs to the rumour that the male proprietor of McHugh's Brews had a notion for Daisy Duke.

'Tea for three, two iced buns and a wee fruit scone, please, Phil.'

'Right youse are, cuddies. Ah'll be back over in a minute.'

As soon as Phil left, Maeve leaned in close to Aoife and Caroline. 'Well? What's the verdict on Handy Andy?'

Aoife looked confused. 'Andy? He's alright, I suppose.'

Caroline gleeked around before speaking. 'I know he's a chancer, but he's not bad for his age!'

'He'd lovely hands,' Aoife said. 'Nice clean nails.'

Of course Aoife'd noticed Andy's nails, while Maeve'd been distracted by his crotch. 'I get the feeling Andy's never had to get his hands dirty,' she said.

She'd timed Aoife's interview: it'd lasted ten minutes. Afterwards, Aoife'd clopped out and stuck her thumb up. Maeve'd smiled back with her hands jammed firmly in her pockets. Aoife was really fucking smart, but she was a complete muppet. 'Did Andy not float your boat?'

Aoife shook her head. Maeve sighed. If Aoife fell into a barrel of cocks she'd come out sucking her own thumb. She'd no bother attracting fellas: she was a magnet for gentle, sensitive chaps – the long-haired, skinny-dicked boys who sometimes assembled at Aoife's house wearing Pantera or Metallica T-shirts. Maeve liked practising her snogging on them, though for fellas who claimed to be into Satan they were awful drips – when she squeezed them the right way between her thighs, they came in their pants.

Maeve doubted Andy'd be so easily pleased. 'So, how'd your interview go?'

'Andy looked over my CV and asked a few questions,' Aoife said in a voice as bright as a shop bell.

Maeve wanted to spit nails in Aoife's shiny wee face. She hated how stuff worked differently for her and Aoife. Aoife came from money. She was the sort of pupil teachers dreamed of. The sort they said would *do well for herself* (as if the doing well was all Aoife's own work, and not bolstered by living in a fancy house with loving parents who could afford stuff like piano lessons, eating in fancy restaurants, holidays abroad, and patience). 'What sort of questions?'

'Oh, he wanted to know where I'd applied. He said he studied engineering science at Oxford but prefers to practise management. I told him I was hoping to read law in Cambridge but I've Oxford down as my second choice.'

Maeve remembered the sound of Aoife's heels click-clacking down the metal staircase. Then Caroline'd got to her feet and plunged into Andy's office. Maeve'd played D:Ream's 'Things Can Only Get Better' on Deirdre's old Walkman to distract herself. But Caroline'd barrelled back out of Andy's office, all pink and sweaty, before the song was over. They'd both flinched as the office door sprang shut behind her.

'And how was Handy Andy when you were in with him, Caroline?' Maeve asked.

Caroline shrugged and started to shred her napkin.

'Well, he didn't really go over my CV much. He asked about my attendance at school, ye know – sick days and that. He wanted tae know which estate I'm from and I said that me and you come from Riverview.'

Maeve hated that Andy knew where she lived. The houses in their estate had got indoor toilets installed in the council's last big upgrade, but living there was still only a step up from squatting in the caravan site out the back of the chapel.

'Was Andy civil enough when you were in yourself, Maeve?'

She remembered how Caroline had mouthed *Good luck* at her as she'd stuffed her headphones and Walkman into her bag. She remembered putting her hand on the door to Andy's office. She wanted to tell Aoife and Caroline what had happened after that, to shock them with her cheek and Andy's bullshit. But she couldn't. She didn't want Aoife to know that Andy hadn't bothered to read her CV. She didn't want Caroline telling her that Andy'd fuck her sideways if she didn't keep her eyes peeled. Andy made Maeve feel grubby. She knew he could treat her any way he liked and get

9

away with it. Her factory job – like Philomena Maguire's waitressing work – had an unwritten duty that'd earn her no overtime or bonuses: stay out of arm's reach of your boss.

The next morning, Maeve perched on the windowsill outside the shop, waiting for Aoife and Caroline. She'd begged them to get her Coke and crisps because she was buzzing too much to walk around the shop saying, 'Hiya,' or 'Och, hello,' or 'So, what's the craic?' to whoever was going about their business.

She was torn between wanting to preserve the town forever, exactly as it was that morning, or taking fifty pounds of Semtex and blowing it all to smithereens.

All of a sudden there were no empty weeks stretching out ahead of Maeve, no long lie-ins spent staring at Deirdre's empty bed, with fuck all to get up for. She wouldn't waste hours dandering around the town broke or mucking about down by the river. The summer that'd yawned before her, dank with boredom, was now sliced up into work days, while her free time fluttered with bank notes. She'd soon be like the older girls she'd watched for years heading for the factory, smoking fags and carrying handbags instead of rucksacks bulging with homework. Just one thing felt the same: the ticking time bomb of her exam results, primed to go off in August.

Maeve trembled, then reached into her bag for a fag. She lit up, blowing smoke at the blue sky stretching out of reach above her head. That's when she noticed the sign above the shop.

2 BEDS TO LET
JP DEVLIN
78234

Maeve chanted, *Seveneight-twothreefour, seveneight-twothreefour* over and over in her head until Aoife and Caroline emerged. She pointed up at the sign.

'To let?' Aoife said. 'So what?'

'It's about time I got a place of my own,' Maeve replied, stubbing her fag out.

'Can you afford it?'

'Not on my own. But *we* could afford it.' Maeve linked arms with Caroline.

'Oh, God, ah don't know about that now, Maeve!'

She dragged Caroline over to the phone box and opened the door. A smell of pish and chips stung her nose. She kicked a soggy takeaway out the door, then checked the receiver for gum before putting it to her ear. The line purred and crackled.

'Aoife?'

'Yep?'

'Lend us 20p.'

Maeve dropped Aoife's coin into the slot, then punched JP's number into the keypad.

'Seveneight-twothreefour, JP Devlin's office. Louise speaking, how can I help you?'

Bang on half twelve the girls arrived outside the shop to meet JP. At ten to one, they were still waiting. Suddenly the dogs up the road started to howl. The hairs on Maeve's neck prickled and her nipples stiffened. 'Brits,' she hissed, giving Caroline a dig in the ribs.

Caroline perked up like an enthusiastic puppy. 'Where? Where?' she panted.

Maeve muttered, 'Quit staring!' then nodded in the direction of the patrol. Her and Caroline crossed their arms under their diddies for a bit of a boost. But Aoife just stood gawking at the soldiers with her mouth hanging open as if she was one of the holy Americans who were flown in on peace trips from time to time. Maeve watched the patrol out of the corner of her eye, doing her best to look indifferent with just a hint of hostility. A few of the soldiers winked like they were doing something dangerously sexy, while one of the younger, cockier bucks aimed his gun at them – a move that reminded Maeve of the way Header Doherty used to wave his dick around in class before Fatty Dolan'd got him into the special school.

Maeve eyed the oldest Brit. He was a hardy fucker who looked like the sort of gristle her Granny Murray liked to chew on after a good Sunday roast. You could tell by the way he handled his gun that he'd tucked several tours of duty under his belt. Brits like him didn't play around at the winking-aiming shite: they were the ones to watch.

The dogs tailed the soldiers down the street at a safe distance, snarling and barking. The patrol stopped just out of earshot, each of them crouching in a different vantage point so they could get a good look around. Caroline released a long, hot breath. 'Phwoar! Did you see the black fella?'

Maeve cringed. Caroline was always pure thrilled when she saw a black or brown face under the camouflage face paint, because everyone in the town was blindingly white. But it annoyed Maeve to see coloured fellas in the British army. It felt like they were on the wrong side. She wished they'd join forces to fight for freedom, instead of displaying as much sense as their collective ancestors, who'd been too busy tearing lumps out of each other to stop the English from stealing their lands.

'I think it's sad,' Aoife said, gazing at the Brit squatting nearest to them.

Maeve got a bad feeling that Aoife was about to let the side down. 'What's sad?'

'The way the UK military recruits.'

'What are you shiting on about?'

'The UK's the only country in Europe that routinely recruits minors.'

Maeve closed her eyes. Aoife was off on one. 'And? So what?'

'They recruit boys from the age of sixteen. And anyone who signs up at sixteen or seventeen has to serve until they're twenty-two.'

Caroline stared at the Brit on the corner, her lust liquifying. 'Jesus. Imagine becoming a soldier before you're allowed to drink or see a dirty movie.'

'And imagine being stuck in the army for *six* years!' Aoife said, as if she was auditioning for an Amnesty International documentary. 'The British army's recruitment policy is the same as Zimbabwe's, Iran's and North Korea's!'

Maeve didn't like where Aoife was headed. On the one hand, she was comparing the UK to places run by dictators, which was fair enough; but on the other, she seemed to be saying that the dickheads swaggering around their town with guns needed some kind of protection, which was a bit of a headwreck. 'Aoife,' Maeve said. 'If there's a North Korea, there must be a South Korea. Kind of like East and West Germany, right?'

Aoife nodded.

'So. Any time I hear of a country using the points of the compass in its name, I know there's a border. And borders need soldiers. The younger they are, the more gullible they are. That's why the Brits give kids guns. The IRA does it too. Because it works.'

Aoife frowned. 'I'm not sure I'd say "this" is working for anyone in particular.'

The Brit on the corner lifted his rifle and peered at them through his gunsight. Maeve gave him the finger. Which was, of course, the exact moment JP pulled up in his BMW.

'Fuck,' Maeve said, dropping her hand.

JP got out and leaned on the roof of his car, appraising the girls like they were cattle at the mart. Maeve tried to look demure, a look she hadn't practised since her First Holy Communion.

'Miss Murray. Miss Jackson. And Miss O'Neill?'

It was no shock that JP had already sniffed out who they belonged to, or that he was surprised to see Aoife.

'Mr Devlin, how are you?' Maeve said.

'Grand, grand,' JP replied, squinting up at the misty sun.

She seized the opportunity to demonstrate her maturity by commenting on the weather. 'Well, sure, it's a grand day, anyway.'

JP blinked down at Maeve. She felt him take the measure of her, from her scuffed bomb-sale boots to her cracked leather jacket.

'It's not so bad now, altogether,' he said, begrudgingly, letting Maeve know that the day hadn't quite met *his* personal standards for the title of 'grand'. 'So youse want to take a look at this place?'

'We do, aye.'

'And who is it that's looking?' JP asked, glancing at Aoife. 'Not all three of youse, surely.'

'No, Mr Devlin. Just myself and Caroline. We got a start in the factory and this place'd be very handy for us.'

'The factory, eh? Under Andy Strawbridge?'

Maeve nodded, trying not to picture herself under Andy Strawbridge.

JP tossed his head back in judgement but said no more. He locked his car, then walked towards the flat. He paused in front of the snarl of litter in the doorway and fingered a bundle of keys. Then he unlocked the door and loped up the narrow staircase with Maeve close behind him. He stopped abruptly at the top of the stairs to search for the next key. Maeve stopped awkwardly near to his buttocks, so she turned her head and held her breath to avoid the whiff of JP's arse crack.

After he eventually entered the flat, she leaned against the door frame, taking a couple of deep breaths.

'Bedroom one,' JP said, pointing. 'Kitchen. Bathroom. Bedroom two. And your living room.'

The flat smelt of fresh paint but was carpeted with what looked like grey pubic hair glued onto a bed of thick black mould. The first bedroom sat in the shadow of the house opposite and was crammed with a stained-pine double bed, wardrobe and chest of drawers. Maeve left Caroline there, checking under the bed, while she took a quick look at the kitchen. There was no window, but it had the basics: a microwave, washing machine, cooker, toaster and kettle. Next she ducked into the bathroom. It was so small Maeve reckoned she could vomit in the sink while shitting in the toilet.

When she walked into the second bedroom she knew right away it was going to be hers. It was lit by a big, west-facing window. A cheap wardrobe slumped heavily against a chest of drawers, and the double bed already had a defeated look about it. But its main selling point was what it didn't have: a doll-sized statue of the Infant Child of Prague, and her dead sister's empty bed.

The living room was occupied by a saggy sofa, two hardy-looking armchairs, and a coffee table that seemed to have survived an interrogation that'd left it knock-kneed and scarred with cigarette burns.

JP stood at the window, staring down at his BMW with an expression similar to the Virgin Mary gazing at the baby Jesus. Maeve looked out of the window. Strawbridge & Associates Shirt Factory squatted right across the road. The blinds were down in Andy's office, but she could see onto the empty factory floor. In the distance, a squall of rain was bearing down on the town, blotting out the hills that dipped and rose like waves all the way to the Atlantic Ocean.

'So, Mr Devlin, how much is it?'

JP tore his eyes away from his car. 'Twenty-five quid a week. I need two weeks in advance and two weeks' deposit. Heating and light's on top.'

Maeve did the sums. They needed a hundred pounds.

'No parties,' JP said. 'No drugs.'

Maeve fired him a wounded as-if-I-would stare – instead of the more accurate I-friggen-wish look. 'Does the fireplace work?'

'Wouldn't chance it.'

'Can we put pictures up?'

'Blu Tack. No nails.'

Next door, Aoife flushed the toilet and switched on the shower. Then she padded into the living room in her socks. 'Mr Devlin.'

'Miss O'Neill.'

'I was wondering how this place is heated?'

'All-electric Economy 7 heating. The storage heaters and water tank heat up overnight.'

'Dear enough to run.'

'Easy to maintain.'

Aoife and JP nodded at each other, as if they'd played a respectable tennis volley. Then Aoife turned to Maeve. 'The water pressure's not great. Want to see?'

At home Aoife had what Mrs O'Neill called an 'on sweet' bathroom. She'd never queued up for what passed as a shower in Maeve's house, where the water pressure and temperature were comparable to Grandad Murray's urine flow before they'd sorted his prostate problem.

'I'm sure it'll be grand,' Maeve said before retreating to the kitchen. Caroline ventured in after her, then opened a cupboard door as if it were booby-trapped. Suddenly a bed started creaking rhythmically. Caroline clapped her hand over her mouth and stared at Maeve, horrified.

A few seconds after the noise stopped, Aoife entered the kitchen. 'I think that bed's a bit rickety.'

'Sure, it only has to last me the summer,' Maeve said. 'I'll try to go easy on it.'

'It's your call,' Aoife replied, Maeve's insinuation sailing clean over her head.

'So, how much is he looking for it, anyway?' Caroline asked.

Maeve watched Caroline's forehead crumple as she explained the terms. She'd a fair idea that it wasn't the no parties or drugs clause that was bothering her.

'That's fierce dear,' she said.

'Twenty-five pounds a week is market rate,' Aoife said. 'And if you want a short-term lease, you don't have good grounds for negotiating a reduction.'

Maeve opened her mouth to say something to Aoife, but caught herself on at the last minute, and turned to Caroline instead. 'I've got the money in my bank account. I can do the rent and the deposit. You gather up your money in the factory and get me back.'

'But that's your prize money! Are you not saving that for England?'

Maeve's prize money was the best thing that had ever happened to her. At fourteen she'd won the regional finals of a Royal Mail writing competition by penning a letter to Bill Clinton beseeching him to bring peace to Northern Ireland. A reporter had arrived at school with some locally famous poet who smelt strongly of the sheep he immortalised in rhyming couplets. A photographer had snapped the poet presenting Maeve with a cheque for £250 while squeezing her arse. After she'd got over the feeling of his mucky fingers on her, she'd felt friggen brilliant. She'd never had money like it in her life. But before she could spend a penny of it, her mam'd dragged her to the bank and made her open a savings account. And for months afterwards, Maeve had resented the snobby English doll from a posh private school who'd won the national finals. In her prize-winner's interview, the girl had said she was going to piss her thousand quid prize money away on a new saddle for her pony, Phoebe.

'We can save up out of the factory,' Maeve pleaded. 'And ah'll get the deposit back when we go to uni.'

'But if we lived at home we'd save even more!'

Maeve thought of her brothers farting on the sofa, her mam stuck like a thorn in her armchair, the weight of Deirdre's empty bed above their heads. She saw herself ticking the days off on her Trócaire calendar like the hunger strikers scratching their lives away on the walls of Long Kesh. 'Mam's gonna charge me housekeeping when I start in the factory. Sure, I might as well have my own place!'

Caroline hung her head, defeated.

Maeve walked into the living room, where JP was jangling his keys like a jailer. She told him they'd take the flat.

Maeve let herself in the door at home. She went into the living room, where her mam sat in the chair by the fireplace and her two youngest brothers, Paul and Chris, lay on the sofa watching the telly. She went straight over to the fire to toast her arse, which was always freezing. Before Deirdre'd taken to her bed, she'd always got in some barb about fat being colder than muscle and Maeve'd always said something about how at least she had an arse. Then their mam'd lepp in with, 'Ah'm warning the pair of youse,' and after that they had to make do with firing dirty looks at each other.

The news was giving the latest updates on the Chinook crash in Scotland. A forensics team was combing the ground for wreckage as a reporter noted that twenty-something Brits had been wiped out in one go and the search for survivors was being called off.

'Well now,' Maeve's mam said. 'The bucks that died in that aren't the boyos we have tae put up with here in the town. Probably never caught wind of a petrol bomb, never mind dodged a bullet.'

A military expert with a large moustache filled the TV screen, stressing that the tragedy was mostly like an accident caused by a mechanical fault.

'They'd hate to hand that to the IRA,' Paul said.

It reminded Maeve of an old joke. 'I heard that an RUC patrol crashed into a tree in Fermanagh this morning!'

'No way!' Chris said, all delighted.

'Yep. All four of them were kilt!'

'God, that's wild,' Maeve's mam said, shaking her head.

'Aye. The IRA said they planted it.'

Paul dead-eyed her. 'Ye think you're so funny, don't ye?'

'I don't think it,' Maeve said, flicking her hair. 'I know it.'

Paul and Chris turned their heads slowly and with great dignity back to the telly.

'So, where's Mickey and Deci?'

Maeve's mother ground out her fag on the ashtray she kept perched on the chair arm. 'Away down the town with your father.'

Maeve picked up the ashtray and emptied it into the fire while her mam sat rubbing her forehead as if her skull ached.

'Is there any more news after the excitement of yesterday?'

Maeve was pretty sure her mam wasn't being sarcastic: nobody'd expected her to get a summer job. Paddy Slevin – the bollocks – had even turned down her offer to work for free on the *Town Times* saying Maeve'd cost him too much in tea and biccies. There was next to nothing going on in the town at the best of times, and jobs went to connections of people already working. Maeve's parents, most of her aunts and uncles, and her nearest neighbours, had no jobs, so she'd no one to lean on for work. Her factory job was as much excitement as they could count on until the exam results came out in August.

The whole town was waiting for the results. They'd decree who'd get away and who'd be left behind, which families had the hope of a teacher or doctor or lawyer, and which families would be kissing Woody Duffy's hole in the hope of a carpentry apprenticeship.

'Well, I've more news now, so I do.'

Maeve liked how her mam looked up at her. 'D'ye now?'

'Hmm-mm. Oul JP is renting out the flat above the shop. A two-bed.'

Her mam dropped her eyes back to the telly. 'Aye. Ah saw the McHugh lads doing it up. Ah was wondering who he had in mind for it.'

Maeve pulled a set of keys out of her pocket and shook them. Her brothers gawked, then Chris punched Paul in the belly. 'I'm getting Maeve's bed.'

'No way!' Paul gasped. 'Ah'm getting it!'

Maeve watched the pair of them wrestle on the floor. Her four brothers slept in bunk beds crammed into a single room. They shared a chest of drawers and shoved the rest of their shit under their beds. Maeve and Deirdre had always felt special, sleeping in single beds separated by a bedside locker and crucifix, with an entire wardrobe to themselves. But Maeve had been less keen on the room after Deirdre'd been stretchered out of it. 'So, what d'ye think, Mam?'

Her mam lit another fag and raised her eyebrows, observing her creed of *Whatever you say, say nothing*.

'What'll it be like, d'ye think,' Maeve went on, 'with me out of the house?'

Her mam took a few quick puffs on her fag, then exhaled. 'Ah imagine that'll free up a bit of space in the bathroom in the mornings.'

Her mam also believed that *Sometimes you have to be cruel to be kind*.

'Ah'm gonna move out the morrow.'

Her mam raised an eyebrow. Maeve fucking hated being on the far side of that trick.

'A Saturday flit's a short sit.'

'Well, I'm only hoping for a short sit. It's tae do til I get my results, remember? Ah'll soon be away tae study journalism in London.' Maeve dried up as her mam looked at her through narrowed eyes. She could nearly hear her saying, 'D'ye think I know frig all about university now, d'ye?' She didn't talk much about her stint in Queen's back in the sixties, but Maeve knew she was the first in their family to get to university. She'd been studying to be a social worker but had quit after some handling during a civil rights march. She'd ended up in the pig factory where she'd met Maeve's da. But she hadn't lasted long there, either. She'd quit the pork processing after she got pregnant with Deirdre, because she couldn't thole the bokes on the bus to work.

'Mam! Tell this skitter that *I'm* getting Maeve's bed,' Chris said, holding a cushion on Paul's face.

'Shut up the pair of yeez. Ah'll decide what we do after dolly-ann here moves out.'

Chris released Paul while Maeve tried – and failed – to keep her mouth shut. 'But where am I gonna sleep when I'm home at Christmas?'

Her mam looked up, wearing her may-God-help-your-inno-cent-wit face. 'I'm sure thon Caroline doll'll still have the flat come Christmas. She's a Jackson and the Jacksons sit tight. She'll not go far out of the town, results or no results.'

Maeve's throat clenched. Sometimes she felt like she was a female version of Icarus, spending hours collecting feathers, sticking them into wodges of hot wax to make the wings she needed to escape. Only instead of helping her, like Icarus's da did, her mam kept picking at the wings, plucking the feathers out the way healthy hens peck at a sick bird. 'I thought ye'd be pleased,' she said, 'that I'm trying to stand on my own two feet.'

Her mam took a long, hard look at her, interested at last. 'Ah'll be pleased when you eventually learn that ye didn't lick your notions up off the street.' She ground her fag out and turned back to the telly, where a small male frog was climbing a very tall tree in order to mate with a female.

David Attenborough was explaining to Chris and Paul how this brave male frog was undertaking an arduous journey in order to impregnate his female of choice, a journey that required a great deal of strength and persistence.

Maeve wished someone like Oprah Winfrey'd butt in to explain what the poor female frog – who was rapidly running out of tree to climb – might be trying to tell the male.

In the end, Maeve didn't flit that Saturday, for Caroline's mother wouldn't let them. 'No Jackson is after a short sit,' she'd said, her arse glued to a sofa in the county she and her ancestors had occupied since they'd worn animal skins and slept under bushes. So Maeve had spent all day mooching around at home, trying to pack for her move.

Packing the basics was easy enough, for Maeve didn't have a lot more than the basics. But she hadn't counted on dealing with Deirdre's stuff. Maeve knew from Granny Walsh's death that you were supposed to sort through the deceased person's stuff at the right time – not so early that you came across as a vulture, but not so late that you looked rare.

In the start, Maeve's mam had said she'd sort everything after the month's mind mass. But it came and went and her mam didn't lay a finger on Deirdre's stuff. Over the following weeks, Maeve's aunts came and went, one by one, in pairs, and once in a group, but her mam refused their offers to help 'sort' Deirdre's stuff, saying everything'd be of use to Maeve. But the look on her mam's face whenever Maeve walked into a room wearing one of Deirdre's T-shirts or skirts told a different story.

Maeve opened Deirdre's jewellery box and picked up the charm bracelet that their parents had bought for her tenth birthday. Maeve had offered it to maggoty Joe Whelan the undertaker when he was preparing Deirdre's body for the wake. But he'd said it was too tacky for the coffin, and asked for a pair of rosary beads. Maeve'd gone upstairs, put her hand under Deirdre's pillow and pulled out the rosary beads that Auntie Mary'd brought back from the Holy Land the time she took the coach tour from Strabane to Jerusalem. Deirdre'd fired the beads on her bed after Mary left, saying, 'It's not a stick of rock ye get from Jericho.' Maeve had hated the way Joe knotted the beads around Deirdre's cold fingers, as if to keep them from moving.

She snapped the jewellery box closed and put it back in their bedside locker. Then she pocketed Deirdre's bracelet, and started to get ready for a night out.

When she was dressed, she walked into the living room, where her da was sitting on the sofa with one hand tucked behind his head. He gave her a wink while she waited for her mam to say, 'What've ye got on under that coat the night?' like she always did. But her mam just slouched in her chair, staring at the fag she'd nipped between her fingers.

'Are ye not gonna check what I've got on under my coat, Mammy?'

'Ye can go buck naked down that town for all I care,' her mam said, flicking fag ash into the fire.

Maeve didn't know what was eating her mam alive but she knew she couldn't afford to care. She turned on her heel and left the house in a rage. She walked the short distance over to

Caroline's house, then rang the front doorbell. Mrs Jackson opened the door with a loose sort of a smile.

'Och, now, Maeve how are ye?'

Caroline's mam always looked how Maeve's mam looked when she was on the Valium, but according to Caroline, Mrs Jackson only ever did the rosary – a drug that totally missed the mark for Maeve.

'I'm grand, Mrs Jackson, grand. Not a bother on me! What about yerself?'

'Och, sure, I'm grand, grand.' Mrs Jackson ushered Maeve into the living room, where Caroline's da and Nana Jackson sat in front of the fire.

'Hiya, Mr Jackson. Hiya, Nana Jackson!'

'Maeve.'

'Och, now, Maeve!'

The heat wrapped around Maeve and she fought an urge to sink into the sofa, for fear she'd wake up in her fifties wearing an Aran cardigan and a look of mild confusion.

'Great day we had today, didn't we?'

'We did, aye, thank God. Maybe summer's here at last?'

'Well, sure, we can only hope, eh?'

'Well now, wan good day's better than none.'

'And the forecast's looking rightly. RTÉ was giving it good.'

'Aye, right enough, but UTV was giving showers.'

'Well now, your man Fish on the BBC was hopeful enough.'

Everyone in the town triangulated the Irish, Northern Irish and UK weather reports several times a day in order to figure out what sort of rain was coming their way. There was a patriotic consensus that RTÉ had the most accurate forecast, and that the BBC was the worst. UTV was considered fairly accurate for the Protestant majority living east of the Bann, but unreliable for the Catholic majority to the west of it. Maeve's Granny Murray was convinced that the wild inaccuracy of the BBC's forecast was a ploy; she believed that the British wanted to catch Catholics off-guard in bad weather, and so to spite them she wore a good, warm coat, summer and winter.

'Aye, well, sure – now we'll see. Cool enough at night still.'

'Aye. You cuddies'll have to wrap yourselves up when youse head out.'

'Aye, we will. Fresh enough out there already.'

'Aye, it is now.'

The squat wooden clock on the mantelpiece tick-tocked in the silence. A blinkered china horse strained against the weight of a wooden cart loaded with miniature beer barrels. Nana Jackson stretched her bent fingers out to the fire and sighed. A door slammed upstairs and Mrs Jackson looked up at the ceiling with affection.

'There's our Caroline now out of the shower.'

'Is she only out of it?'

'Well, ye know our Caroline. She'd be late to her own funeral.'

At the mention of a funeral, Nana Jackson blessed herself and shook her head of blue-rinsed curls.

'Well. Ah'd better head on up,' Maeve said, getting to her feet. She left the room and thumped up the stairs to Caroline's bedroom. She knocked on the door. 'Ye decent?'

'Aye. 'Mon in!'

Maeve entered the room and quickly shut the door to keep the heat in. The curtains were closed and the bedside lamp was lit. Caroline was wrapped in a towel, finger-drying her hair in front of the blow heater. Her bed was heaped with clothes, make-up and perfume, while Nana Jackson's bed lay neat as a fresh snowdrift, under a figure of Christ being crucified. Maeve'd heard Nana Jackson snore when she fell asleep on the sofa after dinner. She wondered how Caroline slept through that racket at night. And she'd no clue how Caroline faced the ever-increasing chance of finding Nana Jackson lying dead in the bed next to her each morning. Maeve shuddered, then removed her coat in front of the mirror. She was wearing black trousers, a purple bodysuit, a black corduroy jacket, a black choker with a purple jewel at the throat and Deirdre's purple fourteen-hole Doc Martens.

'Ooooooo, look at you! You look deadly!'

Maeve sucked her belly in and pushed her boobs out. 'I'm not bad the night, sure, ah'm not?'

'Ye just need to get the warpaint on and the hair sorted. Sure, sit down on Nana's bed and crack on.'

Maeve didn't like sitting on Nana Jackson's bed – she'd a fear that the old-lady smell would seep into her knickers and shrivel her flaps. Luckily, the doorbell rang. Maeve raced downstairs and opened the door. Aoife stood there, wearing her Nirvana T-shirt. 'Awwwwwwk! *Love* that Nirvana T-shirt.'

Maeve didn't really love Aoife's Nirvana T-shirt. She was pure jealous every time she saw it. Aoife'd seen Nirvana when they'd come to Belfast back in '92. Maeve'd been willing to sell her left tit to buy a ticket, but then Deirdre died and she was forced to observe something called *mourning* – an experience she felt was not far off being buried alive in a mass grave.

'Awwww, thanks!' Aoife did an awkward sort-of-bob-al-most-a-curtsy thing.

Maeve kept smiling while cringing inside. She often had to remind herself that one of the main benefits of being friends with Aoife was that it allowed her to practise speaking with a fancy accent, eating posh stuff and tolerating gamminess – all skills she hoped would come in handy for living in England.

She did wonder, as they climbed the stairs, why Aoife was friends with her.

When they got into the bedroom, Maeve stuck some Smashing Pumpkins on the stereo, then poured three glasses of vodka and Coke. She loved that Mrs Jackson still believed that they were mad for Coke at their age – even going to the length of bringing up a tray of ice-cubes for them on hot evenings.

'Any craic, Aoife?'

'Not really. James is home for the weekend. Him and Daddy are fixing up the boat.'

Maeve smoothed a blob of Rimmel's Pale Porcelain across her forehead while thinking about Aoife's big brother. He was up in Queen's, doing medicine. Maeve liked James, though he wasn't for the likes of her. He was like the good china she saw in John the Jook's jewellers with the snotty wee sign saying 'Don't Touch What You Can't Afford'. Maeve hoped it would cost her nothing to look. 'Is he heading out the night?'

'Nope. We've got feis tomorrow. I'm taking it easy. He's staying in.'

Aoife and James had been on the trad scene for years before Aoife became a grunger. Now she was wild for anything Kurt Cobain-related, and always had James on the hunt up in Belfast for B-sides or rare recordings. He was the sort of big brother Maeve dreamed about having – nothing like the four hallions she lived with, who grunted instead of speaking, and stank of Lynx sprayed over a week's worth of wanking.

Maeve took a gulp of vodka, then stood in front of the mirror holding her fag like she was Kate Moss (if Kate Moss was a couple of stone heavier, and shopped at Primark). Her nylon trousers cut into the podge of her belly, her bodysuit was wedged up her hole and her boobs were straining against the too-small bra she'd inherited off Deirdre. But Maeve knew, despite the odds, that she looked well and was wasted on the cubs she'd meet down the town. Some filthy urge wormed its way down through her guts and into her crotch, making her wish she could waste herself on Andy instead. It was the same impulse that made her fantasise about getting caught by Father Goan while sucking off a uniformed Brit at the back of the barracks. She suspected it wasn't a particularly wholesome desire. She turned her attention back to her vodka and before long, they'd finished their quarter bottles. Maeve passed around some chewing gum, then they traipsed down to the living room.

'Och, now, youse look lovely!'

'Took youse long enough!'

'D'ye think those wee jackets are warm enough?'

Maeve loved how the Jacksons never said stuff like, 'I can see what you had for breakfast in that skirt,' or 'Black's wild draining on you, fer you're the colour of yer Auntie Mary.' She loved how Mrs Jackson let them out the front door and then shuffled to the porch window to wave them off. She loved waving back before linking arms with Aoife and Caroline for the walk to the pub.

As they passed the garages, Mickey Campbell shouted 'Lesbians!' at them. Maeve turned, raised her middle finger and shouted 'Smell your ma.' She dodged the stone he sent flying and walked off laughing towards the Old School Bar.

The next morning, Maeve's mam jerked her bedroom curtains open saying, 'It's half nine.' This was shorthand for, 'Get your lazy arse out of bed for ten o'clock mass before I do something we'll both live to regret.'

Maeve hid her head under her pillow. She was pure dying. But getting up for mass was like standing for the Irish National Anthem: non-negotiable, no matter how drunk, disabled, fucked up or horny you might be.

When the toilet flushed, Maeve hauled herself out of bed and went to stand guard at the bathroom door so she'd get in before her brothers. The smell of toast wafting up the stairs set her stomach heaving.

The door squeaked open and Maeve's father looked at her with a twinkle in his eye.

'Up late socialising?'

'Och, Daddy...' Maeve leaned her head against the wall.

'Warmed the seat for ye!' he said, patting her on the shoulder with a heavy hand.

She ducked into the bathroom and locked the door. She avoided the mirror and settled her arse on the toilet seat. Her stomach was swirling. Mass was going to be even worse if she didn't sort that out. After pishing what felt like raw vodka, she grabbed her toothbrush, took a deep breath and stuck the handle down her throat. She boked stringy yellow bile and grey peas into the toilet – there were more peas in the bowl than Maeve could remember seeing in her curry the night before. She shuddered, then flushed the toilet. She reversed her toothbrush, squeezed out a maggot's worth of toothpaste, and started to scrub her teeth.

Maeve somehow made it through the standing, sitting, kneeling and processing, the 'Amening' and 'Thanks being' in mass with everyone else. But by the time Father Goan started droning out the parish announcements, she was fading. Then, in the mouth of the final blessing, Damien O'Hare came speed-walking up the aisle. He genuflected in front of the altar, and sidled up to Father Goan. There was a rustle of excitement as the priest inclined his ear towards Damien's lips: last-minute announcements were usually something interesting or useful, like a sudden death or a bomb alert.

Father Goan waited until Damien had sat back down before clearing his throat. 'I have been informed that there is a British army checkpoint at the chapel gates.'

The whole congregation sagged. They could be trapped in the chapel for hours. Father Goan gave a meaningful glance at Mouldy Macken, the organist, who was quivering like a dog waiting on a bone. 'Miss Macken, while we're waiting, perhaps we could go through "Seek Ye First"? All three verses.'

Mouldy Macken nodded and struck the opening chords on the church organ.

The BBC's *Songs of Praise* had left Maeve with the impression that church organs were the Protestant equivalent of a hair vest, a genteel instrument of torture. Organs put Maeve in mind of ruddy-cheeked English people lustily singing about how much the Good Lord loves Sheep, England, the English and Wet Weather. Everyone in the town preferred Peader Breen on his guitar with the folk singer choir (whose repertoire outside mass included an impressive range of rebel songs).

'And now perhaps everyone can stand up and join in?'

Maeve hauled herself to her feet, relieved that Father Goan had chosen a hymn everyone knew by heart. Only choir members had hymn books, so things got shaky when they went beyond the first couple of verses. Prods, of course, had hymn books not just for their choir, but for everyone in the congregation. Maeve had discovered this on a cross-community visit to a Protestant church down in Enniskillen. The Prods had glowered at Maeve's class as they marched up the aisle and slouched into the pews opposite. While the priest and vicar demonstrated how to play nicely by taking turns preaching, Maeve had flicked through a hymn book. There was page after page of posh hymns she'd never heard before. And the hymns she did recognise had slightly different words to the version she knew, or extra bits, like the Proddie 'Our Father'. Stuff like that rattled Maeve on her 'Meet a Protestant' excursions. These compulsory trips weren't part of the curriculum and weren't graded, but she always felt she was being tested. During the forced interactions, she'd do whatever she'd been taught to do since she was a wee toot of a thing, but then the Protestants would go and do something slightly different and she'd be left feeling like someone'd taken her chair from behind her just as she'd committed to sitting down, sending her sprawling on the floor.

Father Goan and Mouldy Macken warbled their way through 'Saint Patrick's Breastplate' and 'Be Not Afraid' before working up a lather singing 'Faith of Our Fathers' ('Holy Faith! In Spite of Dungeon, Fire and Sword!')

Finally, Damien O'Hare brought word that the Brits had cleared off. The congregation promised to go in peace to love and serve the Lord before surging out of the chapel. Linus McMurphy and a few other head-the-balls ran up the road after the Brits for a bit of craic.

Maeve slid away from her brothers as her mam and dad tramped them outdoors for a round of the graves. She couldn't bear how they started praying over their longest-dead relatives – people buried years before Maeve'd been born – moving from grave to grave to the most recent, where Deirdre lay. Maeve headed to the shop, bought a bottle of Coke, then sat on the shop windowsill in the blinding sunshine. She cracked the bottle open and put it to her head. It didn't cure what ailed her, but she knew, from the Lourdes water they'd poured down Deirdre's throat, that miracles rarely come bottled.

Maeve eyed her Sunday dinner: some dried-up spuds and a cardboardy Yorkshire pudding, with a lump of beef cooling under a slabber of congealed gravy. Her mam was walloping portions onto plates, while her da was holding a newspaper out at arm's length. He was in bad need of reading glasses, but it was clear he'd sooner have an arm extension than wear specs. Her mam clipped Paul around the head so he'd remove his elbows from the table, then dumped a plate in front of him.

Maeve's da eyed her as she tried not to smell the food squatting under her nose. 'How's the appetite the day?'

Maeve fired him a dirty look, then picked up her knife and fork before her mam could start into the black babies in Africa who 'wouldn't know what a feed was, never mind a feed of vodka.' She choked her dinner down, grateful it wasn't her day to do the dishes. When Deirdre'd been alive, chores were easy: everyone had a day of the week for doing dishes, for cleaning the bathroom, for mopping the floors. Even Maeve's da took a turn at the dishes despite the fact that it wasn't usual to see a man in the kitchen, never mind one making himself useful in it. But Deirdre's death had fucked all that up.

Maeve remembered the first Monday after the funeral, the way her mam had got to her feet after dinner, taken the dishes from the table, and dumped them in the sink. Maeve'd wanted to scrab the skin off her own face watching her mam scrub the plates Deirdre should've been washing. But she hadn't the guts to get up and help. So her mam mopped the floors Deirdre used to clean on a Monday, before bleaching the toilet and scouring the bath. She stripped the beds and rammed the sheets into the washing machine and hung the wet laundry – lighter by a load – out to dry. Maeve's mam hadn't been mad about Monday before Deirdre's death. She was even less keen afterwards.

'Right,' Maeve said. 'I suppose I'd better shift my bags across to the flat.'

'Yessssss! We can move rooms!' Paul said, jumping up.

Maeve's mam pointed a knife at his nose. 'Sit yer arse back down in that chair if you know what's good for you.'

Paul sat down, his bottom lip trembling.

'I'm sure that sister of yours left the room a disgrace. So youse bucks'll move nowhere until I get it redd up.'

Maeve thought of Deirdre's clothes, hanging in the wardrobe; her old schoolbooks piled up under the bed. She wondered what her mam'd do. She couldn't donate the clothes to St Vincent de Paul for fear they'd meet one of the Dirty Murphys wearing them down the town. But maybe she'd cram everything into the attic, along with the Christmas decorations and Granny Walsh's old sewing machine. Maeve knew if she'd her way, she'd pile up all Deirdre's crap in the backyard and set it on fire. Fuck whatever the neighbours would think.

'Do you have to go right this very minute?' her da asked.

Maeve shrugged.

'So sit tight for now. I'll flit you over the road later, so I will, after the game.'

Maeve didn't want to wait that long. She wanted to get the fuck away from their tired-out house, to slam the door shut on the tick-tock clocks, the smell of meat, the flimsy curtains, the wood-chip wallpaper and grit of Ajax scourer under her feet in the shower. But she followed her da into the living room and sat with her brothers as the Liverpool team jogged onto an enemy pitch.

Caroline was hanging a pair of pink polka dot curtains in her bedroom when Maeve and her da arrived at the flat.

'Hiya, Caroline!'

'Och, hiya, Maeve! Hello, Mr Murray.'

'Nice curtains!' Maeve said.

'Och, Mam got me them as a wee housewarming present,' Caroline said proudly, smoothing the material with her hand.

Maeve waved down the hallway at Mrs Jackson, who was cleaning the kitchen. Then she gleeked into the living room, where Caroline's da was peering up the chimney. Nana Jackson was sitting on the sofa gazing at the spot where the telly should be, humming the theme tune to *Coronation Street*. Maeve wondered how they'd got Nana Jackson up the stairs and, more to the point, how they were going to get her back down.

She went into her bedroom and dropped her bags. Then her da came in, set down a box and took a slow look around the room. He stared at the double bed for an excruciatingly long time before turning his eye on Maeve. 'Thon bed looks like it could do with a good sleep,' he said, firing her a wee smile.

Maeve licked it up, for she loved having her da all to herself. Then they went through to the living room, where her da settled himself in the armchair by the window. Caroline was cosied up on the sofa beside Nana Jackson, while Mr Jackson stood nodding out of the window.

'Some view, eh?' he said.

'Only the Brits see more,' Maeve's da said.

'Well, our blades are damn near as high as a helicopter up here. Haven't they done well for themselves?' Mr Jackson asked.

'Though with a bit of luck, now, they won't clock long here,' Maeve's da answered. 'Won't be long before these exam results are out and youse'll be away!'

Maeve's heart contracted as the fear came on her again. What if she didn't get good results? What if she ended up stuck in the flat, working in a factory? What if everything she'd worked for fucked up and she became just another scald to her mam's heart?

'Well, there's not much we can do now other than wait,' Caroline said.

'Aye,' Mr Jackson said, sighing. 'It's a different world youse girls are headed towards. There's more opportunities for young people nowadays. Youse won't spend your life on the dole like we did, or throw yourselves away in thon factory.'

'Y'know, Daddy, the factory's not that bad, so it isn't!' Caroline said, frowning. Her da tossed his head back the once, not quite agreeing or disagreeing, which was the closest the Jacksons ever came to open warfare.

'There's nothing wrong with the factory if it's your choice. Ye can thole manys a thing if you choose it.'

'And that's the difference, cuddies,' Maeve's da said, nodding. 'Youse have choices. We'd none.'

After they'd half carried, half slid Nana Jackson to the bottom of the stairs and out the door, Caroline and Maeve unpacked. Then they set up the stereo and lit tea lights in the living room. But when Maeve sat down, she got the trapped feeling she used to get when queuing up for confession with nothing to distract her except for her list of made-up sins.

Father Goan's heart wasn't fit for real sins since the Mother's Day bomb.

'Y'know,' Maeve said, 'I think this is the first time I've ever been in a house without a telly.'

'Oh, my God. Me, too. It's wild, isn't it?'

There was no *Top of the Pops* or *Doctor Who*. No Lois and Clark or *Cagney & Lacey*. No *Golden Girls* or *MacGyver*. No *EastEnders* or *Coronation Street*. Just the pigeons cooing on the roof, weans screeching on the pavement below, and a jeep hooring up the street. Maeve panicked at the thought of what she'd end up doing all summer without a telly to keep her occupied. Her mam's generation had been mad for the civil rights and the marching before the TV mast had boosted its signal and the improved reception settled their heads.

Suddenly, the doorbell rang. Maeve and Caroline exchanged an oh-my-God look, then Maeve gleeked out of the window. 'It's Aoife.'

'I'll get her,' Caroline said, jumping to her feet.

When Aoife came in, she leaned, grey-faced, in the living room doorway.

'Well,' Maeve said, 'how was the head this morning?'

'Not good. I missed mass. I just about managed the feis.'

It sickened Maeve's shite that Aoife's parents treated Sunday mass like an elective social engagement rather than a holy rite. They weren't like her parents, who believed that missing Holy Communion put you at risk of Burning in the Fires of Hell for all Eternity and that mass itself was a fit punishment for being hungover.

'This place looks great now you've moved your stuff in,' Aoife said.

Maeve tried not to look pleased. 'Well, we took the bare look off it, anyway.'

'Can I see your bedroom?'

'Work away.'

Maeve wondered what Aoife would make of her Che Guevara, Rosie the Riveter, Gandhi and 'Smash the H-Blocks' posters. They'd not been hung up since Deirdre's first – and last – year in university. Aoife herself had three big, framed black and white photos of Kurt Cobain hanging from the picture rail in her bedroom. She had posters of KD Lang and Sinéad O'Connor stuck up inside her wardrobe, because Mrs O'Neill didn't like Blu Tack stains on her walls.

'Love your posters!'

'Och, thanks!'

'You've no curtains yet?'

'Naw. But I'll stick some newspaper up for the time being.'

'Would you like me to bring you over some of Daddy's papers?'

Maeve cringed. Having *The Times* plastered to her window would be like writing a giant sign saying BRIT LOVERS LIVE HERE PLEASE THROW ROCKS.

'Och, naw, you're alright, Aoife.'

Caroline bustled into the room with three mugs of tea. 'Sorry, cuddies. We're out of biccies.'

Aoife reached into her bag. 'I suppose it's just as well Mummy sent over a housewarming present, then.'

Aoife called Mrs O'Neill 'Mummy' instead of 'Mammy', and still called her parents 'Mummy' and 'Daddy' out loud, not just in her thoughts. It did Maeve's head in that nobody laughed in Aoife's face about any of that. That nobody dared.

She watched Aoife bring out a big tin of biscuits, the sort that their relatives and neighbours – white-knuckled and tight-lipped – had dropped off, one after the other, during Deirdre's wake. Maeve remembered her mam eyeing them piled up in the kitchen. 'Enough for a barricade,' she'd said, and Aunt Mary'd gripped her mam by the forearm and said, 'Och, now, the barricades.' It'd taken them months to work their way through the biccies, and Maeve'd never felt the same about a jammy dodger since.

'Oh, my God! A whole tin of biccies!' Caroline said, clapping her hands.

'And I got you both a present too.' Aoife clattered a bagful of mix tapes onto the sofa.

'Celine Dion!' Caroline said, pouncing.

Maeve fired a what-the-fuck? look at Aoife as Caroline knelt in front of the stereo.

'It was in Mummy's collection,' she said, pink-cheeked.

Aoife not only owned a CD player, she'd an actual CD collection despite the fact that CDs cost sixteen quid a pop. Her parents and James also had CD collections. The O'Neill house had more books and better music than the town library.

Maeve reached for a fag, got to her feet and lit up out of the window. She blew a tunnel of smoke towards the locked-up factory below as Celine Dion began warbling about distant lights and storms tonight. 'So, cuddies. Tomorrow we start under Andy Strawbridge.'

'I'll not be under him if I can help it!' Caroline said, laughing.

Aoife didn't laugh.

'Wonder what jobs he'll give us?'

Maeve tapped some ash out of the window. 'My guess is we'll be put on the sewing machines.'

Aoife wrinkled her nose as if she'd smelt something on the turn. Maeve knew she was about to say something daft. 'I'd rather service the machines.'

Maeve did her och-would-ye-now? face. Aoife was weird. She wasn't just weird because she was so smart. She was *weird* weird. She loved maths and computers and machines and taking things apart and putting them back together. Maeve loved playing games on Aoife's computer the same as anyone else, but Aoife did shit like coding her own games. She read manuals and computer magazines. The year before she learned to drive, she mastered how to strip down a car engine. For all the size of her, she could jack up a car and change a tyre. She was down for all As on her exams and had offers on the table from every university she'd applied for. But Maeve often had to state the obvious to her.

'The men'll be at the machines, pet.'

Aoife tipped her head like she'd water in her ear. 'But I'm good with machines. I'd be better fixing them than sewing with them.'

'Och, Aoife,' Caroline said. 'Women do the sewing. The fellas do the other stuff. That's how it works. I don't mind, though. I wouldn't mind learning to sew.'

Maeve looked out over the top of the grey factory, towards Donegal where the sun was sinking behind the hills. She was keen enough on learning to sew, but she wished she didn't have to. She knew she'd be content to sit all summer long in the flat, listening to music, reading books and talking shite. But sooner than she liked, Aoife yawned and announced she was going to head on home. Maeve let her out the door, then went into the bathroom to brush her teeth and wash her face. After she said, 'Night, night' to Caroline, she went into her bedroom. She picked up the Mickey Mouse alarm clock that Deirdre'd saved up all the Cornflakes tokens for and set the alarm for half past seven. She wriggled into her sleeping bag and hugged her pillow, which smelled of fags, fire and roast beef. She gazed at Rosie the Riveter glowing fiercely under the orange street lights, listening to Deirdre's clock ticking off the seconds before the jaws of the factory gates would open.

Monday, 6 June 1994

70 days until results

Maeve's nerves woke her at half six. Her bedroom was too bright, and she was foundered with the cold even though it was – at least celestially speaking – summer. She got up and went to the living room, where she huddled under her sleeping bag in the armchair. She loved being three storeys above the town with the sky stretching like a well-washed blue sheet all the way to the sea. She watched Donal McGrath dander up the street to open the shop. Aideen O'Neill and Donna Shiels arrived five minutes later for their shift. Howling dogs betrayed a Brit patrol behind the barracks. A tractor chugged down the street and stopped in the middle of the road. A farmer jumped out and strode into the shop, emerging minutes later swinging a heavy blue plastic bag. Heat seeped into the flat as the roof warmed under the rising sun.

But every time Maeve looked at the factory, her skin twitched. She'd a feeling that a bomb was ticking nearby. She could picture the whole building shattering around her, collapsing into a heap of rubble. Suddenly Deirdre's alarm clock triggered. She leapt up and ran to switch it off, then tramped into the bathroom. She fired a bit of water around her face and rubbed a stick of deodorant in her pits to freshen up, then went back to her room and threw on a T-shirt, fleece and jeans. She opened her make-up bag and considered her options. She decided to keep it low key and patted some powder on her face, drew a flick of black eyeliner over her eyelids and brushed on mascara

37

– just enough make-up to keep her from feeling buck naked. When she was ready, she went to Caroline's door and knocked. 'C'mon, Caroline. Time to get up. Got the factory.'

She didn't answer, so Maeve put her head around the door. Caroline shrank away from the light like a slug recoiling from salt, giving Maeve an insight into how her mam's approach to waking teenagers had evolved. 'Right. I'm putting breakfast on. But I'm not dressing ye. Ye need tae get yourself up.'

When Maeve brought the tea and toast into the living room, she found Caroline hunched over on the sofa, staring at the carpet, zipped up tight in a fleece and jeans. She grabbed a slice of toast and began to chew without saying a word. Maeve wasn't fit to eat. She sipped her tea, wondering how she'd ever get up the nerve to head to London if she was this frigging scared of starting in Strawbridge & Associates. She wished she could whinge to her mam about work so she'd give her a clip on the lug to buck her up. Instead, she bit her index finger until it bled, which felt like a smarter choice than jumping out of the window.

At five to eight, the doorbell rang. Maeve got up and followed Caroline down the stairs. Aoife was waiting outside, wearing jeans and her Elastica T-shirt under her black leather jacket. Maeve was raging that Aoife – a *total* gam – had managed to look cool for working in the factory.

As they crossed the road, Maeve turned her eyes away from the sunlight bouncing off Andy's Jag. His car wasn't just the fanciest one in the car park, it was by far the fanciest motor in the town. She wondered what the interior smelt like. What it'd feel like to sit on the leather seats. She imagined Andy driving too fast down the country roads, blaring his horn at tractors. She knew he'd never be held up for hours at an army checkpoint or starfished against an army jeep while his car was searched from back bumper to front bonnet.

The sight of Mary scowling beside the factory doors brought Maeve back to her senses.

'Right, ladies,' Mary said. 'C'mon with me.'

They followed her through the double doors, then stopped in front of a board full of cards.

'Here's where ye get yer cards. Yer name's on top and they're sorted in alphabetical order. Find yer card, clock in here and put it back where ye found it.'

Maeve found her card and fed it into the machine. It made a wee *thock* noise as it stamped the time deep into the paper.

7.57am

Aoife punched her card, then inspected it before slotting it back into place. Caroline fumbled her card, then apologised to the woman bristling with impatience behind her. The lifers clocked in, then pushed past with bored, resigned faces. When the thick of the crowd was through, Mary growled at them to enter the factory. It was clear that Mary was not a morning person, and Maeve had a suspicion that she might not turn out to be an afternoon, evening or night person, either.

As they crossed the factory floor a bell rang, bringing Mary to a sudden halt. 'Right, ladies and gentlemen,' she guldered. 'It's eight o'clock and youse know what that means!' Mary eyeballed the clusters of murmuring women until they broke up. The machinists squeezed themselves into their stations and the clatter of sewing machines began to ricochet off the bare walls.

Maeve felt like the whirring needles were stitching her skin onto her bones. She dug her fists deep into her fleece pockets against the feeling and allowed Mary to hoosh her into the office. She sagged with relief when the door shut against the racket.

Mary lifted a page from her desk, read it, then frowned at Caroline. 'Miss Jackson, Andy wants you on the machines. Basic training for wan week and then we'll see if you're fit for full production.'

'Aye, grand. Thanks, Mary,' Caroline said, tugging at her curls.

'You two, Andy wants youse on pressing.'

Maeve's mouth opened a split second before Aoife said, 'Pressing?'

'Aye,' Mary said, crushing her eyebrow together. '*Pressing*. Every shirt has tae be ironed before it goes out the door. Andy reckons you'll get the hang of it quick enough. And if ye don't, ye know where tae find the door.'

Maeve's mam had taught her that ironing clothes was a mug's game because most clothes – ironed or creased – looked the same after an hour or so anyway. She only brought their iron out on special occasions, balancing it on top of their rickety ironing board, where it dribbled water before spitting a grey crust onto anything her mam pressed.

'Ah've asked Marilyn Spears tae show youse the boards and irons.'

The name Marilyn Spears was as Proddie as they came. A cross-community experience was looming.

'Youse two should be off basic the morrow.'

Maeve waited for Aoife to pipe up.

'What's basic?'

Mary sighed and took out a fag. 'Basic is yer hourly rate.' She lit up before continuing. 'Ye get paid a set rate for every hour you're here, even if ye never do a tap.' Mary started to cough. She hacked for so long that Maeve got the smack of her lungs on her tongue. 'On top of basic, everyone has a target. If ye hit yer target, ye get a bonus.' Mary lifted a finger at Aoife's opening mouth. 'But don't youse worry your heads about targets for now. When ye're training ye're kept on basic.'

Aoife's mouth snapped shut.

'Miss Jackson here hasn't much hope of hitting a target until well after she's trained in. Sewing's hard work. Professional work.'

'How come Andy has me on sewing, though, Mary?' Caroline said, sliding deeper into her fleece. 'I'm only here for the summer. Is there nothin' easier I could be doing? Like packing? I could fold and box the shirts?'

'Miss Jackson,' Mary said. 'Andy makes the decisions. And he wants ye sewing.'

It killed Maeve that Caroline was reluctant to sew – an actual skill that'd be useful her whole life long, whether she was just fixing her own clothes or making curtains. Pressing was like scouring toilets – one of those things everyone assumes a woman has mastered, but nobody respects. Maeve'd be in no hurry to add 'pressing' to the skills section of her CV.

'Now, you pair,' Mary said, narrowing her eyes. 'By the end of the line things don't flow the way they do at the start. Youse might get shirts through in drips and drabs or in wan big burst. So when there's shirts tae be got out the door, you're expected tae work on overtime for as long as it takes, even if it's past clock off.'

'How much do we get for overtime?' Aoife asked.

'Time and a half unless there's exceptional circumstances,' Mary said with a sniff. Maeve knew Aoife wouldn't be able to resist the bait.

'And what might exceptional circumstances be?' Aoife asked.

Mary shook her head and ground her fag out before answering. 'Ye can cross that bridge when ye come tae it. What ye need tae know fer now is if ye find yerself idle during the day, you're expected tae lend a hand around the factory.'

'Doing what?'

'According to your CV, Miss O'Neill, you're a right clever clogs. So use yer initiative. If the floor needs sweeping, sweep it. If Billy needs a hand with the fabric cutting, go help him roll the material out. If ye see me doing an inventory, check if ye could be of use. Just use yer friggen cop.' Mary sighed, giving the impression that her life had been long and hard, and meeting Maeve, Aoife and Caroline hadn't eased her burden one iota. 'Right. Time for yer tour.'

When the door swung open, the racket of needles, engines and an English radio presenter assaulted Maeve. She hoped she'd harden against the noise, the way she'd hardened to the crash and clang of secondary school. Mary started the tour with the bolts of fabric resting at the back of the factory, ready to be unrolled and cut into shirt pieces. Then she took the girls up through the ranks of sewing machines and demonstrated how the hot plates of the fusing presses were used to sear the tops and bottoms of collars and cuffs together. They toured the racks, boards and tables at the top of the factory, where the shirts were examined and pressed before being boxed.

As Mary was showing them how to use the stain removal gun, the hairs on Maeve's neck prickled. She looked up and saw Andy standing on the mezzanine above them. He raised his eyebrow and grinned at her. She dipped her burning face back into the mist of cleaning chemicals, her head spinning.

Finally, Mary left them in her office with the factory's health and safety handbook. They reviewed where the first aid boxes and emergency exits were, learned which extinguisher worked for what fire, and identified who was trained in emergency first aid. They discovered that they weren't allowed to eat on the factory floor (to avoid staining the shirts) or have sex anywhere on the premises (a rule that Maeve suspected wasn't entirely related to keeping shirts pristine). They scanned a long list of 'contentious articles' that they were instructed not to wear or wave, in the interests of fostering an 'excellent and harmonious working environment'.

'Caroline,' Maeve said, shutting the rulebook with a snap. 'Is a Union Jack flag draped over a sewing station contentious?'

'Is the Pope a Catholic?'

'Aoife, what about wearing a Nirvana T-shirt?'

'Kurt's an international icon! How could he be contentious?'

'Calm down. He's neutral. Caroline, what about a Rangers top?'

'Contentious *and* sad.'

'Correct. Aoife, what about a balaclava and sunglasses?'

'Perhaps permissible when it's below minus 20° and sunny.'

'So, unlikely to happen, then,' Maeve said. 'Caroline, would wearing a Celtic top be contentious?'

'Suicidal more like.'

'What about Union Jack knickers displayed on the premises?'

'Provocative in more ways than one.' Caroline snorted as a
bell rang.

Through the window Maeve saw the women who'd been
squashed into small seats for hours stop sewing. They got up
and tore over to the canteen.

Paddy Quinn, who'd been a bit of a Rah-head when they
were in school – decorating his bag and books with technically
brilliant drawings of Armalite rifles – opened the office door.
'Tea time, ladies. Goes faster than ye think so yeez had better
get a move on,' he said, then walked off.

Maeve, Caroline and Aoife scrambled to their feet, but were
still the last to arrive in the steamy canteen. They joined the
tail end of the queue as the tables filled up with people clutching mugs brimming to the lip with tea, chewing on toast and
smoking fags. Maeve'd never seen so many people work so
hard at eating, drinking and smoking before. Soon she had her
own toast – soggy with margarine – and a mug of scalding-hot
tea in her hands. She sat down at an empty table and started to
eat. She'd only bitten into her second slice when the bell rang.

Across the room, people huffed, crushed fags out, then
scraped chairs back and got to their feet, stretching. As everyone moved towards the doors, Maeve crammed her toast into
her mouth, then eyed Aoife's untouched plate. 'Not hungry?'

'Don't like margarine,' Aoife said, wrinkling her nose.

Maeve grabbed a slice and Caroline snatched the other. Then
she blew on her tea and tried to take a sip, but it scalded her
lips. 'Fuck's sake,' she spat.

'Go heavier on the milk,' a culchie-sounding fella said from
behind, startling Maeve. He sidled up to the table, looking just
as farmer as he sounded. 'Ye want yer tay as warm as cow's
plash,' he said. 'Then ye can pour it down yer throat.'

'Well now, that's something they didn't teach us in school,'
Maeve said, grinning.

43

'There's plenty youse didn't learn in school that ye'll learn the hard way in here,' growled an older woman, who'd the look of a leather glove dried out over a too-hot radiator. She rose to her feet and started hobbling to the door.

'What's cow's plash?' Aoife whispered.

Maeve sighed. Aoife often needed country talk translated. 'Cow's pish.'

Aoife still looked at Maeve blankly.

'He's saying your tea should be the same temperature as bovine urine.'

Maeve took a moment to savour the look on Aoife's face before heading towards the canteen doors, where Mary and Marilyn stood chatting. They stopped talking and glared at Maeve's toast as if it was a particularly contentious article.

'Rule three,' Aoife murmured, nudging Maeve.

'What?'

'No food on the factory floor.'

Maeve shoved the toast into her gob and chewed, but she'd no slabber left, so it stuck to the roof of her mouth the way Holy Communion did when she was hungover.

'Miss Jackson, you're coming with me,' Mary said. 'And youse two, youse are with Marilyn.'

As Caroline slunk off, Maeve felt panic scuttle through her guts. She'd no idea how to be natural with Prods. Thanks to segregated housing estates, schools, churches, shops, pubs, take-aways and Christmas trees, she'd had limited exposure to the fifteen hundred Protestants who made up the Other Side of their town, despite living in it with them for over eighteen years. But, lit by a spirit of peace and reconciliation, she adopted what she hoped was a bright, cheery smile.

'Hi, Marilyn! I'm Maeve. And this doll here's Aoife.'

Marilyn looked sideways at Maeve as if she was messing. 'Just so youse know, as long as ah'm training youse muppets, ah'm on basic. So can yeez get a move on?'

Marilyn barged through the doors and let them swing back in Maeve's face, teaching her factory lesson number one: *Work here long enough and you'll turn into a right cunt.*

Maeve wiped the toast crumbs from her face, then stalked out to the pressing station. The ironing boards were mounted on sturdy bars that were anchored to the floor with fat screws. A thick silvery cushion covered the boards. Maeve pressed her thumb into it and let go. The indent receded like a footprint on the seashore.

Marilyn slammed her hand onto the board. 'Do youse know the run of this place?'

Aoife shook her head.

Maeve was half ready to kill her and half delighted to keep Marilyn on basic for as long as possible.

'Give me strength.' Marilyn huffed. 'Right. Billy's on cutting. And he . . .'

'Sorry, Marilyn – Billy? Which one's he?' Maeve kept her face all innocence while Marilyn released a sigh nearly as long as the Loyalist marching season.

'Him. With the tattoo. Billy,' Marilyn said, pointing at a skinhead down the back.

Maeve eyed the fella's right arm, which was decorated with a bloody red hand tattooed between a Union Jack and an Ulster flag. His left hand was hidden in what looked like a chainmail glove. 'I see him now. What's the glove about? He doesn't look like no Michael Jackson fan.'

'Billy cuts the shirts out. The cutting blade would take the hand clean off ye. Thon glove's for protection.'

Maeve watched Billy unroll a bolt of fabric on the cutting table. There was something oddly hot about him, with his metal glove, paramilitary tattoos and barely concealed hatred of Catholics.

'Billy cuts out the backs, plackets, sleeves, cuffs and epaulettes,' Marilyn said. 'Does them in bundles. Us girls sew our pieces. Mickey there fuses the cuffs and collars. Karen does the buttons.'

Maeve assumed that Karen, with her blonde hair and well-scrubbed face, was a Prod.

'Finished shirts get sent up tae Fidelma in quality control.'

Fidelma Hegarty stopped clipping threads off a shirt clamped to a rack and scowled in their direction. Maeve knew Fidelma in passing, for she'd been a few years ahead of Maeve in school. She lived in a caravan out the back of the chapel and was famous for her sour puss and brawling. Fidelma'd never learned to box formally – she was pure natural. Maeve'd seen her in action a few times, battering some of the lads in her class just for the craic. She'd heard tell of Fidelma taking on full-grown men after she left school. Maeve sometimes saw her with a split lip or a black eye, but she'd never heard tell of her losing a fight.

'After Fidelma finishes with the shirts, youse press them so they're ready for folding and packing. Got it?'

Maeve and Aoife nodded.

'Right,' Marilyn said, cracking her knuckles. 'What pressing have youse done before?'

'I do a fair bit of ironing at home,' Maeve lied.

Marilyn stared at her as if to say, 'Aye, right.' Then she eyed Aoife, who'd gone very pink.

'I haven't really done very much ironing, to be honest.'

Maeve knew that Kitty Kelly 'saw' to the O'Neill house each week, to allow Mrs O'Neill the time she needed to focus on her 'job' of being an artist. While Mrs O'Neill painted canvases in her garden studio, Kitty Kelly ironed acres of blouses, shirts and white linen bedsheets. Maeve'd never seen Mrs O'Neill – let alone Aoife – lift an iron.

'Right, well, *Maeve* is it, you're called?' Marilyn said. 'You need to forget everything ye think ye know, for factory pressing's a whole different show.'

Maeve's ears tingled as Marilyn adjusted the ironing board down to her level.

'First thing ye need tae learn is the vacuum suck,' Marilyn said. She stepped on a footboard that triggered a vacuum. The ironing board sucked in a deep, sort of terrified breath.

'It pulls the shirt tight tae the board,' Marilyn said, rolling up her sleeve. 'Keeps it flat for ironing.' She laid her forearm on the ironing board, then sucked and released her flabby skin as an expression close to pleasure flitted over her face. 'Now, these irons are different to the wans ye might have at home,' Marilyn said, pointing.

The irons were powered by cables that coiled over their heads, clipped in place so they wouldn't catch on the boards or shirts. Maeve picked one up, expecting it to weigh heavy in her hand. But it was light as an empty kettle and ran over the cushioned board as if it were greased. A sudden cloud of steam hooshed in Maeve's face.

'Ye're not trained yet,' Marilyn said, brandishing an iron. 'Put that down.'

Maeve slowly replaced the iron on the board, then folded her arms.

'The steam comes through on automatic when yer iron's on, but if ye need tae give a shirt an extra blast, ye press this but-ton.' Marilyn hooshed a jet of steam into the air, then put the iron down and kicked a large plastic container that was under the board. 'That's the water reservoir,' she said. 'Fill it up in the canteen whenever it's empty.' Then Marilyn took off her fleece and pulled a stopwatch out of her pocket. She handed it to Aoife. 'Time me.'

When Aoife pressed the top button on the stopwatch, Marilyn plucked a shirt off the trolley, unpinned the sticker tag, popped the pin in her mouth and stuck the sticker on her left shoulder. Then she threw the shirt on the ironing board and pressed the vacuum pedal. The shirt clung flat to the board and she ran the iron over the collar. She released the vacuum and twitched the shirt off the board and flicked it so the front left of the shirt stuck to the board. She ironed the front, released the vacuum, then flicked the shirt over to iron the back. She pressed the front right, then did the sleeves and cuffs before throwing the shirt onto the rail.

Aoife stopped the timer. 'Thirty-two seconds!'

Maeve hated that Aoife sounded impressed. She herself was wearing her bored-off-me-tits-here-love expression.

'So,' Marilyn said, wiping a lick of sweat off her forehead. 'Have youse got it?'

Maeve nodded, for now was no time for telling the truth. But she didn't like the sly way Marilyn was looking at her.

'So, show me, ladies,' she said, all smug.

Maeve's heart sank but she picked up a shirt and started to iron like her life depended on it. She felt like she was back in school, in competition with Aoife, only now she had the added pressure of proving to Marilyn that Catholics could be just as fast and accurate as Protestants. So she was pure delighted when she was first to throw a shirt onto the rail. She stood there, waiting for Marilyn's approval.

'What are ye standing there for, ye div?' Marilyn said, as she started examining the shirt. 'You're on factory time! Keep pressing!'

Sweat trickled down between Maeve's tits as she grabbed another shirt. She realised she needed to strip off her fleece but doing that would jeopardise her lead over Aoife.

'Not bad.' Marilyn huffed as she draped Maeve's shirt onto the packing table. 'Good enough for Primark. But a finish like that wouldn't cut the mustard for Ben Sherman.'

Maeve threw another shirt over the rail and picked up her third.

'What the *fuck* is this?' Marilyn suddenly shrieked, pointing at Maeve's second shirt.

'Dunno. What?'

'It's *missing* a *button*!'

Marilyn was so full of outrage you would've thought she'd discovered a severed dick in the breast pocket of the shirt. Maeve hadn't sewn the fucking buttons on, so she used her not-my-circus-not-my-monkeys voice to say, 'And . . .?'

'Ye can't pass a damaged shirt down the line. It has tae go back tae Repairs.' Marilyn flung the shirt into a basket, then bellowed, 'Shite like that shouldn't get past, Fidelma.'

'Aye, well, nobody's fucken perfect, are they?' Fidelma roared back, without taking her eyes off the shirt clipped to her board.

'Aye, well, you're only fucken paid for perfect shirts, so pull that sticker off yer chart and open yer friggen eyes.'

Nobody Maeve knew had ever dared speak to Fidelma Hegarty like that. Marilyn was either much braver or far more stupid than she'd first thought.

'Right. Youse two quit.'

Maeve put down her iron with relief. It wasn't as hefty as their one at home, but it grew heavier by the shirt.

'Youse have tae watch for shite like that,' Marilyn said. 'Fidelma shouldn't let dirty or damaged stuff through. And if she does, youse tell her tae take the stickers off her chart. She hasn't friggen earned them.'

Maeve wondered how many vodkas she'd need to knock into her before she'd feel fit to square up to Fidelma Hegarty.

'The stickers are how you figure out who's done what, right?' Aoife asked, looking at a sticker sheet.

'Aye. Mary can trace every bittay a shirt back tae the person what did it – epaulettes, cuffs, collars, buttons, whatever. And the stickers tell her how much each unit is worth and if you've hit yer target and got into a bonus.'

'My sticker says two and a half p per shirt,' Maeve said, trying to do the sums in her head. *Seventy quid a week divided by four days divided by ten hours.*

But Aoife beat her to the answer. 'So we've to iron seventy shirts an hour to hit our basic?'

'Well, aren't you the wee jean-eee-us?' Marilyn sneered.

Aoife went pink and slightly stiff, as if someone'd given her a mild electric shock.

'Seriously? Seventy shirts an hour?' Maeve said. 'That's more than one a minute.'

Marilyn folded her pudgy arms across her chest. 'That's right. Ye saw me do wan in thirty seconds. D'ye think you're not fit for it?'

Maeve doubted that Marilyn'd be able to keep that pace up all day, but she said nothing.

'Right,' Marilyn said. 'Make sure youse transfer the pressing sticker from every shirt on tae yer sheet. Mary'll calculate the sheets every evening. Any questions?'

Maeve shook her head, lifted a shirt and set to work, relieved that the suck and whoosh of ironing muffled the whirr and clatter of the sewing machines.

When the lunch bell rang, Maeve put her iron down and looked at the pile of shirts to her side. Her legs were cramped, her right arm was numb, and she felt like boking. She'd no idea if Aoife'd done more or less than her. And that felt worse than the pain.

'What are you two doing for lunch?' Aoife asked, massaging her shoulder.

'Sandwiches in the flat. Want tae come?'

They left the factory long after the lifers had stampeded up the street. They crossed the road and climbed upstairs to the flat. Caroline and Aoife collapsed onto the sofa. Maeve recognised the look of people who'd been near enough an explosion to be left with ringing ears, but far enough off to have sustained no injuries.

'Cheese and pickle do yeez?'

Aoife and Caroline nodded. Maeve suspected she could've offered them a suck on a bottle of boiled shite and onions and they would've said, 'Aye, g'wan then.' She threw some sandwiches and milky tea together and served them.

Caroline was first to finish. 'How's it going with the pressing?' she asked, popping the biccie box open.

Maeve looked at the blisters on the back of her hand, where she'd scorched herself with steam. 'Well, it's not easy. My arm's killing me, so it is. What it's like on the machines?'

'Och, I'm just practising on scraps,' Caroline said. 'They won't let me on to epaulettes until I'm ready.'

'What the fuck *is* an epaulette?'

'It's this sort of tab they sew onto the shoulder of a fancy shirt. Looks a bit gammy if ye ask me. But the English like them.'

'Och, sure, the English,' Maeve said, before taking a gulp of tea to swallow down what she was scared of blurting out: that she was stunned by how hard and fast the work was, and exhausted by all the things that kept tripping her up. It felt like starting secondary school – racing to keep up with the big boys and girls, pretending you knew what you were at even though you felt like a complete eejit. Maeve wanted to quit already. But she couldn't. She needed money for rent, and to save for London.

When the bell rang for the second tea break, Maeve dropped her iron into its cradle and shambled towards the canteen. She was last through the door again, but this time she was wise to the set-up. She poured milk into her tea until it slopped at the lip of the mug, then started cramming biscuits into her mouth before she even reached a chair. She was licking custard cream crumbs off her fingers when the bell rang again. She winced as she got up. Her feet had swollen in the few minutes she'd taken her weight off them. She now understood why Fidelma Hegarty trudged everywhere – it was hard to step like a spring chicken when you had hot, spongy slabs of meat for feet. She clumped back to her board and stared at the mountain of shirts piled up in the trolley. Aoife caught her eye and did a Rosie the Riveter pose. Maeve blinked a smile in return, took a deep breath and picked up a shirt.

The final hour seemed to last for all eternity. The English DJ on the radio banged on about drive time and traffic conditions, encouraging motorists on English motorways in the manner of an officer in a wartime movie exhorting soldiers to throw themselves into enemy machine gunfire. Maeve mechanically lifted, pressed and threw shirts from one pile to the next knowing that if she stopped she'd fall down and not get back up. When the final bell rang, she threw her last shirt over the rail and leaned on her board as Marilyn Spears sailed by, smirking. Maeve pressed her face into the ironing board cushion. Then someone touched her hair. She jumped up and knocked the hand from her head.

'You've a sticker in your hair,' Aoife said, pointing. 'There.'

'Och, sorry, Aoife,' Maeve said. 'I thought it was someone messing.' She picked the sticker off and stuck it on her sheet. Earlier in the day she'd thought the sticker sheet was a joke, something a wean could do. But while her first few rows of stickers were straight and neat, by the end it was like a three-year-old had been let loose on it. She folded her sheet over so no one could see the mess, then trudged towards Mary's office door and dropped it into a cardboard box. Everyone had different quantities of sheets. Some of the machinists had bundles of sheets, stiff with stickers from working on doubles of stuff, like pockets and cuffs and epaulettes. Billy had just one sheet. He seemed to get one sticker for cutting out bundles of sleeves or plackets.

Maeve lost Aoife and Caroline in the rush towards the door, so she lit up a fag and stood outside waiting.

When Aoife landed out, she nodded towards the gates. 'Daddy's waiting.'

Maeve turned and saw John O'Neill parked, waiting in his car. 'Nice to get a lift home when you're knackered.'

'Yep.' Aoife nodded. 'Right. See you tomorrow?'

Maeve raised an eyebrow, wondering if Aoife really meant for it to have sounded like a question, rather than a statement. She blew smoke over Aoife's shoulder. 'I don't really think I've got any other choice.'

'Alright,' Aoife said, recoiling from the smoke. 'See you tomorrow.'

'Aye,' Maeve said, stubbing out her cigarette butt on the factory wall. 'See ya.'

52

When Maeve eventually got up to the flat, she dropped into the armchair and stared out of the window. Andy was redding up his desk. He lifted a folder, turned off his desk lamp and left his office. As he came out of the factory's double doors he paused to chat with Mary. Maeve was shocked at the sight of Mary cracking a smile as she looked up at Andy, fingering her wiry grey hair. He laughed, then patted Mary on the arm and jogged over to his car. He didn't look like a man who sat behind a desk or a steering-wheel all day. He looked like he took care of himself.

After his car roared out through the factory gates, Paddy Quinn locked the main doors, then Billy chained the gates.

When they'd all gone their separate ways, Maeve turned away from the window. She wondered what her brothers were having for tea. Maybe some beans on toast with an egg on top. Maybe sausages and bacon and Birds Eye potato waffles. Whatever they'd get would taste good, for they wouldn't have had to cook for themselves.

'Uhhhhhhhhh.'

Caroline, who was lying flat out on the sofa, glanced over at Maeve. 'You alright?'

'Och, it's just I'm so tired out after work, and making you and Aoife your lunches.'

Caroline grimaced and pulled herself upright. 'Toast, egg and beans do ye?'

'Lovely!' Maeve said. Then she looked at the rain coming in over the hills, trying to picture the episode of *EastEnders* she was missing.

By Wednesday, Maeve'd established a lunchtime routine: each morning, she made three lots of cheese and pickle sandwiches and laid out plates, mugs and the biccie box in the living room. When the factory lunch bell rang, she scooted out of the door and over the road as fast as she could with Aoife and Caroline. Once inside, Caroline filled the kettle, Aoife put on the radio and Maeve dropped with a thump into her armchair.

'Jesus. That's us over the halfway mark of our first week.'

'It's getting a bit easier, do you not think?' Aoife asked, as she turned the radio on.

'It's not getting easier,' Caroline shouted from the kitchen. 'We're getting hardier!'

Aoife tuned into RTÉ, a station she said was less 'aggressive' than Radio Ulster. There was no music playing. Instead, an extended news bulletin advised residents and business owners in the Republic of Ireland to carefully check their homes and premises for the presence of incendiary devices. Aoife sat all sombre, as if she was listening to Winston Churchill announce the outbreak of the Second World War.

'What's going on?' Caroline asked, carrying in the tea.

'Och,' Maeve said, 'the Free Staters are losing their heads because some loyalist paramilitaries are saying they've planted a few firebombs across the border.'

'It's not a hoax,' Aoife said, stiffly. 'They've already found one device.'

'That's right,' Maeve said, selecting a sandwich, 'and where was it they found it again?'

Aoife didn't answer.

'It was found in a snooker hall,' Maeve clarified for Caroline.

'I hate that you two get all sneery when stuff happens down south or over in England,' Aoife said. 'It's like you're jealous or something.'

'Fucken right I'm jealous,' Maeve said. 'But not of the bombs. I just wish they'd pay us the same amount of attention when far worse happens up here.'

Aoife put her plate down and frowned at the carpet. 'They've had their bombs down south, Maeve. Dublin. Monaghan. Wasn't there over thirty killed?'

It sickened Maeve's shite that although Aoife had lived up north since she was eleven, she'd had this soft life down south before that. She was always reminding Maeve of the stuff the southerners had gone through, or trying to justify why they

54

stood by and watched shite happen from a safe distance or –
worst of all – pretended it wasn't happening.

'Look, Aoife, the loyalists don't know how to build a proper
bomb on their own – they need the Brits for that. And fire-
bombs in snooker halls don't feel like the work of the Brits.
They're usually classier than that – they prefer moving targets.'
Maeve swallowed the last of her sandwich and reached for her
tea. 'If you ask me,' she continued, 'the loyalists are only going
mad because of the peace talks. They're worried that peace'll
break out and there'll be frig all for them tae do.'

'There's always the drugs and prostitution tae keep them
bucks busy,' Caroline said.

'And what about the IRA? Aren't they already knee deep in
protection rackets and dealing angel dust?' Aoife snapped just
as the news bulletin ended.

Maeve was relieved when 'Riverdance' came on. She
remembered watching the very first performance on the
Eurovision earlier that year. She'd loved how the audience
had jumped to its feet at the end and roared as if something
had changed, as if something powerful had been set free. She
guessed that Riverdance had made the Free Staters feel like
she had that time she went to see *In the Name of the Father*
in the cinema, and the riot scene had come on and the drums
had started belting and the bricks were flying.

She'd felt like she was capable of taking fucking *anyone* on.

Sadly, ironing didn't have the same effect on Maeve. After a
few hours of pressing, she'd had a sickening of the shirts. She
put down her iron and headed to the toilets. She sighed as the
door breezed shut. The blue walls, white tiles and tang of Jeyes
Fluid created an atmosphere poised somewhere between a
shrine and a public swimming pool. She entered the last toilet
cubicle, snibbed the door, then pressed her forehead against the
cold tiles, shivering as the draught from an open window licked
her sweaty neck. She needed a good pish, but before she could

get going, the main door creaked open and a woman entered, coughing so hard she farted.

'Better out than in!'

Maeve didn't recognise the voice. Her bladder clenched as she realised a Protestant had entered the toilets: she'd never urinated near a Prod before.

The woman coughed and farted her way into a toilet cubicle, then closed the door. She rummaged with her clothes, collapsed onto the toilet and began to pish like a horse. 'Och, now,' she said with satisfaction. 'One of life's sure pleasures, a good pish.' After she eventually trickled to a stop, she flushed the toilet, then opened her stall door.

Maeve pished with relief under the cover of the gurgling water as the woman plodded back out to the factory floor without so much as sniffing a tap. Maeve exited her cubicle and scrubbed her hands religiously. She wondered if hand-washing was one of those weird Catholic rituals that Prods weren't bothered with, like drinking Christ's blood and having a wee thing for the Pope. She guessed she'd learn.

On Thursday – somewhere deep beneath the scalded patches of skin, the muscle cramps and sweat-soaked feet – Maeve felt a lick of energy. She realised that she'd get used to the standing and pressing, to the short breaks and long days, and the milky tea and dour Prods. That she'd make it not just to the end of the week, but to the start of autumn. And she'd learned that Taigs and Prods had a couple of things in common: both sides got excited about payday, and they both liked talking about the weather. Everyone got especially het up when they could mash those two subjects together.

'Payday the morrow.'

'Can't come soon enough!'

'Did ye do alright this week?'

'Not too bad, thank God. Plenty of work in.'

'It'd nearly make up for thon rain, would it not?'

'Take more than the shrapnel we earn in here tae compensate me for that.'

Mary'd spent most of the day in her office processing the week's sheets. The chat in the canteen was about what money'd go towards paying back stuff that'd already been worn, drunk or eaten, and what would be set aside for stuff that was needed. Maeve pictured her own wage packets bursting in front of her week after week throughout the summer, paving her path to London in pound coins.

At five o'clock Andy strutted down the stairs and began a round of the factory floor. He called people – girls, mostly – up to his office from time to time. They always came out looking flustered. Maeve'd heard the men laughing about what they'd do if they were in Andy's place, who they'd summon. The women never joked about the same thing. Everyone seemed on alert now that he was out and about on the factory floor. Maeve saw Sharon Rogers pause near Fidelma Hegarty. She murmured, 'Wonder who he'll do today?'

Fidelma snorted and glanced at Maeve. She put her head down and tried to keep an eye on Andy at the same time. He worked his way along the production line, sometimes stopping to have a quick word with someone, sometimes examining a basket of work. She lost sight of him when he entered the line behind her. The next minute Sharon Rogers yelped and dashed towards the toilets, her arms crossed over her chest. Maeve kept pressing: she didn't know what it'd take for her to drop her iron and miss her target, but it was clearly more than a startled Prod.

'You fuck off, Andy Strawbridge,' Fidelma snarled. 'Ah'm warning ye.'

Andy laughed. Then his shadow fell across Maeve's ironing board. Eyes fluttered over her from every angle on the factory floor. Her heart was pounding and a not-unpleasant pressure was building in her knickers.

Andy watched her work for what felt like a long time. 'You seem to have got to grips with the work, Ms Murray.'

Again with the 'Mizz Murray' thing. 'Well, it's hardly rocket science, is it?'

Andy moved closer behind Maeve. 'It's not,' he agreed over her shoulder. 'But you're a natural, Maeve.' Then he slipped two fingers under her arms and made a gentle circular motion that tickled her ribs. Maeve's nipples hardened and she whirled around to face him. Then she realised that her bra was undone. And Andy was looking.

Everyone except for Aoife had seen what'd happened, but nobody said a word.

Maeve crossed her arms over her chest and walked to the toilets, her face blazing.

Sharon Rogers came out of a toilet stall and glanced at Maeve's chest. 'So he did ye?'

Maeve nodded.

'He's a fucker,' Sharon said. 'You watch yerself.'

'I will,' Maeve said, ducking into a stall to fasten her bra. She wasn't sure if she was more unsettled by what Andy had done to her, or by hearing a Prod offer, 'You watch yerself,' as advice, rather than a threat.

When she went back out to her station, she saw Fidelma Hegarty come bulling down the stairs. She then tore into a shirt like she'd a pick against it, leaving Maeve wondering what it was she'd been at up in Andy's office.

Maeve woke on the dot of seven thirty, even though her alarm was off. It was Friday and that meant payday. Daylight shone through the newspaper she'd stuck over the window, the black headline stark against the light.

MURDER LATEST PICTURES AND NEWS

It was a hardy perennial of Northern Irish headlines, relevant week in, week out, year after year. Maeve could never hope to write a better one. She got out of bed and switched on the radio in the hope of hearing a bit of Placebo. But a reporter was talking about some Catholic worker who'd been shot dead in the Harland & Wolff shipyard. Then a union representative gurned on about *working-class solidarity,* saying their union wasn't going to let an *isolated incident* set back relations between the two thousand men who made up the shipyard's integrated workforce.

Maeve knew well that only one hundred of those men were Catholic. Prods and Taigs weren't rubbing together like flour and butter in Harland & Wolff; the Taigs were just a pinch of salt in a big bowl of Proddie dough. She wondered how desperate the dead man had been that he'd taken a job in the shipyard.

Seamus Heaney'd written a poem that had put the frighteners on her own generation. 'Docker' it was called. There were no guns or no explosives in that poem – Heaney'd been writing in the times Maeve's parents still shited on about, before the Troubles, when Catholics were firmly second-class citizens and violence was less coordinated, and far more personal. He'd written about a Protestant docker who'd *drop a hammer on a Catholic.* When Mr Bradley had asked the class for their thoughts on the poem, Charley Kelly'd said that a dropped hammer would be a bit hit-and-miss in terms of injury. Dropped from a fair height, he reckoned you might kill someone – though it'd be harder to hit your target the further up you went. Close up he reckoned you might only cause enough damage to get the victim out of the shipyard on permanent disability. Bradley thanked Charley for his thoughts and asked if anyone else had any observations. So Maeve'd told him that the poem felt like it was from a gentler time, when Prods had to use discretion in their attacks – going to the bother of pretending they were accidents. Mr Bradley, who'd been gradually deflating all year, like an air mattress with a slow leak, had closed his poetry book and asked the class to write an acrostic poem using the word 'rainbow'. He'd collected their work at the end of the class and then gone on sick leave for a few months. Maeve never did learn what he'd thought of her poem, which had opened with the line: *Red like the bloodstains on the grey streets of our town.*

She switched the radio off and went to Caroline's door. 'Caroline?' There was no reply, so Maeve knocked. 'CAR-OH-LINE? C'mon! Rise and shine cos it's payday!' Maeve opened the door and switched on the light.

Caroline groaned and put her head under the duvet. 'Go away!'

Maeve lost the will to drag Caroline out of bed. 'Right. I'm away to have a shower. Get you up and get ready for we have tae head over the road tae collect our cheques.'

Maeve showered and got dolled up. She didn't go too fancy – just black trousers with a black top and her black leather jacket and biker boots. She did Audrey Hepburn eyes and killer lips to soften the biker vibe the jacket and boots were giving off. Then she went into the living room, where Caroline was still sitting in her pyjamas, nursing a cup of tea. 'Och, Caroline, are you not ready?'

'Och, Maeve. I'm wrecked! Ah need me tay.'

'But we hafta go over tae get our cheques.'

Caroline looked up at Maeve with big, sad eyes. 'Could ye not pick mine up for me?'

'Och, Caroline! I don't want tae head over there on me own!'

Maeve looked out of the window. A queue of people was waiting at the factory door. Paddy Quinn unlocked it and everyone traipsed inside. As the yard emptied, Maeve saw Andy's Jag pull into the car park. She watched him climb out and stretch, before he jogged over to the factory. She hadn't thought he'd turn up to work on a Friday. 'Frig it. I'll go then. But you owe me.'

Maeve's hand itched to lift and punch her clock-in card as she walked into the factory. The machines squatted in silent rows and half-sewn shirts lay where they'd been dropped the day before. She joined the tail end of the queue outside Mary's office, and slowly shuffled to the front of her desk.

Mary glanced up at Maeve, licked her forefinger and then flicked through a shoebox containing brown envelopes. She selected one and passed it to Maeve, who carefully avoided the bit that Mary'd touched with her slabbery finger. 'Thanks a million. Can ah get Caroline's too?'

As Mary flicked towards Caroline's envelope, Maeve wondered what Mary'd get up to over the weekend, apart from mass. She'd a horde of sons away in England who rarely visited. And a daughter over in Philadelphia who hadn't flown home even after her da'd blown the head off himself in his shed with the shotgun he'd borrowed off Foncey Logue. Maeve'd overheard someone at the funeral say that at least Mary had the comfort of the wee handicapped child still at home who wasn't likely to up and leave her poor mother, unlike thon snootery doll over in Philadelphia.

'There ye go,' Mary said, holding Caroline's envelope out.

Maeve thanked her, then scooted out of the door.

When Maeve got back to the flat, she ripped her pay packet open and pulled out the cheque.

£83.25

She frowned. There was no way she'd made £13 in bonus. Mary'd fucked up. Maeve checked the figures on her payslip. The one hundred and thirty extra shirts she'd ironed over the week had earned her a bonus of £3.25, which felt about right. But her basic wage was set at £80, and she was sure Mary'd said their basic was £70. She got up and went into Caroline's bedroom. 'How much did ye get?'

Caroline shrugged and reached for her sealed envelope. 'Just my £70 basic, ah'm sure. Why?'

'Go on, check for me.'

'You want me to check me cheque?' Caroline said, bursting into laughter.

Maeve crossed her arms and waited for Caroline to catch herself on. 'Will ye just look?'

Caroline huffed, then opened her envelope. 'My cheque's £70.'

'Gimme a look at yer payslip,' Maeve said. She grabbed it and scanned the figures. 'Och. Your basic's £70. But Mary's made a haemes of mine. She's set it at £80.'

'She has not!'

'She has too. I'd better go and get it sorted.'

'What a pain in the hole.'

'Fucken right it is. It's hard enough looking at Mary when ah'm paid tae look at her, never mind looking at her for free on me day off.'

Mary's cough echoed through the empty factory. Maeve took a deep breath before knocking at her door. 'Hey, Mary.'

'What are you after?' Mary asked, squinting up at her.

'Och, I just need to check my payslip with ye,' Maeve said, laying it on the desk.

Mary looked from Maeve to the payslip and back again. 'D'ye now?'

'Aye. Ah think my basic's wrong. It's a tenner out.'

Mary glanced at the slip, then looked back at Maeve through narrowed eyes. 'Ah don't make mistakes, Miss Murray. I paid you what ah was told to pay you. If ye think that's a mistake, you go and tackle Andy Strawbridge.'

Mary went back to her paperwork, leaving Maeve feeling as thick as pig's shit. 'I don't get ye, Mary.'

Mary sighed, stubbed out her fag, then spoke in the low, threatening voice she used on her disabled child whenever she got rowdy in the crying chapel. 'I pay people what Andy tells me to pay them. If you were expecting an extra twenty quid in yer pay packet, Miss Murray, ah suggest ye enquire with Andy up in his office.'

Maeve's stomach dropped. Andy'd deliberately set her basic ten quid higher than the factory standard. And Mary thought Maeve was in wheedling for even more money.

'Anything else ye'd like me tae do for ye, Miss Murray, or d'ye think ah can get on with me work now?'

Maeve shook her head and left Mary's office. She walked towards the foot of the stairs, then stopped. She didn't have the guts to face Andy, to ask him what the money was about, so she turned to leave. Suddenly the canteen door swung open and Andy walked out. Maeve shrank back as he approached, to let him past, but he stopped a few feet away from her. She looked at the delicate blue pinstripe that ticked down from his shirt shoulder to his leather belt.

'Going somewhere, Ms Murray?'

She shook her head.

Andy took a sip of coffee from a mug printed with THE BOSS in red letters. 'Can I be of assistance to you?'

Maeve shook her head again. She felt trapped but didn't know why. Andy wasn't blocking her way. He was doing nothing she could put her finger on, but she felt pinned to the wall by his eyes.

'Payday today, Ms Murray. I hope you spend your hard-earned money wisely.'

Something shifted and Maeve pulled away. 'That's where you're wrong, Andy. I'm not spending. I'm saving.'

'And what are you saving for?'

'London,' she said over her shoulder, as she walked towards the exit.

'I hope you've got a big piggy bank, Ms Murray.'

Maeve kept walking, thinking of the blood-red piggy bank her da'd brought home from the pig factory before he'd gone on the sick.

Pink & Patterson's Prime Pork Products

The only thing we waist of a pig is the squeal

In spite of the spelling mistake, Maeve had loved her piggy bank. But she'd never had more than a scatter of coins and a few notes in it. She imagined tucking the extra tenner from her pay packet into the pig's belly week after week. One hundred and thirty quid extra she'd have, at the end of her thirteen weeks in the factory. Money that'd make a real difference to her over in London.

Back into the flat, Maeve found Caroline snuggled into the sofa with a cup of tea and a magazine.

'Did ye get yer pay sorted?'

Maeve hesitated. 'Aye. It's sorted,' she said, hating the scratchy feel of her voice in her throat.

'Deadly. Will we head down tae the bank and get these cheques cashed?'

'Aye.'

Hours later, Maeve and Caroline were lying in the living room with a wee community of dirty tea cups gathered at their feet.

'Aoife and James'll be here soon,' Caroline said, yawning. 'It'll be nice to have some company.'

'I'm a bit manky,' Maeve said, stretching. 'I might have an oul shower.'

Caroline eyed Maeve over the lip of her mug as if to say, 'I'm on to you, Missus.'

Maeve tried to look the picture of innocence, pretending that her scrubbing up and the imminent arrival of James O'Neill were totally unrelated.

They'd known James as long as they'd known Aoife. And Maeve'd known since she was fifteen that James had a fancy for her. He wasn't like most men, fancying a fuck. James fancied *her*. He liked being close to her, but he didn't try to grope her. He listened to her stories, laughed at her jokes and engaged with her opinions. And she liked him back. He was smart and kind and funny. He never felt the need to flash the family cash or swing his mickey to act the big lad. She knew James O'Neill would be a catch in any town, never mind *their* town. She loved his blue eyes, his wide shoulders, his fingers on the fiddle. She enjoyed talking to him and tried to learn every lesson he taught her. 'Here, this is how you pour wine, Maeve, like this.'

But James was like the syrup saucers her da set out to drown the wasps at the end of summer: if she wanted to get out of the town, she needed to steer clear.

Maeve switched off the shower and grabbed the towel she'd robbed from home, which wasn't big enough to dry her without going limp with damp. When the towel was defeated, she threw it onto the radiator, then moisturised her face and legs with baby lotion. The scent put her in mind of her brothers when they were still all soft, clean bums and pudgy thighs, years away from the hairy lumps they'd grown into.

When she was finished, she put on her fleecy pyjamas and bathrobe. She didn't look glam, but she felt fresh and clean. She'd a notion James would like that better than a cleaster of make-up and rack of boob. She went into the living room, where Caroline was staring at the corner of the room that was in mourning for a telly.

'*Neighbours* is on,' she said. 'They'll all be watching it over at ours.'

'Och, sure you can watch the omnibus with Nana Jackson tomorrow,' Maeve said, rolling her eyes. Then the doorbell rang.

Maeve looked out onto the street and saw James at the boot of his car, holding it half-closed against the drizzle. 'James is here,' she said. 'I'm not decent. Will you go down?'

'Och ah suppose,' Caroline said with a sigh, hoisting herself out of the sofa.

On the street below Aoife bounced out of the passenger side of the car, said something to James and then hugged him. Maeve felt all weird inside looking at the pair of them. She'd not hugged any of her brothers since putting on her first bra in June 1987.

And not one of them'd laid a hand on Deirdre when they were lined up to pray over her in hospital, as she lay dry-eyed and tight-lipped, dying.

James pushed the car boot wide open and took hold of a big object wrapped in a black bin bag. He hoisted it up and held it to his chest. Aoife slammed the boot shut, locked the car and scooted out of sight.

Maeve sat down just as Caroline opened the door. James struggled up the hall and staggered into the living room, where Aoife helped him lower the bag onto the floor.

'Heavy oul thing that,' he said, all out of puff. Then he looked around the living room. 'Nice place!'

Maeve shrugged like the flat was no big deal. 'It'll do us rightly over the summer, I suppose.'

'It's better than the kip I share in Belfast!'

Maeve didn't point out that the difference between their flat and the 'kip' James shared in Belfast was that she and Caroline were paying old JP rent, while the students James 'shared' with were paying him rent for the house his mummy and daddy'd bought him as a didn't-you-do-well-in-your-exams present.

'What's in that, James?' Caroline asked, nosing at the black bag. 'A wee housewarming pressie?'

Maeve was mortified. She'd been trying to pretend that it – whatever *it* was – wasn't squatting in the middle of their living room.

'Aye. Well. If you want it, it is,' James said, bending down and pulling the bag away, revealing a TV bigger and newer than the only telly in Maeve's family home.

'Oh, my God, a telly!' Caroline squealed as if she'd never set eyes on one before.

Maeve sat a bit deeper in her chair, then looked at James, who was rubbing the back of his head. 'Giving them away free in the cornflakes now, are they?'

'Och, well, I just got a new one for my room, so this one's not needed,' James said, taking a reddener.

'We thought you could use it here and pass it on to St Vincent de Paul when you're leaving,' Aoife said, a prickle of annoyance in her voice.

Maeve got the message and tried to cop the fuck on. 'It'll be deadly to get *Enders* and *Corrie* again!' she said, with a smile that hurt her cheeks. 'Thanks a million!'

The worst thing about her habit of trying to make everyone else feel better about themselves, was that it usually made her feel worse about herself.

'Right, then,' James said. 'I'll get her set up.' He moved the telly into the corner of the room and tuned in the channels. Aoife switched over to a cookery programme in which Delia Smith was demonstrating how one could use the tomatoes and vegetables that were ripening in one's garden in a range of summer salads.

The door hadn't slammed behind Aoife and James before Maeve switched over to *Eurotrash*.

Later that evening, Caroline dozed on the sofa while Maeve cosied into her sleeping bag. The room – lit only by the flicker off the telly – felt warmer and more relaxed, as if it had breathed a sigh of relief. Then the last news bulletin of the day flashed across the screen. Maeve watched footage of over two thousand Harland & Wolff workers striking outside the shipyard gates, protesting at the murder of their colleague. She wondered if their factory would walk out if one of them was murdered – Taigs in support of Prods, Prods in support of Taigs – saying fuck whatever the bosses wanted, whatever the paramilitaries demanded. Tears suddenly pricked her eyes. Despite everything she'd learned from her mam's generation about the hundreds of marches that'd led to violence or nothing more than sore feet; despite having seen movement after movement rise up and crash like waves on a shore, Maeve wished that one demonstration would work. That something'd bring an end to the violence.

She didn't want the reunification of Ireland – anyone with a glimmer of wit knew that the Free State didn't want them: they'd fucked off after Partition, leaving the north in the shit. And she'd no desire to bend over and accept Britain as her lord and master – centuries of British rule had taught her she could trust the Brits as far as she could throw them. But she wished they'd the cop themselves to say, 'Fuck them, fuck the whole lot of them,' before throwing the guns, Semtex, timers and rocket launchers in a pile and pouring the incendiary liquid of their bad memories over the whole frigging lot and setting fire to it. It broke Maeve's heart to imagine being left to themselves – free of the Brits, relieved of the Free Staters, unencumbered by bosses – to grow up and grow old.

But she'd learned to keep a lid on feelings like that. On most feelings. So she dried her eyes and kept them on the prize: getting the fuck out of the town.

New Kids on the Block were blasting out in the living room where Caroline was sitting on the sofa, crushing a cushion against her diddies while imagining snogging Jordan Knight. Maeve was glad she was in the kitchen, making spaghetti Bolognese to say thanks for the telly to James and Aoife.

Pasta had only arrived in the town when Maeve was thirteen. Her Auntie Mary'd told her mam that cooking pasta was dead easy – you just boiled it like spuds. So Maeve's mam'd always boiled their pasta as long and hard as a pot of potatoes. Until Maeve'd learned how to cook pasta in school she'd no idea that pasta wasn't supposed to be a sticky pile of porridge-coloured worms on the cusp of disintegration. That experience had taught Maeve the value of following instructions – or at least reading them to get an idea of how far she could deviate from the rules without things ending in disaster. So, as the Bolognese sauce packet instructed, Maeve sliced an onion while browning minced beef. The packet advised her to splash some red wine on the meat for flavour. She'd no wine handy, so she splashed a bit of vodka into the pan instead, then poured herself a vodka and Coke as the meat sizzled. When it was nicely browned, she put the pasta on to boil, then opened the Bolognese sauce packet and dusted the orange powder over the beef. She added another splash of vodka and stirred until the mixture had turned a kind of fluorescent orange colour. It smelt fucking deadly and Maeve was pleased that the whole thing had taken her under fifteen minutes. She was grating cheddar when the doorbell rang.

Ten minutes later, Maeve sat back in her armchair with a sigh of satisfaction. The spag bol had been great – and though the vodka might've nudged it a shade too far over on the tangy side, she'd horsed it into her.

'God, that was great, Maeve,' Caroline said, putting her fork down. 'Love a good feed of thon cheddar.'

'There's plenty more in the pan,' Maeve replied, glowing with satisfaction and vodka.

Caroline put her hands in a praying position and pulled her face out long like she was pleading to God. 'You sure?'

'Yeah – here, I'll get you some more.'

James and Aoife were still working on their plates. They ate slowly, like proper posh people.

'D'ye want me to leave youse some?'

Aoife swallowed hard. 'Oh, don't worry about me. I've got lots here!'

James held a finger up, his mouth full, chewing. When he eventually swallowed he said, 'I'm grand too, thanks, Maeve. I'd a big lunch earlier. Still feeling a bit stuffed, to be honest. It's delicious, though! Thanks.'

Maeve got the feeling that something wasn't right, which knocked the notion for a second helping right out of her. She brought Caroline a second plateful, then threw a vodka into her and started washing the dishes.

A few minutes later, James came into the kitchen carrying plates. He insisted on helping Maeve wash up. She felt awkward up close to him. She'd the impression he wanted to say something and that she should say – or do – something. But Aoife kept buzzing in and out with knives and forks and glasses and then back in for a glass of water first for her, then for Caroline, then back again for the vodka, so neither of them said or did anything.

After they'd finished redding up, the O'Neills headed home. Maeve switched on the telly and watched the daylight slowly drain from the wide sky that yawned over them from the west, feeling like grit was lodged under her nails, stuck between her teeth and pitted beneath her skin.

Monday, 13 June 1994

63 days until results

Maeve finished her basket of shirts and saw nothing coming her way, so she sailed out for a fag break. She sat down beside Fidelma Hegarty and nodded at Baldy Magee and Mickey McCanny, who were shiting on about the upcoming World Cup matches.

'Ye never know. Ye just don't know how it'll go,' Mickey said.

'Sure, we've a chance, so we do, the same chance as Brazil, the same as Germany,' agreed Baldy.

'And a far better chance than England!' Mickey said, sniggering.

'Fucken hell,' Fidelma said, opening a can of Fanta. 'We can't get away from that oul shite, can we? Who gives a fuck about football, any roads?'

'Sure, we aren't allowed to talk about the World Cup in there,' Mickey said, nodding at the factory. 'The Prods are all sour grapes because neither England nor the Northern Irish team made the tournament.' Mickey spat on the ground.

Maeve wasn't sure if he was making a point or if he was just a bit phlegmy.

'How come we've a Northern Irish soccer team *and* a Republic of Ireland team?' Maeve asked. 'Isn't there only one rugby team on the island? And just the one hockey team? Why isn't there one big Irish football team?'

'Rugby and hockey's posh Brit sports,' Fidelma said. 'They have tae have wan team cos they can't scrape together enough people up here in the north or down south tae make two teams. And even then they still win frig all. Football's different. Every frigger plays football.'

Maeve'd seen Prods play hockey on the telly. It didn't look that different to camogie, but she knew it'd be like their praying and their singing: there'd be some wee detail that'd sink her when she was staring in the mouth of an open goal.

'Back in 1958 and 1982 the Northern Irish squad got tae the quarter finals of the World Cup,' Mickey said, sticking his neck out and shifting around like he'd something itchy down his back. 'They did the place proud, so they did.'

Fidelma glared at Mickey. 'Did *us* proud?' she asked. 'Tell me now, how many Catholics were on those teams?'

Mickey didn't answer.

'In fairness,' Baldy said, 'the Irish football team's no different. It's half full of Brits now that it's managed by an Englishman.'

When Maeve's da had announced that a Brit had taken over the hopeless Irish football team, her ma's jaw had dropped. 'Jack Charlton?' she'd said. 'Sure, he's as English as genocide.'

'Aye,' Mickey said. 'Took an Englishman tae relax the rules on who's Irish. Charlton doesn't give a fuck where ye were born. He'd recruit any footballer – English or Irish or Rwandan – as long as he can kick a ball and dig up an Irish granny.'

'And what about women? Would he hand an Ethiopian lady footballer an Irish passport as quick as a Nigerian man?' Fidelma snapped.

'Och, now, Fidelma, you're some laugh,' Mickey said, stretching. 'Right. Ah'm away back in here, for some of us have work tae do.'

'Aye, and some of us is only here for the good of our health,' Fidelma said, firing a filthy look. 'Fuck away off back in there, will ye, before I fell ye.'

Mickey dandered nonchalantly indoors with Baldy trotting at his heels.

Fidelma ground her fag out with the heel of her shoe, then eyed Maeve. 'You're very young to have such a filthy habit, Maeve. When'd you start smoking?'

Maeve shrugged casually, as if to say, 'Sure, wasn't I born smoking?' She shook back her hair. 'Young enough, I suppose. Sixteen?' She said that like she didn't remember the exact minute she'd smoked her first fag. But it was June 1992. Maeve'd been sitting the last of her GCSEs. They'd buried Deirdre the month before. Every day after the funeral her mam had dragged herself up the road to the chapel to light a candle for Maeve's exams before stumbling out to the graveyard to stare at the plastic-wrapped flowers rotting on top of Deirdre's grave.

'Sixteen? Was it tae keep ye off the biccies?'

Maeve remembered her mam saying, 'Keep yer head screwed on for these exams. Ye've your whole life ahead of ye tae cry.'

'Exam stress.'

'Sixteen's too young,' Fidelma said, clicking her tongue. 'Ye'll do yer lungs no good.'

Deirdre's last pack of fags had been Maeve's first. After the doctors had told Deirdre she'd totally fucked her liver with the paracetamol, Maeve'd asked her if she wanted anything. 'A fag,' Deirdre'd said, looking at the ceiling, 'and tae turn back the clock.' Maeve'd gone home and pulled Deirdre's handbag out from under her bed. She'd opened the bag and found Deirdre's wallet, which contained her student ID, some bank notes, a few coins and a packet of Wrigley's chewing gum. And she found a half-used tin of Urge body mist. She remembered Deirdre, home for Christmas after her first term at university, watching telly with everyone else. The Urge ad had come on, showing a man relentlessly chasing a woman down the street before presenting her with a bouquet of flowers, at which point a posh male voice declared: *Men just can't resist Urges.* That's when Deirdre'd snorted and said, 'It's not flowers they're forcing on ye in the real world.' Maeve could still see her mam's eyes blazing at

Deirdre, willing her into silence, and her lovely, useless da sitting there, oblivious.

Maeve hated that even though she'd got the gist of what Deirdre'd been trying to say, she'd just sat there. But she fucking despised her mam for saying – and doing – fuck all.

She'd dropped the can in the bin.

Then she'd delved back into Deirdre's bag and found an empty pill bottle.

Miss Deirdre Murray
200 paracetamol tablets
Use as directed
Avoid alcohol
4 May 1992

Deirdre'd got the pills for free by getting a prescription from Doctor Molloy in the surgery, and the prescription allowed her to dodge being interrogated by the chemist. She'd kept the sealed bottle in her bag for a fortnight – two weeks that had slipped past Maeve like all the other weeks before.

Deirdre had collapsed four days after swallowing every single tablet.

Nothing'd been the same since.

Doctor Molloy had bawled her eyes out at the wake. 'She told me she'd fierce period pain. Fierce! There was no sign of anything else. I would never've prescribed them if I'd known. Never!'

Maeve's mam'd left Doctor Molloy with Maeve as soon as she could and gone into the backyard to have a fag. She hadn't come back in until after they'd got rid of her.

At the hospital, a watery-eyed chaplain had told Maeve and her brothers that the twenty-second of May was the feast day of Saint Rita, patron saint of the impossible. He asked them to bow their heads to pray for a miracle; which they'd done, for what it was worth.

Maeve had pocketed the empty pill bottle, then carried Deirdre's purse and cigarettes to the hospital. She'd wheeled Deirdre outside and watched her light a fag. When Deirdre took her first puff, Maeve saw a softness come into her eyes for what seemed like the first time in a long time. It turned out to be the last time.

Deirdre never uttered another word about what a man's urges had led to up in Belfast. And Maeve – who'd learned young to obey her community's pact of silence – had never asked.

Maeve realised Fidelma was eyeing her. 'Sure, we could die any minute, any one of us,' she said.

'True enough,' Fidelma said. 'And the Brits'll probably get ye before John Player does.' She stood up, stretched, then headed back into the factory, leaving Maeve underneath the rumble of a hovering army helicopter, missing Deirdre.

It felt like it always did: she was frozen in that split second after a bomb detonates, the moment the light and air is sucked from the world, before the shock wave hits, before the shattering glass, the squealing, the screams and sirens.

Mary had been stalking the factory floor and picking on people for a good half hour before she walked up to Maeve's station. 'Andy wants tae speak tae ye,' she said. Maeve nodded but kept pressing, intent on finishing the shirt she'd just started. 'Now,' Mary snarled.

Maeve did a keep-yer-wig-on face, then put down her iron. She climbed the stairs, conscious of glances from the factory floor, then paused at the top to catch her breath. Her heart was still banging when she knocked and opened the office door.

'Yes, that's right,' Andy said into the phone, while gesturing at Maeve to enter. 'Yes. We're on target.'

She was glad he was on a call: it gave her time to catch a grip of herself.

'Well, they're ambitious targets, make no mistake. So I'm very pleased to be where we are, especially given the challenges we're experiencing using local workers.' It was clear by the big serious head on Andy that he was speaking to someone important. 'Oh, I understand, Lucinda – I know *you* appreciate the challenges inherent in integrating low-skilled workers from a deeply divided community into a modern, desegregated working environment.'

Andy had no gun or and wore no uniform, but his English accent gave him a certain power, and it left Maeve with the impression that he was acting.

'Yes. Absolutely. Your support has been invaluable.' He smiled, nodded and frowned as he spoke. Maeve wondered if all that somehow transmitted down the line to the Lucinda doll.

'Well, I do my best.' He sounded like one of the smarmy English radio presenters Maeve hated, the ones who toyed with the poor eejits who rang in on the phone lines. They got off on leading the plebs down the garden path, using them to make themselves sound smarter and look more important.

'Absolutely, one hundred and ten percent.'

Maeve dropped down into the chair nearest her, and promised herself that she wouldn't end up being just another stupid audience member.

'Lucinda, I just want to say thanks for all your support.' Andy was clearly trying to wrap up the call, but the way Lucinda was purring down the line at him gave Maeve the impression that she didn't want to end the conversation. 'Yes. I'm very much looking forward to our next meeting too,' Andy said, stretching back in his chair and stroking his tie. 'Yes, the same hotel. It suited us quite well the last time, did it not?' He looked at Maeve and adjusted his balls.

She felt a pressure in her jeans. The sort of pressure she normally worked up during a snog.

'Brilliant. OK, Lucinda, I'll let you get on to more important things,' Andy said, loosening his tie.

As Maeve crossed her legs, she felt a slick on her knickers. Yet Andy hadn't even spoken to her, never mind laid a finger on her.

'Not at all. Thanks again, Lucinda. Bye.'

Maeve waited for Andy to do the trail of *bye-bye-bye-bye-bye-byes* that everyone she knew did before they put the phone down. But he acted like a character in a soap opera: 'Bye,' he said, before banging the handset into the cradle. Maeve felt sorry for Lucinda on the other end, saying her *bye-bye-byes* before realising she was bidding farewell to a dial tone.

Andy scribbled something on the notepad in front of him as Maeve shifted in her seat, leaning into the pressure in her knickers.

'That,' Andy said, 'was Lucinda Taylor of Invest NI. She's one of the people who provides the financial support I need to keep this show on the road.'

Maeve dead-eyed him while picturing freakshows and circus horses.

'Lucinda supports enterprises that are committed to building sustainable companies in communities such as this.'

The way Andy said 'communities such as this' gave Maeve the dirty, disappointed feeling she got when reading books like *The Railway Children*. Other communities were nicer than hers. Other communities shot each other less and didn't blow themselves up quite as much. Other communities had less wrist-slitting, kiddie fiddling, wife beating, binge drinking and dog shit. 'So it's our job to prove to your investors that this factory isn't some dodgy business, set up to suck as much money as possible out of them before it goes tits up?'

Andy placed a hand on his notebook and spread his fingers wide before answering. 'You have a gift for translating the Queen's English into your Northern Irish vernacular.'

Maeve nodded, thinking *Fucken right I do*.

'But if you don't mind me saying, Ms Murray, that particular skill won't be of much use to you over in London.'

Maeve's minge shrank like a snail retracting into its shell.

'Looking and speaking as you do will win you plenty of attention over in London,' he continued. 'But I'm not so sure about respect.'

Maeve realised that Andy wasn't like the eejits she'd fooled at her university admissions interview. He didn't buy into her slabber about being a scrappy wee doll who'd fight her way out of the gutter to become a respected journalist. Andy looked at her like the mouthy wannabe she was, all fur coat and no knickers.

'So, how does one earn the respect of the English?' Maeve asked.

'I think learning how to speak English properly would be an excellent start.'

Maeve considered spitting in Andy's face.

'And of course it would help,' he continued, 'if you didn't despise the English quite so openly.'

Maeve's forehead trembled as Andy grinned at her and picked up a book. 'I think you ought to read this,' he said.

'*How to Win Friends and Influence People*. How'll that help me?'

'It'll teach you a thing or two about people skills.'

'And that'll set me up for London, will it?'

'No. But it's a start. And to be frank, Ms Murray,' Andy said, looking at her with amusement, 'the race you think you've entered started generations ago. You need all the help you can get.'

Maeve stood up, grabbed the book, then stalked out of the door. She pounded down the stairs, ignoring the oh-ho-now looks darting between the machinists and Fidelma's 'Aye, right,' stare, and tried to lose herself in the suck and slam of ironing. Minutes later, however, she scalded her left hand with a blast of steam and had to rush to the cold tap in the toilets. As water gushed over her skin she pictured walking out of the factory gates and over the road to her parents. But Maeve knew what her mam'd say if she came running home with her tail between her legs: 'You made yer bed. You lie in it.'

She dried her hand, took a deep breath, then slotted herself back into the production line.

At lunchtime, Maeve fired her new book onto the coffee table in front of Caroline and Aoife. 'So. Andy thinks that's going to help me out over in London.'

'*How to Win Friends and Influence People*!' Aoife said brightly. 'Daddy likes that book too.'

'Really?'

'Yes. It's a business classic. I've read it. Pretty useful, if you ask me.'

Maeve wondered what else Aoife had read while she'd been watching *Eurotrash*.

'So I should actually give it a go, then?' Maeve asked, just as Aoife took a neat little bite of her sandwich. Aoife nodded enthusiastically, clearly keen to say more, but Maeve had to wait for her to finish chewing, for none of the O'Neills spoke with their mouths full.

'Yes, do. It's kind of like a cross-community relations programme, only aimed at helping you get on with everyone, rather than just Protestants.'

'Maybe I should borrow it after ye, Maeve?' Caroline said, reading the blurb.

'To be honest, Caroline, a lot of what the author covers comes kind of naturally to you,' Aoife said.

'But not tae me? Is that what ye're saying?' Maeve said, hating the are-you-starting-on-me? tone in her voice.

'No,' Aoife said, going pink. 'That's not what I mean. It's just you sometimes sound more . . . more defensive than Caroline.'

'Maybe I just have more to be defensive about?' Maeve said, defensively.

Aoife shrank into her seat and took a large bite of her sandwich.

They were on their biccies before she started up again. 'So, Andy must be into his business theory.'

Maeve shrugged, wondering where Aoife was going.

'I wonder if he saw that episode of *Tomorrow's World* last month?'

'Which episode?' Maeve said, as if *Tomorrow's World* was her reason for living.

'The one that explained how computers are going to change factories?' Aoife said, hopefully.

'Och, naw. I didn't catch that one.'

'Oh, that's a shame!' Aoife said, narrowly missing the will-ye-quit? look Caroline was firing at Maeve. 'It showed how in the future robots will do more and more of the manufacturing work while computers will monitor every aspect of the production process.'

'Right,' Caroline said. 'So robots'll be making perfect shirts, the men'll be working the computers, and we'll all be sitting on the dole?'

'No. It's more like the computers will help the managers optimise every second of a worker's time, which will result in maximised productivity and profits. More and better jobs, not less.'

'I can guess who'll be experiencing the productivity and who'll be enjoying the profits,' Maeve huffed, sending a spray of custard cream crumbs flying onto the pubic hair carpet.

'All factories are going down this route,' Aoife said. 'It's not all bad. Imagine how great it'd be if we could schedule food and toilet breaks according to actual human needs.'

'Och, Aoife,' Caroline said, staring at her with the soft eyes she used on the disabled weans when they were wheeled from door to door to collect for charity. 'They'll make everything the same for everybody and it'll suit no one. I don't need the same food and toilet breaks as Mabel Moore or Baldy Magee. What I need is better pay, a decent sewing machine and some hand towels in the loo. It's not rocket science.'

'But imagine a machine that makes tea or coffee at just the right temperature for your break!' Aoife said, putting her empty plate down on the coffee table. 'Or one that creates a snack based on the calories you burn off in the job you're doing?'

'Imagine getting enough time to drink a cup of tea at the temperature you like instead of being rushed out the door?' Maeve said, exasperated. 'Imagine working only five hours a day, so you've time to exercise instead of being glued to a fucking chair or on your feet for nine hours a day?'

'Och, c'mon, cuddies,' Caroline said. 'All this is miles off for us. Sure, we're still putting stickers onto paper timesheets. Mary uses a calculator and writes everything down by hand. Sure, we're even paid with cheques in envelopes that have our names handwritten on the front!'

'Best way to optimise that place is tae put a match tae it!' Maeve said, bringing the conversation to an end. She didn't like Aoife's talk of change. She liked the factory the way it was. She liked sweeping out the dusty corners when she'd no work on. She enjoyed airing her arse in the cool blue of the toilet block after a sweaty hour of ironing. She liked sneaking outside to sit baking in the sunshine on a cracked plastic chair. It was the gaps in the factory system that made everyone's days bearable. It'd be nothing short of torture if Andy Strawbridge filled each last second up with work.

The next day, Maeve listened as a couple of lifers whinged about missing their targets. Though factory targets were a whole new thing for Maeve, she was well used to the general idea of targets – she'd grown up classifying buildings, institutions, organisations and people into types of target, which included the popular categories 'legitimate', 'soft', 'high profile', 'intended' and 'unintentional'. Willie Fraser, for example, was a full-time member of the Ulster Defence Regiment, and came from a long line of what Maeve's mam called 'Deep Protestants' (a title they'd earned a century ago when their ancestors had drowned three Catholic sheep-rustlers in a water trough in the town centre). Willie was clearly a 'legitimate' target. Jody Johnson was a part-time police officer and postwoman, making her both a 'legitimate' and a 'soft' target: the IRA got her one Valentine's morning, when her route was longer and slower than usual because of the glut of cards in her bag. Then there was seventeen-year-old Catholic, Hugh Devine, shot dead the week after he got his driving licence as he filled in for Simon Frost, a Protestant breadman and a part-time soldier. An 'unintentional' target.

British politicians were easy, being both 'legitimate' and 'high profile'.

Any shop, takeaway, garage, company or human who supplied the British army or RUC with foods, goods or services was a legitimate target, as were court buildings, army bases, police barracks and all associated aerial and road vehicles.

But factory targets were a whole different story.

For a start, they were shared. Taigs and Prods had to hit the same level to earn the same money. And they weren't soft.

When Mary'd told Maeve that she needed to iron seventy shirts an hour, she'd felt like an IRA apprentice who'd been handed a hammer and orders to eliminate the British prime minister: hitting the target was possible, but success was unlikely. Ironing seventy shirts in a day – never mind an hour – seemed like a stretch to Maeve. So she didn't see the point in busting a gut trying to iron *over* seventy shirts an hour in order to earn tuppence.

She took the matter up with Aoife: 'So, what about these targets, Aoife? Why should I sweat for an hour to have the chance of earning two and a half pence extra? I'd make more money going down the back of the sofa looking for pennies.'

'Well, I was thinking about targets,' Aoife said, cautious as a cat. 'Let's say I iron seventy shirts in an hour and then do an extra ten shirts. That earns me an extra twenty-five pence.'

'LOADSAMONEY.' Maeve's Harry Enfield impression didn't earn a smile from Aoife. She wasn't mad into him. Maeve'd heard Mrs O'Neill describe Harry as trashy, which showed she both got – and missed – the point.

'OK,' Aoife said, biting her lip. 'But if your basic is £1.75 an hour, you've just awarded yourself a pay increase of over fourteen per cent. Or an extra £2.25 per day.'

Maeve grasped Aoife's satisfaction with the percentage. But it was the idea of pennies adding up to pounds that lit a fire under her arse.

By the end of Tuesday, Maeve was ironing over one hundred shirts an hour. Doing that every working hour for two days would earn her a CD. But she realised her satisfaction wasn't just about the money. There was something kind of nice about the way her target added up with all the other targets so that their combined work hit an overall target. After years of studying and sitting exams alone, it felt good to be part of something bigger than her own self.

Maeve learned the hard way that her targets didn't adjust to account for period pain or tampon changes. The next day, she missed her bonus by a mile, then stumbled home and climbed into her sleeping bag in front of the telly with a hot water bottle. Caroline heated up a tin of Campbell's chicken soup and then sat down with Maeve to watch *Coronation Street*.

The ad break leading into the episode was – as usual – stuffed with images of chocolate, washing detergent and women's sanitary products. The jam rag ad started off with two sanitary towels side by side. One was normal – a long and thin pad, the type that Maeve knew from bitter experience was soon soggy in the middle while the two ends remained clean and dry. The other pad had wings on either side, giving it the look of a stranded flat fish. A clean female hand poured a vial of blue liquid over the normal pad.

Maeve remembered what her da'd said one evening when they were all lying up watching a similar ad: 'Ah see Princess Diana's on the rag again.' Deirdre and Maeve had burst their holes laughing, but their mam'd hissed 'Fuck up!' at him and he hadn't commented on feminine hygiene products since.

Maeve took a mouthful of soup while the blue liquid over-flowed the normal pad and spilled onto the white counter. The same hand then poured liquid onto the branded, winged pad, which of course absorbed every drop.

'D'ye mind,' Maeve said, 'before wings? The branded pad used to soak up the blood?'

'Aye. But suddenly now it needs wings. Would that be evolution?'

Maeve laughed, setting her hot water bottle wobbling on her belly. 'If I'd my way, it'd fly to the bin next, when it was full.'

'Jesus, I'd pay extra for that,' Caroline said, before taking a slurp of soup.

Maeve put her empty bowl on the coffee table. 'When I get tae London I'm gonna find out where they make those ads and I'll give them our notebook.'

Her and Caroline were dead proud of their notebook. They'd used it to sketch out remakes of the terrible ads they saw on telly.

Their favourite was the tampon ad.

They'd got tired of all the tall skinny 'birds' in white trousers flinging themselves around in aerobics classes or draping their bodies over men's cars – not one of them doubled over in pain in a pair of period joggers with a hot water bottle shoved up their jumper. So they'd dreamed up an ad shot in black and white, starring Maeve and Caroline (obviously). The ad would open with them striding out of a village, wearing old-fashioned Dutch girl outfits while the caption '*Holland, 1887*' faded into view. They'd walk to a dyke where a Dutch boy (played by Aoife) would be using his finger to plug a leak so the dam didn't burst and flood the village below. They'd do a close-up of the Dutch boy, sweating and stressed to fuck, but feeling like a hero. Then they'd cut to Maeve and Caroline exchanging a God-help-his-innocent-wit look. Then Maeve would shove the Dutch fella to the side and plug the dyke with a tampon.

Maeve'd decided that the only splash of colour in the whole ad would be the blue string of the tampon blowing in the wind. But she was especially proud that nobody was going to speak in the ad, which reflected how their mothers communicated with them about periods – using significant glances, frowns and sighs – but was mostly a strategy to ensure that she and Caroline wouldn't have to learn any Dutch.

'D'ye really think we could get our ad made?' Caroline asked, looking at Maeve. Her face was drawn after a ten-hour shift in the factory, and chicken soup was dribbling down her chin, but her cheeks were pink with hope.

'Aye, of course,' Maeve said. 'We just have to get in front of the right person.'

She knew that most success in the town was down to who you knew, not what you knew. But she hoped that London would be different, that working there would be like doing exams, where her performance was anonymously assessed by impartial strangers who were keen to reward hard work and talent. She needed to believe that success was possible if only nobody knew who she was or what she came from.

That night she went to bed early and slid *How to Win Friends and Influence People* out from under her pillow. She started reading chapter one: 'If You Want to Gather Honey, Don't Kick Over the Beehive.'

On Thursday, Caroline and Maeve fell in with Proddy Sharon Rogers as they crossed the road to the factory. Maeve said, 'Hiya' in a voice she knew was a wee bit too bright and over-enthusiastic, the sort of voice she'd heard teachers use around school inspectors – the sort of voice she heard in her head when she imagined herself winning friends and influencing people over in London.

Sharon said, 'Hiyas' back, which sent Maeve to her board buzzing with a feeling she supposed was the 'reconciliation' shit that the peace people pushed as hard as Harry the Chew pushed his whacky baccy. She still wasn't used to working with Prods, which wasn't all that surprising, for although the town's population (if not its wealth) was split pretty evenly between Taigs and Prods, she'd got to the age of ten without knowingly meeting a Protestant.

Obviously she'd *seen* Prods down the town, but they went to the litter of churches on their side of it, while Maeve attended the big Catholic chapel that dominated her side. They had separate schools, too, with different start and end times to avoid conflict on the way to and from school, which resulted in the supposedly mixed school buses becoming either Catholic or Protestant.

Maeve's mam shopped in the Catholic newsagent, grocer, butcher and chemist, while the Prods stuck to their own equivalents. But the Prods had a monopoly on enterprises that required serious money, like the hardware shop, jewellers and furniture place. Maeve didn't like those shops. They always had a watchful, anxious sort of a feel about them that Maeve's mam said was because the owners were always on alert for fire-bombs, or worse.

All the housing estates were segregated, though Maeve'd heard that Taigs and Prods had been mixed together in the estates way back in the sixties. Her mam'd said, 'Most Prods were as poor as Taigs, most Taigs were as hungry as Prods. We hadn't the energy to whale the shite out of each other.' But when the Troubles took off, both sides naturally clustered closer to their own kind, and families who lacked that survival instinct were 'encouraged' to leave.

Maeve was seven the night the last Prod was petrol-bombed out of her estate. She remembered the way the graffiti on the wall seemed to flicker in the firelight.

Prods Fuck Off
Vótáil Sinn Fein
Brits out
IRA all the way

She'd watched the flames from the burning house lick the dark December sky, her fingertips tingling as though she'd touched something hot and holy. She'd felt like she was part of a tradition so old it might even be pagan. It had been a good feeling at the time, but she'd felt kind of dirty the next day when the burnt-out house sat like a broken tooth in the terrace opposite.

On the whole – through an enormous effort by the schools, churches, communities and government – the town was almost completely segregated. Which explained how Maeve's first formal meeting with a Prod her own age had taken place in the back of an armoured police car. That day, she'd been chanting her nine times tables with the rest of the class when Charleen McCafferty – whose whole family had an innate radar for the security forces – had shouted, 'Police!'

Everyone gawked out of the window as two armoured police cars pulled up outside the gates. Mrs Boyle tried to restore order by rapping the metre ruler on her desk and threatening murder as a male and female constable lumbered up the school path. The class was under a glimmer of control when a knock at the door sent another ripple of excitement – and fear – around the room.

The headmaster opened the door and gave a stern sort of a look over at Mrs Boyle, who nodded severely back at him. 'Right. Maeve Murray and Stephen McLaughlin, get up now and go with the master.'

Stephen McLaughlin – the wee lick – had got up right away and headed over to the door. But Maeve didn't move a muscle.

'Come on, Miss Murray,' growled the headmaster. 'We haven't got all day!'

Maeve scuttled over to the door and allowed him to herd her down the corridor towards his office. But she stopped dead at the door when she realised the police were lying in wait.

'In ye go,' the master said, shoving Maeve and Stephen into the office. He shut the door, then sat down behind his desk wearing a smile that put the fear of God into Maeve. 'So. This is Sergeant Smith,' the master said, stretching his face in the direction of a partially bullet-proofed policeman.

Sergeant Smith nodded at Maeve and Stephen, one hand resting on a handgun, while the other cradled a submachine gun, like a woman trying to keep a hold of a newborn and an obstreperous toddler.

'And this is Constable Short.'

The policewoman smiled and said, 'Hi' in a weird accent that could've been from as far off as Belfast. Though she also wore body armour, she wasn't armed, for lady policemen weren't allowed guns. Looking at her gave Maeve the sad feeling she got when she saw a docked dog wagging the stump where its tail had been.

'Sergeant Smith and Constable Short are here to escort you pair to a cross-community event,' the master said.

Maeve felt her bowels contract. Cross-community events had scared the shite out of her ever since Deirdre'd come back deranged from a trust-building residential weekend in Corrymeela. She'd told Maeve that on the first morning, a flabby Welshman had split the Taigs and Prods into mixed teams, then given them a sheet of plastic, a few sticks and a roll of duct tape. He'd instructed them to build a raft, which they'd later launch on the lough loaded with several team members. Of course, as soon as his back was turned, the Prods had grabbed Deirdre, taped her mouth and bound her wrists and ankles and thrown her into the water 'to see if it was true that Taigs floated'. Deirdre hadn't floated. The Prods who'd thrown her into the lough got no apple crumble after dinner that evening, something Deirdre'd said mattered not a shite to them, for as everyone knew, Prods weren't into apple crumble as they were mad for the traybakes.

The next morning, the groups had to participate in a trust game that required someone from one persuasion to fall backwards off a stone wall into a net of hands from another persuasion. Deirdre'd said they'd won that exercise before it even started because the Prods lost the toss and had to go first. A small, round Prod by the name of Gillian Gilchrist ended up in A&E with a split skull after the net of Catholic hands she fell into proved equal to their trust in the Prods.

Maeve'd asked Deirdre how her team had got away with the incident, even getting traybakes for dessert that evening. Deirdre'd shrugged and said, 'We just told the supervisor we never understood the rules.' Then she'd paused, narrowing her eyes, before adding, 'But we understood – us and the Prods – we understood the rules. It's *them* who don't understand.'

'The Inaugural Inter-County Inter-School Integrated quiz starts today,' the master said, rubbing his hands together as if he could generate a storm of enthusiasm big enough to electrify everyone in the room. 'You two have been selected to form a team with Lorna and Nigel from the Other School across the bridge to represent our town.'

The master conjoined his hairy eyebrows and glared meaningfully at Maeve and Stephen as he said 'the Other School', as if they didn't know what that meant.

'Where's Lorna and Nigel?' Maeve asked.

The sergeant flashed a look over at the woman police constable, who took a breath before answering. 'Lorna and Nigel are feeling a bit nervous. They decided to wait in the car.' She got to her feet. 'I'll introduce you now, if you're ready?'

'Right then,' the master said, jumping to attention. 'Do us proud!'

Maeve wondered what the master meant by 'do us proud'. Did he want them to win the quiz, or sabotage it? Should she refuse to collaborate with the planters who'd stolen their land hundreds of years previously? Should she sit in silent protest at eight hundred years of English oppression? And she wondered if participating in a quiz organised by the RUC would make her and Stephen legitimate targets? Worst of all, nobody'd mentioned what the prize was. She could only hope it'd be cold hard cash. But it was mostly likely to be some sort of daftness like 'stronger, more resilient inter-community relations'.

She slunk off with Stephen, behind the police. They were split up at the armoured cars. The sergeant directed Stephen into what Maeve thought of as the boys' car, while Constable Short ushered Maeve into the girls' car.

'Lorna, this is Maeve. Maeve, Lorna.'

A blonde girl roughly Maeve's age gawped at her. Maeve hadn't the faintest clue what she was supposed to do. Should she shake the other girl's hand? Say 'Hiya' or 'Lovely to meet you'?

Lorna turned away and stared straight ahead, so Maeve played it safe and did the same. Nobody introduced the grim-faced policeman who drove the silent car down past the graveyard. Properly holy people, like Caoimhe McShane and Catherine Mullan, blessed themselves at the first graveyard wall, then bowed their heads in prayer until they reached the second graveyard wall where they blessed themselves again, but Maeve thought that was weird. She only blessed herself and said *Lord have mercy* silently inside her head while picturing her dead Granny Walsh, like she'd been trained to do at First Holy Communion. But as she did so, she realised that nobody else in the police car traced the sign of the cross on their chest.

Though Maeve had heard that Prods didn't bless themselves, her stomach turned over at seeing this first-hand.

Later that night, Maeve's mam had interrogated her in front of the fire while her four brothers and Deirdre watched from the sofa. Maeve explained things as best she could: she'd been escorted from school in the back of an armoured vehicle to a neutral venue where she'd participated in a Hands Across the Divide quiz that was policed by RUC officers with submachine guns. And they'd won.

'How many rounds are there in this quiz?' Deirdre had asked, her eyes glittering.

'It's a sudden death tournament,' Maeve had replied. 'We're through to the quarter finals.'

'So, they'll be lifting the pair of youse again?'

That hadn't occurred to Maeve. 'I suppose,' she said, panicking at the idea of facing up to three more rounds of cross-community quizzing. But she survived the next three rounds, only speaking to Lorna and Nigel when conferring during team rounds. She believed her mam was proud when their team got to the finals. They were up against four posh Belfast kids, who wore blazers, shirts and ties instead of sweatshirts plastic-printed with a pixelated school crest that the hungrier pupils picked at when they ran out of snotters.

After they'd annihilated their opposition, they were forced to pose for a photo. The two boys got to hold one handle each of a big silver cup, while Maeve and Lorna stood like tools at either side, with Constable Short and Sergeant Smith looming behind them.

The photo had been published in the local newspaper, so Maeve's mam'd written off for a copy of the photo. She didn't frame it (she wasn't the framing type), and she didn't prop it up on the mantelpiece like Stephen's mam did. But from time to time she took it out of the drawer and showed the neighbours, saying, 'Isn't it a shame now, they didn't take a photo of the weans without those pigs in it?'

Maeve was glad all that contrived bridge-building shite was behind her. That *How to Win Friends and Influence People* was the actual answer to getting on with Protestants. She was looking forward to trying out Dale's tricks for relaxing them, and his tactics for avoiding triggering them. She was hopeful that all the practice she'd get over the summer with Protestants would equip her for dealing with the touchy fuckers Ulster Protestants modelled themselves on: the English.

Everyone in the canteen was going at the tea and toast like it was their day's work. Then the door swung open and Mary entered, carrying a wallop of cake.

'Oh ho, Mary!' Mabel said. 'Who are we celebrating today?'

Even before Mary raised her eyebrows, Maeve knew by the colour of Mickey McCanny that he was the focus of the celebration.

'Another year older, hey, Mickey?' Marilyn shouted, as he slid down in his chair.

'Well, he's not a year wiser anyway, still stuck in this kip!' Baldy Magee said.

Mary set the cake on the table, flicked her lighter, and lit the strawberry-striped candles with a shaky hand. Then she started singing 'Happy Birthday' in a quavery voice while waving one hand, summoning everyone to join in.

'Happy birthday to you!

Happy birthday to you!

Happy birthday, dear Mehhhhh-key,

Happy birthday to you.'

Maeve was all ears at the end, expecting the Prods to add an extra line like they did when they were saying the 'Our Father', or to salute the Queen or something equally mad. But everyone started clapping and a thrill went through Maeve – she liked that they'd the 'Happy Birthday' song in common.

Mary doled out the cake onto the blue paper towels that she'd robbed from the senior staff toilet, then everyone ambled up to get a slice, in total slacker mode.

Maeve grabbed a slice of cake and horsed it into her so she'd be finished before the bell rang.

'Lovely cake, Mary,' Mabel Moore said through a mouthful of crumbs. 'You're a good hand with the cakes.'

The bell rang, so Maeve, Caroline and Aoife got to their feet. But everyone else sat on. 'Are we striking or what?' Maeve asked, looking around.

'It's Mickey's birthday,' Fidelma said. 'We get five minutes extra for a birthday.'

Maeve sat down, sorry she'd shovelled her cake into her.

'What age are ye now?' Mary asked Mickey, who kept his eyes on his cake.

'Thirty.'

'Jesus. Thirty.' Baldy whistled. 'Boysadear! The years don't be long flying in now, do they?'

'How old d'ye feel, Mickey?' Maeve asked, curious.

'Ye're only as old as the woman ye feel.' Baldy sniggered. He was pure jealous of the fact Mickey was seeing a nineteen-year-old up in Derry.

'Ah still feel twenty. Honest to God. It's like ah got stuck at twenty. But then ah head out with a gang of twenty-year-olds, and ah suddenly feel the value of thirty.'

As the oul wans clucked and tutted about old age, Maeve considered what it'd be like to reach the age of thirty. She'd turned eighteen in late May. Deirdre'd made it to nineteen. In her head, Kurt Cobain had lived as long as a human possibly could while remaining hot and relevant. Thirty was frigging ancient – Maeve couldn't picture making it that far, never mind deeper into a hellscape populated by wrinkly oul fuckers who couldn't hold their drink, pish or farts.

Mabel Moore limped towards Mickey and laid her hands on his shoulders. 'Just you remember,' she said, as he wilted under her grip, 'the older the fiddle, the sweeter the tune.' She leaned down and gave him a big smacker on the cheek. He rubbed his face with the back of his hand as Mabel cackled above him, her face puckered into a riot of wrinkles.

That afternoon, Maeve was warbling along to Whigfield when the main doors swung open. Three men walked in and paused at the top of the factory floor. Marilyn Spears stopped sewing and gawped at them, porridge-faced. One of the men pointed at Billy, who put down the roll of fabric he was working on. As the men walked towards Billy, Marilyn squeezed out of her chair and ran after them. There was a short, intense conversation, then Billy pulled off his chainmail glove, fired it on the ground and stormed out of the side door. The three men and Marilyn followed not far behind.

Maeve – and everyone else – kept working. Billy didn't come back, but about five minutes later, Marilyn reappeared and gathered up a few of her Prod cronies. As she marched them out the door, Maeve caught Caroline's eye. She nodded discreetly at the toilets. Caroline gave a tiny nod and got to her feet. Maeve waited twenty seconds before following her in.

'What the frig's going on there?' Caroline's eyes were wide.

'No idea. I only saw what you saw.'

'So who are them fellas?'

'No idea. Hardy-looking boyos, any roads. Wouldn't want them coming in after me at work.'

Caroline checked her watch. 'The news'll be on soon. Might be worth listening to.'

'It's the English news,' Maeve said. 'Whatever's bugging Billy probably won't feature.'

'Right enough. But we need tae get back out there anyway, before Mary hunts us.'

Maeve scanned the room from time to time as the newscaster on the radio gravely described the rail strike that was *crippling Britain*. A series of English commuters came on air whinging about the *economic devastation* being *wreaked* on Britain because they couldn't hop on a train to work. Maeve wondered sourly how they'd feel if they had to live in her wee corner of British-occupied Ireland, where the Protestant-majority government had ripped the railways out of the Catholic-majority counties decades earlier. Then, right at the tail end of the news bulletin, the newscaster noted that reports were coming in of a multiple shooting in Belfast. Glances leapt like flames across the factory floor. Mouths hardened, eyebrows twitched. Maeve doubted *How to Win Friends and Influence People* would have a chapter that'd help her smooth over this situation. The best she could do was put her head down and try to keep her focus on her own targets.

A few minutes before the four o'clock news, Paddy Quinn and Fidelma Hegarty marched out of the fire doors. Maeve slunk out after them. They didn't say a word as Paddy fiddled with his pocket radio. When he caught the crackle of the Radio Foyle news jingle he sat down, strangely still, staring at the radio as if something might appear in the speaker. A grave newsreader announced that the Irish National Liberation Army had shot several men outside the headquarters of the Ulster Volunteer Force on the Shankill Road. One man had been killed outright, another critically injured, and a few others wounded. A local politician condemned the violence as *a scurrilous attack on innocent Protestant people.*

Maeve sighed. That sort of shit put her right off journalism: she didn't get how the reporter could stand idly by letting someone describe the people who hung about a paramilitary HQ as 'innocent'. She was relieved when Paddy switched the radio off.

'So the INLA's decided tae fuck things right up for everyone,' Fidelma Hegarty said, growling from deep in her throat, like one of those big cats Maeve loved watching on nature documentaries.

'But why are the INLA starting up now when there's all this talk about peace?' Maeve asked. 'Are they feeling left out?'

Fidelma snorted, making her feel about one foot high. 'Them bucks in the INLA aren't fit to suck their own fingers. That's no INLA attack. That's the IRA settling scores before they give up their guns.' Fidelma paused and looked down at Paddy as if waiting for him to agree or disagree. He looked her in the eye but said nothing. 'And here's another thing,' she continued. 'The UVF'll not be long in retaliating. They'll be after another Greysteel. And if ah've worked that out, ye can be sure the IRA's well aware of the fact.'

A weight sank into Maeve's guts. She remembered the UVF attack on the Rising Sun bar in Greysteel the Halloween before. 'Trick or treat!' the gunmen had roared before opening fire. They'd run off laughing, leaving eight dead and nineteen wounded.

Paddy stood up and collapsed the radio aerial with a slap. 'The IRA can't be held responsible for the actions of the UVF,' he said, quietly.

In the silence that followed, something clicked inside Maeve. 'The IRA must be serious about a ceasefire if they're at shit like this,' she said.

Paddy looked at her, then tucked the radio into his jacket. 'Have ye not learned yet that the IRA's always serious?' he asked, then turned on his heel and headed back indoors.

Fidelma sat with a thump on the blue plastic chair and frowned. 'We'll have tae lie as low as Larne Catholics for the next while,' she said.

Maeve nodded. She knew the drill. Head down. Back against the wall. Emergency exits noted.

The bell rang for tea break, and Maeve and Fidelma went in and joined the silent procession towards the canteen. No one said a word as they collected their mugs of tea. The Prods sat munching their biscuits aggressively at Maeve's side as if to say, 'We have our eye on youse.' And her side crunched their biccies right back at the Prods to say, 'Aye, and we're watching youse.'

The UVF shot a Catholic taxi driver that Friday, then gunned down a couple of Protestant builders they'd mistaken for Taigs. Maeve had the same sick feeling everyone else had: the UVF was only warming up. She was pure relieved when Aoife said that James was willing to drive them over the border for a night out. She was dying to get out of the town and into a Free State pub where she could sink a pint without flinching every time the door opened. The plan was perfect until James revealed his plot to go for a brisk walk on the beach before going to the pub. 'It'll do us good,' he'd said, when he saw the look on Maeve's face. 'Blow the cobwebs away!' Aoife'd added. But when they arrived at the beach, it was raining so hard that even James balked like a horse refusing a fence.

'Let's sit here until the rain blows over,' he said, after parking his car facing the sea.

Maeve rubbed a peephole in the steam on her window, but all she could see was the rain hopping off the glass.

'Rossnowlagh in Irish is "Ros Neamhlach",' Aoife said, opening her window and taking a deep breath of salty air. 'That means "heavenly headland".'

'If that's Donegal's idea of heaven,' Maeve said, wiping rain spatters off her face, 'I'd hate to experience hell.'

She shivered and hunched deeper into her seat, watching James fiddle with the radio. He was wearing a fancy shirt. She'd begun to judge the boys and men she met by their shirts. Not just by the brand, but the cut and fabric. It took her just seconds to dissect the shirt on a man's back now. She could price the cuffs, cut and buttons. She knew the value of the fabric and how a button-down tripled the cost of the collar. She knew which shirts should be tucked and how many buttons should be left open. But for all the specifics, the men she met in shirts could be boiled down to one of two types: bootleg culchies in checked shirts, and fellas with notions in Ben Sherman's.

'Is that a new shirt, James?' she asked.

'Yep. Aoife got me it for my birthday.'

'Looks well on ye,' Caroline said. 'Is it a Ben Sherman?'

James shrugged and lifted his two hands into mid-air, looking at his cuffs as if he could see the brand there.

'It's a Ben Sherman,' Aoife said. Then she added, 'James is a large,' as if that meant something special.

Maeve hated how women's clothes came in extra small, small, medium and large while men's shirts came in medium, large and extra-large – like there was no such thing as a small man. 'I sometimes picture the sort of Englishman who wears the shirts we make,' Maeve said. 'They're all called Bob or Dave and they start most sentences with the words, "The thing about me, right, is…" and say stuff like, "I'm the sort of bloke, right, who"—'

'Och, Maeve,' Caroline said. 'Leave the English alone. It's not right slagging them like that.'

'I will not. Can ye not see them wearing our shirts down the pub to watch soccer and drink pints, trying to pull birds but ending up roaring "ENG-GRRRR-LAAA-NNNNND"?'

'Well, if they'll pay M and S or Ben Sherman good money to keep us in food and drink, I'm not complaining.'

'They're still wankers,' Maeve said, opening her window a crack. She was gasping for a fag, but James had this weird no smoking in the car rule.

'Have you ever wondered if our shirts end up being worn by British soldiers?' Aoife asked. 'Like when they're off duty?'

'Och, Aoife!' Maeve said, her head falling backwards as if she'd been shot. Trust Aoife to ruin the craic.

'But have you not?'

The worst thing was that Aoife seemed genuinely curious.

'Ah haven't, naw,' Maeve said, hoping she'd put an end to the conversation.

'Well, it's crossed my mind, so it has,' Caroline said. 'There we are on one hand sewing shirts for the English while on the other we're boycotting Newtowncoote butter because it comes from Protestant cows.'

'Yeah,' Aoife said, turning around in her seat. 'The IRA blew up the Chinese takeaway in the town because they served the police one night. And they're always targeting the Shorts factory.'

'Shorts make bombs, Aoife! We make shirts!' Maeve snapped.

James turned the radio off. The sound of depressed waves flopping onto the beach filled the car. 'Look,' he said, 'I don't know why the IRA doesn't blow up factories for processing chickens or making clothes for the English. Maybe it's because the chickens and the clothes get boxed up and shipped off and we don't really know who eats what or wears what in the end. Maybe the IRA hasn't classified clothes and chickens as integral to the struggle.'

James said 'the struggle' the way the O'Neills always did: ironically, as if it was a tussle between toddlers. Maeve stared out of the window, digging her fingernails into her arm, wishing he'd shut the fuck up.

'Whatever the reason, I'm glad the factory is left in peace. I'm glad you can all earn some money over the summer. I'm glad that the likes of Marilyn Spears and Mary can earn a living in the town. And I'd love it to last.' James flicked a lever. The wipers swept over the windscreen, then a prickle of drizzle settled on the glass. 'Well, it looks like it's easing,' he said. 'Will we give up on the walk and make a run for the pub?'

Maeve flung open her door and sprinted to the Sandhouse.

They ended up staying for hours. Aoife and James had brought their fiddles, which meant their table had free drink carried to it. Caroline got drunk enough to sing 'Only Our Rivers Run Free', which made all the oul fuckers wet-eyed, and gave the younger lads a hard-on.

Maeve couldn't bear how everyone missed the frigging point of the song so she took herself away outside for a fag. She was staring at the waves smashing off the rocks to the front of the hotel when the door behind her opened, pouring yellow light, music and the stink of beer into the night. Maeve's hackles rose as she readied herself to deal with the sleazebag who'd followed her out of the door.

'Are you not freezing?'

It was just James.

'Where there's no sense there's no feeling.'

He moved closer to her. 'Are you tired? Do you want to head home?'

Maeve shook her head. 'I'm fucken tired of home, is my problem.'

'Well, not long til you get the results. You'll be away before you know it.'

'If I get the results.'

'You'll get the results.'

The waves crashed in the silence.

'Will you miss nothing about the town when you're gone?'

Maeve took a drag on her fag. She wasn't going to admit she was scared she'd miss everything and terrified she'd miss nothing. 'I'll miss Caroline. But I'm hoping me and Aoife'll see each other when we're in England. She can visit me. I'll visit her.'

'And maybe I can visit you too, when I'm over to see Aoife?'

Maeve tried to imagine James in London. It wasn't an easy thing. He looked at that moment the way she liked him: salt-slicked by sea spray, his fingertips hot and red from the fiddle strings, wearing a look of such hope that her heart near broke. 'I'd love tae show you around London.'

James smiled and took a step forward just as the side door opened.

'James?' Aoife stood in the doorway, light haloing her body. She squinted at Maeve and James. 'They've been asking for Morrison's jig. I need you to keep me right on it.'

'Coming,' James said, stepping into the light. Then he paused and glanced at Maeve.

'I'll be in after this,' she said, waving her fag.

When the door closed, she took a last drag, then flicked the glowing butt out into the ocean, where it was swallowed up without a sound. She knew James didn't approve of smoking. And she had this feeling that Aoife didn't approve of her.

Maeve put the finishing touches to the sparkly shamrock she'd drawn on her cheek with some emerald eyeshadow and blew herself a kiss in the mirror. She was still hungover to fuck after the night before, but Ireland was playing Italy in the World Cup. Her and Caroline made their way down to the Old School Bar. Maeve rapped on the locked door using the I'm-a-Taig-Open-Says-Me knock they used when times were tense. The letterbox rattled twice in response, so she slid her ID through.

After a few seconds, Iggy Loughrey opened the door just wide enough to let them squeeze in, then bolted it shut again.

Maeve and Caroline settled down with their drinks well away from the door and windows. They'd no hopes for the match. They were only there for the craic. But twelve minutes into the game Ray Houghton chipped the ball into the corner of the goal and Maeve and everyone else in the bar jumped to their feet and roared before guldering 'The Fields of Athenry' along with the sixty thousand Irish fans in the Giants Stadium.

When the final whistle blew, Maeve collapsed back in her seat like she'd been concussed by a blast. She'd tasted winning. And she liked the smack of it.

The next morning, Maeve dragged herself down the road home for Father's Day. The news had given her a worse sickening than the booze. She knew nobody wanted to watch footage. But nobody could switch over. They owed the wee men who'd died in a bar in Loughinisland while cheering for Ireland that much.

. . . direct reprisal for the INLA shooting at the UVF headquarters on the Shankill Road . . .

Maeve's da loved Father's Day. When she was younger she'd always ask him what he wanted. And every year he'd give the same answer: 'Sure, what would I want when I've six weans?'

'Daddy!' she'd squeal, delighted.

. . . one of horror, one of sadness, we are undoubtedly now in a spiral of tit-for-tat killings . . .

Maeve's mam would watch out of the corner of her eye, half smiling.

'Ah've wan daughter to wash dishes and clothes. And wan tae cook and clean.'

Maeve'd complain that she wasn't his slave. Deirdre'd say something around women's rights.

'And I've four lumps of cubs who'll play for Tyrone.'

. . . Eleven people were shot in the back. Six men are dead . . .

They'd all hand over their usual presents: aftershave from Deirdre, Jelly Babies from Maeve, a bottle of stout from Chris, socks from Paul and a jumper from Deci and Mick.

. . . no retaliation . . .

He'd open his presents, dabbing on the aftershave, offering the sweets around, trying on his socks and jumper before easing open his bottle of stout and taking a sup.

. . . The RUC never gives up. You will be caught and you will spend long years in prison. We will leave no stone unturned . . .

Maeve's mam clucked her tongue. 'Well, now, at least they saw the goal scored, before they were kilt.'

Her da bit the head off a Jelly Baby. 'Ye have to wonder, though. Would that've happened if we'd a united Irish team?'

. . . yet another community brought to the edge of despair by the paramilitaries . . .

Maeve stared at the telly. Thought of the civil wee man with his comb-over, the undrunk pints sitting flat on the bar.

Monday, 20 June 1994

56 days until results

Maeve had sandbags in her belly. When shit had happened before, she'd only had to share streets with the other side. But that morning she'd be sharing the air she breathed. And there was Aoife to think about. When she'd first moved to the town from the Free State, she'd been pure clueless. Maeve had to teach her stuff like how to tell which bomb alert was obviously a hoax, and what might be the real deal; what death threat was a deadly serious paramilitary plan, and what was more likely to be some dickhead trying to put the wind up you. Aoife – as usual – had been a star pupil. She learned the ropes fast. But she'd never mastered keeping a cool head, and made a real show of herself when Arnie McArnold was shot dead. Maeve was sad herself when Arnie was shot – it was a shitty enough thing to happen – but he wasn't the first person from the town to be killed – and they'd long worked out a template for dealing with shite like that.

Och, did you hear so-and-so was shot?

Och, he was not, was he?

Och, aye. Shot dead in his bed/car/outside the shop/inside the shed/up the bog/down the road.

Och, naw. It's not right, so it's not.

Och, it's wild. Shot him in front of his mammy/daddy/children/boss/animals.

Och, God help them.

Och, now, when will it ever end?

Lord only knows.

Maeve didn't know most of the people killed locally, for they were generally Protestants. When she was younger she always headed down the town after a bomb or gun attack to watch the reporters. She liked the way they were lit up when they spoke at the cameras – shining through the drizzle like moving statues. Later, on the telly, however, the reporters looked ordinary, while local people swam in and out of focus in the background, like fish lurking in muddy waters, their expressions shifty, as if they suspected that they were suspects.

Maeve's mam always said the same thing at the end of a report: 'Ah don't care who he was or what he was doing, that's a sin, so it is.' Her da would nod and grumble: 'Two wrongs don't make a right.' Maeve was unnerved by how personally her parents took those murders. She didn't feel the deaths in her teeth and bones the way her parents seemed to. She suspected it was because she'd grown up in the Troubles – neighbours shooting neighbours was just the way things had always been for her. It was the older generations who were more easily disturbed. But a few murders did get under her skin. Like when the IRA shot Samuel Frost in his clock shop. Even the sheep on Muckish hill knew that Samuel was a civil wee man who didn't make a living from his shop, for as he said himself, clocks were on the way out both on mantelpieces and in car bombs: everything was going electronic. Samuel fixed clocks for the love of it. The IRA hadn't even been after him – they were after his son, whose part-time soldiering role made him a full-time target. Twenty-six bullets missed Samuel as he stood in front of his son. One struck him in the chest.

Samuel's shop was always cluttered with mechanisms, the air flickering with tick-tocks, so the device the gunmen left sitting on the counter went unnoticed until it triggered half an hour later, taking the right arm off the ambulance man who'd just given up resuscitating Samuel. The explosion was later described as 'miraculous' because nobody'd died in it.

Maeve'd grown up thinking her town was the site of more miracles than Lourdes.

For a while she hadn't liked walking past Samuel's shop and she was sad when Granny Walsh's clock stopped ticking and nobody could fix it. But in the end she got used to the silent clock and could walk past the boarded-up shop without it taking a flinch out of her. She'd learned long before Aoife moved to the town that she could get used to almost anything, eventually.

But it was a different story when the IRA shot Arnie McArnold.

He'd been a sports coach who'd got money from the Peace People to run a free course of trampoline lessons in the local leisure centre. Aoife'd begged Maeve to do trampolining with her, so Maeve had to drag her mam down to the leisure centre to speak to Arnie. He'd described trampolining as, 'Acrobatics, sort of,' and reassured her mam that there'd be no rackets, batons or physical contact, and no requirement to share changing rooms with Prods. Maeve was dead chuffed when her mam reported back to her da saying, 'They'd want to be really keen on killing each other to manage it in thon class.'

After the free course was over, Arnie formed a team out of the four Catholics and Protestants who could scrape together fifty pence each week for a paid class. He split them into Taig–Prod pairs, so once a week Maeve bounced in time with a Prod under the glaring lights of the leisure centre.

It was all going grand until the IRA ambushed Arnie one murky December morning on his farm up near the border. Maeve's mam had crossed herself and muttered, 'God help them, whatever they did,' when the blue lights of the ambulance flickered over them as it screeched through the town. Later, her da came in with the papers and the news he'd picked up in the shop. 'Some fella shot dead on his farm. Was out milking the cows. Part-time soldier, I hear.'

'It's not right, targeting them like that,' her mam said, frowning. 'Like they're poaching rabbits.'

Tears had trembled in Maeve's eyes when she saw the footage of Arnie's widowed mother being steered past the security cordons and helped up the path to her house. But she knew better than to cry: sympathy for a dead Protestant was one thing, grief was quite another.

Aoife hadn't yet learned that lesson. She came to Maeve's door later that day, white-faced and wet-eyed. She'd cried more over Arnie in a few hours than Maeve'd yet cried for Deirdre. In the end, her mam had to ring the O'Neills and tell them to come and get Aoife. Maeve didn't see her for a few weeks after that, for Mrs O'Neill carried her off to Dublin for a 'break'.

If the UVF attack in Loughinisland had gotten under Maeve's skin (that wee old man and his comb-over), she was sure it'd lodge in Aoife's bones.

But Aoife didn't mention the shooting. Nobody did. And it wasn't on the radio because the English were pure gagging for the latest on OJ Simpson. There was zero craic on the factory floor, but things were bearable until they filed into the canteen for the first tea break. Maeve, like most people, kept her head down and avoided catching anyone's eye. The sound of toast being chewed and mugs clunking on tables was the only sound, until one of the swing doors nudged open and Mary scuttled in with a cake. She placed it on a table and lit the candles without saying a word. Then she picked up the cake and presented it to Karen Gilchrist from the button machine.

'Och, Karen, is it your birthday?' Marilyn Spears asked, perkily.

Karen nodded miserably.

'Och, and what age are ye now?'

'Thirty-three.'

'Still a rose with the dew fresh on ye.'

'C'mon, that's enough oul chat.' Mary scowled. 'These candles have no last in them.'

Maeve gripped her mug as Mary took a wheezy breath and started singing 'Happy Birthday'. She couldn't bring herself to sing. And Caroline had her mouth zipped. So did Aoife. Fidelma Hegarty was sitting with a big purple head on her, pure raging, beside a thin-lipped Paddy Quinn. Marilyn was belting out 'Happy Birthday' as if she alone could make up for the half-silent room. After a spatter of applause, Mary cut up the cake and doled it out. Aoife recoiled from her slice as if it was a plateful of warm dung, then she pushed her chair back and got to her feet. Fidelma Hegarty also stood up, and so did Maeve and Caroline. As they walked back to the factory floor, they were joined by Paddy Quinn, Mickey McCanny and every other Catholic in the factory.

Every Catholic except for Mary.

Maeve picked up a shirt and began to iron. The torrent of shirts pouring through the production line that day came as a relief. Her body and factory time disappeared as she went into autopilot. She didn't have to think about the frigging factory or who was working in it when she became a part of it. Bottlenecks were the bad bit. That's when the thoughts came skittering back: their exam results lying in wait; Deirdre's dark eyes staring at the ward ceiling; the latest news. When she ran out of shirts, Maeve mooched over to Caroline, where she sat reversing her pile of sewn-up epaulettes, to try and help speed her up. But every time Mary clocked her sitting with Caroline she'd hoosh her away off to sweep the floor or clip buttons off the damaged shirts.

Mary never bossed Aoife around, for she'd attached herself to Paddy Quinn. In the start Aoife was like a wee shadow stuck to him, handing him screwdrivers and watching him strip down the broken machines. She asked enough smart questions to keep him entertained, and soon became his mascot. Before long Paddy had Aoife fixing things. Sometimes, during tea break, he'd tell the other men what she'd done, saying she was 'some hand' with the machines, noting, 'She's a useful woman to have around.' Aoife'd glow pink above her mug of tea, not noticing that Paddy was treating her much like a pet monkey that he'd trained to shit in the toilet instead of on the floor. After a while, when Paddy was busy, the machinists started shouting at Aoife to come look at their machines when something went wrong, for as often as not, she could fix minor glitches and keep them off basic, though it fucked her own bonus. Maeve'd asked Aoife about it one day. Asked her why she stopped pressing to help someone else make a few pence more. 'It's not about the money,' she'd said, without explaining what the fuck it *was* about.

On Wednesday morning Maeve caught sight of Mary limping down the stairs from Andy's office. Although Mary was up and down to Andy's office the whole time, nobody ever accused her of flashing her flaps at him. *Perhaps nobody wants to think of Mary's flaps*, Maeve thought, thinking of Mary's flaps.

'Maeve Murray,' Mary guldered, 'in tae my office.'

Maeve finished the shirt she was working on and slung it over the rail before slouching into Mary's office like she didn't give a fuck, even though her legs were shaking.

'Sit down,' Mary said, nodding at a chair.

Maeve sat down in the other chair and crossed her arms. She wished she'd some chewing gum. Chewing gum always made her look like she gave zero fucks.

'So you're here what, two weeks, is it now, Miss Murray?'

Maeve hated it when people from the town called her by her surname. It was only ever an insult.

'Aye.'

Mary paused to light a fag.

'And how are you finding us?' Mary said, all arsey attitude.

Maeve was sick of arsey attitude. Everyone from the town had an attitude for anyone from the town who'd an attitude about the town. Everyone resented anyone who'd hope of getting out, especially – Maeve knew well – someone like her, who came from a shite family. It was alright for Aoife O'Neill with her accountant father and artist mother to have notions, but

Maeve's da had been invalided out of the pig factory when he got sick of the guts and gore, while her mam'd swapped her marching and civil rights for the fags and bennies. Her da's side had been landless farm workers who'd wintered in the town before heading to Scotland to work most of the year as hired farmhands; her mam's side called themselves factory workers, though they'd spent more of their lives on the dole than the factory floor. There wasn't a single shopkeeper, publican, priest, nun, teacher or doctor in Maeve's family, and looking at the cut of her brothers, there wasn't much hope of one in the future. They couldn't afford to buy their council house. Nobody as poor as Maeve could afford to have notions about herself. Which was why she treasured them.

'The factory's great for me personally. I'm learning loads.'

Mary cocked an eyebrow, giving Maeve the feeling she was about to piss all over what she'd said. 'And what is it ye think you're learning?'

Maeve was dying to say, 'I'm learning how not tae be a sad oul bitch like you, counting the years off before I'm buried by weans who've forgotten the way I like tae take my tay.' But she didn't. 'Well, there's the obvious stuff. Designing a shirt's one thing. Producing it is a whole other thing. It's interesting to see how the design affects production. Like epaulettes. There's no point to them at all, they're a pain in the hole to sew, and they add an extra ninety-five pence to the shop price of a shirt. And still the English are after them.'

Mary nodded, but said nothing.

'Then there's the skills,' Maeve said. 'Billy cutting the material, the machinists sewing the pieces, stitching the whole thing together. It's pure magic watching everyone work together.'

Maeve knew by the dead look in Mary's eyes that she hadn't yet said the right thing.

'But I haven't a clue about the bigger picture. Like who designed the system in the first place. Or how contracts come in the door. Or how this place is financed.'

Mary puffed on her fag. 'And what about the way people work?' she asked. 'D'ye think ye've got a handle on that?'

Suddenly, Maeve wasn't so sure of herself. 'What d'ye mean?'

'What ah said. D'ye have a handle on how the people work in here?'

'Like how it's a mixed workplace? Catholics and Protestants all working together?'

'Ah wouldn't go as far as tae say we work together,' Mary said, squinting. 'Side by side's more like.'

Maeve thought of the way the factory jobs were distributed, like a see-saw for Taigs and Prods. Billy was on cutting – a prestigious, skilled job; so Paddy Quinn was on machine maintenance – which probably paid about the same. Fidelma was on quality; Sharon was on packing. Mickey McCanny worked the fusing press, so Karen Gilchrist operated the button machine.

'And d'ye know who runs the place?' Mary asked.

'Well, you and Andy manage the factory, don't youse?'

'Aye. We manage it alright,' Mary said, crushing her fag into the overflowing ashtray. 'But what you need to figure out, Miss Murray, is who runs it.'

On Friday morning Maeve ripped her envelope open and pulled out her payslip, hoping to see £123 – the amount she'd figured she was due. But the total was just £92.65. She squinted at her basic, wondering what sort of a dirty trick Andy Strawbridge was playing on her. It was £70, not £80. And her bonus was a shitty £22.65. A second later she noticed the name on the payslip: *Marilyn Spears*.

'Ah, fuck. Fuck fuck fuck fuck FUCK!'

'What's up?' Caroline called from the kitchen.

'Mary's mixed my payslip up with Marilyn Spears.'

'Well, how much does Marilyn earn?' Caroline said, hurrying in, all biz. 'Gimme a nosey!' She snatched the payslip and scanned it.

Maeve pictured Marilyn Spears exhibiting her payslip all round the Proddie side of town. News like that wouldn't rest long over the bridge. Soon everyone'd know about the extra tenner Andy was paying her.

She was fucked.

Later that day Maeve tried to explain to Aoife why she was so fucked. But Aoife didn't get it. Of course she didn't.

'It's Andy's factory. He can pay people whatever he likes,' she said, imperiously.

Caroline looked up from her bag of cheese and onion Taytos and sighed. 'That might be true, Aoife, but Marilyn Spears's been in the factory a lot longer than Maeve. And she's got three weans.'

'Well, I know it doesn't seem fair. But it's still Andy's right to pay Maeve what he wants.'

'Nobody's going tae be thinking about Andy's rights!' Maeve snapped.

'There'll be bad feeling about Maeve's pay,' Caroline said, licking crisp crumbs off her fingers. 'And people'll talk shite.'

'Like what?' Aoife asked.

'They're going to say Maeve's not getting something for nothing,'

'But what does that mean?'

'Oh, for fuck's sake,' Maeve spat at Aoife. 'They're going to say I'm shagging him.'

Aoife's mouth popped open. Maeve felt like shoving a pool ball into it to shut her up.

'But you're not!'

'Well, I know that!'

Caroline looked glumly into her empty crisp packet. 'Nana Jackson always says "No smoke without a fire".'

'Well, if Nana Jackson's joining the lynching party I've no hope at all!' Maeve said, prowling over to the window.

'But why did he give you extra?' Aoife asked, quietly. Maeve turned and glared at her. Aoife wilted, but her shoulders stayed stiff. 'Well, why did he?' Aoife asked again. 'And why didn't you tell us?'

Maeve turned to face the window. 'Look. The first week I thought Mary'd made a mistake. I went over the road and checked with her. She said she doesn't make mistakes and told me to tackle Andy myself.'

'And did you?'

Aoife wasn't quite on the attack, but she was like one of those nice RUC officers you sometimes got questioning you about something, trying to make a call on whether or not they were going to lift you for an interrogation.

'I chickened out the first day. And when I tackled him he said he reckoned I could do with all the help I could get.'

A glint of agreement flickered over Aoife's face.

'But why didn't you tell us?'

'Ah, dunno,' Maeve shrugged, tears prickling her eyelids. 'I just felt really funny about it all. It felt dodgy and I didn't want any shite off him or youse or anyone else. I thought I could keep it quiet until we got our results and I get away.'

'Ah wish you'd told us, though,' Caroline said, softly.

'Me too,' Maeve said, collapsing into her chair. 'Just I need the fucking money. And I don't need no drama.'

She waited for Aoife to relent, to say everything would be OK. But Aoife sat in silence, her knuckles clenched white on her knees. Maeve realised if her own best friends were this sore on her, the factory would be a hundred times worse.

Later that evening Maeve headed home, hoping to have a quiet word with her da about her payslip. But her mam was sitting alone in the living room, watching a special report on the high unemployment in Derry. Her mam always tuned into hardcore shite like that when they weren't around to keep her on the soap operas and the holiday shows.

'Where are the boys?'

'Training,' her mam said. 'At least, they'd better be.'

'And where's Daddy?'

'On his way tae Belfast with Toot Maguire.'

'What? Did he get on tae a new trial?'

'Aye. A two-week one. Him and Toot. They're delighted.'

Doing the drug testing was easy money. Thousands her da got for a couple of weeks of lying in bed, popping pills, pissing into test tubes and letting nurses drain his blood and monitor his heart rate. There was always the chance of things fucking up, like they'd done for her cousin, Josey, who'd taken a reaction to the injections he'd got on a trial and ended up with bad kidneys. The compensation was good was the only thing. As her Auntie Mary'd said: 'Sure, half the young wans these days end up with the kidneys gone after a night out at the pills. At least this ways he got a lovely wee house outtay it.'

'He hasn't had a trial this ages,' Maeve said. 'Are they getting harder to get in to?'

'Could be his age. They want the younger fellas. Less chance of things going wrong.'

'Fingers crossed he gets the placebo.'

'Well, now, you know yer father. No luck at the horses. But he's done well with the drugs.'

They fell silent as some thin strip of misery that'd been dug out of the Bogside whinged on the telly about the lack of jobs. *There's no jobs now. All the jobs is gone.*

'Och, dry yer fucken eyes, would ye?' Maeve's mam spat at the telly.

Maeve eyed her mam as she jabbed the mute button on the remote control.

'At least they had fucken jobs in Derry at wan point. They built some decent houses and schools. They'd some nice stuff. What've we ever had? Hardly a leaf to wipe our arses with, never mind a pot to piss in.' She got to her feet and flung the contents of her ashtray into the fire. 'Ah'm away out for a walk.'

She slammed the door when she left. Maeve wished her mam didn't get so wound up when her da was away up to

Belfast. It'd been the same when Deirdre headed to university. She always said they'd be better off out of of the town, but never lifted a finger to leave, and hated it when someone else did. It was a bit like her attitude towards actual life – an attitude she'd assumed her own children held. Which was why Deirdre's suicide came as such a shock. Maeve remembered what her mam'd said when the young English psychologist who'd been assigned to them asked how they felt about the fact that Deirdre was dying. 'Sure, she's as well off dead. What future does she have, anyway?' The psychologist started explaining that suicide rates in Northern Ireland were actually on the low side, because of what he called 'the conflict situation'. He was doing research on the phenomenon, and had also studied in Malawi, the Yemen and Lesotho (countries Maeve was only familiar with from the FIND THE FORMER BRITISH COLONY word searches they got to do in history class when Master Devlin was hungover). The psychologist explained that his hypothesis was that if peace broke out in Northern Ireland, suicide rates would soar. Maeve's mam had eyed the psychologist for a good five seconds before saying, 'Och, sure, at least we've that tae look forward to.' He'd gone red and then spouted some shite about hope, about how 'one never knows'. Maeve'd looked at Deirdre lying sedated in the bed, her skin that yellow colour they'd seen on Squirrel McHugh the few desperate weeks he'd clung on after his liver cancer diagnosis. She knew Deirdre's chances of a new liver were slim even if she was at the top of the transplant list. But Deirdre never made the list, because despite her age, the doctor had told them that her deliberate use of paracetamol had made her a risky bet. 'There's no knowing,' he'd said with a sniff, 'what she'll do if we give her another liver.'

The next day, Aoife picked up Maeve and Caroline for a day of window shopping in Derry. Mrs O'Neill had been a bit iffy about letting them go, for there'd been a riot the night before in protest at Prince Charles's upcoming visit. But Maeve was pure desperate to get out of the town, and she'd assured Aoife's mother that it'd all be tidied up by the time they arrived.

After Aoife parked her car at the Diamond, Maeve climbed out and sucked in a lungful of Derry air. She loved the tang of smoke and spilt petrol.

'Isn't it wild?' Aoife said, picking her way through the broken bricks and bottles littering the road.

'What's wild?' Maeve asked. 'That British troops murdered fourteen unarmed civilians during a civil rights protest? That the people of Derry have to wreck their own town to express their discontentment with a lack of justice?'

'No,' Aoife said, going pink. 'I meant it's wild the council hasn't cleaned the place up yet.'

Maeve kicked a broken bottle, sending it skittering down Shipquay Street.

'Och, look!' Caroline said. 'There's a sale on in Primark!'

Maeve tramped to the shop window with Caroline. Aoife stood assessing the riot damage in the street instead of the special-offer leggings on the shop dummy. But then Aoife'd never been in a riot. It was another one of those wee differences between her and Maeve.

Maeve had been in her first riot when she was five years old. It was a pure accident, for her mam and dad weren't one of the Republican families who reared their children hardy, sending them out to riot as soon as they could toddle, starting them off with stones before they progressed to petrol bombs, and then graduated to the IRA. Like most people, Maeve's parents wanted a quiet life and tried to keep their weans on the straight and narrow.

And, boy, was Maeve's path straight and narrow. She felt like the Brits were manning a permanent checkpoint in front of her while the Catholic Church breathed hellfire down her neck. And crowded all around her, jostling and elbowing her, were her neighbours and teachers, the paramilitaries and her family. With all these other folks telling her what not to do, Maeve barely had space to breathe, never mind figure out what the fuck she wanted to get up to. Which she supposed was the point.

Mind you, at five years old all Maeve wanted was a Barbie doll house and to go to heaven when she died. She still believed in Santa and heaven back then. Her first riot happened the day her mam and dad had left the four of them at home so they could go Santy shopping. Mick was a bright-eyed baby. Deci was a dump truck of a three-year-old. And Deirdre was an anxious seven-year-old, all sharp elbows and bony knees.

Their mam and dad had left strict instructions not to leave the house under any circumstances. But by dusk, after hours of Deirdre telling everyone to pick up their toys, eat their beans and say their prayers, Maeve was bored. She'd stood at the window, watching anyone fit enough to walk or lucky enough to have someone to push them, making their way down to the Diamond, where the town's first Christmas tree stood. It had come about because some Plastic Paddy who'd done well for himself over in Chicago had brought his Yank wife to visit the year before and she'd been so horrified by how bleak the town was she'd sponsored the erection of a communal tree at its heart to bring cheer to everyone left behind.

Earlier in the week, Maeve'd sat watching Princess Sonja of Norway on the telly, illuminating the seventy-foot tall Norwegian fir tree in Trafalgar Square. The tree had burst into light at the centre of London, above a crowd that shimmered under the glittering decorations. Maeve'd asked her mam if she and Deirdre could go and see the lights being switched on in their town but she'd said no, for there'd be ructions instead of illuminations. But even at five years old, Maeve knew that riots – like picking raspberries and getting sunburnt – happened in the summer, when the nights were warmer and the evenings brighter (you'd catch your death rioting in December). So she'd turned back from the window and tortured Deirdre with whining until she'd said, 'Alright, alright – we'll head.'

They'd bundled themselves and the boys up in coats and mittens, then they'd trotted down the town together, Maeve clutching Deci's hand, Deirdre pushing Mick in the buggy.

Maeve had imagined that the town would sparkle with thousands of fairy lights reflected in glass baubles, tinsel shivering in the breeze, a star shining at the top of the tree. She'd pictured a cloud of frosty breath rising as the crowd sang 'Silent Night, Holy Night'. But, in real life, the Diamond was packed with two silent crowds, lit by orange streetlamps and patrolled by RUC men cradling submachine guns. Deirdre kept well away from the cops and Land Rovers, and parked the buggy in the thick of their own side. Maeve gazed up at the tree, which had the air of a butchered animal, drooping towards the crowds, its branches outstretched as though asking, 'What did I do to deserve this? What?' A thick rope of lights strangled the tree, twenty lightbulbs weighing the branches down. There was no tinsel, no star. Maeve could almost hear the workmen from Strabane District Council who'd been employed to decorate the tree saying, 'Sure, that's a grand job now, altogether.'

But she was young and daft enough that hope was still in her heart. She trusted that when the tree was illuminated it would transform, just like a skivvy or a rat in a Disney movie. She watched a thin man step up to the microphone. He tapped it and said, 'Testing, one two three, testing,' before informing them that Santy was on his way. He spoke in the tone of someone phoning in a bomb warning, which Maeve realised, years later, had been his way of managing their expectations. 'We'll all sing a few carols now tae warm us up,' he'd said, before bleating:

'Jing-ill bells, jing-ill bells,
Jing-ill all the way.
Oh what fun,
It is to ride,
On a one-horse open sleigh-hey!'

It was a bit like mass – a few eejits or ones with notions joined in with the singing, but most of the crowd stood around awkwardly, shuffling with the cold and mortification. But despite the shite singing, things were reasonably jovial until a white van drove up and Santy emerged from behind a sliding side door like B.A. Baracus. The man with the mic roared, 'Here's Santy! Santy's arrived!' Then Santy pulled out a sack and shouted, 'HO HO HO!'

The two crowds surged closer to the tree, and scuffles broke out where they merged.

'Easy now, folks! Have a bit of manners. Let Santy through tae the tree.'

Maeve tried to keep her eye on Santy, who was a gash of red in the brownish-grey crowd. She noted that he was carrying a sack that didn't look magical enough to contain enough gifts for her own family, never mind the whole town.

'Lift me up!' Deci'd said, tugging Deirdre's hand. 'Lift me up so's I can see!'

Deirdre'd hoisted Deci up as Santy pushed his way over to the Christmas tree, flanked by three RUC men who were hugging their guns tight to their bellies. Maeve saw a couple of armoured Land Rovers roll slowly down from the head of the town. Back then, she'd thought every small town in Ireland had a heavily fortified police barracks, watchtowers, helipad and an army base, in addition to the usual shops, pubs and hairdressers.

Then Santy threw a switch and the Christmas tree burst into light.

Everyone in the crowd looked up at the drooping tree, shivering in the wintry breeze. Santy opened his sack, shoved his hand inside, said, 'Ho ho ho,' again, and threw a fistful of glittery objects at the crowd.

People flinched as the projectiles hit them and pattered onto the ground.

'Quality Streets!' Deirdre said, awestruck. 'Santy's firing sweeties!'

But when Santy threw a second handful, the crowd surged around them and the RUC raised their riot shields and batons. Deirdre put Deci down beside the buggy, clutching his hand. A glass bottle shattered on the wall beside her head as she kicked the brake with her foot.

'Maeve! Take Deci! We need tae go!'

Maeve turned just as someone fell into her from behind. She got shoved forward and swallowed into a forest of legs. She couldn't see the Christmas tree. People thrashed, shouted and screamed all around her, but she was somehow untouched. Somewhere, miles off it seemed, Santy appealed for calm as the Christmas tree was pulled to the ground. She couldn't see Deirdre's bony knees or Mick in the buggy. And because she couldn't make herself any bigger to see better, she tried to make herself smaller. She curled up in the gutter, with her back to a signpost. Then she saw something glinting on the grate beside her. She stuck her hand out and grabbed it. It was one of the sweets Santy had thrown into the crowd. Five-year-old Maeve thought that people were fighting over these sweeties, and that she'd found something delicious but dangerous. She closed her fist around it, shut her eyes tight and sang 'Silent Night' inside her head.

Even after she got the sense that the crowd had thinned she stayed where she was. Eventually someone picked her up, saying, 'The poor child!' Maeve's eyes had sprung open, but she stayed curled up, and let herself be passed along the street from one stranger to the next like a parcel at a party, until she landed in the arms of an RUC woman. She clung to her like a monkey, the sweet melting in her fist. Finally, she heard Mick wailing. She looked down and saw Deirdre pushing the buggy towards her while dragging Deci by the hand.

Deirdre stopped in front of the policewoman, then said, 'That's my sister.'

The RUC woman raised her eyebrows at Maeve and tilted her head to the side. Maeve nodded and the policewoman gave her a wee squeeze, then bent down and put her on the ground, at which point Deirdre pursed her lips and spat. She was only tall enough to splatter the RUC woman's bulletproof jacket but, as their mam said later, it was the effort that mattered.

'Paninis!' Caroline crowed, salivating over Thran Maggie's menu.

'Cheese and ham, or cheese and chicken, or cheese and tomato!' she said. 'Oh, my God, I don't know what tae get.'

Maeve loved the way Derry was pure fancy, with its paninis.

'One of each and then we can try each other's?'

Caroline dropped the menu, then sat back and stared at the waitresses with her hands clasped in prayer position, her face wearing the look of devotion she'd once reserved for statues of the Virgin Mary. Her summoning worked and soon Maeve and Caroline were chewing, while Aoife leafed through the accommodation pages in a greasy copy of the *Derry News*.

'My God,' she said. 'You can get a room in Derry for next to nothing!'

'Ah wouldn't call £50 a month next tae nothing, Aoife!' Caroline said. 'My student loan is £740 for the year.'

'Och, I don't mean nothing. Just, compared to England, Derry's really good value.'

'Aye. Well. Clearly there's better value in Derry, what with there being a civil war on.' Caroline wasn't usually so riled up over stuff like this. Maeve wondered what was eating her.

'We can get in the car and take a run out to Magee if you want, Caroline?' Aoife said. 'Take a look around?'

'You're alright, Aoife, thanks. Ah'm sure I'll see enough of it tae do me in the years to come.'

'OK. If you're sure.'

'I'm sure.'

'Well, look,' Maeve said. 'At least you'll still have some of your student loan left over for eating and shopping. Me and Aoife'll be broke once we've the rent paid over beyond.' Maeve looked over at Aoife for back-up, but she said nothing. 'I was looking at the rents in London,' Maeve continued. 'I'll be lucky to get a room for £200 a month. And that's me sharing a bathroom with fuck knows how many.'

'Ah still think you should take up my Auntie Joan's offer of a room, Maeve,' Caroline said. 'She'd see ye right on the rent. She'd look after anyone from the town, let alone a friend of mine.'

Caroline's Auntie Joan had put Maeve up when she was over in London for her interviews. She'd met Maeve off the bus at Victoria station, looking like an extra off *In the Name of the Father*.

Everyone said that Joan lived in London, but it became clear to Maeve pretty quickly that Joan lived nowhere near Buckingham Palace or Trafalgar Square. It took a good hour and a half to get to UCL from Joan's house in Woolwich. An hour and a half that Joan had mostly spent talking about the traffic.

But it wasn't just where Joan lived that depressed Maeve. It was *how* she lived.

Even after twenty-one long years in England, Auntie Joan's accent was still as broad as the Foyle – still all 'aye*s*' and 'naw*s*' and 'Sure, God bless us, now*s*'. Joan attended a church that had an entire mass just for Irish emigrants. She still had Irish hair, for she had it done every Saturday morning by a woman who'd fled to London from the riots in Derry the summer of 1972. Every Saturday evening, Joan nursed a shandy in the local Irish bar with her husband, then returned home to her terraced redbrick house with its tick-tock clocks, Belleek china Celtic crosses and shamrock bowls, her crocheted doilies and spider plants, and photo after photo of relatives at christenings, First Holy Communions, confirmations and weddings, to fall asleep after a nice cup of tea under a figure of Christ dying on a crucifix. Though Joan burned coal instead of turf, and her grown-up sons spoke with London accents, her house could be transported – lock, stock and key – back over to Strabane and you'd never know she'd been away. Maeve couldn't fucking face that.

'Well, sure, now, if I'm stuck ah'll take her up on her offer,' she said. 'Just til ah get on me feet, like.'

Maeve had pictured herself on her feet in London. She was going to live in a house with a mix of students from Ireland, Scotland and England, with a nice French or Spanish lad in there for good measure, and hopefully somebody properly foreign, like an Indian or African. They'd all be studying for different degrees – like medicine and music and zoology – but they'd have loads in common and would hang out all the time, sharing books and CDs and stories about their lives. Maeve would have a sofa in her bedroom, big enough for Aoife or Caroline to sleep on when they visited. They'd have the time, money and energy to go drinking before dancing, and would be friends even after becoming rich and famous. She'd imagined all this, and more.

'So, how much d'ye reckon your rent'll be, Aoife? Did ye check yet?' Caroline asked.

Aoife had gone very pink. 'I won't be renting.'

'Oh,' Caroline said.

Aoife was quiet for not nearly long enough. 'It's just Daddy thinks that rent money is dead money. He'd saved up to buy a house for me and James to share. But then he didn't get into Cambridge.'

'But didn't they buy him a house in Belfast?'

'Yes, but Belfast's cheap as chips. Cambridge is a different story. It'll be a bit of a stretch for them, but we'll find something. And it won't just be me on my own. We can get other students in, you know, to help with the mortgage.'

The way Aoife explained things, it sounded like her tenants would be thrilled to help her pay off her mortgage, rather than being like Maeve – resenting every last penny she'd begged, borrowed or scraped together disappearing into the pockets of a landlord.

Maeve grabbed her purse. 'Ah'm away for dessert. Might as well get me cream horns in while I can still afford them.'

Monday, 27 June 1994

49 days until results

Maeve swallowed a few Syndol with a mouthful of tea. It was a trick her ma'd taught her after Deirdre's funeral, to get her through the last of her GCSEs. The codeine melted her guts enough that she could manage a slice of toast and a fag, but Maeve wished she had a few of her mam's bennies. They'd float her over the road the way her mam'd drifted through Deirdre's funeral, like she was the frigging ghost.

At five to eight Maeve trudged down the stairs with Caroline, her legs trembling. She opened the door and saw Aoife standing waiting in the drizzle. 'I was thinking I could fill your reservoir and warm your iron when we get over the road.'

Maeve nodded, her heart scrunching up. Then she took a deep breath and crossed the road. When she entered the factory, eyes slippery as snake tongues flickered over her. She dandered over to the office like she was on a day out and knocked on the open door.

Mary looked up at her over her glasses. 'What d'ye want?'

'There was a wee mix-up with the wages on Friday,' Maeve said, tugging Marilyn's payslip out of her pocket.

Mary's eyebrows shot up. 'Did ah get something wrong?'

'Well, my cheque was grand. But I'd the wrong payslip. I got Marilyn's.'

'Well, sure, that's no big deal,' Mary said, shrugging. 'Just a wee mix-up. Marilyn probably has your payslip. Sure, why don't ye go down tae her now tae check?'

Something about the way Mary looked back down at her order forms, pure deliberate, told Maeve that a mistake hadn't been made. That Mary'd deliberately swapped the payslips. Blood pounded in Maeve's ears. Then Mary looked back up at her. 'Still here?' she asked, all innocence.

'Not for long,' Maeve said, then she turned and walked out of the door.

Marilyn Spears was standing beside her machine, giving out yards to Mabel Moore, who was tutting and shaking her head. 'Och, now, sure there's no justice in this world, so there isn't, none at all,' Mabel said.

Then Marilyn spotted Maeve. She slowly folded her arms under her diddies and glared as if she was about to start spitting nails at her. The other machinists stopped sewing and gawped over.

'Mary seems tae have made a wee mistake with the payslips,' Maeve said. 'Mixed yours and mine up.' She offered Marilyn her payslip.

'Thanks,' Marilyn said, snatching it and throwing it on the table. Then she picked up Maeve's payslip and glared at it. 'Though ah have tae say, ah'd far rather have that fat cheque you're getting, not to mention the big basic you're on.' Marilyn brandished Maeve's slip in the air. 'Says on here,' she guldered over the machinists' heads, 'that Maeve Murray – a temporary worker with a couple of weeks' experience – is on a basic of £80.'

Almost everyone stopped and listened.

'And apparently,' Marilyn continued, 'she earned herself a bonus of £43.45.' Aoife's iron whooshed as Marilyn picked up her own payslip. 'Marilyn Spears,' she screeched, 'mother of three! Full-time machinist with ten years' experience!' Her bingo wings flapped as she waved her payslip in Maeve's face. 'Basic: £70. Bonus: £22.65.'

'Marilyn, I . . .'

'Ah don't begrudge ye a penny of yer bonus, Maeve Murray, for ah saw what ye did to earn that. But what ah want tae know is, what the fuck you're doing behind closed doors for Andy Strawbridge that's earning you an extra tenner a week?'

It felt like the factory had sucked its breath in and was waiting for Maeve to deck Marilyn. She tensed her arm. She'd only ever battered her own brothers and Deirdre. She'd no idea what it'd feel like to hit a Prod.

'WHAT IS GOING ON DOWN THERE?'

Maeve closed her eyes and breathed out, 'Fffffffffuuuuuuuck.'

'IS THERE A REASON WHY THESE MACHINES ARE NOT PRODUCING?' Andy rapped the metal railings with a ruler and a few sewing machines kicked back into action.

'Oh ho! I see your fancy man's keeping an eye out for you,' Marilyn said, flicking Maeve's payslip at her.

'I don't need no man tae look out for me,' Maeve answered, watching her payslip flutter to the ground. Then she picked it up and walked back to her board.

The light on her iron was glowing green and her basket was full. Mary started yelling about something that Maeve could not give two fucks about. She grabbed a shirt and plunged into a blizzard of cuffs, collars, sleeves and backs.

Going to work the next morning, Maeve clocked Andy standing in silence at the top of the factory, watching everyone come in. There was no gossip. No craic at all. Everyone kept glancing up at Andy, then exchanging looks. Billy Stone and Paddy Quinn stood with their arms crossed in opposite corners of the factory, like bouncers at a nightclub. At eight o'clock, Mary closed the main doors with a clump that Maeve felt in her spine.

'OK, you lot,' Andy said, sniffing. 'Later today some men from McAllister's will drop in. I've convinced them to check this place out. If they like what they see, a nice big contract will come our way.'

Murmurs of approval eddied around the factory.

'Is that the big McAllister's factory outside Ballymena?' Marilyn Spears asked.

'Yes. They've just won a significant contract and need sub-contractors to help them through.'

'There's no security in subcontracting,' Mabel Moore croaked. 'Ah've seen it all before.'

'There's no security in factory work at all these days,' Andy said. 'Times have changed. We work with weeks in hand, not months or years, like you did back in your heyday.'

'So if this comes in, will we see a better basic? Or maybe a bonus?' Fidelma asked.

Andy sighed as he looked around the factory floor. 'I'm not going to lie to you. You're competing against Asian factories with thousands of workers who'd kill to do a week's work for what I pay you per hour. Cheap labour. Cheap materials. Cheap rent. Newer machines. These are lean times for factories in this part of the world.'

Discontentment rumbled through the crowd like a bad dose of gas.

'Right,' Andy said. 'Here's what I need from you lot: your best work, a clean factory floor and no backchat. When the McAllister's arrive, you'll speak when you're spoken to and keep your heads down. Any questions?' Andy looked around, unaware that Mary was standing behind him, glaring. 'No? Well, back to work then,' he said, clapping his hands at them like they were pre-schoolers.

The McAllister's bucks arrived shortly after the first tea break. Mary intercepted them at the front door, then fired a hard, wide-eyed stare at Maeve. 'Miss Murray, would you let Andy know the gentlemen from McAllister's are here?'

Maeve dropped the shirt she was ironing and sprinted upstairs. She burst into Andy's office without knocking. 'The men from McAllister's are here.'

'Right. How many?' Andy said, closing an accountancy book with a snap.

'Just the two. A big one and a wee one.'

He pushed the book under some paperwork, then straightened his tie.

'I'll be down shortly,' he said, dismissing her.

Maeve went back to her board, disappointed. Some part of her had been hoping for more from her interaction with Andy, for him to comment on her appearance, or to discuss the contract. She ironed slowly, distracted by the McAllister's bucks. The tall, fat, redheaded one was scanning the machinists. He looked like he'd been parboiled before being squeezed into his suit: his flesh bulged out at the cuffs and collars. He had what Maeve's mam called 'a bad eye' in his head. He was carrying a bundle of samples, a roll of fabric and an air of menace. The other fella was a sleekid, skinny wee runt, with glasses and oily grey hair. He was lugging a briefcase near as big as him, and stood with his head slightly raised, as if he were sniffing the room, two ratty yellow teeth poking out from between his lips.

Andy jogged down the stairs and walked briskly towards the men. The big redhead loomed over Mary and pumped Andy's hand. Then Andy leaned down and shook the wee fella's hand, before escorting them both up the stairs. They stood for a while on the landing, eyeing the rows of machinists before retreating into the office.

They landed back out just before lunch, skittering down the stairs in high good humour. Mary walked them to the door, a big gammy grin splitting her face, but she came back scowling. She stopped in front of the packing table and guldered, 'Right, yous'uns. Stop what yiz are at and get up here!'

Maeve put her iron down and joined the awkward huddle at the packing table. Ten identical shirts lay in front of Mary.

'Right. Ah'm sure youse've all seen the men from McAllister's.'

'You couldn't miss thon big lump of a redhead,' Fidelma Hegarty said, glowering.

'He's some bruiser,' scoffed Baldy Magee. 'Wouldn't want to get in his road!'

'And that wee croil at his side,' Mabel Moore said. 'There'd be more juice in a gooseberry.'

Everyone laughed until Mary slammed her hand on the table. 'The McAllister's fellas said they're happy enough with the look of the premises and the equipment.' She paused and glared at them. 'Now they want to see what youse can do.' She selected a shirt and smoothed it out on the table. 'They want one hundred of these. By the end of the day.'

'Och, for fuck's sake, Mary!' Marilyn Spears groaned. 'We'll all be on basic.'

Mary glared at her over the top of her glasses. 'If youse get this right and we win this order, we could switch tae a five-day week.'

Mary'd played her trump card. An extra day's pay would be life-changing. Anything from a fancy takeaway on a Friday, to a new pair of shoes in the month, or money towards a sofa.

Maeve leaned in to hear Mary dissect the shirt. 'It's a slim fit shirt in poplin. Cutaway collar. Breast pocket. Two-button single cuff. Single placket and a pleated back.'

She passed the shirts around. Maeve fingered the material. It was good, thick stuff that'd press and box well. Karen Gilchrist examined the buttons with a frown. Caroline was surrounded by machinists who were going over the seams.

'Right,' Mary said, scowling at her watch. 'Time tae crack on.'

Billy snapped on his metal glove, then hefted the fabric roll onto his shoulder like it was an unconscious woman and carried it down to the cutting table. Maeve watched him dump the fabric onto the table, torn between wishing he'd throw her submissively on a feather bed before ravishing her, and picturing him hefting a corpse into a shallow grave.

As soon as the first bundles were cut out, Mary distributed them throughout the factory. Then she buzzed from machine to machine, scrutinising the material as it rippled under needles, inspecting the seams at each stage of sewing. She hovered over

Mickey McCanny as he fused the cuffs and collars and fussed over Karen Gilchrist on the button machine. By the time she brought the first shirt to the ironing boards, her nerves were shredded. She handed it to Maeve, then watched her like a hawk before snatching the ironed shirt out of her hands. She flew over to the packing table, where she pulled the measuring tape from around her neck and snapped it from underarm to cuff, button to button, shoulder to tail. Her frown softened on the second check. Then she passed the shirt to Sharon Rogers for folding and packing.

Ten loose shirts lay on the packing table and another ninety sat folded and boxed when Andy and the McAllister's fellas burst back through the factory door later that afternoon. The red-head's tie was sideways and his face was several shades brighter than before.

The ratty wee fella took out a tape measure and began to examine the loose shirts. The big redheaded buck picked a few shirts at random from the boxed pile, then tore them loose for examination. Maeve caught the smack of booze on their breath as they joked between themselves. An agreement was reached, then Andy helped them carry the boxed shirts out of the door. When he returned he snapped his fingers at Mary, and they both climbed the stairs to his office. Although Mary came back down the stairs later, Andy didn't reappear.

Maeve was trudging out of the canteen the next morning after tea break when she spotted Andy standing on the balcony. He watched everyone settle back at their stations, then cleared his throat. 'I heard back from McAllister's.' He paused, clearly enjoying the way the whole factory was hanging on his words. 'Looks like they're as foolish as I am. Prepared to take a chance on you lot.'

A hiss of satisfaction filled the room. Something like annoyance flickered across Andy's face.

'We've won the contract,' he said, louder, clenching his fist in the air, as if he was Nelson Mandela.

Applause splattered across the crowd like a skift of rain. Maeve joined in as it swelled to a shower, smiling like a fool. But when she caught sight of Andy's smug face, she stopped clapping and dug her fists into her fleece.

'Alright, alright,' Andy said, holding his hand in the air. 'There's a lot of hard work ahead of us. I might need more hands on deck. So you can spread the word about that for me.'

'Houl on a minute there, Andy Strawbridge,' Fidelma Hegarty said. 'I thought there was talk of a five-day week.'

Andy looked aggrieved, as if it pained him that Fidelma'd decided to wreck everyone's buzz.

'I'm afraid I can't commit to that just yet, Fidelma. Maybe on the next contract.'

'If we last that long.' Fidelma snorted.

'Right,' Andy said, ignoring her. 'By way of a celebration, I'm putting some dosh behind Kelly's bar tomorrow night. You're all very welcome to join me.'

The promise of free booze triggered a few yips from the country ones.

'Kelly's?' Marilyn Spears squawked, as if she was hard of hearing.

The Prods had shrunk back in on themselves, eyeing each other. Arms were crossed, eyebrows raised.

'Yes. Kelly's bar,' Andy answered, briskly. 'In the centre of the town.'

Maeve liked drinking in Kelly's. It was laid back. Had a wee bar that farmers liked to stand in, clabbered to the knee in shite. There was a lounge with a telly and jukebox that always had a good mix of ones in it. And then it had a function room, which was only opened for private parties, like funerals and birthdays. Jackie and John Kelly liked to steer clear of politics, so they didn't welcome fundraisers or special quizzes. That meant Kelly's was the one bar in the town you'd take a visitor to, where there was the least chance of a stranger having their head kicked in, or worse.

'We were hard-pressed tae find a bar that'd take both sides,' Mary said, gleeking over at Paddy Quinn. 'Kelly's were the only wans. We've booked the function room. We've our own toilets. It's nearly as good as drinking in the factory.'

'Still a fucking Taig bar, Mary, no harm tae you or Andy,' Billy said. 'What's wrong with drinking at the Cromwell?'

'They wouldn't take all of us,' Mary said. 'Not after that business at the Millar wedding.'

Maeve remembered that business at the Millar wedding, which had starred an eejit Free Stater who'd accepted his Proddie girlfriend's invitation to a wedding in the town. Maeve's mam had seen him down the town when she was out shopping. She'd said he'd had the look of a man on safari, him sticking his fingers in the bullet holes on the walls and posing for a photo beside a Brit, hours before he was found out the back of the Cromwell with a beer keg dropped on his skull.

When the coroner ruled 'death by misadventure', Maeve's da'd said, 'Well, he's not far off the mark' while her mam'd said, '"Suicide" would've been more accurate for a Free Stater drinking in the Cromwell.'

'Right, you lot. Back to work!' Andy snapped. 'Go on! Back to it!'

Maeve picked up her scorching iron and slammed it onto a shirt collar. She wondered what it'd be like to go drinking with a squad of Prods. And Andy.

Maeve's end of the production line quietened down later in the day. Aoife'd gone over to Karen Gilchrist to learn about the button machine while Maeve'd started onto stain removal. She was keen on stain removal since Fidelma Hegarty'd shown her how to apply the chemicals so she could get as high as she used to when sniffing body spray in the school toilets. After her third stain, though, Maeve'd got a bit too giddy, so she grabbed a Coke from her bag and headed out via the side door for a bit of air.

Mary and Mabel Moore were basking in the sun while Sharon Rogers was leaning into Baldy McGee for a light. This gathering wasn't Maeve's idea of sound company, but now she was out, she couldn't turn on her heel. She pressed her back against the hot brick wall, watching Baldy squint up at the sun.

'Best wee country in the world we'd be, if we'd weather like this every day.'

Maeve wondered where it was Baldy'd travelled that led him to form that opinion.

'It's all go, isn't it?' he said. 'McAllister's in with the big contract and Andy taking on more people?'

'Andy Strawbridge wouldn't be the first stranger in the town to make big promises,' Mabel Moore huffed.

Baldy's eyes widened and he scratched under his chin with the look of a man thinking bigger thoughts than he was used to.

Suddenly a shot echoed across the yard.

'What's that, now?' Sharon Rogers said, clutching her chest.

Another shot rang out. There was an awkward silence before Mary spoke. 'Sounds like Foncey Logue up shooting at the crows.'

They held still. Another couple of shots blasted across the yard.

'It's not crows he's after, if he's still shooting,' Mabel Moore said, frowning.

Again they listened. But all they heard was the caw of crows settling back into the thrum of the town.

'Ah'm away in,' Mary said, standing up. 'Youse'd do well not to be too far behind me.'

As soon as she disappeared, Baldy settled into her seat with a grunt. 'Ye hafta wonder how she does it,' he said, shaking his head.

'Does what?' Sharon asked.

'How she endures the sound of Foncey Logue and that gun going off,' Baldy said, raising his eyebrows and tucking his chin into his neck.

Maeve suddenly understood what he was driving at: Mary's husband had borrowed Foncey's gun to shoot himself. Foncey'd gone up to the barracks the day after the funeral to get his gun back from the cops. He was out later that evening, back at the crows.

'She's hard as nails, that doll,' Mabel said. 'She has tae be.'

'Well, ah wouldn't be fit fer it, ah can tell ye that much,' Baldy said.

'It's not normal, so it isn't,' Sharon said.

Mabel got to her feet and hobbled forward a few steps to ease the stiffness in her hips before fixing her watery blue eyes on Sharon. 'And who among us is normal?' she asked, before limping back into the factory.

The next morning there was a party feeling in the factory. The country ones, God help them, had come in already dressed up under their fleeces, with make-up stashed in their handbags. Maeve's one actual privilege in life was that she hadn't been born a culchie. The town was shite, but the country was full of actual shite.

Not everyone in the factory was in good humour. Billy Stone spent much of the day pacing around the yard, smoking, looking like some hot bit of stuff in a prison drama. In fairness, Maeve thought, training for jail was probably no big waste of Billy's time. She just hoped that nobody she knew would be the cause of his incarceration.

They got as far as the afternoon break before Billy exploded. 'Free beer or no, ye'll not find me darkening Kelly's door,' he snarled, before standing up. His chair teetered, then fell behind him. 'The rest of ye can do whatever the hell youse want.'

The whole canteen fell silent, even though he was only addressing his own side.

'Billy,' Marilyn Spears said, 'there's manys another person sitting here that feels like you. But you're only cutting yer nose off tae spite yer face if ye don't show up. Drink's drink, wherever it's swallowed.'

The bell rang. Maeve scraped her chair back and joined the rush for the door. Marilyn, Mary and Billy stayed behind. He strode out of the canteen much later, with Marilyn trotting after him. Mary scuttled into her office and closed the door, then shut the blinds.

When the final bell sounded, the machines stopped and the country girls dived into the toilets with their make-up bags. Andy came out onto the mezzanine and surveyed the factory floor with a colonial air. Maeve couldn't decide if this was turning her on or pissing her off (it was probably a bit from column A and a bit from column B, she thought, which was kind of exhausting).

'Right you lot,' Andy barked. 'The free bar starts at seven. That should give you enough time to get cleaned up.'

'Some of us'd need more than half an hour to scrub the muck off,' jeered Baldy Magee, whacking Mickey McCanny on the back.

'If your face was as clean as my arse ye wouldn't lie so lonely in yer bed at night,' Mickey answered.

A few of the lads sniffed their pits, then sprayed Lynx as if the hole in the ozone layer was nowhere near big enough. Maeve watched Billy Stone stalk out of the factory. As soon as he was out of the door, Paddy Quinn walked from the back of the factory and climbed the stairs up to Andy's office. Maeve saw Andy nod at Paddy before jerking his head at his office door. Then Andy looked down directly at Maeve and winked at her. Blood surged into her chest as Paddy Quinn followed Andy's gaze. She dipped her head and grabbed her fleece, then raced out the door to get ready for the pub.

Half an hour later, Maeve tottered into the living room in the only pair of high heels she owned. Caroline was sitting on the sofa in blue jeans and a black top.

'God,' she said, staring at Maeve's scarlet bodysuit and black pencil skirt. 'That's some get-up for Kelly's. Who are you trying to impress?'

Maeve wiggled and pouted and said, 'Baldy Magee' in her best Marilyn Monroe voice. She knew it wasn't right laughing at poor oul Baldy, crippled as he was with man-diddies, a monobrow and bad breath. It wasn't right, but it was fun.

Aoife didn't laugh. She sat there, looking much the same as she had half an hour earlier, doing that natural thing that she got away with. Suddenly, under her gaze, Maeve felt brassier and wobblier than usual.

'Right,' she said, pulling her black cardi tight over her chest. 'Will we head?'

Maeve's feet were killing her by the time they reached Kelly's bar. They passed the front door on the street, and entered the alleyway that led to the function room. Alleyways gave Maeve the creeps, for they were always featuring on the news, cordoned off and filled with white-suited forensics experts fussing over bloodstains. She shivered and followed Caroline and Aoife down to the door. She let them go in first, but this tactic failed to render her invisible, like she'd hoped.

'Jesus, but you scrub up well, Maeve Murray,' Mickey McCanny said. 'You must be going somewhere fancy.'

Maeve rolled her eyes as Mickey cracked himself up, then she sailed over to a corner table with Aoife while Caroline went to the bar. Most people had settled into the same company they kept in the canteen. Fidelma Hegarty was sitting on high stools at the back with Paddy Quinn, with a good view of the room. A group of machinists was watching a pool game. Marilyn Spears was cradling her diddies at a table, deep in conversation with Billy Stone. Mabel Moore sat opposite, guzzling stout. Mary was frowning in a tight knot of Proddie machinists, them all knocking the drink into them.

Then Maeve saw Andy.

He was sitting on a high stool at the end of the bar in his work suit, with a glass of something clear in front of him, watching the room like there was a one-way mirror between him and everyone else.

'He doesn't really fit in, does he?' Aoife said.

'Naw. He looks a bit of a dick,' Maeve said, though she felt like she was the bigger dick for saying that. *How to Win Friends and Influence People* advised against slagging people off, even behind their backs.

Caroline put their drinks on the table, then slid in beside Maeve. 'Jesus,' she said, 'ye'd have more craic at tea break.'

She was right. The Prods were quieter in Kelly's than they were in the factory (though for all Maeve knew, maybe Prods were dryshites when they were on the lash).

'Our side's very relaxed,' Caroline observed. 'D'ye think they're just showing off because we're on home turf?'

'Not sure.' Maeve shrugged. 'Maybe it's just less dicey, drinking in here tonight. UVF's not likely to hit Kelly's when it's full of Prods.'

'You're not wrong!' Caroline laughed. 'Marilyn and her lot are our human shields!'

Once they'd settled themselves, Aoife nodded in Andy's direction. 'Do we know how much money he's put behind the bar?' she asked.

Maeve wished she knew what was in the kitty so she could watch Aoife do one of her freaky wee calculations, where she'd figure out how many pints and shorts could be bought for the total and predict at what time the money'd run out.

'No idea. So we'd better crack on,' she said, clinking glasses with Aoife and Caroline. Then they started at the drinking like they'd targets to hit and bonuses to earn.

Maeve was more than a few sheets to the wind by the time she found herself at the bar beside Andy.

'You're looking rather well tonight, Ms Murray,' he said, eyeing her. 'Good to know you've better dress sense out of the factory than in it.'

Maeve eyed Andy. He was still in his work clothes. 'Wish I could say the same for you, Mr Strawbridge.'

'I see you've been studying that book I gave you.'

'And I see you can't be bothered to practise what you preach.'

Theresa swiped at the counter in front of Maeve with a cloth. 'What are ye having?'

'Three vodkas with a dash of orange, please, Theresa.'

Maeve watched the vodka drain from the bottle as Andy continued to eye her. She liked him looking at her. But she hated that he was so obvious. A blind man on a galloping horse – let alone a function room full of nosey factory folk – would realise he was letching over her.

'Vodka and orange, eh?' Andy said. 'I would've thought you were more of a cocktails woman. A mojito, maybe.'

Maeve had no clue what a mow-hee-toe was, but she wasn't going to admit that. 'I prefer a Cosmopolitan.'

She knew about cocktails from an article in *Select* magazine. One of their writers had been paid to get pissed on Cosmopolitans and Sex on the Beach in some fancy London bar. It had given Maeve the impression that writing articles for magazines was far better craic than investigating paramilitary murders.

'Good luck getting a Cosmopolitan in here,' Andy said.

Maeve was drunk enough to laugh, before a flicker of eyes from the tables deeper in the room sobered her up. Theresa splashed orange cordial into the glasses, then plonked them in front of Maeve.

'Thanks a million, Theresa,' Maeve said, pushing the drinks together and lifting them.

'Trust me on the mojitos, Maeve,' Andy said. 'You're definitely a mojito woman.'

'Andy,' she answered. 'I'd trust ye as far as I could throw ye.'

She basked in his laugh as she walked off. But when she put the glasses down in front of Caroline and Aoife, they slid their drinks towards them without saying, 'Och, thanks, dotes.'

'What was going on there?' Caroline asked, running a finger through the condensation on her glass.

'Just Andy being a dick.'

Caroline took a careful sip of her drink. 'You mind yourself around him, Maeve. He's too fly for the likes of us.'

'Ah, fuck Andy,' Maeve said, raising her glass. 'Here's to free drinks!'

Aoife gripped her glass hard, then raised it. 'Let's not fuck Andy.'

Caroline laughed and clashed her glass off Aoife's. 'Ah'll drink tae that!' she said. 'Sláinte!'

The Prods began to loosen up as the drink flowed, so Caroline went over to some of the machinists she knew for a chat. Then Aoife went up to the bar to get a round in. To Maeve's surprise, she struck up a conversation with Andy. Maeve emptied the ice from her glass into her mouth and crunched it between her teeth as they chatted. Aoife stood on after Theresa had served their drinks, chatting to Andy for far longer than Maeve had. When she couldn't thole it any longer, she got to her feet and walked over to the pair of them.

'Hey,' she said.

'Hey,' Aoife said. 'There's your vodka.' She pushed a glass towards Maeve.

'Och, thanks,' Maeve said, waiting. She didn't like how Andy was looking at them. Like they were entertainment.

'I'm speaking with Andy about optimisation,' Aoife said.

'Awww, right,' Maeve said, picking up her drink. Then Aoife turned her back on Maeve and resumed her conversation with Andy.

Maeve was mortified. Aoife'd never cut her dead before. She turned away, took a gulp of her drink and looked around the room. Fidelma was sitting on her own. Maeve staggered over and plopped down beside her. 'Fidelma. What's the craic?'

'Not a wild lot,' Fidelma said. She was eyeing Billy, who was smoking at Marilyn's table. Maeve'd seen him get up to play a fierce game of pool every now and then, destroying whoever he was up against before firing the pool cue on the felt and heading back to his pint. But as hot as Billy was, drinking with him looked about as much craic as a holocaust.

'D'ye think Billy's loosened up with the drink?'

'Billy?' Fidelma said, as if she hadn't been watching him.

'Aye. He was in wild bad humour about drinking here.'

Fidelma took a drink of her pint. 'What d'ye know about Billy?'

'I know he likes his tattoos,' Maeve said, taking another gleek at Billy's right bicep.

'Remember your man, Cedric Moore? The milkman that got the works up by the border?'

Maeve nodded, though she'd never known the man himself. What she remembered was how their milk deliveries were disrupted while undertakers picked Cedric's flesh off the hedges and sifted through the broken bottles they'd shovelled off the road for shards of bone. 'UDR, wasn't he?'

'Aye. Thirty-two-years-old. Mabel Moore's youngest. And Billy Stone's uncle.' Fidelma glanced over at Marilyn, then back to Maeve. 'Marilyn Spears married into them. Dunno how, if it was a cousin or whatever. Course, she lost her own father in an ambush way back before our time. He was RUC.'

'Fuck.' Maeve had never really connected the blurry faces she'd seen on the news over the years with the names of the Protestants she now worked with.

'So they're touchy sometimes, them wans,' Fidelma said, frowning. 'Course, the Twelfth coming up doesn't help.'

'Naw, it doesn't.'

'Ye can see why Billy's kept out of the security forces. Factory's an awful lot safer than the police or UDR. You're the target when you're in the forces.'

Maeve knocked her drink back, glad of the sting of it in her throat. 'Ah sometimes get the impression Billy's signed himself up tae another organisation. A loyal wan. No pension to speak of though.'

Fidelma turned and eyed Maeve, then knocked her own drink back. Maeve took the hint and lurched to her feet. 'Can ah get ye another cider?'

Fidelma nodded. Maeve turned and the room twisted around her. She did her best to hold a steady line to the bar, and clutched the counter in relief when she arrived.

'A tad tipsy are we, Ms Murray?'

Maeve turned to face Andy, surprised by how much effort it required to lock eyes with him. 'Us Nordies don't do tipsy, Andy.'

Theresa landed over in front of them. 'What're ye having?'

'A Bulmer's and a double vodka with a dash of orange.' *Because why the fuck not?*

About half an hour later, Andy stood up, held a glass in the air and rapped a spoon on it. The buzz in the bar quietened down and everyone peered in his direction.

'Congratulations, ladies and gentlemen. You've exhausted our celebratory fund.'

'It might be exhausted,' Fidelma Hegarty grumbled, 'but there's life in me yet.'

Andy waited for the room to settle back down. 'I'm sure you'll all continue having a marvellous time together,' he said, saluting the room with his glass. 'Enjoy the rest of your night.'

A few people – Prods mostly – raised their glasses in response. Maeve watched Andy set his glass down and stroll out of the door. She felt like running after him and hijacking him, forcing him to drive her over the border to some seaside town where she'd demand a moe-hee-toe and a bag of bacon fries.

Caroline dunted Maeve with her elbow. 'What are ye thinking?'

Maeve was thinking that Andy was the one more likely to do the hijacking. He'd park up some dead-end border road to have his cock sucked while keeping an eye out for Brit patrols.

'Och, nothing. Am bollixed, is all.'

Caroline leaned back and sighed in contentment. 'Sure, we're all bollixed. It's great.'

Mabel Moore drained the last of her pint, then wiped her mouth with the back of her hand and yawned. She said something to Marilyn and Billy, then hunted for her handbag. A notion took Maeve. The sort of notion that only entered her head after reading *How to Win Friends and Influence People* and drinking more than her fair share of free vodka.

She got to her feet and staggered over to Marilyn's table. 'You away on, Mabel?'

Mabel's faded blue eyes were bloodshot. 'Ah'm away on tay me bed. Not fit fer this shite no more.'

'Well, sure it was craic while it lasted.'

'Hmmmugh,' Mabel grunted, standing up. 'Ah'm awful stiff from sitting so long.'

Maeve caught the whiff of old lady pish. She'd never worked up the nerve to ask anyone of Mabel's generation why they stank of pish. She wasn't sure she'd like the answer.

'Ah'm sure the dander home'll loosen ye up again,' Marilyn clucked.

'Ah doubt walking will lubricate the parts the stout didn't reach,' Mabel said. 'Ah'm away, any roads.'

As Mabel hobbled towards the door, Marilyn gestured at the empty chair. 'Will ye not sit down?'

There was something rattish about Marilyn's smile. But Maeve remembered Dale Carnegie's advice that winning friends begins with friendliness, so she sat down heavily. The seat was oddly warm. Maeve was thankful that Mabel's Proddie buttocks were warmer than her coul Taig arse.

'So, yeez've had an alright night?' Maeve asked. Billy didn't look at her, never mind answer.

'Well, free booze tastes better than cheap booze,' Marilyn said. 'And every penny counts with the wages some of us is on.'

Maeve shifted as Marilyn wobbled her head at her. Her arse cheeks felt prickly.

Billy picked up his pint and looked sideways at Marilyn. 'Ah'm clearing the fuck outta here as soon as ah fire this down me.'

Marilyn nodded at him, then got to her feet. 'Ah'll put that song on the jukebox for ye.'

Maeve was left alone at the table with Billy. She knew *How to Win Friends and Influence People* had taught her that she should converse with Billy in terms of his interests. But his obvious hobbies, such as flirting with loyalist paramilitary activity and working out, were not Maeve's specialist subjects. So she defaulted to what she thought was a safe bet. 'Lovely weather we're having, any roads.'

Billy's eye scalded her for a couple of seconds. When he looked away, Maeve reminded herself of Dale Carnegie's words: 'Don't criticise, condemn or complain.' Then took a gulp of her vodka to fuel another try – a tactic that was sadly absent from *How to Win Friends and Influence People*.

'Sure, Kelly's isn't so bad, is it now, Billy?' Maeve said, using his name like Dale had advised. 'It's a friendly wee bar. Some of your side even pay tae drink in here the odd time.'

Billy gazed at Maeve with interest this time. She noticed how blue his eyes were. A bit close together maybe, as Prods' eyes tended to be. But pure intense. She got the feeling Billy was seeing her for the first time. And she liked the feeling of being seen.

'Nice enough place,' he said amiably, looking around. Then he locked eyes with her again. 'No real cover in here, though, is there?'

Maeve knew exactly what Billy meant. A gunman'd only have to open the door to have a 180-degree angle on the room.

'It was real good of youse tae invite the likes of me in here,' he said, reflectively. 'Learned a lot, so I did.'

Maeve suddenly felt sick. She stood up. That's when she felt a chill on her arse. She clutched her hand to the back of her skirt. It was wet through.

'The toilets are that way, I believe,' Billy said, nodding.

Maeve ran into the toilets, slammed into a cubicle and shut the door tight. When she pulled off her skirt her clammy skin goose-bumped in the cold. Her stomach was turning even before she sniffed her skirt. It stank of pish. Proddie pish. She laid the skirt on the water tank of the toilet and boked. When she was done, she wiped her mouth and flushed. Then she pressed a wad of loo roll into her skirt over and over again to soak the worst up. When she ran out of bog roll, she sprayed air freshener over the back of her knickers before pulling her skirt back up around her waist. Then she went to the sink and washed her mouth out with water and scrubbed her hands until they were numb.

Maeve slunk back to her table where Aoife was deep in conversation with Paddy Quinn and Baldy Magee. It was obvious Baldy thought he was onto a good thing, but Maeve knew by the look of Aoife she only thought she was having a thrilling conversation about machine maintenance.

'Ah have tae go,' Maeve said quietly to Caroline.

'Awww,' Caroline said. 'It's only early.'

Maeve picked up her bag and squeezed it under her oxter. 'Och, ah know. But ah have tae go. Now.'

'What's wrong?' Aoife asked.

A gust of laughter rose up from the Prods sitting at Marilyn's table. Mabel's chair was conspicuously empty.

'Ach, ah just have tae go,' Maeve said. 'I'll head on myself if ye want tae stay.'

Caroline and Aoife exchanged looks and picked up their glasses. Then the bass line of 'Simply the Best' thunked from the jukebox.

'Ohhhh, I love this one!' Caroline said, clutching Maeve's arm. 'Och, stay for this song, Maeve! We can go straight after.'

Maeve collapsed onto the warm velvet cushion as Caroline started to sing along with Tina.

'And who put that on?' Paddy Quinn asked, frowning over at the jukebox.

'Marilyn, I think,' Maeve said.

Marilyn, Billy and some of the other Prods were singing along.

'She waited until the money was spent before starting, did she?' Paddy said, before downing his drink and standing up, stiff as a board.

The buzz in the bar started to die down as the singing got louder and louder. Billy Stone was walloping the table like it was a drum. When Tina lashed into the chorus about being simply the best, Marilyn and her cronies responded by roaring, 'SECOND BATTALION OF THE UFF!'

Everyone in the room knocked back their drinks and tightened their shoulders as Theresa rammed shutters down over the bottles of alcohol before grabbing empty glasses and stashing them under the bar.

'I think we need tae get outta here,' Maeve said. 'Fast.' She stood up, the whiff of piss and toilet freshener bitter in her nose, then staggered into the alleyway. The night air tasted sweeter and colder than anything she'd drunk all night. She gulped it down until she couldn't breathe, then vomited in the gutter.

Maeve crept in the door home late the next afternoon. Music was pounding upstairs.

'Lo,' she said to her mam, who was sitting on her own in the living room, staring at the telly.

'Lo,' she replied.

'Where's the boys?'

Her mam rolled her eyes at the ceiling.

'Some difference having two bedrooms for four boys, eh?' Maeve said. 'Some peace for you and Daddy?'

'It's a different shade of shite, tae be honest.'

Maeve was dying to ask about Deirdre's stuff. She wanted to know what her mam'd done with it. 'When's Daddy back?'

'The morrah, ah believe.'

'Have ye heard from him?'

'Naw, but Toot's wife said she was chatting to him on the phone. Toot says he reckons they both got the placebo.'

'That's some relief,' Maeve said.

'A great relief,' her mam agreed, looking not one bit relieved.

'Would ye not think of getting the phone in yerself? Be nice tae hear how Daddy's doing when he's away on the trials. Or for me tae be able tae ring home when I'm over the water.'

Her mam didn't answer right away. Then: 'Didn't they teach ye how to write in school?'

A log crumpled in the grate.

'What about a cuppa tay?' Maeve said.

'Aye. G'wan then.'

Saturday, 2 July 1994

44 *days until results*

Mrs O'Neill had invited Maeve and Caroline over to dinner, to thank them for having Aoife over for lunch every day. Visiting Aoife's house was an honour not commonly granted. It wasn't the biggest or oldest house in the town, but it was the best. Mrs O'Neill liked to note that it'd been built by a widowed doctor in the late Victorian era who'd retired back to the town after forty years in Kent. He'd imported a team of English builders to construct a redbrick house by the river. After the doctor's sons were killed on the Somme, the house had passed to the local vet. His artificial insemination programme for cattle had been a lot more successful than his own attempts at breeding: after he and his wife died childless, the house had stood empty until the O'Neills paid through the nose to be the first Catholic owners.

Maeve was obsessed by the house. Each wall in every room was painted a slightly different shade of white. Mrs O'Neill had once shown Maeve the colour cards, which had included colours like Bone White, Frost Breath and Linen Dust. Maeve'd cracked some joke about Cocaine White that'd made Mr O'Neill (or John as she called him, when herself wasn't in earshot) crease up before he wilted under Mrs O'Neill's gaze. Maeve'd always thought white was boring. But these not-quite-whites ('qwhites' she called them, privately) played with her eye in the same way that scents on a breeze teased her nose. The hue of each wall changed according to the time of day, the weather conditions, the number of candles lit, the colour of the rugs or the glow from the stained-glass lamps. Mrs O'Neill made white work.

But then, everything in her house worked.

It was the only house in the town that'd ever featured in magazines.

In one article there was a photo of Aoife's mother making jam with berries *handpicked from their walled kitchen garden* while standing barefoot in their *large but cosy* family kitchen.

'Can she not afford slippers?' Maeve's mam had asked (she'd never heard of, never mind experienced, underfloor heating).

There were shots of the staircase that *loops up through the heart of the house before falling like a wave in the reception.* There were photos of the *bright, high-ceilinged rooms* where *heavy curtains fall like a respectful silence, pooling on the floor*, snaps of John and James repairing the summerhouse, of Aoife curled up reading in the library in a puddle of sunlight.

Mrs O'Neill shared her tips on interior design.

The storage bench in the kitchen is actually an artisanal pig's trough that we stumbled across during a family ramble. The farmer almost paid us to take it away! It's Irish oak. It took months to dry out in my workshop before I could sand it. I fed it with wood oil recommended by a family friend in Denmark. Months of terribly hard work, really . . . but worth every min-ute!

And that was Aoife's family. They were so fucking rich, so smart and secure, they could dig a pig's trough out of the shit and do it up for a seat and no one would laugh. People *sneered* at their pig trough alright, but every last one of them was jeal-ous of it.

Which was why Maeve also hated going to Aoife's house.

It wasn't just that her house was so big that it could've fit-ted Maeve's entire house into their two front reception rooms. It wasn't just that the front garden was bigger than the bare scrubby square of grass Maeve's family shared with fifty other council houses. It wasn't just that Aoife's family only closed their curtains when it was cold or dark, not feeling compelled – like Maeve's family – to shut their curtains against Brit patrols and nosey neighbours. It was because Maeve felt fatter, itchier, poorer and thicker when sitting opposite Mrs O'Neill's ash-blonde hair, ice-chip eyes, white linen shirts and faded blue jeans.

In Aoife's house, Maeve felt like a mattress stain waiting to happen.

She sat at the huge mahogany dining table, prickling with the impression that the dead doctor and his doomed sons were breathing down her neck, ready to rap her knuckles if she licked her knife.

'It's not long now until youse are off to France, is it, Mrs O'Neill?'

It sickened Maeve's shit that Caroline was even lovelier than her usual lovely self in the O'Neills' lovely house. Watching her lick their arses sent Maeve's own tiny reservoir of loveliness dribbling down her leg, where it puddled on the floor.

'No. We get the ferry on Wednesday.'

'And are yiz going for long?'

Mrs O'Neill looked stung for a moment, but kept smiling. That was her specialty; a trick Maeve had vowed to master.

'Well, this year, what with the exam results, we won't take our usual two months. We'll just stay a month.'

'Still, a month in France!' Caroline said. 'And just the two of youse?'

'Well, Aoife is determined to make the most of her . . . *time* . . . in the factory.'

Mrs O'Neill spoke indulgently, as if Aoife's factory job was an interesting one-off experience, instead of a trap she had to fight to escape.

'And James is staying for the internship he secured in Farring's Pharmaceuticals. He'll go to France in September, with that nice new friend of his, Scott.'

'So it's just Aoife here, all on her own?' Maeve asked. She couldn't imagine her mam trusting her alone in their house, never mind one that'd fit half the town if you wanted to party.

'James has promised to drive home every weekend, to keep an eye on this place. And of course, he's off the week of the Twelfth.'

Maeve had to admire the way Mrs O'Neill didn't need to don a balaclava and brandish a sawn-off shotgun in order to issue a warning.

'Don't you have any holiday plans of your own, Maeve?'

Maeve shrugged like holidays were a bag of shite she'd zero interest in. 'The whole factory shuts for the Twelfth week. Caroline's heading to Donegal with her lot. So I've the flat to myself.'

'Imagine the view you'll get of the parades!' Caroline joked.

Despite the fact that over two thousand Orange parades happened every year to commemorate the victory of some Proddie king over some Taig king back in 1690, Maeve'd never actually seen a parade in real life. That's because her family – like every other Taig family with an instinct for self-preservation – headed across the border when the marching reached its height around the twelfth of July. When they couldn't scrape together the money to take refuge in the Free State, they hid in the house with the curtains closed, a stash of Tayto crisps and the TV turned up full blast against the flutes and drums.

'Almost as good as the view of the bonfire from here!' Maeve said.

'That monstrosity,' Mrs O'Neill said, in a tone that made Maeve feel she was the monstrosity for talking about the huge bonfire the Prods built on the riverbank opposite the O'Neill house every July. Of course none of the O'Neills had ever seen it burn – they'd always evacuated to France before things kicked off.

John O'Neill entered the dining room and placed a sizzling duck in the middle of the table.

Maeve remembered the first and last time she'd tasted duck. Deirdre'd taken her to the Chinese one weekend she was home from university, one of the good times before the run of dark days. She'd told Maeve to 'quit whinging about chicken balls', then she'd ordered the most expensive item on the menu: a carton of crispy duck. Maeve'd never felt bad about eating chicken balls, for she doubted what was in the batter was anything close to meat, never mind a hen. But duck was a different matter. As she stood waiting for their order, she kept hearing a wee duck say *quack quack quack-quack-quack* over and over again. It wasn't the best feeling. But when Deirdre had opened the carton beside her on a bench in the town centre, and the smell of roasted duck had wafted up her nose, all thoughts of *quack* had been driven out of her head. They demolished the carton in minutes. She could still see Deirdre sitting, smiling in the drizzle, sucking the duck fat from her fingers.

The Chinese was blown up a month later for serving Brits, putting an end to crispy duck dinners in the town.

Maeve was trying to make a sliver of home-made apple pie last her as long as it was lasting the O'Neills, which she was managing by drinking a whole lot more than them.

'This young lady here,' John said, pointing a fork in Aoife's direction in case anyone had a shadow of a doubt as to who the young lady at the table might be, 'wanted to be a nun for a while!'

'No way!' Caroline laughed.

'It was only for a year or so,' Aoife said, with great dignity.

Maeve didn't laugh. Aoife wasn't so far from a nun, or something like one. She was never horny for boys in the way that most other girls were.

'Caroline. Let me guess,' John smiled, 'You wanted to be a . . .'

Caroline sat wide-eyed, waiting for the punchline.

'. . . a train driver?'

'Och, Mr O'Neill! The trains were long before my time!'

Mrs O'Neill took a sip of wine. 'My grandfather was on the last train out of the town in August 1959.'

Maeve'd seen the picture in the hall – before its departure, the last train had been filled with a selection of local VIPs. None of Maeve's relatives had made the picture. Not even to shovel coal.

'So, what *did* you want to be, Caroline?' John asked.

'She'd a notion of being a shepherdess for a while,' Maeve tattled.

'A shepherdess, Caroline?' Mrs O'Neill laughed. 'Wherever did you get that idea from?'

Caroline – pure red in the face – fired a dirty look at Maeve. 'Nana Jackson has a collection of china shepherdesses and I liked the look of the uniform.'

'I'm not sure shepherdesses have a uniform in real life.' Aoife said, getting to her feet. 'But I've got a copy of the *National Geographic* that features Mongolian herders and their traditional costume. I'll go get it now!'

'Sit where you are, Aoife,' Mrs O'Neill snapped.

'Well, sure, it doesn't matter now, anyway,' Caroline said. 'I've applied for politics in Magee, for Mammy was saying Belfast's a good three hours up the road. Magee's only an hour. I'm counting on converting to the teaching after graduation. Then it's only a year I'll have tae spend up in Belfast.'

'You'll make a great teacher,' John said decisively, before turning to Maeve. 'So what did you want to be?'

The O'Neills eyed Maeve as if she was a monkey in a lab who'd been given a brush and paints. Would the subject eat the paints or create a work of art?

'Well, your Aoife was there the day I decided to become a journalist.'

'Really,' Mrs O'Neill said, folding her napkin and placing it beside her plate.

'Yep. My thirteenth birthday.'

'Was that the day Linus McMurphy found the booby-trap bomb?' John asked. 'The one he carried home to your estate?'

Maeve nodded and eased into the tale of what happened when Linus McMurphy found a bomb up the Killeen Road, a couple of miles outside town, and carried it the two miles home, before defusing it with his bare hands on the green. Maureen Mackey was on her way to the chapel when she clocked what Linus was at. She hauled him off by the lug, then got a few of the local hard men over to check out the situation. After some discussion, they agreed to inform the police.

One minute Maeve was sitting in the kitchen, eating cake and drinking minerals with Deirdre, Caroline and Aoife, the smell of burnt matches singeing the air; the next, she was being evacuated out of the back door. With frig all else to entertain them, Maeve's mam and dad joined the crowd at the security cordon, about two hundred and fifty yards back from the bomb. There was a festive atmosphere, for with the bomb scattered in bits on the green, there was no danger of an explosion.

But then the bomb squad arrived.

Deirdre and Aoife had shrunk back into the crowd, white-faced as the Brits manoeuvred the bomb disposal robot towards what was left of the device.

'It's alright,' Maeve had said to Aoife. 'It's going to be fine.'

Then the controlled explosion detonated and blew in most of the windows in the estate.

There wasn't a scratch on Aoife when Maeve's mam handed her over to Mrs O'Neill an hour later. But she was still trembling, her eyes swollen from crying. That evening, after Maeve's da had taped plastic to their front windows and her mam had shaken the glass from their bedsheets, they watched the news. A reporter described how cowardly IRA bombers had planted a viable device in a crowded residential area.

'But Linus McMurphy found it up the Killeen Road!' Maeve exclaimed. 'It was never planted anywhere near the town!'

Her da'd shushed her with a wave of his hand. A reporter explained that bomb disposal experts had bravely carried out a controlled explosion on the device, saving local houses from massive destruction.

'But it was already defused!' Maeve had whinged, her lesson not yet learned. 'Linus had it in bits!'

Her da'd flicked over to the RTÉ news. But they didn't feature on it. 'We should've just bucked it in the bin ourselves,' her da'd said, watching the plastic on the windows bubble in and out with the wind. 'But sure we'll know for the next time.'

'Is there any word from the council on how long it'll be before we get our windys back in?' her mam'd asked.

Maeve thought of the remains of her birthday cake, lying in the bin, riddled with glass shards. And she realised that she wanted in on this shit. That she wanted to broadcast the truth, instead of parroting the government's agenda.

Of course she'd framed things a bit differently for the interview panel over in London, and for the O'Neills. 'After witnessing that incident I decided to become a journalist so I can share the hurt behind the headlines with readers and viewers across Britain and Ireland.'

The panel in London had looked kind of itchy after Maeve said that. She suspected they were more comfortable with the English candidates, whose journalism portfolios were stuffed with twee shite like village fêtes and dog shows.

'Journalism's not an easy job, Maeve,' John said. 'But I'd say you're well able for it.'

Maeve took a reddener. It felt important, having his endorsement.

'But it isn't just tough,' Mrs O'Neill said. 'It's dangerous.'

Something like mercury tilted inside Maeve, connecting a circuit that triggered a series of small explosions in her brain.

'I mean, I'd worry if Aoife started working on the sorts of stories you see in the news or read about in the papers these days,' she said. 'I'd be terrified to think of her investigating people like Michael Stone. Or worse: people like him coming after her.'

Mrs O'Neill had pinpointed what Maeve'd been trying to hide from everyone, including herself: journalism put the shits up her.

'Well, I wouldn't mind working on a fancy magazine instead of crime investigations,' Maeve said. 'But it's not easy to break into them.'

Not for the first time, Maeve felt Mrs O'Neill's eye slide over her synthetic fibres and serving-wench cleavage. Mrs O'Neill gave her the impression that she was too loud and wobbly to fit into fancy places, not the right kind of shabby to be anywhere near chic; that nobody was going to pay Maeve good money to write about drinking cocktails or wearing the latest trends. They'd have her digging the dirt in paramilitary drinking dens while they sat chatting shite in some fancy glass office in London.

'Sure you can write on the side,' John said, 'until you're established. Make a name for yourself before you end up saddled with a husband and kids.'

Maeve nodded and smiled at the stains she'd made on the tablecloth. They talked the talk, the O'Neills did, all jobs and marriage and babies. Her mam never shited on like that. She'd a suspicion her mam's highest hope was that Maeve would live long enough to graduate.

Monday, 4 July 1994

42 days until results

Because of Independence Day, the radio was all Bruce Spring-
steen, Aerosmith and Jimi Hendrix. Maeve thought it was a bit
weird that the English joined in on the fourth of July celebra-
tions – gate-crashing a party thrown to celebrate the end of their
supremacy. But then the Yanks celebrated kicking the English
out with style – all barbecues, parades and beer. Independence
Day was way better craic than the Twelfth, which always left
Maeve feeling like she'd been forced to swallow a gutful of broken glass before being kicked in the stomach.

Just then a wee doll pushed open the factory door, and stood
there knock-kneed, looking like she was dressed for helping
out at a wake.

'Who're you looking?' Maeve shouted, without missing a
stroke of the shirt she was on.

'I'm here for an interview,' the wee doll answered. 'With
Andy Strawbridge.'

'He's in the office up the stairs.'

Maeve watched the wee doll creep up the stairs, as if she
was scared to make a noise. Her interview lasted a good bit
longer than Maeve's had done. After twenty minutes she came
bouncing down the stairs a changed woman, all smiles and hair
flicks, like she'd had the craic. Maeve decided she hated her.

During tea break, Maeve slumped into her chair, avoiding eye
contact with anyone who'd start into her about wet seats or

bonus tenners. There were a few nudged elbows and smug heads at Marilyn's table, but nobody said anything. She slurped her tea in peace until the double doors burst open and Andy strode in.

'Good morning, everybody. Keep eating.'

Maeve was broke to the bone for him. Like anyone needed to be told to keep eating?

'I've conducted an analysis of our production line. And after some deep consideration, I've drawn up a floor plan that should optimise not just our production, but your experience in the factory.'

Maeve looked at Aoife, who went bright pink and sank her gaze into her mug.

'Give that tae us wan more time, Andy,' Fidelma Hegarty said. 'This time in English.'

'Andy's had a look at how the machines and tables is set up,' Mary said, 'and he reckons we can move stuff around so it's easier tae get the shirts through.'

'But we've been working like this since the factory reopened,' Marilyn Spears said. 'The set-up was like this when we were under William McFarland.'

'Yes. Which is why it's time for a change.'

Andy clicked his fingers at Mary. She shuffled to the back of the canteen and taped a huge sheet of paper to the wall.

'Any hope a moving my machine intil my house? Ah reckon I could be fierce productive working from me bed,' Mabel Moore cackled.

Andy folded his arms and stared at the floor, waiting for silence. 'This, ladies and gentlemen, is the plan. We're putting it into action first thing tomorrow morning. I suggest that you take a few minutes to look over it. Feedback to Mary if you've any observations.'

He strode out of the canteen before anyone else could get a dig in.

Maeve eyed the cluster of people grumbling in front of the plan. 'The future starts now, eh, Aoife?'

Aoife put her mug down. 'I didn't *ask* him to change things.'

Maeve swallowed the last of her tepid tea thinking Aoife didn't have to ask for what she wanted. Things just seemed to land in her lap.

All day long, girls continued to arrive for interviews. Maeve noticed that the ones in tracksuits and T-shirts spent no more than five minutes in with Andy, but the girls in skirts or nice trousers stayed much longer.

Late that afternoon, Fidelma shoved a trolley full of wrinkled shirts towards Maeve, then leaned in close. 'What're the months of a Proddie calendar?'

'Dunno.'

'January, February, March, March, March, March, March, September, October, November, December.'

Fidelma slapped Maeve on the back and let a big hearty laugh out of her. Maeve knew that sectarian jokes weren't right. But telling one was like knocking back a shot of vodka or slipping a wee Valium – it helped ease the tension, gave you a quiet laugh behind the Prods' backs. And she knew the Prods did the same, only they reversed the religions so the Taigs were always the ones getting served up to crocodiles or blowing themselves up. Jokes like Fidelma's marching one – jokes that ripped the piss without being vicious – were the ones Maeve liked best. But those jokes were few and far between.

She remembered Mr Orr, the substitute chemistry teacher who'd taught for one year in St Jude's. He was a refugee from Ardoyne who became known for his oral end-of-class tests, during which he'd stare dead-eyed at the back wall of the classroom, firing questions over the top of their heads. 'Nitrogen reacts with hydrogen to form which caustic and hazardous gas?'

They'd learned early that they weren't supposed to raise their hands to indicate they wanted to answer. Mr Orr preferred for them to wait as he paced around the class like a caged bear before he pointed at someone – like Andrea Murphy – expecting an immediate answer.

'Is it pneumonia, sir?'

Despite being from Ardoyne, Mr Orr never hit anyone for getting the answer wrong. Instead he'd say, 'Wrong,' before reciting the right answer in a tone of a man who is suicidally bored. 'Nitrogen reacts with hydrogen to form *ammonia*, a caustic and hazardous gas.'

Nobody took notes. Aoife didn't need to. Everyone else just accepted where they were, having long ago given up on improvement.

'Why does iodine have a higher boiling point than chlorine?' Mr Orr might point at Mary McDaid of the smelly McDaids.

'Because it's a different colour?'

'Wrong. Iodine has a higher boiling point than chlorine because the forces between iodine molecules are stronger.'

Mr Orr livened up these end-of-class quizzes by inserting rogue general knowledge questions to keep the class on its feet. 'What do you do if you see a Protestant with half a face?' He'd point at the like of Jimmy Kennedy, who'd been in the remedial stream in school since he was four years old, and had five uncles who'd all done time in Long Kesh (a measure of both their burning patriotism and incurable stupidity).

'Reload and fire again.'

Mr Orr's delivery was the same whether he was testing general sectarian knowledge or GCSE chemistry. 'Hypothetically, how would you save a Protestant from drowning?'

'Ye'd take yer foot off his head, sir.'

Mr Orr paced about – skinny and itching for a fag – never expressing approval if someone got the answer right. 'Is a British soldier an example of a hazard, a risk, or both?' he'd once asked before pointing at Louise McGrath, whose family had the reputation of being hazards themselves, not just to the Brits, but residents on both sides of The Divide.

'Neither, sir?'

'Wrong. A Brit is an example of a hazard and a risk. The risk to your personal safety goes up or down depending on the soldier's mood, his personal experience, orders from his superiors, and what you are doing when you encounter him. Right. When atoms collide and react, what is it that meets and interacts?'

'The neutrons, sir?'

'Wrong. The outer electrons.'

Sometimes Mr Orr stopped mid-prowl and put his two hands to his head, as if he was in great pain. After a few seconds, he'd take a breath, and resume pacing. 'How do you know ET is Protestant?' He might point at Eddie Maguire.

'He looks like one, sir.'

In a way, Mr Orr's quizzes were inclusive. Eddie Maguire wasn't able to give Mr Orr an example of the only giant covalent substance that can conduct electricity, but he sure as hell knew how to tell if it was a Protestant that was looking at you through a keyhole.

'What's the only guaranteed way a Catholic can gain entrance into Queen's University, Belfast?' Mr Orr had pointed at Maeve for that one.

She'd parroted the answer she'd learned in Careers class, even though she knew it wasn't what he was looking for. 'By completing the UCAS form correctly and studying hard enough to get the required exam results, sir?'

'Wrong. The only guaranteed way a Catholic like you can gain entrance into Queen's is to donate your body to science.'

Mr Orr moved on, but Maeve kept thinking about the joke. Did it mean Catholics were so dumb that the only way Queen's would accept one was as dead meat? Or did it mean Queen's was so sectarian that they'd only take useful Catholics – ones that could be used for dissection? She didn't ask Mr Orr for clarification. By the end of the year, he'd ensured that most of the class had a passing knowledge of chemistry, and nearly everyone had a remarkable repertoire of sectarian jokes.

Maeve wondered if the Proddie school Sharon Rogers had gone to had had a teacher like Mr Orr, a real-life Mr Keating from *Dead Poets Society*, someone who stuffed the gaps in the curriculum with what the pupils really needed to survive the real world. Thanks to Mr Orr, Maeve had been reasonably well equipped for GCSE chemistry and working in the factory. She felt less equipped for London. Part of her wished she could trust Andy enough to do more than read the book he'd given her. But the safest thing she could do was save money. Something she'd do a better job of, she knew, if she could only quit the frigging fags.

On Tuesday morning they started rearranging the factory floor. Because Maeve and Aoife's ironing boards were already optimally placed they'd nothing to do. So they helped the machinists move their stations into place following the plan. Then they installed paper hand towels in the toilets. Aoife made a big show out of conducting a comparative hand-drying performance test. She had Fidelma Hegarty time her and Maeve washing and drying their hands, only Aoife had a paper hand towel and was done in ten seconds, while Maeve stood for a minute rubbing her hands under the hand-dryer – which was as warm and powerful as a gentle fart – and still wasn't done. Aoife was thrilled until Fidelma observed that if the people who currently skipped hand hygiene now stopped to wash their hands, toilet breaks would take even longer than before.

Back out on the factory floor, Maeve noticed that someone had moved the stain removal station over beside a window. Aoife explained that the window could be opened when using the chemicals, so nobody would get dizzy from the fumes. Maeve nodded while wondering how much closer to the nozzle she'd have to get for a high – a comparative performance test she knew Aoife would never approve of.

The buzz died when everyone sat back behind their stations and got back to work. Things didn't go well. They kept messing up, reverting again and again to the old system that seemed to have burned itself into their muscles as well as their minds. Improvement, Maeve noted, wasn't as easy as just shifting chairs and tables around.

Maeve and Aoife were outside having a break with Baldy Magee when Fidelma Hegarty appeared. She jerked her head at Baldy to indicate that he should get the fuck off the plastic chair. He jumped up and Fidelma collapsed onto the seat.

'Wan more day in this dump, then we've a week off,' she said, rubbing her calves.

'Are ye going any roads, Fidelma?' Baldy asked.

It hadn't occurred to Maeve that Fidelma would go on holidays during the Twelfth. She'd just presumed she'd lie low in the town.

'Naw. From the frying pan in tae the fire, I suppose, stuck here in this shithole. Youse going anywhere?' Fidelma looked at Aoife and Maeve. They shook their heads.

'Still and all, ah'd say you've a great view of thon bonfire from your mansion, hey, Miss O'Neill,' Baldy Magee said.

Aoife shrugged.

'But ye would now. Best view in town. And how big is it now?' Baldy asked. 'Would it be anywhere near as big as the bonfires up in Belfast? Hmmm?'

'I'd say it's close to twenty foot,' Aoife said, unable to resist an imperial estimation.

'Twenty feet, hey?' Baldy said, sucking air in between his teeth. 'Gets bigger every year.'

'I don't have a pick against the bonfires,' Fidelma said. 'There's nothing like a good fire. Drums are grand too. Ah wouldn't say naw tae a go on a lambeg. It's the marching, flutes and bowler hats I don't understand. Why are they intay all that?'

'They say it's a celebration of their culture,' Aoife said.

'Wish they'd learn how to celebrate without making me feel like they're trying to rub my nose in a hot steaming pile of Protestant supremacy,' Maeve huffed.

'I think they're just insecure,' Aoife said.

'Kind of like Andy and his dick and that car?' Fidelma asked. Aoife went pink.

'We outclassed the Prods centuries ago,' Baldy said, shoving his hands in his pockets. 'It's only a matter of years before we outbreed them.'

Maeve distanced herself from the disturbing mental picture of Baldy breeding by trying to calculate how big and hot the bonfires would be by the time the Catholics outnumbered Protestants.

'You know,' Aoife said softly, 'I do sometimes wonder what it's like to be a Protestant, feeling the foundations of your power crumble beneath your feet.'

Fidelma eyed Aoife with her ye-what-now? face. 'Probably no worse than it feels never tae have had foundations in the first place?'

Maeve knew what Fidelma meant. It was hard to feel sorry for the Prods when they were building their bonfires higher and beating their drums all the harder. You didn't need to be Dale Carnegie to know that wasn't the best way to go about winning friends and influencing people. But the Prods – like the English – hadn't clung to power by being nice to the folk whose arses they'd kicked centuries ago. Bosses, landowners, aristocrats and CEOS weren't studying *How to Win Friends and Influence People*: it was written for people like Maeve.

When the lunch bell rang on Thursday signalling the half day was done, Mabel Moore held her two arms up and roared, 'Praise Be!' The machinists stood up laughing and stretched their cramped muscles. Mary came onto the floor and looked around her, beaming. Then Maeve heard Andy's office door spring shut. She looked up, her heart racing. He leaned on the mezzanine banister.

'Ladies and gentlemen,' he said, like a ringmaster at a circus, confident he could draw all eyes to him. 'McAllister's will deliver the material we need for our new contract on Monday the eight-eenth. And I want you lot to show them what we're made of!'

'Well, ah reckon ah'm about ninety-nine per cent tae, toast and Tennent's at this point of me life,' Mabel Moore cracked. 'But how are ye gonna prove that tae McAllister's?'

Andy waited for the cackling to die down before continuing. 'I hope you all enjoy your time off with your families and loved ones. I want you all to come back here refreshed and ready for our new contract.'

'Fuck that,' Mickey McCanny said, raising the Coke bottle he'd poured vodka into earlier that morning. 'Ah'm away tae get wrecked.'

A cheer went up from the factory floor.

'Of course,' Andy said. 'I'll still be here, working behind closed doors to secure the contracts that will help us expand our operation.'

'No rest for the wicked,' croaked Mabel.

Andy threw his hands up in mock surrender. 'OK. Jog on you lot. See you in about ten days.'

They surged through the doors. Caroline had to rush home to mind Nana Jackson to give her mam the chance to go and clean the chapel, so Maeve loitered at the gates. Mickey McCanny was brandishing a copy of the *Sunday Tribune* and slabbering on about a ceasefire.

'Where'd ye get that rag from?' Sharon Rogers asked.

'Ah get it off Father Goan's housekeeper for the crossword. Fair good crossword in it.'

'Southern news,' huffed Sharon. 'Shows ye what them Free Staters think they know.'

Fidelma Hegarty glared at Sharon. 'Well, what ah know is it feels frig all like a ceasefire up here the way your side are going at things.'

'Well, Billy says a ceasefire has tae be in the works the way your lot are settling old scores before they have tae lay their guns down.'

Maeve watched the group splinter into two packs, snarling and snapping, hackles raised, teeth bared.

'Well, ah think the only road to peace is to shoot the whole damn lot of them,' Mickey said. 'Politicians, gunmen, the whole lot.' Mickey's other pet solutions included: 'burn it to fuck', 'fire it in a ditch tae rot' and 'race the hoor up the road'.

'Can I borrow the paper, Mickey?' Maeve asked.

'Work away,' he said, handing it over.

Maeve hunched her shoulders against a sudden squall of rain. Fidelma Hegarty eyed the sky like she might hit it a slap. 'Fuck this weather. Ah'm away tae the School Bar to warm meself up a bit. Who's coming?'

Maeve suspected that drinking with Fidelma Hegarty'd be more dangerous – but much better craic – than daytime television. 'I'll join ye.'

An hour later, Maeve was on her third pint, losing her fifth game of pool, and throwing shapes to 'Should I Stay or Should I Go?' Drinking with Fidelma was deadly. Nobody was going to fuck with Maeve when she was on the batter with Fidelma. And she had this powerful feeling that she could fuck with whoever she wanted.

A couple of hours later Fidelma was telling Maeve about the time she'd fallen for a traveller fella in Ballyshannon when Johnny the Squawk came in the side door, all biz. 'God-oh, so there's where ye've got tae, Fidelma.'

Nobody liked Johnny the Squawk, for nothing got by him and what he didn't know for sure, he made up as he went along.

'And who's interested in my whereabouts?' Fidelma growled.

Johnny took a step back as if he was scared of her, which was all for show, for she wouldn't waste her time battering a croil like him. A fart would send him flying.

'Ach now nobody's looking ye. But ah thought ye might be interested in the whereabouts of yer nearest and dearest.'

'What are you shiting on about?'

Johnny rubbed his stubble, then sat one arse cheek on a bar stool. 'Well, there's ructions, so there is. In the Diamond. The loyalists out with flutes and our side out with fists. And ah seen yer da in the thick of it.'

Fidelma's face darkened. 'Fuck away aff, will ye, Johnny, before I fell ye.'

Johnny scooted up off the stool like he was feared then ducked out the door, grinning.

Fidelma sank the remains of her pint and got to her feet. 'Ah'm away for a pish. Then ah'll have tae go see what the craic is.'

Maeve nodded, downed her own pint, then followed Fidelma.

Outside it was still bright and rain was spattering the pavements. Every shop in town was shuttered and padlocked against the possibility of ructions later on. The Diamond was snarled with knots of teenagers and men, roughly divided into Prods and Taigs. A few of the Prods were in band outfits, and a couple of them were whistling away on flutes. Suddenly sunlight struck the Diamond, filling the puddles with gold and splintering in the falling rain. It was one of those moments when even the town looked beautiful, when Maeve felt she didn't have the strength to rip herself out of the heart of everything she knew to start over, all alone in a huge city crawling with strangers and their weird ways of doing stuff. But then a cloud sailed over the sun, plunging the street back into grey. Living with Irish weather was like shacking up with one of those arseholes Maeve read about in her mam's magazines – getting flowers one minute, and having ten shades of shite knocked out of you the next.

'Och, now,' Fidelma groaned. 'What the frig is he at?'

Her da was pure blootered. And he was squaring up to a Prod, staggering rings round him, throwing shapes. The Prod was, in fairness, trying to dodge the fight. It was their own side who were keeping Fidelma's da going.

'Them wans egging him on, the fuckers,' Fidelma said. 'They know the kind of him.'

The Prod landed a punch on Fidelma's da and a cheer went up from his cronies. Fidelma's da swung around, but stayed on his feet, swaying as he tried to focus on the fella who'd hit him.

'Are ye not going tae get him?' Maeve asked, her heart banging like a drum, a wee bit horny, if she was honest, to see Fidelma flying in with her fists swinging.

'Fuck, naw. Ah have tae let him work his bad humour out.'

Maeve stood by Fidelma's side, watching her da get a hiding. The Prod he was up against was decent enough to only hit the man hard and often enough to eventually land him on the pavement, where he lay spitting blood and curses.

'Right, he's more civil now,' Fidelma said. 'Ah'll make some of them friggers help me carry him up the road. You enjoy your holiday now.'

'You too,' Maeve shouted, as Fidelma waded into the thick of the crowd. She bent down and put her arms under her father's oxters, hoisting him to his feet. As she turned away, Maeve wondered if Fidelma's face was red only from the effort of hauling that big wreck of a man upright.

Monday 11 July 1994

35 days until results

Scott Fitzpatrick and Maeve were sitting at opposite ends of the old, scrubbed-soft kitchen table in the O'Neill house. James was stirring a pot while Aoife was staring out of the window at the Proddie kids and teens swarming around the bonfire across the river.

'When are they lighting that?' Scott asked, looking at Maeve.

'How would I know? I'm normally hiding in the house with the curtains closed for fear I'd end up on top of it.'

Maeve'd got her first taste of Scott down the town the day before. She'd bumped into James and his friend while shopping with her mam. After they'd walked off, her mam'd said, 'God-oh, if thon was an ice cream, he'd lick himself.'

'So, Maeve,' Scott said. 'Where is it you've applied for again?'

Scott was studying medicine in Oxford and had told Maeve that he'd an ambition to 'practise' as a gynaecologist. But she knew by the cut of him that no matter how much he'd learned about textbook pussies, he wasn't qualified to handle one in the wild.

'UCL.'

'Ah. UCL. My grandmother read medicine there.'

What in hell could Maeve say to that? That her Granny Walsh'd left school at thirteen? That her mam'd dropped out of uni? That her da'd even failed at the pig factory?

'Fantastic place, UCL,' Scott continued. 'You'd do well to get in there. I hope you've a fallback position.'

'Goldsmith's,' Maeve said, shutting him the fuck up.

James brought a big pot over to the table, and began serving spaghetti. It slithered onto Maeve's plate, slick with olive oil. Then he ladled a rich red meaty sauce on top.

Maeve was dying to get stuck in, but she noticed that Scott was sitting back, watching James grate a lump of dusty cheese onto a plate, so she held her horses. James passed the cheese to Maeve. She sniffed it, then recoiled. 'Jesus Christ. What's that then?'

'Fresh Parmesan. I brought it down from Belfast.'

Maeve wasn't keen on Parmesan. It had been one of Deirdre's university affectations. There was still a grubby wee cellar of it mouldering away in their kitchen cupboard at home.

'Well, if that's what it smells like fresh, I'd hate to catch the ming off it when it's rotten.'

'It's nice, though,' James said. 'Try some.'

Maeve scattered a few flakes onto her meat, then passed the plate to Scott. As soon as James lifted his fork, she tore into the food. They didn't talk much during the meal. As Maeve ate, she scuffed her feet on the warm terracotta floor tiles (Mrs O'Neill had salvaged them from a derelict chateau in France – the town's equivalent of the Elgin Marbles). She finished first, of course, then pushed her empty plate away.

The problem with James's spaghetti Bolognese wasn't that it was awful. Of course it wasn't. The sauce was meaty and melty at the same time. Aoife had praised the pasta for being 'all dawn tay', which probably meant that James had *intended* it to be half-cooked. Even the cheese worked (in the same odd way that Maeve quite liked the sour smell of Granda Murray's old socks, while she couldn't thole the vinegary ming off Granny Walsh's pits). The problem was James's spaghetti Bolognese didn't taste like anything she'd ever eaten before. Specifically, it tasted nothing like the spaghetti Bolognese she'd made him using a packet of powder.

She knew he hadn't meant to ruin spaghetti Bolognese for her. She knew he thought he was doing her a good turn. But even if she could afford the fancy ingredients he'd used, she'd never be footered to spend two hours over the stove for herself or anyone else.

'James, that was unbelievable,' she said, doing this kissy-fingers thing she'd seen on *The Godfather*. 'Absolutely amazing.'

Scott was mopping up sauce with a piece of bread. 'You'll make some woman a fine wife!'

Nobody laughed. But Maeve suspected Scott didn't care. He wasn't trying to raise a laugh. He was just a sneery cunt, like the scummy lawyer in *Pretty Woman*. She poured herself another drink and wondered what was for dessert.

After dinner, they went onto the balcony to watch the bonfire burn. Scott was slouching in his chair wearing a quilted jacket, with one foot resting on his thigh. He looked like he belonged. Maeve was wrapped in a blanket like a hunger striker. She looked over the river where the flames from the bonfire licked the trees, while the giant, lumbering heartbeat of a Lambeg drum pulsed under a scrape of flutes. Her blanket slipped down. James leaned forward and pulled it up around her shoulders. She dipped her head at him to say thanks, then took a sip of her Irish coffee.

'So, Aoife,' Scott said, 'you never told me about your entrance interview for Cambridge. James said it was quite the interrogation.'

'Hmmm. It wasn't as much fun as I'd hoped.' Aoife described how she'd been ushered into an oak-panelled room where three men sat in a row. They'd asked her a series of questions that she'd 'quite enjoyed' answering, before one old fellow expressed interest in the 'unusual' fact that Aoife was attending a mixed comprehensive secondary school.

'So I had to correct him of course – I explained that St Jude's isn't mixed. It's all Catholic.'

'And how did he take to correction?' Scott asked.

'Well, nobody said anything for *ages* so I started panicking that I'd come across as sectarian, so I told them I would've loved to have gone to a mixed school, but we'd no choice.'

'Really? But your nearest school is mixed. I've seen the sign. It says "Integrated High School".'

'That's just for show, Scott,' Maeve snapped. 'They say they accept Catholics to get additional funding. But no Catholic'd dare go there.'

'Anyway,' Aoife said, 'the two old fellows sort of smiled at each other like I'd said something funny. Then the younger man, he said, "He meant mixed sex."'

'Embarrassing,' Scott said, displaying his talents for stating the obvious and being a total dick in a single word.

'Well, yes. Mortifying, in fact. And, of course, that's when they asked me about the appendix.'

'The appendix?' Maeve said in her what-the-fuck? voice.

'The appendix,' Aoife confirmed, gravely.

'OK,' Scott said, all interested, as if this line of questioning wasn't total lunacy.

'They asked me to imagine that my body was society, and the appendix was a part of society.'

Maeve sighed and took a gulp of coffee. This was the sort of oul shite that put her clean off university.

'So then they said' – here Aoife put on a surprisingly convincing posh English accent – '"What might you do if the appendix were causing the rest of society pain or was threatening the wellbeing of society as a whole?"'

Maeve wondered what she'd say to that. There didn't seem to be a smart answer, let alone a right one.

'I was panicking because I know all about the appendix, what with James here,' Aoife said, glancing at him.

'A painful old business that, appendicitis!' James said, wincing.

'All I could remember was what the surgeon said about the appendix: it's basically a vestigial body part that has no purpose, no point – and no influence on you – unless it gets infected. Then you're in trouble.'

Maeve's coffee was running low, cooling to near blood temperature. The plume of smoke over the bonfire thickened and darkened as flames reached the tyres at the top.

'So.' Scott sniffed. 'Of course one should simply cut the appendix out and incinerate it, correct? But only to save a life. To reduce pain. One wouldn't interfere, otherwise.'

'Well,' Aoife said, 'The surgeon said to Mummy and Daddy that a blockage was to blame for James's appendicitis. And Mummy – being Mummy – asked what the blockage was. And the surgeon said, "It's calcified faeces" and Mummy was kind of mortified so he said, "Oh, but it can be a tumour or parasites, so really, calcified faeces is a good thing."'

'Great name for a band, that,' Maeve said. 'Calcified Faeces.'

'Anyway,' Aoife said, looking revolted, 'I remembered all that, and said that the appendix itself isn't really to blame for the pain.'

'It's only reacting to the crap that's got stuck in it,' Scott said, draining his glass.

'Well, I didn't put it *quite* like that. But I said that ninety-nine per cent of the time, the poor old appendix is fine. It's just a vestigial relic that wants to be left to itself. Removing and incinerating the part of society that seems to be causing you a problem is not necessarily the best solution. I said, where possible, society should work together to remove the blockage.'

'Or at least keep the shit flowing smoothly!' Maeve said, feeling inspired.

'I used the term "waste product",' Aoife said. 'But yes – that's the idea. Keep the waste flowing. Find and destroy the parasites. Cut the tumours out. But leave the organ intact.'

'And what did they say to that?' Scott asked.

Aoife's chair creaked as she shifted position. 'Nothing, actually. They were pretty poker-faced. They took a few notes and wished me well in my exams.'

'Well,' Scott said, yawning. 'I suppose it was an acceptable answer, for you got an offer.'

Aoife closed her eyes. Maeve knew exactly how she felt – her heart being squeezed by hope and fear. They both had offers. But if they didn't get their projected grades, they'd get stuck in the dead end of the Six Counties. Stranded in a vestigial relic that had become a massive pain for both the Free State and the Brits. Maeve put her empty glass on the floor and gazed at the black smoke billowing into the sky. Incineration was a no-brainer.

The next morning the scorched grass around the smouldering bonfire was lumpy with unconscious loyalists. The castle car park was full, and the bucks in bowler hats had already started up at the flutes and drums again.

Maeve began drinking early that morning. It was in the air: the Lambegs pounding, the breeze thick with the stench of the bonfire. She was drunk by lunchtime, but she kept going. They all did, drinking quietly and steadily, the alcohol climbing in their bloodstreams like river water rising against a flood wall.

It was dusk when Scott started a conversation that Maeve'd been bored of by the time she was fourteen. 'One of my friends in Oxford, he's got this idea that if he removed a couple of his ribs, he'd be able to suck his own dick.'

Scott made Maeve seal up like a Barbie doll.

'What's he studying?'

'He hopes to become a surgeon. So I imagine this is something he'll be able to research. He'll make a fortune, if he's right.'

'Doubt it.'

'Why?'

'If that ever took off, first thing I'd do when meeting some lad I'm interested in would be' – Maeve leaned over and squeezed James's rib cage. He curled up against her, laughing – 'to do that. It's hard to prove a man's a motherfucker, but an op like that'll make it obvious who's a cocksucker.'

Scott's face darkened. Maeve couldn't tell if he was angry or horny or – like most men she knew – both at once. 'To be honest,' she said, 'I don't know why lads are so interested in sucking their own cocks. I mean, every girl I know can lick herself out and you don't hear us crowing about it.'

Scott gazed at Maeve, his mouth open like he was trying to say something, but had forgotten what.

'I mean, it must be the difference in our rib cages and genitalia that makes it possible, right, Aoife?' Maeve knew there was a good chance that Aoife would ruin the joke. But she just went pink, which was a great help. 'It's a bit of stretch, mind you,' Maeve continued. 'Kinda like a cat. But you get better at it the more you practise. Makes perfect, as they say.'

Scott laid his shredded napkin on the table. 'So what happens when you're menstruating?'

Everyone winced. Maeve'd never heard a male say the word 'menstruating' in real life before. She hoped she never would again. 'What d'ye think happens?' she asked Scott, licking her lips.

He shrugged, his face blazing, while James stared at the carpet.

'Oh, Maeve, stop! Stop it!' Aoife said, putting her face in her hands. 'This conversation is not appropriate for the dinner table!'

Maeve picked up her spoon and dug out a mouthful of apple crumble. She waved it at Aoife. 'Good crumble this,' she said, then sucked on her spoon while staring at Scott.

Maeve realised later that evening she was bored of everything and everyone – herself included. And being bored of herself felt much worse than being broke, or feeling trapped, or having your whole heart blister over with grief. And she wondered if what had driven Deirdre to sit silently among her family for four days with the contents of a bottle of pills melting her liver wasn't whatever had happened up in Belfast, but how she felt afterwards. Being bored of it all. Bored of being treated like shit and then feeling like shit. Maeve wanted Fidelma Hegarty to charge in and make mincemeat of Scott before dragging Maeve out on the lash with her. She wished she had the guts to run the gauntlet of streets full of drunk, riled-up Orangemen so she could land at Fidelma's door with a bagful of cider and have some proper craic.

But instead she hung on in the O'Neills' house. She did OK – she was fucking managing – until Scott suggested they play 'Truth or Dare', at which point Maeve made a gun of her hand, pulled the trigger against her temple and collapsed on the sofa.

'You could just say "No, thanks", Maeve?' Scott said, sheathing himself in his armchair.

Maeve pulled herself upright and took a gulp of vodka. Then she asked, 'What about we play a game of "If I was…"?'

Scott perked up like a dumb but keen guard dog. Maeve could almost hear him snarling in his throat. 'How does it work?'

'Right. So. Someone says something like "If I was ice . . ." and then the person they choose has to finish the sentence with what they'd be, like – "I'd be in a Diet Coke", or something like that.'

'So I understand the concept,' Scott said, preening. 'But isn't the grammar off?'

'What do you mean?' Maeve asked, giving Scott the rope he needed to hang himself.

'I mean, we ought to be saying "If I Were" not "Was". "Was" is poor grammar. An aspiring journalist ought to know better.'

It was clear to Maeve that although Scott knew the grammar was wrong, he hadn't a good enough grasp of it to explain why. She was about to eviscerate him when Aoife jumped in.

'Maeve's well aware of how to use the subjunctive mood, Scott. She's asserting her right to use Hiberno-English in our private domestic setting.'

'Just like he's asserting his right to sound like a dick by using the word "ought" in West Tyrone.'

Maeve bristled at Scott and he sneered back. In a romcom, their characters would go their separate ways after that summer, have terrible love affairs throughout their twenties, then be the singles invited to a couples' dinner party in the hope they'd hit it off. They'd hate each other all over again before learning how they'd changed: Maeve'd be a famous but hard-as-nails investigative journalist, and Scott'd turn out to be a sensitive paediatric oncologist, on the cusp of a breakthrough cure for some hideous childhood cancer. They'd reminisce about their grammar row, then kiss in the rain and live happily ever after. But Maeve felt like she was starring in a Northern Irish documentary – more likely to end up missing her knee-caps or buried in a bog.

'OK. Let's get going. Aoife: if I was a pub . . .?'

'Ummmm . . . I'd be closing time?'

Maeve should've known Aoife wasn't going to be happy hour.

'OK, Scott . . .' Aoife said, looking around the room for inspiration. 'If I was a wine glass. . .?'

'I'd be a 1989 Bordeaux. Room temperature.'

Maeve wondered what she'd started.

'Maeve, if I were English . . .?' Scott asked.

'I'd be George Washington,' she said. 'Riding a white horse.'

Scott narrowed his eyes at her.

'James,' she said. 'If I was snow . . .?' She expected him to say something like 'antifreeze' or 'Christmas Day'.

But he didn't. 'I'd be dusk.'

Maeve found herself transported to one winter evening, years before, standing outside the chapel at dusk, her breath frosting the air. The graveyard was glowing under a fresh snow-fall. It looked as if an alien had laid a spectacular blanket over the bodies sleeping below the ground. It was the last time she could remember believing there was something sublime, something divine, hovering just out of sight, slightly out of reach.

'Scott,' James said, his ears pink. 'If I was a pot of pasta . . .?'

'Linguine or fusilli?' Scott asked, like any of it fucking mattered.

Hours, perhaps days, later, Maeve was trying to open a bottle of Smirnoff she'd nicked from the pantry. It slipped and smashed on the floor.

Suddenly she was back in their kitchen at home, in a smog of baked beans and burnt fish fingers, with Deirdre screaming in her face over a bottle of smashed ketchup. Their mam clipped them both around the back of the head, then snarled, 'Draw yer horns in and tidy up that mess.' Maeve had started to clear the table while Deirdre dropped on her knees before the broken bottle. The next minute their mam hissed, 'Oh, holy fuck.' Deirdre was staring at a neat red line across her left wrist. Maeve could still see the colour. It was the red of fairy tales. Of Snow White's lips. Of poisonous berries. Of ruby slippers. Of still-beating hearts steaming in the winter air.

'Stupid, selfish wee bitch,' their mam had said, pulling Deirdre to her feet.

Deirdre's eyes were glittering – not with tears or anger, but with relief. Her skin was pale but she was relaxed, like she'd let go of something icy cold or boiling hot. Their mam wrapped a wet tea towel around Deirdre's wrist, tight as a noose, then tied a hand towel around that and dragged her into the living room.

'What now?' their da asked.

'She's cut. She'll need stitches.'

He saw the blood seeping through the towel wrapped around Deirdre's arm and his jaw went slack. He was no good with the blood. Not after ten years of the pig factory.

'Fuck,' he said, getting to his feet. 'I'll go out and call a taxi.'

'Call McNabb's,' her mam said. 'Not Gallagher's. Tell them to pick us up below the Cromwell.'

Their da nodded, then headed out of the door to the telephone box.

'And you,' her mam'd said, pinning Maeve to the wall with her eye, 'you're going with us.'

A fair-headed Protestant drove them to the hospital in silence, then charged them a good five quid more than a Gallagher would've. Maeve watched a nurse stitch Deirdre as she lay on a white bed in a blue cubicle. Because of the nature of Deirdre's injury, a doctor was summoned to speak with them before discharge. He checked Deirdre over without saying a word, then walked their mam down the corridor. That was the last Maeve saw of him. Their mam stalked back five minutes later, jerked the curtains around the bed closed and sat down on the blue plastic chair by Deirdre's bed. She sat gently rocking for a while, then she caught a grip of Deirdre's good wrist.

'You try that again…' she hissed, blinking back tears and swallowing loudly. 'You try that again and ah'll fucking kill ye myself.'

'Are you OK, Maeve?'

Maeve blinked. James was standing in front of her.

'Broke the bottle.'

'I can see that.'

'Sorry.'

'It's OK. I'll clean it up.'

'I'm so, so sorry. Broke the bottle.' Maeve noticed she was crying. That meant she was pure bollixed.

'Maeve. Honestly. It's no big deal.'

She knelt down to pick up the shards of glass.

'Here,' he said, grabbing her wrists. 'Leave that. You're only going to cut yourself.'

Tears splatted into the puddle of vodka.

'You need to lie down,' James said, putting his arm around her waist. He led her up the stairs to bed.

She was sure he only kissed her to stop her from saying 'Sorry' over and over again. She'd never tell him she only kissed him back to see something other than pity on his face.

The next morning she woke in her clothes, the sour tang of cum in the back of her throat, her head pounding. James lay on his stomach beside her, sound asleep. She allowed herself to stay for a few moments, observing the acne scars pitting his shoulders, the skimmed-milk shade of his eyelids. She remembered the way he'd let her kiss him, as though he was on the ropes in a boxing match, praying for the bell to ring.

She climbed out of bed, smelling of his aftershave and sweat, and gathered up her things. She'd a bad feeling she wasn't done being sorry.

Monday, 18 July 1994

28 days until results

Caroline'd bounced back into the flat that weekend, all freckles and smiles, with a stick of rock for Maeve that said:

DONE

GAL

And Maeve did feel done. Sitting indoors for a week breathing bonfire smoke and guzzling booze had given her the anaemic look of a seedling that'd tried to sprout under a rock. As they crossed the road over to the factory, she glanced up at the factory sign. The 'R' in the factory sign had come loose and was hanging upside down.

STRAWBRIDGE AND ASSOCIATES SHI Я T FACTORY

Paddy Quinn and Baldy Magee were standing in the drizzle at the door, smoking.

'Well. Did yeez have a good break?' Maeve asked, scanning the car park. Plenty of culchie cars were in, but Andy's Jag was nowhere to be seen.

'Aye,' Paddy said. 'Ah took the weans and herself down tae Sligo.'

'I'd a week in Bundoran,' Caroline said. 'And Nana Jackson won the jackpot on the fruit machines!'

'No jackpot for me,' Baldy said, mournfully. 'Ah stayed with the mother.'

'I was stuck here too,' Maeve said, though she felt that was a bit of a cheat. Watching the Twelfth from inside the O'Neill house and being fingered by James O'Neill wasn't quite the same as being trapped with your mam in a wee house on a big council estate.

'Too bad for yeez,' Paddy said. 'Ah suppose the town was black with Prods.'

'It was, aye. But ah learned how ye can get twenty Orangemen intil a telephone box,' Baldy said, all sly.

'How d'ye do that then?'

'Tell them they're not allowed.'

They all cracked up. Then a big truck with an Antrim numberplate pulled up at the gates and blasted its horn. Baldy rushed over and started directing it in as if it were an oil tanker entering the Suez Canal.

'What's in the truck?' Caroline asked Paddy.

'It's the McAllister's material,' he said. 'At least they've delivered that much on their promise.'

'What are ye saying?' Maeve asked.

Paddy gleeked around before answering. 'McAllister's would be a fairly Protestant set-up,' he said. 'There's no wild reason for them tae be loyal to the likes of this place.'

'Mixed, ye mean?'

'That.' Paddy nodded. 'And then there's our management. We're an unusual set-up.' He raised both eyebrows and pulled his mouth to the side, critically, as if to say, 'We'll say no more about that now.'

Maeve nodded back like she'd understood what he was saying, though she hadn't a clue what he was driving at. She watched him follow the truck around to the back of the factory, then she turned and did big eyes at Caroline, who shrugged back at her. They burst into giggles and clocked in.

Maeve shivered as she entered the factory. The air felt thin and cold, for the warmth of fags, tea and toast, Lynx and farts had leaked out of the factory during their week off. She heard the big double doors at the back of the factory creak open. Baldy walked in, then energetically waved the truck up tight to the entrance. Maeve wondered how the driver had the restraint not to run him over. Once the truck's back doors were opened and the ramp lowered, Billy Stone and Paddy Quinn began to unload the bolts of fabric. They stacked them high at the back of the factory while Mary watched, checking off a list on her clipboard.

'How much is that now, Mary?' Fidelma Hegarty asked, eyeing the mound of fabric. 'Looks like only a fortnight's worth of work! No more than that, any roads.'

Mary rubbed her forehead with the heel of her hand. 'A wee bit over a fortnight. Enough to keep ye busy.'

'Only two weeks, though?' Mabel Moore asked. 'There's room enough in this place for a month's worth a fabric. Do they not trust us or what?'

Billy heaved a roll of fabric onto the cutting table. Maeve felt a tingle on her neck as he ran his hand appreciatively over the material.

'Ah dunno what the agreement between Andy and McAllister's is,' Mary said. 'It's my job tae make sure they deliver us the fabric, and our job tae make sure we deliver them the shirts.'

'Well, ah suppose ah'd better crack on,' Fidelma said, scissoring her clippers in the air.

'Aye, that's right,' Mabel agreed, sitting down with a puff. 'Tay doesn't drink itself and shirts don't sew themselves.'

Billy slipped on his chainmail glove and switched the cutting blade on. Maeve watched him shear the blade through the fabric until the green light on her iron clicked on. Then she sent a puff of steam into the air, pulled a shirt to her board and got back to work.

Andy arrived in the door at eight fifteen, escorting the nervy wee doll Maeve'd seen at the interviews. He walked her over to Mary's office, where he said something that left the wee doll tittering. Then he dashed up the stairs and stood on the mezzanine, stroking his tie in a way that made Maeve picture him admiring his own dick.

She caught Fidelma's eye. 'Aye, right,' they said with their eyes. 'Aye, right.'

Maeve got back to her shirt. Now that her muscles had warmed up, it felt like she'd never been off, but the atmosphere had changed. A good bit of the tension that'd ratcheted up before the Twelfth had evaporated. Most of the Prods had the look of a bled goose, like the marching and drumming had helped them work something out of their system. But everyone was narky. They were all still fucking things up with the new system – the machinists passing baskets full of finished pieces the old way, people reaching for bundles in the wrong places. It was a relief when the tea break bell rang, for there were no wreck-the-head changes in the canteen – it'd always been optimised for tea, toast and fags.

Maeve hung back to finish a shirt, listening to a newscaster rattle the latest details from the Fred West case across the factory floor. She wondered what it was about the English that allowed serial killers to flourish – did they not notice people disappearing from under their noses, or were they just too polite to say anything? Nobody in the town had a hope of being a serial killer, for everyone knew the shade of your last shite before you'd wiped your arse.

She put down her iron and draped the finished shirt over the rail. Then she noticed that the new girl was sitting like an eejit behind a sewing machine. Maeve remembered Dale Carnegie's advice: 'Winning friends begins with friendliness.' She took a deep breath. 'Tea time,' she said. 'Goes faster than ye think so ye'd better get a move on.'

She walked into the canteen with the new girl skittering behind her.

'It's tay and toast first thing. It's tay and biccies in the afternoon,' she said, picking up a mug. 'Go heavy on the milk. Ye want yer tay lukewarm, so ye can pour it down yer throat.' Then she grabbed a plate of toast. 'Ye get yer toast here. And you've about five minutes tae bate it into ye.'

'Thanks, missus,' the wee doll said.

Missus? Maeve thought, as she lifted her plate. *Cheeky wee bitch.*

That afternoon, the first of the new shirts reached Maeve. She enjoyed pressing the good thick fabric, sliding the iron over the back, steaming the collar stiff. These shirts were a pleasure to iron, exposing Maeve to another wee way in which having money greased your way through life. She was surprised when the home bell went – the working day had gone in faster than her week off.

Aoife and Caroline ducked into the toilets, so Maeve picked up her bag and joined Fidelma on her way out. The new doll was loitering at the door.

'Have ye no home tae go tae?' Fidelma asked, shrugging on her denim jacket.

'I'm waiting for a lift from Mr Strawbridge,' she answered, flicking her hair.

'Are ye now?' Fidelma said, eyeing Maeve.

'Aye. He says he'll drop me home. It's dead handy,' the wee doll said.

'Aye,' Maeve snorted. 'Andy's known for that. Being handy.'

'Eh?' said the wee doll. 'Ah don't get ye.'

Fidelma sighed and rubbed her nose. 'Sweetheart, if ye want my advice, ye should take the bus. Or get a lift with a neighbour.'

'Aye,' Maeve said. 'Mind yourself around that buck.'

The sound of Andy's office door springing shut echoed across the empty factory floor.

'Ye know something?' the wee doll said to Maeve. 'I think you're just jealous.'

Maeve's jaw dropped. 'What did you just say?'

'I see you're putting into practice Mr Carnegie's book, Ms Murray,' Andy said, from behind them. 'Making friends with your new colleague.'

'Och, you know me, Mr Strawbridge. I'm that rare individual who unselfishly tries to serve others.'

'Unconscious, of course,' Andy said with a twinkle in his eye, 'of the enormous advantage that might confer upon you.'

The new doll and Fidelma looked at Maeve and Andy as if to say, 'What are the pair of youse shiting on about?'

'Strikes me, your latest employee could do with reading the book and all.'

'Well, perhaps you can pass it along to Wendy when you're finished, Ms Murray?'

Maeve rolled her eyes at Andy, remembered what Dale'd said about a person's name being the sweetest, most important sound to them. He grinned back, then put his hand on Wendy's shoulder and steered her out of the door. He paused in front of his car, joggling in his pocket for his car keys. Wendy glanced back at Maeve with a fuck-you face. Maeve crossed her arms and raised an eyebrow at her to say, 'You and whose army?' Andy's Jag winked and clunked as it unlocked, then they climbed inside.

'That wee doll's like manys before her.' Fidelma sighed. 'She'll not make her first pay cheque.'

'Do any of them listen tae ye, Fidelma? When ye warn them?'

Fidelma took a long look at Maeve. 'Ah think a lot of folk find Andy Strawbridge more persuasive than the likes of me,' she said, then she plodded off up the road towards the caravan park.

Maeve stood smoking with the lifers at the factory gates the next morning, watching Andy park. They fell silent when Wendy got out of his car, swinging her hair. Maeve felt jealousy surge through her. They watched Wendy cross the car park with Andy. He stopped in front of the group, tapped his watch and raised his eyebrows. Then he walked into the factory with the Wendy doll giggling at his side.

'Weans shouldn't play with matches,' Mabel Moore clucked.

'Aye, well, some people hafta learn the hard way,' Maeve said, hoping she wasn't one of them. Then she crushed out her fag and clocked in.

Later that afternoon, Andy stopped at Maeve's pressing station and watched her work for several minutes.

'Ms Murray?'

'What?' she said, without taking her eyes off her shirt.

'Call up to my office later,' he said, then strode off.

Maeve's nerves weren't good after that. She didn't want to head to Andy's office, for she was nowhere near finishing his stupid book, having got wound up reading chapter twelve: 'If You're Wrong, Admit It.' But after the last tea break, she climbed the stairs and put her head around his door.

'Yes. Certainly,' he was saying, down the phone. 'I'll check that too.'

He beckoned her in with a wave of his hand. The door snapped shut behind Maeve as she sat down in front of his desk.

'Yes, yes. Look, I have someone with me in the office here, so I can't go into that right now.' Andy tugged on the phone line, then tucked the handset between his shoulder and jawline and unbuttoned the double cuffs on his shirt. 'Yes, yes, yes,' he said, rolling up his sleeves.

He'd a nice tan, like many of the soldiers Maeve saw on the street. He wasn't the blue-white colour of James, the greenish-grey of most of the men in the Town.

'I'll see to it,' he said, taking the handset back into his hand.

Maeve looked at the litter of Invest NI grant forms covering his desk. There were a lot of pound signs and figures.

'Right. I'll let you know. Bye.' Andy dropped the handset back down on the cradle with a clatter, then smoothed his tie. 'Ms Murray.'

'Mr Strawbridge.'

She wondered about his name: *Straw bridge. Not something with any last, you'd think. Not something you'd trust your foot on.*

'I'd like to hear how you think the optimisation plan has gone.'

'Why are ye asking what I think? That's all Aoife's idea.'

'I'm interested in your opinion, Ms Murray, which I imagine is quite a novelty for you.'

Maeve sat back and folded her arms. 'Well, no harm to you or Aoife but the whole thing's been a friggen disaster.'

Maeve'd been pure delighted that the reorganisation had failed, with everyone whinging and looking to go back to the old way of doing stuff.

'Change never goes smoothly,' Andy said, with a shrug. 'People always prefer to stick with what they know.'

Maeve didn't want to stick with what she knew. She was sick of cornflakes for breakfast. She was tired of cheese and pickle tucked between slices of white bread 'buttered' with margarine. She was bored of egg, beans and toast for dinner. She wanted to get lashed on moe-hee-toes instead of vodka stained with orange squash.

'I have great confidence that this new system will work,' Andy continued, 'once you lot get used to it.' He tipped back in his chair and looked at Maeve. 'I have to say that Ms O'Neill is quite the clever clogs. She'll go far.'

Maeve felt like Andy had twisted a valve open in her chest, letting the air hiss out of her.

'Now you,' he said, looking straight at her. 'I'm curious about just exactly what *your* potential is.'

'Reading my CV might help you out with that.'

'I did read it, actually. Some pretty impressive grades predicted there – Bs. Not quite as spectacular as Ms O'Neill, but surprisingly good, considering your background.'

Maeve didn't like how she needed to make a conscious effort to keep breathing.

'You know, Ms Murray, I've a suspicion you're not all that different to me.' Andy considered Maeve in the same way her mam eyed up the special-offer joints in the butcher's window.

'I come from nothing,' he said. 'I've been treated like dirt. I've had to claw my way out of the muck.'

Maeve's fingers itched to play a teeny-tiny invisible violin in Andy's face. She wanted to know what he thought of as muck. She wouldn't be surprised to hear he'd an uncle in prison but she'd bet a week's wages that the last violent death in his family went back to the Second World War. Andy had the sheen of someone who'd had a hot dinner every day, piano lessons once a week and fat stockings on Christmas morning. And in the heel of the hunt, even if Andy had been through proper shit, he was a man. No matter how shitty things got for a man, they were always shittier for a woman.

'Seems to me,' Maeve said, 'that you've swapped muck for shit.'

Andy narrowed his eyes and sighed. 'Northern Ireland's potential might not look magnificent to the casual observer,' he said. 'But with these peace talks, there's the chance of change.'

Nobody Maeve knew believed that the talks about talks would lead anywhere other than more shite talking about shite talking. 'You're telling me you believe in the peace process?'

'I didn't say that. I said I sense there's *opportunity* over here. With the American influence bearing down on the province, the British *and* Irish governments need to find solutions. Europe too. They'll invest in anyone who can provide solutions to problems like your town.'

Maeve wasn't keen on some of the solutions that men had dreamed up for various historical 'problems': chastity belts; lobotomies; lunatic asylums; concentration camps.

'I'm working in this underprivileged community,' Andy continued, as if Maeve was holding a mic in front of him, 'to create a model for community integration and prosperity that will shine as an example for other workplaces across Northern Ireland.'

'Good luck with that, Andy,' Maeve said.

He smirked, nudging her back onto familiar territory. 'Oh, I don't need luck, Ms Murray. Just time. A little more time.'

He got to his feet and walked around to where Maeve was sitting. He pulled her to her feet, then brushed her hair from her face, and kissed her.

Maeve walked down the factory stairs using the same level of attention that she put into pretending she wasn't drunk in front of her mam, then went into the toilets and locked herself in a cubicle. She stripped off her fleece and flapped her T-shirt. She froze when the main door opened. Someone clumped in and stopped outside Maeve's toilet. She pulled down her joggers and pants and tried to pish, but a fart escaped instead. She wiped the slick between her legs and flushed the toilet. When she'd organised her clothes, she opened the door.

Fidelma Hegarty was standing there with her arms crossed.

'Hey, Fidelma,' Maeve said, ignoring the look on her face. She walked to the sink, turned on the tap and let the cold water nip her fingers.

'So what the fuck's going on between you and that Andy buck?'

'Nothing.'

'Don't fucken bullshit me, Maeve Murray. You out there yesterday warning the wee doll, and you up there today.'

Maeve turned off the tap, then tugged a rough blue paper towel out of the dispenser and rubbed her hands.

'Ah know what ah'm talking about with Andy,' Fidelma said. 'For ah had a ride off him. Half the factory has. And he's not as good a ride as he thinks.'

Maeve dropped the paper towel, soft with damp, into the bin.

'Ye could do better, Maeve. An awful lot better. Leave the likes of Wendy tae Andy. You steer clear.'

Maeve stared at the water droplets splashed on the floor tiles.

'Y'know something?' Fidelma said, sighing so hard that she seemed to deflate. 'Ah'm fed up with this shithole. Maybe ah shoulda worked harder at the book learning. It'd be nice to have some friggen options.'

'There's time enough yet, Fidelma. There's night school.'

Fidelma looked at Maeve balefully. 'Aye. And there's Harvard and all.' She turned her back on Maeve and left.

Maeve and Aoife were standing at the factory gates waiting for Caroline. Wendy was leaning against Andy's car, examining her nails.

'I imagine she'll be sucking his cock before I've a mouthful of baked beans,' Maeve said, putting herself right off her tea.

Aoife hesitated before responding. 'It sounds like you hate her more for that than him.'

Aoife's dig landed neatly under Maeve's ribs.

'Don't think much of either of them, if the truth be known.'

Aoife looked at Maeve quizzically. 'So what was your chat with Andy about? Were you two discussing the book?'

Maeve felt her nipples harden. 'Nope. He was asking what I thought of the optimisation, funnily enough.'

Aoife's shoulders stiffened. 'And what did you say?'

Maeve tried not to think of Andy's cock, hard against her hip. 'I said it was all a bit of a disaster, so far.'

A cloud sailed over the sun. Maeve felt like the sky was holding its breath, getting ready to spit needles of rain.

'New things don't go smoothly,' Aoife said. 'Particularly at the start.'

Wendy perked up like a puppy when Andy emerged from the factory.

'Some new things go smooth enough it seems.'

Maeve hated the sour tone in her voice. And she hated Andy for kissing her like he owned her, for anchoring her to his desk with an attention she'd never experienced before, a focus that narrowed the town, the factory, the office, down to his mouth and her lips. It had lasted only seconds, but'd left Maeve feeling like he'd sucked the dust and grit of ordinary life from her lungs and bones and filled her with a hot, dark, combustible

liquid. She'd never been kissed like that before. Never let herself be kissed like that before. Never been on the ropes before.

'I don't get your thing for Andy,' Aoife said.

'What thing is this?' Maeve asked, watching Wendy laugh at
something Andy'd said.

'I don't know how to describe it,' Aoife said, flushing pink.
'But there's something going on between you. It's like you both
hate each other, and yet you both want more of each other.'

Maeve watched Andy's Jag glide out of the car park and roar
off up the street.

'Andy's English,' she said. 'And I've been raised to hate
the English.' Maeve remembered standing inches away from
Andy's chest in his office, knowing that if he tried to fuck her
on his desk, she'd drop her knickers for him.

'I get that bit, Maeve,' Aoife said. 'It's the whole sort of
fancying him thing that I don't understand.'

Andy hadn't tried to fuck Maeve. He'd stepped back from
her and rolled his shirt sleeves down before saying, 'I think
you've got a lot of potential, Mizz Murray.'

'He told me he thinks I've got potential, Aoife. And maybe
that's what I'm horny for. Someone believing in me.'

'Yes, but potential for what?' Aoife asked, looking worried.

When Andy arrived on Thursday morning, there was no sign
of Wendy nipping at his heels. Fidelma and Maeve exchanged
an 'oh ho now' look. But they didn't get the bars off Mary until
tea break.

'Andy says her work wasn't up to scratch.'

'So she's gone for good, then?' Marilyn Spears asked.

Mary nodded and nobody said another word until after
she'd left the canteen.

'Ah heard he banged her like a Lambeg drum,' Marilyn cackled, everyone joining in.

'Ach, fuck up, will youse?' Fidelma said, rattling the newspaper she was reading. 'She's more than likely learned her

lesson.' She put her head down when the crowing settled, and glowered at a photo of the Labour Party's latest hope, Tony Blair. 'Would ye look at the cut of that?' she said to Maeve. 'If Maggie Thatcher was still fit for a ride, thon's the very fella she'd hop on.'

'Ye think?' Maeve said, looking at the picture. Blair looked like the sort of toothy creature you'd see in a Free Presbyterian church, a man who believed way too hard in the wrong thing.

'Aye, she'd be pure wet for him, all right, with all his chat of weakening the trade unions,' Fidelma said.

Maeve knew little about trade unions. They seemed to be organisations mostly made up of red-faced men shouting on behalf of other men who worked in car factories or coal mines. She remembered Thatcher locking horns with the coal miners during their strikes. In fairness to her, she was as much of a cunt to working-class Englishmen as she was to the hunger strikers she starved to death in Long Kesh.

'Are we unionised?' Aoife asked.

'Ye are, surely,' Mabel Moore shouted over from the next table. 'You're in the best union there is. The United Kingdom of Great Britain and Northern Ireland!'

Mabel clutched Marilyn's arm laughing while Fidelma dead-eyed her with a stare.

'I meant a factory union,' Aoife said, pink-faced.

'There's no union rep here,' Fidelma said. 'We've been told we don't need one.'

'By who?' Maeve asked.

Mabel eyed Billy and glanced at Paddy Quinn before answering. 'By them that's in charge,' she said, in a voice like a shutting door.

Fidelma pushed the newspaper over to Maeve. 'Here. Ye can finish the crossword for me.'

'What are ye stuck on?'

'Seven across. Ten-letter word for unity and support. Starts with S. Ends with Y.'

Maeve frowned at the paper. 'Simplicity fits but that's not right.'

'I think it's solidarity,' Caroline said, quietly. Aoife nodded.

Maeve filled in the boxes with a feeling that she'd failed a test she hadn't wanted to take.

Caroline left the flat to take Nana Jackson to Thursday night bingo, leaving Maeve alone with her sleeping bag and *How to Win Friends and Influence People*. She'd just started chapter eighteen: 'What Everyone Wants' when the doorbell rang. She shuffled to the window and looked out.

Fidelma was standing on the street, a blue bag hanging heavy in her hand.

Maeve opened the window and shouted, 'Hey Fidelma!'

She squinted up at Maeve through the rain. 'Ah've a rake of tins bought.'

'D'ye want me tae come down?' Maeve said, struggling out of her sleeping bag.

'Do ah look like ah want tae go drinking tins under the bridge? Wise up and let me in.'

Fidelma nosed around the flat before settling herself into Maeve's armchair. Then she dipped into her bag and brought out two tins of cider. She fired a can at Maeve, who felt ridiculously relieved when she caught it. Fidelma's tin hissed with satisfaction as she pulled the ring. She put it to her mouth and guzzled, then put her tin down with a sigh. 'God, ah needed that.'

'Aye. Hard enough week,' Maeve said, sipping from her own tin.

'Not long now til yer results?'

'Monday two weeks.'

'Within spitting distance. So it's England you're heading tae, assuming ye get the results?'

'Aye. London.'

'Och, London. Ah've not been.'

'Ah only was over myself fer me interviews.'

192

Maeve found herself speaking broad dialect when she was talking with Fidelma, the opposite of the way she tried to speak fancier when she was chatting with Aoife or Andy.

'Be some change for ye, London.'

'It will, aye. Would ye head over tae England yerself if ye had the chance? Or the States, maybe?'

'The States is awful far. And there's visas to think about. Ah'm not mad about England. But it's an easier lepp.'

'When were you in England?'

'Ah was over in Liverpool a while back.'

'Och, were ye? How'd ye find it?'

'Och, grand. Good enough craic once ah got the abortion over with.'

Maeve took a gulp of cider. She'd never heard anyone other than a priest say the word outside religion class. And priests never simply said the word. They hissed or thundered it.

'Och, right,' Maeve said, wondering what the frig she was supposed to say next. 'Was that a handling?'

'Well, figuring out how tae get over the water and paying for the whole shebang was a handling. But d'ye know something? Fer all that oul shite that the Holy Joes talk about regret, ah was grand afterward. Ah was only annoyed the wanst. And that because ah was over beyond, drinking and bleeding in some fucking Irish bar in England instead of being in my own bed.'

'Sure that's no craic.'

'No craic at all.'

Fidelma went quiet. Maeve thought about the posters their RE teacher had stuck around the blackboard showing black bin bags full of dismembered, aborted babies whose teeny bloody hands had reached out to her for the five long years she'd been forced to study religion.

'They knew well enough why ah was over. They knew by the cut of me.'

'Ah'd say.'

'And they left me well alone. No oul shite from no one. But then this streak of piss came up to me, towards closing time.' Fidelma glanced fiercely over at Maeve. 'Just tae warn ye, they only serve wee measures over in England, in the pubs. You'd need tae be on the doubles if its shorts you're on. And they close fierce early.'

'I've heard it's wild, right enough,' Maeve said, nodding.

''Tis. Eleven o'clock.'

'Sure, ye'd only be getting going.'

'Ah was, in fairness. But yer man anyway, he sidles up to me and drops the hand.'

'Like ye'd be up for that even if you were in the form?'

'Too right. And ye know – ah was tired out, what with the travelling and them hoovering me out and then the bleeding. I was feeling a bit twitchy. So ah took his hand out of me jeans and says "naw" to him. Civil enough ah was. But he wouldn't quit.'

'Fucken hate that.'

'Aye. Wan thing ye should learn is, when tae quit.' Fidelma paused as if remembering something. Then she shook her head and went on. 'So, anyway, he was buzzing round me like a fly round shite so ah told him to fuck right aff.'

'Good woman yerself.'

'And didn't he come up to me then, real close, and say he wouldn't fuck me anyway, for he didn't fuck baby killers.'

'He did not.'

'He did too. And sure what could ah do then? Sure ah had to batter him. Which was no hard job fer he was such a streel of gristle. But ah was done in afterwards. Ah'm not usually done in after giving someone a hiding. It usually gets me blood up.'

'Och, but sure ye weren't the full strength of yerself.'

'Ah wasn't, naw. Lucky for him,' Fidelma said, darkly. She stared at her tin for a few moments. 'Ah thought ye should know that Andy Strawbridge put up the money for me trip.'

Maeve swallowed a mouthful of cider, felt it sizzling in her stomach. 'Did he?'

'Fuck knows it probably wasn't his. But when ah tackled him about it, he was quick enough tae put money on the table. Sterling notes too.' Fidelma said, nodding approvingly.

'It was kinda thoughtful of Andy tae give ye sterling,' Maeve said.

'It was, surely. There's not much worse than standing arguing in an English shop with an Indian fella, trying tae get them tae take yer Ulster Bank notes,' Fidelma said.

'Aye. It was considerate, in the circumstances,' Maeve said.

'Well, ye could take it that way. Or ye could say to yerself I probably wasn't the first woman that buck's sent over the water for an abortion.' Fidelma took a mouthful of cider and swallowed it like she was downing a pill. 'And I doubt ah'll be the last.'

Maeve was still in foul form on Friday night, even though James and Aoife had given her and Caroline a lift up the road to Dicey's bar.

Dicey's had two things going for it: first, it was kind of grungy so the music was good; second, it was upstairs where no fat bastard UVF gunman would be fit to climb for a random shooting. Aoife was off chatting to one of the cuddycubs who hung about at the back. They weren't quite Goths, and they weren't total lesbians, but they were the sort of odd wee dolls who wore mostly black and kept their tits hidden under band T-shirts. Winona Ryder types. *Aoife* types.

James was sitting slightly too close to Maeve, watching her and Caroline beat a slabber of drink into them. She'd no idea how he could sit there stone-cold sober, nursing a Coke, but she'd a suspicion it was the sort of character trait that'd help him survive years on a children's ward, telling parents that their only child's cancer was incurable before asking them if they'd like to donate its brain to science.

Suddenly Maeve realised that Caroline was sitting utterly still and super alert, like a cartoon dog pointing at a sitting duck.

It was easy to see who'd caught her attention.

A tall fella was standing at the bar, in bootcut jeans and a checked T-shirt, his hair carefully spiked with wet-look gel. As Maeve assessed him, he turned around and locked eyes with Caroline, who, instead of doing her normal thing of look-ing away, giggling, while elbowing Maeve, sat still and gazed straight back at him. The next thing Maeve knew, your man was walking over to them, bold as brass. And he didn't bother with any oul shite-talking.

'Can I get youse ladies a drink?'

And Caroline didn't waste a single second. 'We're both on the vodka and orange.'

When he came back five minutes later with Smirnoff vodkas and two tiny bottles of real Fanta, Maeve had the measure of him. By the end of the next song, he and Caroline were snog-ging the faces off each other.

Maeve sat stiffly beside James. He'd not mentioned what'd hap-pened the Twelfth night (a fact that both annoyed and pleased her).

'Well, they seem to be getting on well,' he shouted in her ear.

Maeve nodded and grimaced.

'Does Caroline know about, you know . . . us?'

Maeve stiffened up. 'No. And she doesn't need to know.'

James flinched slightly, and Maeve felt like she'd given Nana Jackson a slap.

'Sorry, James. Just, y'know . . .' she said, struggling for words.

'I know,' he said, nodding.

Maeve watched Aoife lean in to the wee dark-eyed cuddy she was chatting to. There was something childish about the way they were going on. Something kind of innocent. Aoife hadn't been like that around Maeve since Deirdre'd died.

'And does she know?' Maeve asked, jerking her head over in Aoife's direction.

James shook his head. 'No. She's enough on her mind.'

Maeve nodded, then sculled her drink and stared at the empty glass until James got the hint.

Something jagged Maeve's insides as the rear lights on James's car faded into the drizzle. She turned and climbed the stairs up to the flat behind Caroline and her buck, then went straight to her bedroom. She lay on her bed, the room swinging around her as Garth Brooks twanged on about unanswered prayers in the room next door.

Because Maeve's blowjob tally had been considerably higher than Caroline's for several years, she'd always presumed that she'd be the one who'd Do It first. She'd pictured arriving in London and meeting some musician who wouldn't be able to keep his hands off her. And she'd imagined the call she'd make the next morning, in which Caroline'd call Maeve a dirty bitch and she'd answer, 'It's love not lust' before comforting Caroline with the thought that one day she too would meet someone and Do It. But not twenty minutes later, she was listening to Caroline and her new man riding while she lay staring at the ceiling (her still-intact hymen the only thing quivering between her legs).

Tuesday, 26 July 1994

20 days until results

Caroline was in her bedroom, getting ready for her first official date with Martin. He'd promised to take her for a bite to eat in Strabane, then over to Lifford for the cinema. Maeve and Aoife were listening to Pearl Jam in the living room, pretending not to be jealous. But then Caroline let a wail out of her.

Maeve looked at Aoife, then turned Pearl Jam down a notch. 'You OK, lovie?'

'I can't do up my trousers!'

'What?'

Aoife turned the music off.

'I CAN'T DO UP MY GOOD BLACK TROUSERS!'

They went through to Caroline's room. She was standing in her bra with a V-shaped pudge of belly bulging out of the open zip.

Maeve took control. 'Lie on the bed, suck your gut in and try again.'

Maeve held her own breath as Caroline threw herself on the bed, then drew in her belly and pulled the button towards the hole. After ten seconds of straining, she let go. 'Oh, my God, I'm soooooo fat!'

'You're not fat,' Aoife said. 'It's probably just PMS.'

'It's not PMS. I'm *fat*. It's alright for you two – you're on your feet all day. Sure, look at youse – youse've lost weight! But I've an arse on me like a busted sausage.'

Maeve was kind enough not to point out that she hadn't just lost weight – she'd also tightened up. Her stomach, arms and legs were leaner than they'd been just a few weeks earlier. She'd never looked so good. Mind you, Aoife was pure heroin chic, with an inch gap between her thighs and hip bones that jutted out at the top of her jeans. Maeve knew that even if she was mainlining the heroin, she'd never lose the big-boned look that lit a fire in the eye of the farmers drinking in Kelly's bar after a good day at the mart.

'Darlin, you're not fat,' Maeve cooed. 'You've just put on a bit a weight. C'mon. Get in tae your other trousers and we can start walking the roads tomorrow.'

'I am not taking to the roads like some sad oul biddy. No way!'

Caroline rolled over and mashed her face in the duvet. Maeve saw her point: having to walk the roads was a dismally public admission of your age, weight and social status. Still. She was worried for Caroline. She'd seen how big the other female factory workers got after a few months of being crammed behind a sewing machine for nine or ten hours a day, fuelling themselves with biccies, crisps and Coke.

'Well, look. You'll be out of the factory soon enough. You'll be at uni and you'll soon lose the pudge. For now ye could quit the biccies and focus on the slap.'

Caroline pulled a pillow over her head and crushed it around her ears.

Aoife glared at Maeve, then sat down beside Caroline. 'Caroline. Martin's really not going to care what you're wearing.'

'But I do,' Caroline said from under her pillow. 'It's not all about him.'

'You know, I always think it's kind of strange,' Aoife said, 'that we live here, in this town, where going to the pub is taking your life in your hands, and yet we're supposed to care about what size our bums are.'

Caroline snorted under her pillow. Then Aoife laid her hand on Caroline's shoulder and rubbed it gently. 'I think you should love yourself as much as Nana Jackson loves you.'

Caroline sat up and said, 'Och, Aoife,' then threw her arms around her.

Maeve left the room before she boked up in her own mouth.

On Friday, Caroline went bowling with Martin, which would've been no big tickle if Aoife wasn't away to Belfast to see some film James was mad for. Maeve was left facing one of the biggest problems she had with living in a small town: she'd run out of people she wanted to talk to, never mind fuck. In pure desperation, she walked over the road home and let herself in the door.

'Lo!'

'Whisht, Maeve, will ye! The news is coming on.'

Maeve crept into the living room and sat down beside her da.

'That mortar attack in Newry'll be on,' he said to her, patting her knee.

'Wonder now, will it be as bad as the parish hall mortar was?' Maeve asked.

'I heard nobody was dead,' her da said. 'But they reckoned over forty injured.'

'Well now, we'd over seventy hurt,' her mam said, with a certain amount of pride.

A plummy BBC reporter described the mortar attack as an *emphatic terrorist response* to Sinn Fein's rejection of the Downing Street Declaration. Maeve wasn't mad about mortar bombs; she preferred ordinary bombs. They usually came with warnings, which didn't always get the timing right, or the location dead on, but you'd get the gist that there was a bomb nearby that'd go off sooner or later, giving you time to evacuate, or at least draw the curtains to stop the worst of the glass from cutting the lugs off you. Maeve'd learned early on to sit still after an explosion. She liked listening to her ears ring while her mam or dad scrambled to the phone box to call Granny Murray before the lines were cut by the Brits.

Sometimes the electric'd be blown out, and they'd sit around the battery radio, with candles lit, waiting for the official news reports that supplemented (and often contradicted) the word they'd got from their neighbours.

By the time Maeve was ten, however, the walls around the RUC barracks at the heart of the town were so well reinforced, bomb blasts deflected outwards, annihilating any nearby houses and humans. Getting bombs inside the barracks was a tricky business, one that involved bribery, hostages and timing devices. A mortar bomb rocket-launched over the barracks walls was some bright spark's answer to the dilemma.

The problem was, the time between launching a mortar and it landing was just seconds, so nobody issued warnings about mortar attacks, not even the nod and wink kind of caution you sometimes got before an ambush, warning you to avoid a certain road at a specific time or to stay indoors longer than you might usually do on a particular morning. That meant that 'The Parish Hall Mortar Attack' (so christened in order to differentiate it from 'The First Mortar Attack' and 'The Really Bad Mortar Attack') came as a surprise not just to the RUC, but also to Father Goan, the residents in the nearby old folks' home and everyone who had been involved in the dress rehearsal of the Christmas show.

Miss Magee had wanted to raise money for the Rwandans, who, she'd explained, had recently gone buck mad and were killing each other at a fierce rate. Because the primary and secondary schools performed a mini and big version of the Nativity, Miss Magee was allowed to put on a secular show. Every teenage girl in town pleaded with her to do *Dirty Dancing* (despite the town lacking anything close to a man who could play Patrick Swayze) but Miss Magee – ever the realist – had chosen *The Wizard of Oz*. Deirdre and Maeve had got parts playing Munchkins. ('Well,' Maeve's mam had said, 'it's hard tae see either of youse stepping into Judy Garland's ruby slippers.')

The dress rehearsal was taking place in the parish hall. Deirdre and Maeve had pushed their way in through the big double doors with a crowd of other weans. The hall was warm and bright, buzzing with excitement. Miss Magee closed the curtains on each of the windows that ran the length of the hall so nobody'd get a gleek of the rehearsal.

Maeve and Deirdre had lined up with the other Munchkins for their costumes. They were all scundered by the make-up, which was slapped on by middle-aged women who'd learned their craft in the sixties. They cleastered the same orange foundation on everyone before applying blue eyeshadow and red lipstick with a heavy hand. Their cheeks were stamped with rouge at the very end, leaving them looking more like Oompa Loompas than Munchkins. Then they queued up at the refreshments table for the stubby bottle of warm lemonade and packet of crisps that would fuel them throughout the rehearsal. They sat on the plastic chairs lining the walls and watched Miss Magee put Dorothy, Scarecrow, Tin Man and Lion through key moves from their role while in costume (a safety check she'd implemented after *The Sound of Music* scandal, in which Maria had burst her dress during 'So Long, Farewell', forcing Father Goan to drop the curtain early and start into five decades of the rosary).

When Miss Magee was satisfied that her stars were safely double-stitched into their costumes, she clapped her hands together above her left ear with her head down to get a bit of quiet, then directed everyone into place.

The curtain rose to reveal Róisín McGrath's Dorothy chatting to a toy dog in a basket, while Linus McMurphy crouched under the stage yipping and barking in response (a genius casting that kept him both occupied and safely confined). As much as Róisín sickened Maeve with her singing and dancing and dreams of being a star over in Hollywood, something inside her lit up as Róisín glowed like that bit in the movie where everything goes Technicolor, shining like nothing in their town ever had before or after.

'Auntie Em said to find a place where there isn't any trouble. Where do you think I should look, Toto?'

Róisín listened with her head cocked, while from under the stage Linus McMurphy barked something that, if you were feeling cynical, might've translated as 'Try my hairy hole.' Róisín looked out into the hall, letting her eyes drift over their heads and began to sing 'Somewhere Over the Rainbow'. She had a voice, back then, Róisín did. And she was gorgeous. Fifteen years old, getting ready to sit her GCSEs, at the singing and the dancing even when she wasn't cast in local productions. She was a total dose. But even though Maeve'd heard about that magical place over that frigging rainbow week in and week out for months, Róisín was good enough to pin her and everyone in the hall in the moment with her voice: the longing in it.

Which was when the first mortar had hit the parish hall.

Maeve learned later that the IRA had fired three mortars. The second one had bounced off the barrack walls and exploded in the bookies next door. The third one had sailed over the walls and landed inside, but failed to explode. The news reports had said the children were 'lucky', for despite being packed together in the parish hall, they'd received only minor injuries.

Before that evening, Maeve'd thought 'lucky' was when you paid five pence to get a go at the lucky dip barrel and you dug your arm oxter-deep into a barrel filled with polystyrene balls and caught a hold of something that was worth more than five pence. 'Lucky' was finding fifty pence in a coat your mam'd bought from the St Vincent de Paul shop. 'Lucky' was winning a box of chocolates at the Christmas raffle. Maeve had loved what she'd thought 'lucky' had felt like.

She didn't feel lucky when she felt the slap of the explosion, the air sucked from the hall, and then blown back in around them, glass shredding first the curtains, then their clothes and finally their skin. When the lights went out, someone, somewhere in the dark, starting at the squealing, then others joined in, like they'd rehearsed it.

The women who'd been doing the make-up started reading from the scripts they'd learned by heart for this sort of occasion. Maeve heard voices she recognised repeating phrases in the dark:

Oh, Mary, Mother of God. Mother of God. Mother of God
Sweet Jesus
Oh, God help us. God help us now.
Then the crying and the shouting started.
Bernie, Bernie, where are you?
Joe? Joe, are you there?
Maaaa-meeeeeee . . .
C'mere to me, Brendan!

The streetlamps were blown out. Moonlight shone through the shattered windows, spotlighting the glass glinting underfoot, on clothes, in hair. Maeve stood up. Glass crunched under her shoes. Her legs trembled as though they weren't sure of the weight of her. She had that stupid fucking 'wish upon a star' line stuck on repeat in her head.

She put her fingers on her face. It felt slick with make-up. Everything and nothing hurt.

'Deirdre?'

Maeve's voice didn't carry over the screams, the squeals, the shouts. The fire station siren wailed and shop alarms throbbed in the background. She wanted to go home, but she knew her mam'd kill her if she went back alone.

'Deirdre?'

Maeve could hear herself whining. She knew she was an awful embarrassment to herself. The sound of grown-ups crying annoyed her. She wanted them to be brave. To be quiet.

She searched for Deirdre in a chorus line of faces, shining with make-up, blood and tears, and eventually found her cowering against the wall, her eyes wide open. Maeve stumbled over and sat beside her. They held hands as Frankie McCanny carried Róisín McGrath off the stage. Grown-ups with torches arrived and led them into the chapel, where Maeve observed the wounded being triaged like she was watching a Christmas special of *Casualty* until her mam rushed in, without her coat. She explained later that she'd been washing dishes when she'd heard the blast. She'd said she'd left the immersion on before running out of the door because she knew – she just fucking knew – that they were all right, but that they'd need a hot bath.

Their mam had scanned the chapel, then locked her gaze on them, and came at them like a guided missile. 'Youse alright?'

Maeve had nodded, but Deirdre kept doing her staring thing. Their mam pulled them to their feet and shooed them towards the door. Nurse McKenna shouted over to say if she'd wait five minutes, she'd check them over. Maeve's mam shook her head, saying, 'They're grand. Not a bother on them.'

And they were grand too, once they were sitting on top of blankets on the sofa, drinking Ovaltine and watching *Miss Marple*. Maeve was called up to the bath first. The smell of Dettol scalded her nose as she entered the bathroom. She stood on top of an old newspaper, which caught the glass fragments that fell as her mam peeled her costume from her back, as if it'd been Pritt-sticked onto her.

Her mam took a breath, then ordered her to get into the bath. Maeve eased herself into the hot water.

'Yer back's cut. This is going tae sting.'

She scooped water up with a jug and poured it over Maeve's back. The disinfectant sang in her sliced skin. Her mam showered the glass from her hair, then, instead of giving Maeve's scalp a good scutching, as she usually did, she gently massaged shampoo through her hair. She told Maeve to keep still while she drained the bath. Then she wiped up the slivers of glass so Maeve had a safe spot to stand up in. After she was rinsed and dried, her mam dabbed Germolene onto her cuts, before handing her pyjamas warm from the radiator. Maeve left the bathroom as her mam filled the bath again for Deirdre. Oddly, Deirdre – who'd been right beside Maeve when the mortar bomb hit – didn't have a scratch on her.

The next day, they heard that Róisín McGrath'd been kept in hospital overnight, though she'd "only" suffered what the media'd dismissed as *cosmetic injuries*. She was filmed on her hospital bed, describing how she'd been singing when the mortar hit. That news segment was Róisín's fifteen minutes of fame, for you knew looking at her face that her life'd never be the same.

Maeve watched a BBC news reporter speak in front of a shattered street in Newry, summing up the latest mortar attack.

. . . this attack will further deepen gloom in Northern Ireland about the prospects for progress . . .

Then the newscaster moved smoothly to a story in which the Ministry for Defence was disputing the *massive payments* awarded to the women they'd sacked for getting pregnant.

Maeve thought of the mortar attack survivors – the people who were carried out and the ones who walked away on trembling legs – and wondered if they'd sleep. She thought of how their mam had packed her and Deirdre off to bed, smelling like Dettol, their ears singing in the dark. She'd stayed awake for hours that night, watching Deirdre blink in the bed opposite, her eyes glittering like broken glass.

Monday, 1 August 1994

14 days until results

There were no shirts for ironing first thing that Monday morning, so Mary sent Aoife and Maeve to the canteen to make up big cardboard boxes for transporting the packaged shirts. It was a job Maeve enjoyed, apart from the paper cuts. She liked flicking the flat cardboard open, pushing it into a cube shape, then folding the flaps so it became a box full of air. It was more craic than the fiddly individual boxes for the fancy shirts, which required close attention and were easy to mess up.

Aoife stacked a box, then turned and picked up another flat-pack. 'Did you notice anything about the material this morning?'

Maeve shrugged.

'It just looks to me about half the material they delivered two weeks ago,' Aoife continued. 'Looks like about a week's worth of work.'

'As long as I've enough work to see me through to our offers, I don't care how they deliver it to me.'

Aoife fiddled with a flap that had bent the wrong way, then got frustrated and dropped the box. Maeve picked it up, fixed the flap, then stacked it.

'Can I talk to you about my offer?' Aoife asked.

'Course you can.'

'It's just when I was up in Belfast with James, Scott said something to me.'

'That dick.'

Aoife selected a new box and popped it into shape, then stared through it. 'He's not that bad, Maeve, once you get to know him.'

Maeve suspected that Aoife's tolerance for dicks, wankers and bullshit was the core skill Dale Carnegie was trying to teach people like Maeve. 'I'll take your word for it.'

Aoife took a sharp breath in through her nose, then released it while saying the word 'Anyway . . .' She continued: 'He asked me if I realised that Cambridge gave me my offer to improve their diversity record.'

'Aoife, last I looked, you weren't black.'

'Oh, I don't think Cambridge is *that* far down the diversity path yet.' Aoife then blushed, as if she already felt crap about bad-mouthing the college that had conditionally accepted her.

'So what did he mean?'

'He said that because I went to St Jude's, my college will be able to count my admission as being from an under-repre-sented background.'

Maeve placed a box on the wall they'd built up, then took a long look at Aoife. 'They're hard up for diversity if they're counting you.'

'I don't think they measure diversity based on national representation. It's more about who goes to Cambridge. It's my understanding that – historically – Cambridge hasn't admitted many people from comprehensive schools, let alone mixed-sex comprehensives.'

Then Maeve understood. Aoife didn't need to have dark skin to tick a diversity box for Cambridge. She'd be the girl from a troubled town in 'Ulster' who went to a 'comp' with people of the opposite sex. Although Aoife had grown up with money and a loving family in a fancy house, her background would seem deprived when juxtaposed against private schools, family piles and cut-glass accents. 'I see. Posh is relative.'

'Yes, it is. You think I'm posh. And I think Scott's posh. And Scott thinks the people he hangs out with are posh. And they think the people above them are posh.'

'And so it goes, the whole way up to the Queen,' Maeve said, throwing the last box onto her barricade. She pictured Aoife in Cambridge, wearing beige and using the right knife at the right time. She'd start spelling her name 'Eva' and flattening her accent. She'd marry an Englishman whose surname she would adopt. She'd become what Cambridge wanted her to be. Maeve would never fit in like that. And poor students with dark skin had no hopes at all. Aoife was just different enough – just about 'deprived' enough – to make the folk in Cambridge feel good about their charitable intentions without having to make much of an effort.

'But diversity won't get me in the door if I don't get my grades.'

'You'll get your grades,' Maeve said, staring at the empty boxes waiting to be filled with folded shirts that would in due course be stuffed with Englishmen.

'Actually, Maeve, there's a chance I won't get my grades. And things aren't the same for me as they are for you. Our families are different.'

'Tell me something I don't know.'

Aoife let her hair fall around her face before closing a box. 'It's perfect As I need. In my world, two As and a B is failing.'

Maeve pushed a single cardboard box with her finger, thinking about how in her world, letting your sister die was failing. The box slid backwards, then dropped to the floor, leaving a gap in the wall. She slowly pushed another box backwards, contemplating how her mam couldn't even keep her daughter alive. The box fell to the floor. Maeve placed her finger on a third box, remembering the biggest, most spectacular failure in her family so far: Deirdre, who'd failed to keep breathing, which was all they ever wanted her to do. The wall of boxes wobbled, but held, as the third box fell.

'I guess failure is like posh,' Maeve said. 'Relative.'

Then she slammed her foot through the wall of boxes, bringing the whole thing crashing down. Aoife flinched as they tumbled across the floor.

'Look,' she said. 'I know with everything you've gone through, it's not easy for you to listen to me going on about my own wee problems.'

Maeve tensed up.

'And I'm sorry I do that. It's just I've got no one else to talk to, Maeve. Only you and Caroline ever gave me a chance in this town. If it wasn't for you two, I don't know what I would've done.'

Maeve suddenly felt very, very tired. She sat down in a chair and looked at her trainers, trying to herd a scatter of words through her mind and out her mouth.

'I'm probably wrong,' Aoife continued, 'and I don't want to make a mess of things between us. But we're going to go our different ways soon. And I want you to know, I'll always be there for you. No matter what.'

Maeve lifted her head and gave Aoife what she needed: a wee, thin-lipped smile. Just enough to wave the white flag between them. She accepted the offering with an intense nod. Maeve could almost hear Dale Carnegie clap.

'Will we pick all this up before Mary comes in and has a conniption?'

Caroline was going for a drive up to the TV mast outside Strabane.

'Martin's such a dote. I said I'd only ever seen the red light at the top of the mast and he said, "C'mon then, I'll take ye up" and he's as good as his word. He's taking me up tae Legfordrum this evening. To watch the sun set.'

Maeve'd waved them off, pure annoyed at being left to make her own tea. In the end she'd decided to head over home to see if she could scrounge some fish fingers. She ducked into the shop and picked up some Mr Kipling's French Fancies so she wouldn't arrive with her two arms the one length, then she let herself in the door.

'Lo!'

'C'mon in, Maeve. Sarah's here.'

Maeve's heart sank. Sarah McCanny – the oul scrounge – would've already hoovered up the last of the fish fingers.

And, right enough, when Maeve put her head around the door, there Sarah was, lying up on the sofa eating a fish finger.

'Lord God now, but it's hard tae beat a good fish finger.'

The telly was off, because Sarah was of that generation that couldn't manage to chat shite and watch shite at the same time.

'Well now, yer luck's in this evening, Sarah, for it looks like our Maeve has brought dessert and all.'

Sarah flashed her NHS dentures at Maeve. 'Would they be French Fancies? Nothin like a wee French Fancy!'

Maeve nodded at Sarah as she edged her way to the kitchen clutching her bag.

'Are ye putting the tay on there, Maeve? Ah'd have a wee cup.'

'Me too!'

'Sure, ye might as well put a pot on and bring cups for everyone. Yer father's over at Toot's place, helping out with thon bike. He'll not be back til late.'

'Sure thing,' called Maeve, clenching her jaw. 'Are there any waffles left?'

'Naw, love. We had the last of them. Plenty of white sliced there, though, and yer da got some crisps in if ye want a wee sandwich.'

'Och, lovely, thanks.'

Maeve, like everyone else in her house, had to be on best behaviour when Sarah was over, for she reported the manners of every house she visited all around the town ('And sure you wouldn't believe the hoo-hah over in the Dolans' last Wednesday. And all over the head of a tin of sardines!'). She went into the kitchen in a pure rage and fired the French Fancies onto the worktop. Then she unplugged the kettle and slung it under the tap, all the time seething at the roundy belly on Sarah, who hadn't made her own tea since the autumn of 1982 when her only son was arrested at Manchester Polytechnic and was given three concurrent life sentences for running a bomb factory (something everyone knew he was innocent of, for – as his own father said in his defence in court – though Dermot had a face for modelling balaclavas, he hadn't the wit to run a piss-up in an Irish bar, never mind manufacture and distribute bombs from a bedsit in Cheetham Hill).

Since then, Sarah had saved every penny she had for her seasonal coach and ferry trips to an English jail. Maeve knew feeding Sarah her tea every day and donating a few quid to have pictures of Dermot printed on T-shirts and posters was her community's way of supporting the family during this miscarriage of justice. But it didn't take the edge off her hunger, or her rage. She plugged the kettle in and flicked it on. Then she buttered a couple of slices of bread, bust open a packet of cheese and onion Tayto crisps and made herself a sandwich. She doled milk and sugar into five mugs, then made a big pot of tea and brought everything through to the living room on a tray.

Sarah beamed at Maeve when she left the pot in front of the fire to brew. 'Aren't you the quare cuddy, now? A great help tae yer mammy even though you've left home?'

'Och, now, sure I'd do anything for Mam.'

Her mam scowled over as if to say, 'If ye lay it on too thick ye'll suffocate in it.' Maeve shoved Chris, forcing him down Sarah's end of the sofa.

'So, tell us this now, are ye still in thon factory?'

Maeve braced herself for an interrogation as intense as anything the Brits had put Sarah's son through over in London. 'I am, aye.'

'God now, isn't it great these days with the opportunities youse young wans get. Imagine now, a factory job in the town.' Sarah shook her head in wonder while Maeve's mam stubbed a fag out.

'Thon tay'll be ready now, Paul,' Maeve said.

Paul made a face but got up to pour. Sarah watched Maeve take a bite of her sandwich.

'What's that now you're having? A wee crisp sandwich?'

Maeve nodded, holding her sandwich close, for Sarah wasn't above asking for a bite.

'You'll fade away tae nothin if ye don't have something more substantial than that for yer tay,' she clucked, as Paul handed mugs around. 'So, not long now til the results, eh?' Sarah said, as if the end of the world was nigh.

Maeve shook her head for it was hard to talk with a mouthful of Tayto and sliced pan.

Her mam glared at her for being so rude. 'Naw. She'll get them . . . when is it? This week?'

'She gets them mid-August! Like every year!' Chris said. He'd acquired a keen interest in exam schedules since starting his GCSEs.

'Two weeks, eh?' Sarah said. 'So, what's the plans then? Heading over the water, are ye?'

Maeve dreaded this bit. She knew the drill, for Deirdre'd gone through it before her. All the neighbours had asked her what she was going to study and she'd said media studies and they'd looked at her blankly, so Deirdre'd tried to explain what media studies was and what job she'd be qualified for in the end, but after she'd stopped talking they avoided her eyes and said to their mam, 'Well now, with the help of God she could surely convert to the teaching after she's finished the mee-jah studies.' Brainy children from families like the Murrays were supposed to aim for steady careers that'd raise the stock of the whole family: medicine, law, dentistry, accountancy or teaching. Careers that'd land a mortgage and husband, boosting them a rung up or two up the ladder. Nobody knew where in hell you'd end up after doing media studies.

'Ah hope tae head tae London tae do journalism,' Maeve said.

Sarah turned the corners of her mouth down and squashed her chin into her neck, creating a stack of skin that rippled disapproval from her forehead all the way down to her vest top. 'Journalism, is it? No easy job for a woman. And only a skite away from touting.'

'Och, it's probably London I'll work in after I graduate. Wouldn't want tae risk working over here!' Maeve said, stuffing the last of her sandwich into her mouth. Then she picked up her half-empty Tayto packet.

'Well now, ye need tae mind yourself over beyond, and all. Think on my Dermot. Think on the years he's been rotting in an English jail.'

Maeve did sometimes picture Dermot, rotting like a spud in a dark cupboard, a cautionary tale of a Taig with notions who flew too close to the Imperial sun.

'What was it he studied now, Sarah?' her mam asked.

Maeve knew that her mam knew damn rightly that Dermot McCanny had got nowhere near the grades he needed to do teaching in Ireland, so he'd ended up having to do a history degree in a polytechnic in England.

'History. Dermot wanted tae be a history teacher.'

For the umpteenth time, they contemplated the irony of an Irish history student becoming a minor footnote in the long history of British miscarriages of justice.

'And is there any word yet of Dermot being wan of those prisoners they're transferring back over here?'

Sarah put her mug down and blessed herself. 'Not yet. Not yet. Ah've the knees wore outtay me tights praying they'll send him home. Ah'd get tae see him every week if only they'd let him in tae Long Kesh.'

'Och, now, sure, wouldn't that be great for the both of youse?'

'But, sure, the English. Ye couldn't trust them tae pour pish outtay a shoe and the instructions on the heel.'

Maeve wondered, as she licked the Tayto crumbs off her fingers, if Sarah's house felt like theirs. Like there was something missing. Like time had both frozen and yet somehow streaked past them. She got to her feet and went out to get the French Fancies.

'Och, now, the French Fancies,' Sarah said, when she came back in. 'Sure, ye can't beat a wee French Fancy.'

Maeve smiled at the fish finger crumbs trembling on Sarah's whiskers, wishing she was up the top of Legfordrum, getting the hole rode off her underneath the TV mast.

Aoife had invited Caroline and Maeve over to her house Saturday night. 'Mummy and Daddy get back from France on Sunday evening,' she'd said, meaning that'd be an end to them having the run of the place. But Caroline'd declined the invitation. She'd already arranged a 'night in' with Martin.

Maeve couldn't stomach the bokes she got from watching Caroline light candles and hoover the pubic hair carpet near bald, so she grabbed her leather jacket and said, 'Ah'm away.'

'Och, have a lovely evening, dotes,' Caroline said, pressing play on Garth Brooks's 'The Thunder Rolls.'

Maeve was approaching Aoife's front gate when she spotted Billy driving towards her on the road out of the town. Just in time, she diverted the hand she'd instinctively raised to wave, and used it instead to tousle her hair as if she was starring in a shampoo ad. She caught a glimpse of the men Billy was with. They looked like the tight fellas who'd crashed the factory after the UVF headquarters shooting earlier in the summer. Something like an ink stain spread through Maeve's body as she remembered Billy's words about casing Kelly's bar. She was glad he was heading out of the town, and even more relieved she was going to drink in Aoife's house.

When she swung the back door open a wave of 'Molly's Lips' hit her. Aoife and James were sitting at the kitchen table with a bottle of wine, instead of thrashing round the kitchen in bare feet like Maeve'd be doing, if she'd access to all that booze and underfloor heating.

'Hiyas!'

'Hey, Maeve!' James said, smiling. And for some reason Maeve took a total reddener (which Aoife noticed, because Aoife fucking noticed everything). 'Vodka and orange?' he asked, getting to his feet.

'Go on then,' Maeve said, sitting opposite Aoife, who was playing with a red cellophane fortune-telling fish.

'It's a shame you didn't come up to Belfast last week,' James said. 'I think you would've liked *Reservoir Dogs*. It was a better viewing experience in the uni film theatre than the big cinemas.'

Maeve let her gaze scald Aoife for a couple of seconds. 'Och, sorry, I just was wrecked after work. I woulda been no craic. I don't know how this doll had it in her,' she said, firing a *Really?* look at Aoife.

'Another weekend, maybe?' James asked, holding out a drink.

Maeve nodded, watching the fish in Aoife's open palm curl up and turn over. 'So what does that mean?' she asked.

James consulted a piece of paper. 'Seems Aoife's false.' He laughed, peeling the fish off her palm. 'Here,' he said, reaching for Maeve's wrist. 'Let's see what you are.' He pulled her hand close, then placed the fish onto her palm. They watched the head and tail quiver and twitch on her palm as though it was being shocked by a current running between its top and bottom.

'So. What am I?'

'Apparently you're in love,' James said, avoiding her eyes.

Maeve pulled her wrist free and sat back.

James placed the fish on his palm. It curled up as if it was trying to protect itself from a kicking.

'And what are you?' Aoife asked.

James hesitated before answering. 'The fish thinks I'm passionate.'

Maeve's heart scrunched. James was as passionate as the sweaty cellophane fish on his palm. She didn't need a crystal ball to see the future he was doggedly plodding towards. First he'd graduate with a respectable 2:1 in medicine from Queen's University. He'd become a doctor, then a consultant in the NHS. He'd take out a small mortgage on a huge house in a bigger, better town than the one they'd grown up in. If she married James, they'd have two boys and twin girls who'd speak with an accent they'd never need to lose. James would quietly, selflessly save lives at the hospital twelve hours a day while Maeve'd be bored off her tits at home, choking down the bennies so she could be numb enough to take care of their weans without walloping them. They'd make excruciating visits 'home' to the town, where they'd stay with his parents. Maeve'd need a Valium to help her walk down to dinner past the *glorious* stained-glass window on the landing (which featured as a double-page colour spread in a landmark book on Ulster glassware) without putting a brick through it. Mrs O'Neill would pick on her clumsy, redheaded granddaughter for laughing too loud or dropping her Denby or losing her coat for the umpteenth time, but would dote on her tall, blonde grandson who'd be so very good with numbers and sharp cutlery. Maeve saw herself lying wide awake at night despite dangerous quantities of wine and pills, staring up at a frost-breath ceiling while James slept soundly at her side. Even imagining that future put a thirst on her. She was relieved when James laid the fish gently on the table and stood up.

'Aoife tells me you haven't seen *Schindler's List*.'

Maeve shook her head. She didn't know much about the Jewish holocaust – for GCSE history they'd studied the decimation of the Native American population by the Europeans who'd stolen their lands, spread killer viruses and destroyed their traditional way of life. It was nearly always the Prods who studied the concentration camps, which Maeve found kind of unsettling.

'That's the one with Liam Neeson and Ralph Fiennes?'

'Yep. It's set in a factory. I thought perhaps you'd be interested in that.' James said it as if Aoife wasn't working in the factory.

Maeve got up from the kitchen table and followed James and Aoife down to the TV room. James pushed the tape into the player, then told Maeve to keep an eye out for the girl in the red coat.

Maeve knew that the child was fucked from the second she appeared. So she did what she'd done to get through Deirdre's funeral – she detached herself and sat dry-eyed, watching the wee cuddy skip to her death.

Monday, 8 August 1994

7 days until exam results

There was no banter that Monday at clock in, zero craic as the machines warmed up. Maeve found it hard to get in the swing of things, her mind replaying the footage of the latest murder. She followed Fidelma out via the side door for a fag at half nine. Mickey McCanny was pacing up and down.

'Ah heard she was left lying in the bedroom, with her four wee boys around her,' he said, spitting on the ground. 'Was hours before their da came home. An' the babby in the cot roaring for his mammy.'

'Wild. A wild thing.'

'Can ye imagine coming home tae that? Your cubs running out tae you at the door, and them in their pyjamas, covered in blood?'

'Wild too, tae think of that wee child that'll never be born now.'

'Savage. Shooting a pregnant woman and her putting her weans to bed. *Savage.*'

'Bad as our side is, ye wouldn't catch them shooting a woman seven months expecting.'

Maeve said nothing. Years of lip service to collateral damage and accidental civilian deaths had created a fuzzy impression that the IRA wasn't happy about the men, women and children who were wounded or killed during its operations. That they'd some kind of moral high ground, compared to the UVF, who were happy to kill as many Catholics as they could manage. The IRA almost blamed their 'legitimate targets' for the deaths of civilians caught in the crossfire. It wasn't that the IRA didn't kill pregnant women in front of their weans. But at least they said it was 'regrettable'.

Maeve didn't know for sure what the UVF would say about this murder. But she'd a fair idea that regret wouldn't feature.

'What really fucks me off is all this shite talking about peace,' Fidelma said. 'Christ, sometimes the only thing that gets me over the threshold of this place in the morning is the thought that maybe the IRA'll get a few of them in the back some night.'

As Paddy nodded in agreement, the side door opened and Billy stepped outside.

Fidelma stared at him with a look of hatred so strong Maeve was surprised that he didn't combust on the spot. She remembered Billy driving past her the night of the shooting. Saw the faces of the other men in the car flash in front of her. She doubted there'd be a chapter in *How to Win Friends and Influence People* relevant to this situation. For any of Dale's advice to work, you needed to believe that your colleagues didn't consider you a legitimate target.

On Wednesday, Aoife dropped in to the flat with her serious head on. She kept going to speak, but her words bottled up in her throat at the last second. Maeve doubted it was the latest shooting that was nagging her.

'Anyone want a sneaky wee vodka?'

Caroline looked at Maeve as if she'd suggested they home-pierce their genitalia. 'But, sure, it's a school night!'

'We don't have to go mad. Just a couple! I've a drooth on me.' Maeve got to her feet and looked over at Aoife.

She twitched, then nodded. 'Just the one.'

Caroline collapsed her face back into her neck and raised her eyebrows.

'I'll do you a Coke, Caroline.'

Maeve brought in a bottle of Tesco Value vodka, some glasses and two litres of real Coke. She knew their loyalty to real Coke was weird. Even though Tesco Value cola cost twenty pence for one billion litres, they always bought actual Coke, which (Aoife had calculated) cost almost as much – on a drink-by-drink basis – as Tesco Value vodka. But Maeve had been reared on real Coke. Her family had taken Coke's side in the Coke vs Pepsi war. (Maeve's mam believed Pepsi was like Protestants – a Johnny-come-lately brand trying to pretend it was the real deal.) Maeve suspected that her taste for real Coke was the nearest she got to having good taste.

She handed Caroline and Aoife their drinks, then clashed glasses before enjoying a gulp. 'So, I reckon I'm about two hundred shirts to the good so far this week. That's an extra fiver! Where are youse at?'

Caroline rolled her eyes. 'Yeah, well, I managed about three extra epaulettes so, you know, nine p.'

Maeve handed Aoife a fresh, stronger drink. 'I reckon I've done about two hundred and twenty extra shirts.'

'An extra £5.50? Nice!' Maeve said, like the star *How to Win Friends and Influence People* pupil she was. She knocked back her drink, then held her hand out to Aoife for her not-yet-empty glass.

Aoife obediently sculled the last of her drink and passed her glass back to Maeve.

'What're you looking so miserable about, Aoife?' Caroline asked. 'I'd kill tae earn an extra £5.50! Ye can swap tae epaulettes if ye want.'

'It should be an extra £7.50.'

'Huh?' Maeve said, handing Aoife a fresh drink.

Aoife took a big swallow before continuing. 'I've been looking at the cost of a shirt. What we get against what they cost in the shops.'

Maeve sighed. Aoife was going to tell them that they were being shafted by Andy. That the shirts they got pennies for working on were going for £30 and £40 in the shops. That Andy was on a fortune while they slaved for a pittance.

'So ye found out Andy's doing us. Tell us something we don't know.'

Aoife took another big slug of vodka, leaving her near the heel of her drink. Caroline put her head to the side, like a bird eyeing a worm. 'Och, Aoife. What's eating ye?'

Aoife emptied her glass, then put it on the table. 'I wrote down what everyone gets for all the pieces,' she said, pulling out a notebook. 'Cuffs. Collars. Plackets. Backs. Sides. Fronts. Epaulettes.'

'And?'

'So. Those basic work shirts we do for Marks and Spencer cost £30 in the shops. And Andy pays us about a fiver for every one we make.'

'Aye, but sure, we know what we're paid isn't the whole story,' Maeve said, pouring Aoife another drink. 'He has to pay for the material and the cost of running the factory – electricity and that – transport and all? Sure, that all adds up.'

Aoife tossed her notebook on the table and picked up her glass. 'Yep. I dug into all that. Billy told me about the cost of fabric. The lovely shirts we're doing for McAllister's are made with expensive fabric. The standard M and S stuff is a good bit cheaper. Primark shirts are bargain basement.'

Caroline picked up the notebook and read a few pages. 'Well, even considering wastage,' she said, sticking her jaw out at Aoife, 'Andy's doing well on the raw materials!'

'Yep. So I asked one of Daddy's friends about the cost of running the factory – he used to do the books for it before Andy took over. And when Daddy got back from France, he looked up the grant Andy got from Invest NI – it's public domain.'

Maeve nodded like she knew what 'public domain' was.

'So then Daddy and I did a rough calculation of stuff like tax and pensions and things like that.'

Maeve thought of the sort of stuff her and her da did together. Picking horses for a flutter during the Grand National.

Reading the TV guide so they could make the best choice between watching the *Antiques Roadshow* or *Family Fortunes*. Farting competitions on the sofa. 'Right. And?'

Aoife pushed the notepad across the coffee table. Maeve scanned the figures. 'So he's screwing us.'

'He's screwing us really badly,' Caroline snorted.

Aoife nodded. 'Daddy explained that the grants Andy won are supposed to help him to develop a sales pipeline and build up his workforce.'

'What's that mean?' Caroline asked.

'Well, basically, the grant buys him time to make sales, build up a client base and train enough people so the factory becomes self-sufficient and can scale up.'

'But he's only got McAllister's on board,' Maeve said. 'One client.'

'Daddy said he wouldn't be confident the McAllister's are a real client. They might be colluding with Andy.'

Maeve remembered the way the ratty wee fella had sniffed the factory out. The greedy eyes on the sweaty big redhead.

'And Andy did a pile of interviews,' Caroline said, 'but he only hired that Wendy doll.'

'But she didn't last long,' Aoife said. 'And for all we know, she's still on the payroll.'

'Andy's not running a shirt factory,' Maeve said. 'It's a fleecing parlour.'

'Aye,' Caroline said, 'and we're the sheep.'

Maeve didn't say, 'Well, what are we going to do about this?' Because, really, what the fuck could they do? Knock at Invest NI's door and rat Andy out? Blackmail Andy for more money? Organise the whole factory to strike?

'Ah need a drink,' Caroline said.

Maeve passed her the vodka, then got up and went to the window. She stared down at the factory, pure raging.

She wasn't raging at Andy for ripping them off. She wasn't raging at Aoife for ruining their summer. She was raging with herself. She was the one who was supposed to be training for a career in journalism. She'd had the same opportunity as Aoife to figure things out. But it was Aoife who'd uncovered the scam under their noses.

'I asked Daddy what we should do about all this,' Aoife said.

Maeve turned around and saw the concern on Caroline's face.

'And what'd yer da suggest?' Maeve asked.

'Well, he said it's very hard to do anything without hard evidence. Everything we've got is just circumstantial.'

'Aye,' Caroline said. 'And even if we had evidence, who's going to listen to the likes of us?'

Aoife flicked through her notebook again, then threw it on the table. 'But it doesn't feel right to stand by and do nothing,' she said.

They fell silent. Then Caroline spoke, all soft. 'Och, Aoife, even if we had hard evidence, would it really be right to tout on Andy?' she asked. 'The factory'd be shut down. We'd all be out of a job. And just speaking for myself here, low wages are better than no wages.'

Aoife sighed and sat back on the sofa. 'I suppose working in the factory has turned out to be a lot more interesting than we anticipated.'

Maeve grabbed the vodka bottle and wondered what sort of lessons they were yet to learn. She thought about Master Bradley, her old English teacher. He'd grown up locally, and though he'd married a dose from Cavan, who never stopped whinging about the Troubles, he was considered sound. He was no Robin Williams from *Dead Poets Society*, but he knew how to get around Maeve and most pupils in his classes.

One day, hungover to fuck, he'd read them the fable of the emperor's new clothes.

Maeve'd found it easy to get on board with the story: a vain man with more money than sense having his arse kissed by a load of lackeys who all pretended to see his suit of invisible clothes, so they couldn't be accused of stupidity or dishonesty. But she was annoyed when it came to the emperor parading around town buck naked until a wee fella points out he's wearing no clothes. In real life, Maeve knew it'd be some blade like her who'd be the first to state the obvious. But the telling of tales didn't work like that. The men writing the stories grabbed the starring roles. The women made up the scenery.

When Master Bradley finished reading the story, he asked the class to picture themselves at the scene watching the emperor marching down the street in the nip.

Maeve imagined standing in the crowd, gawping at the man striding towards her with his balls swinging like a big naked Orangeman.

'Now, I want you to write a version of this story, from your viewpoint,' Master Bradley said, picking up his newspaper and flicking to the racing section. 'You can be the mayor, or someone in the crowd, or a horse, or a flea on the horse, for all I care. You have half an hour.'

Maeve liked when Master Bradley was hungover and let them do shit like that. Everyone knew they could write one line or a whole novel – he wouldn't give a frig as long as they let him nurse his hangover in peace.

Maeve'd started scribbling.

Obviously, she cast herself as a busty wench, skivvying in a smoky tavern, carrying frothy flagons of beer to randy old merchants. Then some wee skitter bursts in shouting, 'The emperor's coming!' and everyone rushes outside. Maeve the tavern wench lays down her tray and follows them, pushing her way to the front of the crowd. She spots the emperor marching down the road, his wife sitting beside him in a carriage, grey with mortification. Then the wee skitter shouts, 'Sure, he's buck naked!'

In the silence that follows, no one can unsee what they'd been pretending not to see. Some people gawk harder, some look away, most wave flags with a smile frozen on their faces.

And that's when Maeve the tavern wench shouts out: 'And he's got a tiny cock.'

In Maeve's fable, the emperor crumpled under the eruption of laughter from his subjects while the empress stared daggers at Maeve the tavern wench.

Maeve had got as far as the tavern wench being dragged off by soldiers when Master Bradley droned, 'Time's up. Pens down.' Then he eyed the class, considering who he'd pick on to share their story.

Maeve panicked. As much as she'd enjoyed writing her fable, she didn't want to read it out to the class. Master Bradley started with Jamesy Kelly, who read his story in one breath: 'Born blind, I missed the only craic ever tae happen in Bare-buttston.'

Maeve shrank into her seat, trying to be inconspicuous, as Master Bradley lit on people at random until the class bell rang. 'Leave your work on my desk on your way out.'

At the end of the week, he dropped their stories back on their desks, passing comments as he went, so everyone knew who'd done a good job, and who'd been shite. But he released Maeve's story without saying a word. On the front page he'd written *See me after class.*

She made sure she was the last person to get to her feet after the bell rang, then slouched over to Bradley's desk, which she knew annoyed the shite out of him.

'I read your story.'

'Did you, sir?'

'I did. And I'd like to know if there's a happy ending.' He pushed the story across his desk. 'Finish it.'

Maeve picked it up. 'Yes, sir.'

'Next Friday will do.'

'Yes, sir.'

Maeve lay awake that night, wondering how to end the story. She considered a happy ending, like something out of Disney, where the emperor's son would ride in on a white horse to save

Maeve the tavern wench from the empress's dungeons. He'd wash, dress and wed her, before sitting her on a golden throne wearing a gleaming crown. Together they'd replace the liars and flatterers of the old court with plain-speaking ordinary folk, who made their own clothes, rules, and crisp apple pies.

But that was balls.

She considered a triumphant ending, with the townsfolk raising a rebellion, rescuing Maeve the tavern wench, and toppling the throne before forming a socialist democracy. But Maeve knew only too well where her firebrand female heroes had ended up:

Joan of Arc, burnt at the stake.

Emily Wilding Davison, trampled under the hooves of the king's horse.

Bernadette Devlin, shot nine times as she bathed her weans.

At fourteen, Maeve knew her story wouldn't be a happily ever after.

The following Friday, she dropped the finished story on Master Bradley's desk, then sat down and listened to him drone on about the division between court and peasants, magic and reality in *The Tempest*. He split the class into groups and asked them to outline the changes they'd enact in Northern Ireland if they had magic powers, which was the sort of shite that made Maeve wish she lived some place normal. Then he picked up her story. Maeve was so distracted, she wasn't fit to shoot down Kevin Browne's suggestion that they use their magical powers to transform the town's Protestants into sheep that could be shared equally among the Catholics (Maeve wanted a sheep even less than she wanted a Protestant). She watched Bradley flick to the last page of her story. He frowned, then looked down at Maeve. She didn't like the look in his eyes so she hid her face in *The Tempest*.

At the end of the class, Master Bradley held out her story without comment. She mumbled, 'Thanks, sir,' then ran to the toilets and locked herself in a cubicle.

Strong ending, he'd written in red ink. *Shame it's not a happy one.*

Maeve sat on the toilet seat for a while, wondering what he meant. Did he want her to rewrite the stoning bit? Was a happy ending better than a strong ending? For weeks afterwards she tried to come up with a happy ending she could believe in. Or at least a not-incredibly-violent-and-tragic ending. But – not for the first time in her life – her imagination failed her.

It was nearly home time when Maeve knocked on Andy's door. She'd taken all day to work up the nerve to confront him. He tidied away some paperwork as she walked in.

'Well, this is an unexpected pleasure, Ms Murray.'

Despite herself, Maeve felt a surge through her body, a pressure in her knickers. She tried to distract herself by eyeing his desk, which was strewn with a stash of factory paperwork and Invest NI forms.

'Well?' he asked. 'What can I do for you?'

Before she could speak, the phone rang. Andy frowned. 'Answer that.'

Maeve folded her arms and tried to channel her inner Fidelma Hegarty. Andy looked up at her, then raised both eyebrows and nodded in the direction of the phone. She caved and picked up the receiver. 'Andy Strawbridge's office. How can I help you?'

Mary's voice rasped back at Maeve. 'Miss Murray, can you send Mr Strawbridge down to my office when you get a moment, please? Tell him there are some insurance gentlemen here to see him.'

'Can I ask who's calling?'

'Now, Miss Murray. This very minute,' Mary said, hanging up.

Maeve put the receiver down. 'Mary says there are some insurance gentlemen down in her office who want to see you.'

'Fuck,' Andy said, throwing down his pen. It skidded across the desk and fell on the floor. Maeve picked it up like the tool she was. 'Stay here. Don't answer the phone. I'll deal with you after I speak with these gentlemen downstairs.'

The way he said *gentlemen* gave Maeve the impression that the fellas in Mary's office didn't meet Andy's standards for the title. He stood up, smoothed his tie over his shirt front, then walked out of the door.

Maeve'd never been alone in Andy's office. She sat down in his chair, enjoying the feel of the warm leather under her arse. She looked at the paperwork on his desk. Andy was filling in an application for the final 10 per cent payment of a grant. Maeve sucked in her breath: £21,000. Money like that would buy four council houses in her estate or a couple of houses in a studenty area of Belfast. She picked up a sheet of paper, printed with a list of names. Her own name jumped out at her, alongside a row of numbers. As Maeve scanned the figures, she realised it was an accurate record of what she'd been paid each week in the factory. She looked for Aoife and Caroline's names. The knot in her stomach relaxed as she realised their pay matched what she knew they'd been paid.

But then she noticed how long the list ran on.

Hugo Arkinson
Mary Bradley
Brenda Coyle
Frances Duffy
Miriam Frost
Cecil Jones

The list read like the captions under the old school photos the *Town Times* printed from time to time.

But instead of a name having the word 'deceased' in brackets after it, half of these names deserved the label 'fake'.

Maeve realised that she'd got proof that Andy was defrauding the government. And that put the shits up her.

If she was a character in a Nancy Drew novel, she'd steal the payroll printout and walk out of the factory door with Aoife.

They'd take the printout and Aoife's notebook to a big newspaper, who'd piss their pants to break the exclusive story.

COLLARED: DODGY SEW AND SEW STITCHED UP BY MILLIES

Maeve would be rocket-launched into the world of investigative journalism, while Aoife's fledgling legal career would be gold-stamped by Andy's criminal conviction.

But the only reporter Maeve knew was Paddy Slevin in the *Town Times* and his expertise lay in identifying who was who in vintage First Holy Communion pictures or interpreting the significance of the spring lamb mortality rate. And she'd be kneecapped or worse if she went to the police.

Tell-tale tit. Your mammy cannae knit. Your daddy cannae go to bed without a dummy tit.

Which left her with the only other 'law' enforcers she could think of: the IRA.

Maeve was well aware of their stance on occupying Ireland (criminal), riding a Brit (criminal), doing drugs (criminal), joyriding (criminal) and being gay (criminal). But she'd no idea what they thought of financial fraud.

She tried to imagine what Aoife would do. What Bernadette Devlin would do. What Fidelma Hegarty'd do. Then she folded the printout, shoved it down her knickers and trudged back to her ironing board.

Maeve knew which house she needed to visit. It was funny that she knew. It's not like Ciarán Friel's name was listed in the Yellow Pages under 'Community Justice'. She just knew that his bell was the one she needed to ring.

One of his sons – a skinny strip of a lad who they said had hopes of making the senior Tyrone team – opened the door.

'Ah need to speak to yer da.'

Maeve could imagine the sort of people this lad had seen asking to speak with his da.

'He's in the living room.'

Of course he was in the living room. Men like Ciarán Friel didn't sit in the kitchen, perched on a chair, cupping a mug of tea in their hands. They sat in front of the telly, waiting on the cups of tea their women brought in to them without being told. Their hot dinners were made and their dirty dishes washed. Their pants were laundered, aired and folded before being placed in the right drawer. The carpets under their feet were hoovered, the toilet they shat in was scoured, and their Long Kesh harps, their Belleek china Celtic crosses and Tyrone Crystal candlesticks were dusted. Not that Ciarán Friel noticed. The like of him only noticed when their womenfolk failed to keep up with one of the endless tasks that allowed him to devote his time and energy to planning a bloody end to the British Occupation of Ireland.

Maeve went into the living room where Ciarán Friel sat in the armchair nearest the fireplace, his three teenage sons sprawled across the sofa. A car engine revved on the telly. Ciarán looked up at Maeve, expressionless.

'I need to speak to you.'

Ciarán nodded and raised a hand at his sons, who got up and left the room. Then he turned the TV volume down. 'Take a seat.'

Maeve found herself perching like a young priest on the edge of the sofa. Ciarán looked her over. She'd tried to dress for the occasion – wearing bootcut jeans and a black top under a big black cardigan. She'd nipped home and lifted a gold Celtic cross necklace and St Brigid's cross earrings from her mam's jewellery box. She'd enough make-up on to look like she'd made an effort – to look like a tidy cuddy – but not enough to look slutty. Or so she hoped.

'You're Seán Murray's daughter.'

'Maeve.'

'And you're working in that factory over the road.'

Maeve nodded.

'I was very sorry to hear about yer sister a while back.'

'Thanks.

They sat in respectful silence for a few moments.

'I heard you might do well in your A-levels.'

'Well. Fingers crossed.'

'So, where'll ye head?'

Maeve knew that Ciarán Friel knew where she'd applied to. The whole town knew exactly where everyone wanted to go. They even knew where the best of the Prods hoped to head. She'd a bad feeling that Ciarán Friel was about to make a point.

'University College London.'

Ciarán's gaze went back to the TV where some big-haired English git was zipping along a country lane in a small red car, shouting into a camera.

'Over tae London, eh?'

'Aye. London.'

Ciarán rubbed his nose. 'Ye couldn't have got into some place in Derry maybe, or Belfast, or even Dublin?'

'The careers teacher told me to try for UCL and Goldsmith's,' she said, dropping Dusty McDonnell in the shit.

'Well, us Irish have a long tradition of that, now. Sending our brightest and best over the water.'

Maeve nodded and tried to look mournful. She wasn't sure if she should be staring at the slabber in the red car like Ciarán Friel was or staring at Ciarán Friel himself, so she glued her eyes on the Long Kesh harp on the mantelpiece.

'Centuries now we've been doing that. We built London for the Brits, did you know that? And rebuilt her after the war.'

'We did, right enough. I've uncles who worked on the building sites.'

Ciarán glanced at Maeve with a cold eye. 'Wasn't just hospitals and houses and office blocks we put up for them. We built roads. Tunnelled sewers. Laid railways. Thon new Eurotunnel's the honest work of Irishmen.'

Maeve knew better than to speak of the toilets Irish women scrubbed, the English arses they wiped, the slack elderly mouths they spooned food into, the medicines they doled out, the beds they made, the food they cooked, the nappies they changed, the pupils they taught, the letters they typed, the floors they mopped. She nodded along like she'd been trained to do, trying to demonstrate that she not only knew her place in the scheme of things, but that she was grateful for it.

'So, what is it ye wanted to speak to me about?'

Maeve took a deep breath. 'The factory.'

His eyes were suddenly on her. 'What of it?'

'We reckon Andy Strawbridge is lining his own pockets.'

'Who's *we*?' There was gun metal in his gaze.

'Me and a couple of the other girls working there.'

'And tell me now, how did you cuddies come to that conclusion?'

Maeve swallowed hard. 'Well, there's big Invest NI money flowing into that place and other than his fancy car, we can't see where the money's going, for it's not in our pockets. So we took a look at what we're paid for our shirt pieces. What our wages are. The rent. Can't say we're sure of the electric. But his costs don't tally with his grants. And then I found this.' Maeve unfolded the payroll printout as three English gits walked around a white jeep in a television studio.

'Did you take his insurance money into consideration?' Ciarán asked, gesturing for the paper.

'Is insurance so wild dear?' Maeve asked, passing the payroll over.

'Well,' Ciarán said, scanning the paper, 'the factory being where it is, there are high premiums to pay, locally, like, to make sure nobody'd break in and rob those machines or wreck the place.' Ciarán looked up at Maeve. 'Ye wouldn't want that, would ye? For him tae forget his dues tae both sides of the local community? And for that factory tae be put at risk, and all these hard-won jobs lost?'

The penny dropped. Andy was paying protection money. And because of the way the town was divided, he was paying it to both sides.

Maeve realised Ciarán was sitting, waiting for her to show that she'd understood. 'Naw,' she said. 'He should be paying his dues.'

Ciarán turned his gaze back to the telly.

Maeve knew it was time for her to thank him for educating her on financial points she'd been ignorant about. But some streak of madness made her think that perhaps Ciarán Friel hadn't got the full picture.

'But another problem with Andy Strawbridge is that he has no respect for women.'

Ciarán took a deep, slow breath and let it out before turning to look at Maeve. 'I've found myself,' he said, 'that respect has tae be earned. The hard way.'

His insult sizzled in the air between them for a few seconds. Then Maeve felt her flytrap open again. 'Andy Strawbridge gropes his female employees on the factory floor,' she said. 'He picks and chooses who he drives home in return for sex. He assaults girls in his office. I'm wondering if all this protection money stretches as far as protecting us.'

Ciarán Friel's face and ears turned red. Maeve wondered where else the blood was pumping.

'Them's some big allegations coming from a very wee girl.'

On the telly, the camera zoomed in for a close-up of the audience, cheering something the big-haired git had said.

'And who's going to back your story up, sweetheart?' Ciarán asked, crumpling the payroll in one hand. 'What evidence do you have to bring against this businessman who has brought employment and funds into our economically disadvantaged area?'

He chucked the payroll into the fire. It burned as the big-haired git on the TV drove through a sunny city in yet another car. Maeve stood up and walked to the door.

'Where d'ye think you're headed, wee girl? I haven't finished with you.'

Maeve turned around. 'Ah'd say you're not finished with me alright, you and your kind. Ye have us where ye want us.

Youse have done for years. But ah'm finished with you. Ah'm finished with you and this shitty wee town. You're welcome to it. Ah hope ye frigging well die for it.'

Thinking she might as well be hung for a sheep as a lamb, Maeve slammed the front door behind her.

Sarah McCanny gawked over from next door, where she was sitting sunning herself outside her porch. 'God save us now, Maeve Murray, but what is it that's wrong?'

Maeve walked off without answering, wondering whether or not she'd make it to London with both her kneecaps intact.

Monday, 15 August 1994

Results day

Maeve and Caroline were walking through the school gates when Aoife's mother swerved out past them in her blue 2CV, like she was a getaway driver.

'Suppose she's picked up Aoife's results,' Caroline said.

'Suppose,' Maeve said. But she didn't care about Aoife right now. She was eyeing a few of the lads they'd shared a classroom with for years. They were slouching against the wall, looking years older than just a few months before, lean and brown from their labouring or farming, from shifting beer kegs or footing turf. She nodded at them, then pushed through the front doors of the school. She was swamped by the reek of Jeyes Fluid, sweat, nicotine and boredom. Christ was still bleeding on the three-foot cross hanging over the gym entrance, and the Virgin Mary was peering in wonder at her feet, as if she'd only just noticed that someone had gloss-painted them peach.

Maeve and Caroline's trainers made little kissy noises as they walked towards Fatty Dolan's office. They stopped at the door and eyedballed each other. Caroline shook her head and crossed her arms. Maeve rolled her eyes, then knocked and put her head around the door. Fatty was sitting at her desk with a box of brown envelopes in front of her, looking much like Mary on payday.

'Well,' Fatty said, 'come on in.'

Maeve entered the office, fighting an inexplicable urge to curtsy.
'I hope you'd a good summer,' Fatty said.

'I got a start in the factory, miss.'

'Well, I hope you had the good sense to save, rather than spend,' Fatty said, raising an eyebrow.

Maeve nodded, wishing she'd just hand over her results to frig. Fatty flicked through to 'M', selected an envelope, then held it out to Maeve. 'Best of luck.'

Maeve thanked her and left the office.

'Ah'll see ye at the lockers,' she said to Caroline, then blundered down the stairs. She sat on a bench, holding her unopened envelope, wondering what Fatty'd meant by, 'Best of luck'. Was she consoling Maeve because she'd got shite results? Was she wishing her luck because she reckoned Maeve'd need it for heading over the water to England?

A few moments later, Caroline sat down beside her. The bench trembled beneath their arses.

'Ready?'

Caroline shook her head.

'Me, neither.'

They sat staring at their envelopes.

'I'm gonna wet myself if we clock much longer,' Caroline said, squirming.

Maeve tried to catch a grip of herself. 'Alright. Will we open them together? On the count of three?'

Caroline nodded.

'OK. One. Two. Three . . .' Maeve ripped open her envelope, then stared at her results in disbelief.

'Jesus, Mary and Joseph,' Caroline said, 'I got all Bs!' She squealed and beat her feet off the ground the way they used to when they wanted to show approval during school assemblies or indoor sporting events.

'How'd you get on?'

Maeve passed her slip over to Caroline without saying a word.

'Three As!' she squealed. 'Holy Mother of God, Maeve!'

Maeve hadn't just done it. She'd overdone it. Three. Fucking. As. She stood up and roared, '*YESSSSSSSS!*'

'Ladies.' Fatty Dolan was standing at the top of the stairs glaring almost fondly down at them. 'I know you're all moving on to more glorious things, but I would appreciate it if you could keep the peace in St Jude's one last time.'

'Yes, miss, sorry, miss!' Maeve said, grinning up at Fatty. 'Just, you know . . .'

'Yes. I know,' Fatty said, smiling. 'Feel free to make some noise outside.'

Maeve and Caroline bounced past Fatty and burst out of the front door. They joined a crowd of their old classmates who were slabbering on about what they'd got and where they were or weren't going. Maeve gave zero fucks, for all she was thinking was *Three As!*

She was going to get the fuck out of the town.

Maeve tried to steady herself before opening the door to her house. She remembered the last time her family were waiting on A-level results. Deirdre'd been a nervous wreck for weeks beforehand. Maeve's da had gone out the road to St Jude's to pick up her envelope. Then he'd slipped it – unopened – under Deirdre's duvet. She'd said nothing and didn't come downstairs for hours. They'd all sat around, assuming the worst, not answering the doorbell because they'd frig all to tell anyone. In the end, Maeve's mam had headed up the stairs, grabbed the envelope and ripped it open. Deirdre's results were really good – they were her ticket to Queen's. But Maeve sometimes wondered if she'd still be alive if she'd failed and stayed in the town.

She took a deep breath and turned the key. When she entered the living room her da looked up from *Breakfast TV* and gave her a wee smile. 'Well. How'd ye do?'

Maeve gave her da the envelope, then started to shred her split ends.

He pulled out her results slip and scrutinised it at arm's length. Then he laid it carefully on the arm of the sofa and nodded. 'Well now. That's my cuddy.' He stood up and clamped Maeve under his oxter, beaming. 'My own cuddy.'

Maeve's mam eyed them. 'Did she do well?'

'She did,' he said, patting Maeve.

'And how'd she do?' her mam asked.

'Three As,' he said, pronouncing the letter to rhyme with baa. 'Three As, eh?'

'Three As?' her mam said, the English way. She stood up and bucked the contents of her ashtray into the fire. 'And how'd that Aoife O'Neill do?' she asked.

'I haven't seen her yet. And I heard nothing.'

Then Maeve's mam took a step forward and clutched Maeve. She breathed in the reek of fags, tea and Sure deodorant, letting herself be hugged until her mam let go and reached for her fags. 'Three As. Well now. How'd that Caroline doll do?'

'Three Bs.'

'Well,' her mam said. 'The Jacksons aren't as slow as they walk easy.'

'But you did a good bit better than three Bs, eh?' her da said, beaming. 'And you probably did as well as that Aoife O'Neill, eh? Good cuddy. Good girl yourself.'

'Aye. But ah hafta get back over tae the factory.'

'Ah'll walk ye over the length,' Maeve's da said, reaching for his jacket. 'And ah might take a wee dander on down the town afterwards.'

'A wee dander in tae the School Bar's more like!' Maeve's mam huffed.

'Well, if ah can't lift a glass on a day like this, ah dunno when ah'll next be able tae!' he said, in high good humour.

Then Maeve heard what sounded like a phone ringing from the hallway. She looked at her mam. 'What's that?'

'Well, it's not a jukebox anyway,' her mam said.

Maeve looked at her da.

'Ah got paid for the trial there,' he said, beaming. 'Thought we should look into a home improvement.'

'Ah suppose ah better go answer this for no one else'll bother their hole,' her mam said, getting up and going into the hall.

Maeve watched her pick up the receiver and say, 'Sevenninetwosixsix . . .?'

Maeve heard a tinny version of her Aunt Mary's voice gabbling from the earpiece.

'Aye . . . aye . . . we did,' her mam said, rolling her eyes at Maeve. 'We got the results.'

Mary chattered back like a tiny, enthusiastic machine gun.

'Aye, well, she did well . . . she did, aye. Three As.'

An explosion of congratulations burst from the phone as Maeve's mam smile-frowned at her and jerked her head at the door.

'Aye. She's near enough launched now. We'll see how far she gets.'

Maeve smile-frowned back at her mam, picturing herself sailing up and over the town like a mortar bomb. She hoped she was on target.

Between the sun splitting the stones outside and the exam results gossip, the whole factory felt lifted. But Aoife didn't come into work. Maeve imagined she was off gallivanting with her parents, celebrating her imminent entrance to Cambridge some place fancier than McHugh's Brews.

When the tea bell rang, Maeve fell into the queue behind Fidelma Hegarty.

'Results day, eh?'

Maeve nodded.

'Did ye get what ye needed tae get outta this place?'

'I did,' Maeve said.

Fidelma hit her a slap on the back that near sent her flying. 'Good woman yourself. Great job.'

Fidelma waited for Maeve to pick up her tea and toast, then plodded with her over to Caroline. 'So how'd you do?'

'All Bs.'

'Them's some results! Where are you off tae now?'

'Magee,' Caroline said, miserably. 'Politics.'

Fidelma didn't need to say anything: her face said it all.

'So you'll be away tae London next, will ye, Maeve?'

'I will.'

'Coach and ferry, I suppose.'

'Aye. My ticket's bought.'

'And how much did that cost ye?'

'Twenty-five quid with my student discount.'

'It's not for free, a ticket tae London.'

'Far cheaper than flying, though.'

'And when are ye leaving?'

'Mid-September.'

'Mid-September,' Fidelma said, quietly. 'Not long now.'

Later on, Maeve dragged Caroline outside for a fag. They found Mabel Moore sitting on the plastic chair with her legs wide apart and her skirt hitched up over her knees.

'Ah heard you cuddies did well,' she said.

'Och, aye, we did well enough,' Maeve answered, all casual, like her results were already last week's milk.

'Ye don't do much better than three As now, do ye?' Mabel said, clamping a cold, watery eye on her.

Maeve shook her head, feeling like a bit of a dick.

'Naw. Ye don't,' Mabel continued. 'So don't fucken do yerself down. There's manys another'll do that fer ye.'

Right on cue, Mary appeared in the doorway. She lifted her hand, shading her eyes against the sun. Mabel dropped her fag and mashed it out with her heel. 'Tell us this and tell us no more, Mary. What's going on with them McAllister's fellas?'

Mary stiffened and said, 'Heh?', as if she'd never heard tell of McAllister's before.

'Them McAllister fellas shoulda been back by now. Or sent word back. We've pushed plenty a shirts their road.'

'Ah dunno anything about them, Mabel.' Mary shaded her eyes again. 'Andy's on the phone til them the whole time. All seems grand tae me.'

Mabel stood up and scratched her chin. 'Whatever ye say, Mary. Just doesn't feel right tae me. All this work we're firing out the door and the big mad push on it. Doesn't feel steady.'

'From what I see, things are as steady as ever they'll be, what with the factories in Asia hoovering up all the work.'

Mabel tossed her head and hobbled back indoors. Mary followed her.

'What d'ye think's going on?' Caroline asked.

'No idea,' Maeve said. 'I just hope Andy can keep us in work for the next four weeks.'

Maeve took her time smoking her fag

'Where d'ye think Aoife is?' Caroline asked.

'Probably out celebrating with her lot,' Maeve replied. 'While I break my back doing her ironing.'

'S'pose. Will we head back in?' Caroline said, moodily.

Maeve stubbed out her fag and got to her feet, wondering what was eating Caroline: she wasn't carrying on like a woman who'd got better than expected results.

When they went back inside Maeve caught sight of Andy standing on the mezzanine. He gestured *come here* at her with his hand. Her heart pounded and she took a few steps forward before realising he was signalling at Mary. She put her head down and walked back to her ironing board.

She didn't know what it was about Andy that made her feel like a fish on a hook, but she hoped she wouldn't be like that with every Englishman she met, otherwise London'd be pure exhausting.

Maeve and Caroline walked over to the Jacksons' after their shift ended, the heat from the day's sun still warm in the road.

Martin was helping the Jacksons load Nana Jackson into the back of his ancient Vauxhall Astra so they could drive to the Fir Trees in Strabane to celebrate Caroline's exam results.

'Shame there's no room for you in the car, Maeve!' Caroline said, slipping her arm around Martin.

'Och, I'll be grand. Mam said to come over for dinner. And I might ring Aoife and see what the craic is with her.'

'Yeah. It's weird we haven't heard from her. Or about her.'

'Och, I'm sure we'll find out soon enough. Youse go enjoy yourselves,' she said, waving the Jacksons off.

At home, Maeve discovered her da hadn't been seen since he'd headed down the town earlier in the day.

'And how'd that Aoife doll do?' her mam enquired.

Maeve explained that Aoife hadn't landed in to work and she hadn't heard how she did.

'Have you not, now?' her mam said, slicing through the crisp chocolate layers of a Viennetta. 'Sure, why don't you ring her from the phone there til we see how she did?'

Maeve didn't want to speak to Aoife with a whole audience of brothers and her mam. She wanted the privacy of a phone box. 'Och, naw. Sure, she'll probably drop round to the flat later this evening for a chat.'

Her mam tossed her head, then gave Maeve a huge slice of Viennetta.

'How come she's getting the biggest slice?' Chris whinged.

'Cos I done well,' Maeve said. 'What've you ever done?'

She dug into her Viennetta, thankful that Dale Carnegie had never said anything about being civil to your siblings.

An hour later, Maeve dialled Aoife's number in the telephone box up the road, and hung up after three rings. Then she pushed her back against the door, ignoring Dervla Daly, who was waiting to use the phone. Maeve didn't really expect Aoife to be in, but she was happy to hog the box for a couple of minutes to annoy Dervla. She got a shock when the phone rang just moments later.

'Maeve?'

'Hey, Aoife. Didn't see you at the factory today. Are you alright?' Maeve mouthed *Fuck off* at Dervla as she waited for Aoife to answer.

'I'm OK.'

Aoife was clearly not OK.

'You sure you're OK?'

Dervla Daly started tapping on the window, pure wrecking Maeve's head.

'I got two As and a B.'

Maeve's heart beat like a balloon bobbing at a ceiling. 'Och, Aoife!'

She didn't reply.

'Och, Aoife, I'm so sorry. Does that mean Cambridge is out?'

'Oxford too.'

'Och, but sure you'll get to Trinity with two As and a B.'

Dervla Daly battered the telephone box door behind Maeve.

'Probably,' Aoife said.

Maeve covered the mouthpiece, opened the telephone box and roared, 'Will ye fuck off?', almost missing Aoife's quiet reply.

'But I didn't want to go to Dublin.'

'Och, Aoife. I'm so sorry.'

'And I'll have to learn Irish.'

'Och, but sure you still have some Irish from your primary school days down south.'

'"An bhfuil cead agam dul go dtí an leithreas?" won't help me get to the Irish bar.'

Maeve had no idea what 'On will key yade a gum dull go dee on leth-russ' meant for she'd never been taught Irish in school. The British government had made sure of that.

'Awwwww. But sure you can move to London after you finish up in Trinity. Loads of people do that!'

'I suppose.'

Dervla stuck her middle finger up at Maeve. She mouthed, *Dead meat* back at her.

'Mummy said you did well.'

'Well, I could've done worse.'

'But you couldn't have done better,' Aoife said, bitterly.

They fell silent. Maeve wondered what Dervla'd do next. Wished she knew what she should say to Aoife. 'D'ye want me to come over?'

The line crackled.

'OK. But just for a bit. Mummy wants to talk to me.'

Maeve did the *bye-bye-bye-bye-bye* thing until Aoife cut the line dead. Then she hawked in her throat, spat in the earpiece and placed the phone back in the cradle. She opened the telephone box and aimed a kick at Dervla, who skittered out of reach, laughing.

Instead of going around the side of the house and rapping at the kitchen door, Maeve rang the front doorbell. It echoed deep into the house, as though trying to summon a servant from bygone days. A shadow passed behind the stained-glass panes, then the door opened.

'Maeve,' Mrs O'Neill said, smiling a smile that didn't reach her eyes and fell from her face as soon as she finished speaking. Colour splashed their clothes and the floor as she closed the door, like someone'd murdered a rainbow. 'Aoife's just having a shower. Would you like to wait in the kitchen?'

Maeve nodded and followed her through. 'Didn't Aoife do well?'

'She did. She'll be the first of us to get to Trinity.'

'You must be so proud.'

'Immeasurably.'

Maeve liked how Mrs O'Neill had the nerve to lie through her teeth. To pretend she wasn't fucking devastated by Aoife's slightly less than perfect grades.

'Do you want a coffee?' Mrs O'Neill said, waving her hand at the French press.

Maeve was no etiquette expert, but she suspected Mrs O'Neill was supposed to offer her congratulations on her results rather than a coffee. But she remembered Dale Carnegie's advice on controlling her temper from chapter ten: 'You Can't Win an Argument.'

'Naw, you're grand, thanks.'

Mrs O'Neill nodded slightly, as if to say, 'Yes, yes, I am.' Then she continued: 'All in black this evening? Are you regressing to your Goth phase?'

Maeve chose to interpret Mrs O'Neill's comment as an opportunity to bond over a shared interest. 'Nope. I suppose black's my favourite colour. Like yourself and the white!'

Mrs O'Neill looked at Maeve, then took a sip of coffee. 'Black isn't actually a colour, Maeve. If you ever study colour, you'll learn that in the visible spectrum, white reflects light, making it a presence of all colours. But black simply absorbs light. It's the absence of colour.'

Maeve realised that nothing she'd read in *How to Win Friends and Influence People* would ever make conversing with Mrs O'Neill bearable.

'Black was first used by the cave painters of Lascaux in France. They burned wood until it was charred carbon, then used it to draw bulls. Later on, someone discovered that burnt bones held a deeper, more intense black than wood. That's where the shade "bone black" comes from.'

'And have you ever painted with bones, Mrs O'Neill?'

Mrs O'Neill looked at Maeve, her pupils tiny dark pools of hatred, which was a bit annoying as she wasn't entirely taking the piss. She could picture Mrs O'Neill photographing a cow from its birth through to its slaughter, then burning its bones in a fire pit by the summer house. There'd be a hefty price tag on her monochrome portraits of cows painted with the charred marrow of their own bones.

'I use Windsor & Newton,' Mrs O'Neill said. She poured a half-mug of coffee, then picked it up and swished the liquid around and around.

'So what you're saying is that midnight isn't black. Guinness isn't black. Grapes aren't black, and neither are people or berries?'

Mrs O'Neill finally took a sip of coffee. 'That's right.' She placed her mug on the table before continuing. 'What I find interesting is that some ancient cultures have two words for black. One to describe that luminous, glossy black you see in a piece of polished ebony—'

'I wouldn't know what ebony is.'

Mrs O'Neill explained that ebony was much the same as the black inside a split coal. Maeve could picture it then. The gleam of a hearse.

'So what's the other black?'

Mrs O'Neill gazed at Maeve, suddenly seeming tired. 'It's the flat, dull black of soot. Of outer space.'

'Or depression,' Maeve said, suddenly seeing herself as Mrs O'Neill saw her. A black hole at the heart of her family, sucking in all the light and love, always needing more.

'I think Aoife might be out of her shower now,' Mrs O'Neill said.

'I have to go,' Maeve said. 'There's something I forgot tae do.' She hurried out the back door, leaving Mrs O'Neill sitting like a sphinx at the kitchen table.

Maeve'd passed the caravan park every week her whole life long on her way to mass, but she'd never gone in before. The only people who went into the caravan park were folk with no other choice.

'Hey,' she said, to a blank-looking wee cub who was baiting a dog with a live rabbit. 'Where's Fidelma Hegarty?'

The boy pointed at a caravan at the far end of the park. Maeve walked over and rapped on the door.

'Fuck off, Tony. Louise isn't here.'

'S'not Tony. S'me. Maeve.'

The caravan trembled as Fidelma moved about inside. Maeve heard Fidelma growl something. A woman answered, also low.

'Ah brought cider,' Maeve said, feeling like a total dick.

The caravan door opened. A woman Maeve didn't recognise stepped out.

'Ah'll have a can, so I will,' she said, nodding at Maeve's bag.

Maeve handed one over.

'Thanks,' the woman said to Maeve. Then she shouted back into the caravan, 'Ah'm away.'

Fidelma came to the door. 'Right, Louise, safe home,' she said awkwardly.

Maeve noticed Fidelma'd a bit of a lather worked up.

'Ah'm not disturbing ye, am ah?'

'Naw. Get in,' she said, glaring at the wee cub who was taking in the whole scene.

Maeve entered and handed Fidelma the bag of cans. Fidelma gave Maeve a can, kept one for herself, then stacked the rest in the fridge. 'Sit down there.'

Maeve sat on the window seat and opened a can. She'd only ever been in a caravan on holidays in Bundoran. But Fidelma's caravan smelt of perfume and Calor gas rather than the sea.

Fidelma closed the fridge, then folded the plastic bag and stashed it in a drawer. 'At a loose end, are ye?'

'Caroline's away tae the Fir Trees. And Aoife's not in the form for celebrating.'

'Did she not do well?'

'She did well enough. Two As and a B.'

'But not as good as you.'

Maeve shook her head. She wasn't sure how she felt about doing better than Aoife. She wasn't sure what she was supposed to do with that.

'And not good enough for over the water, naw?'

'She'll get Trinity. She'll get away to Dublin.'

'Well sure, it's an ill wind,' Fidelma said, opening a can.

'Your caravan's lovely, so it is.'

Fidelma stared at Maeve all prickly, trying to suss if she was ripping the piss. 'It's no palace,' she said, relaxing. 'But ah keep it decent.'

'Who's that, then?' Maeve said, pointing at the only photo in the caravan.

'Mammy.'

Fidelma's mother'd died young. Deirdre'd been one of the group of pupils who'd got the morning of her funeral off to stand a guard of honour at the chapel. She'd told Maeve about Fidelma and her sisters trooping past arm in arm, holding their da up between them, his bloodshot eyes darting around, as if looking for an escape route.

'How long's she dead now?'

'Ten years,' Fidelma said, sitting down heavily on the seat furthest away from Maeve.

'You're not like her.'

'Naw. Ah take after me shithead da, for me sins.'

Maeve said nothing. Fidelma's da'd been known for knocking seven shades of shite out of his wife while she was living. He'd moved on to his daughters after the funeral.

'When'd you move in here?'

'When ah turned seventeen. Got sick of me da. Ah'd have ended up crippling him if ah'd stayed.'

'And is your woman I met there living here too?'

'Jesus Christ, Maeve Murray, is this an interrogation or what?' Fidelma asked, her face darkening.

'Sorry, Fidelma,' Maeve said, sitting back.

'Och, naw. I'm sorry,' Fidelma said, crushing her tin. 'Ah'm fed up, is all. Ye can't fart in this town but someone wants tae know the flavour.'

'Tell me about it,' Maeve said.

Fidelma got up and went to the fridge for another cider. 'Ah live here on me own. The rent wouldn't kill ye. But I'm sick of it.'

'Would ye think of taking the flat after me and Caroline leave?'

'JP Devlin wouldn't rent tae the likes of me. Ach, no. Thon shirt factory's on its last legs. When it goes tits up, I'll find something else tae keep me occupied.'

'Sure, you're already well occupied. We have been for eight hundred years!'

Fidelma laughed her big hearty laugh as the rain started bouncing off the caravan.

The next morning, Maeve woke to a dig in the ribs.

'Maeve.'

She groaned and curled up into a foetal position.

'Maeve!'

Someone shook her by the shoulder, giving her the bokes.

'Get up tae fuck, Maeve Murray, or we'll be late!'

Maeve realised she was lying on Fidelma's sofa. And she was fucking dying. She'd no memory of the night before beyond her and Fidelma playing 'Only a Woman's Heart' and bawling their lamps out. She'd a notion that Fidelma wouldn't be mentioning that at tea break.

She washed her face, then trudged down the road to the factory. They landed in, reeking of cider and fags, just in time to clock in. Maeve went to her board and found her iron stone cold and Aoife nowhere to be seen. She stared at the trolleys full of shirts that were waiting to be ironed, and the whole weight of her sagged into her boots. She picked up her water reservoir and headed to the canteen to fill it. A long, hot, hard day was just beginning.

She lasted an hour at the shirts before she needed a break. She slunk past Fidelma, who was going at the shirts like she was Edward Scissorhands, then ducked out of the emergency door. Mabel was hogging the seat outside, flapping her skirt up and down to air her knickers. Mary was hunched over a fag.

'Hiyas,' Maeve croaked.

They nodded at her, then Mabel dropped her skirt, closed her eyes and put her face up to the sun like she was a daisy on a lawn. Maeve put the bottle of Coke to her head and poured it down her throat.

'Some drooth on you this morning, hey?' Mabel said, cracking an eyelid open.

Maeve nodded. She wasn't sure she was fit to speak.

'Hungover tae fuck's more like,' Mary said. 'And on a day where we're short staffed and already behind.'

A white van drove in through the factory gates and parked at the double doors. Mabel shaded her eyes and watched the delivery man unload a couple of bolts of fabric. 'Is that all we're getting?'

'We're on daily deliveries this past while,' Mary said. 'Material in every morning.'

'And ah see myself the shirts go out every evening.'

'Aye, they do. Straight up to McAllister's for distribution.'

'He doesn't keep much on the premises, does he?' Mabel said, sitting up.

Mary hunched around her fag. 'I suppose not. He says he's trying to be lean, whatever that might be.'

'Hmmmm,' Mabel said. 'Ye would think that wan big lorry delivering all the fabric over of a Monday and taking the shirts back would burn less petrol.'

'What would ah know about transport costs?' Mary said, flicking her half-smoked fag onto the tarmac. 'It's my job tae keep youse on yer toes. That's a big enough job for ten of me.'

She prowled back into the factory.

Mabel eyed Mary's fag. 'Hand that up tae me, will ye?'

Maeve picked up the butt and handed it to Mabel. She clamped her lips around it, saying, 'Waste not, want not.'

Maeve surreptitiously wiped her fingers on her jeans, wondering if Mabel could taste the tang of Mary's spit on the fag.

When the home time bell rang, the machinists stretched, pushed back their chairs and reached for their bags. Maeve collapsed over her ironing board. She'd killed herself all day, but was still drowning in shirts. Another mound had gathered beside Fidelma. Mary and Andy were frowning at the folding table beside Sharon Rogers.

'Fidelma. Caroline. Maeve,' Andy said. 'Over here, please.'

Fidelma set her jaw and bulled over like she was going to box Andy. Maeve walked over beside Fidelma, her hands balled in fists inside her joggers.

'Ladies, we need to see these shirts out the door tonight.'

'Ye mean *you* need tae see these shirts out the door tonight,' Maeve said. She felt braver than usual, standing beside Fidelma.

'We are all moving parts in this factory, Ms Murray,' Andy said. 'We all need to pull our weight to meet our targets.'

Maeve tried to arrange her face in the sort of fuck-you expression she imagined Fidelma was wearing.

'I'd like you three to stay on and finish up this load of shirts so the McAllister's chap can drive them up the road.'

Fidelma put one hand on a shirt lying on the table, slowly smoothing it flat. 'What's it worth to ye, Andy?'

'You'll get paid overtime.'

'Overtime's time and a half. Ah don't want overtime. Ah want double time. We all do.' Fidelma jerked her head in Maeve and Caroline's direction. They nodded and folded their arms like they meant business.

'Just this once,' Andy snapped. 'Double time in your next wage packet.'

'And a fiver each in our hands as we're going out that door so we can get a feed down the Indian.'

Maeve loved the cheek of Fidelma. The cop on of her. The way she knew they'd the upper hand – something that did not happen a lot – and how to use it.

'There's about two hours' work here,' Andy said, eyeing Fidelma. 'You get that done before eight o'clock you'll get your double time and an Indian. If you miss this target, you get single time and no Indian. Deal?'

'Deal,' Fidelma growled, with satisfaction.

Maeve and Caroline tore open the Indian takeout and dished it up while Fidelma cracked open a tin of Fanta and took a good slurp. Maeve liked how Fidelma made herself at home. How she sat on her arse, put her feet up and let someone else see to her.

'Ah hear you've a new fella,' Fidelma said to Caroline, who nodded. 'And is he good tae ye?'

'Och, he's lovely. And he's so good to Nana Jackson. Brings her wee treats and stuff.'

Fidelma shot Maeve an oh-God-save-me-now look. 'And he's a taxi driver?'

'He is. Though it's not safe, the taxi-ing. He'd be better off out of it.'

Maeve wondered how Martin had the balls to keep at the taxis, working late night after night, wondering which call was just another carload of blootered workmen, and which might've been placed by a loyalist paramilitary in possession of a handgun and instructions to kill another Taig.

'Sure there's plenty of opportunities open tae him if he's got a car. He can drive any roads.'

'He can, aye,' Caroline said, nodding. 'He's looking for something new. He's got his eyes open, Martin has.'

Maeve fired Fidelma a wee 'boke' face.

'Ah'd have wider horizons myself if ah had a car,' Fidelma said.

'Didn't know you had your driving test,' Maeve said. She couldn't imagine Fidelma behind the wheel of a car. She'd be lethal.

'Och, now, naw, ah don't have a licence or that. But I'd an uncle over the border there that taught me how tae drive. Ah've driven the length and breadth of Donegal. Sure, you'd hardly need a licence at all in the Free State – it's not like up here with the Brits.'

'Them fuckers,' Maeve said, shovelling a mouthful of korma into her.

'Ah keep trying tae imagine you living in the thick of them over there in London,' Fidelma said, before chomping on a poppadom. 'Hard tae picture.'

'I think I'll manage it. At least, I hope so.'

'Are ye sure, now? Ah mind you the day thon peace choir came tae St Jude's.'

'Och, Fidelma!' Caroline said. 'Maeve was only fourteen!'

'Aye, she was. But she still put the frighteners on them.'

Maeve always felt a bit sick when she thought of the Middleton Male Peace Choir. She'd gone as usual that day into the gym for morning assembly along with the whole school. Fatty Dolan'd been standing on stage like she always did, staring everyone into acceptable behaviour. But their form teachers had flanked the rows of seats like guards. Seats were only brought out for special events, like a bishop's visit, or a talk by a past pupil on how to emigrate. But they'd not had word of an event, which made Maeve suspect that a British politician and a load of troops was going to be parachuted in on top of them for a five-minute photo opportunity. Fatty Dolan blessed herself, rhymed off a few prayers, then gave out yards to the whole school for something everyone knew Linus McMurphy had done. Eventually she paused and clasped her hands together so tight Maeve wondered if she'd break a finger.

'This morning,' she said, using her special voice, 'we will experience an extraordinary performance by some visiting musicians.'

The gym doors squeaked open. Maeve knew without turning her head to gawk that Jon Bon Jovi hadn't entered the building.

A bluster of smiling men trooped up the hall, shiny with sweat. She could tell by the cut of their jeans, their soft bellies and the big heads on them that they were English.

Behind Maeve, Cormac Kelly rumbled, '*FEE FI FOE FUM*,' triggering the line, *I smell the Blood of an Englishman* in everyone's head. Fatty Dolan eyeballed Cormac, who slunk down in his seat, grinning.

The men climbed onstage and formed into lines.

'I'd like you all to welcome the Middleton Male Peace Choir to the school,' Fatty said. Fatty and the teachers clapped thunderously while a skift of applause swept through the pupils. Mr Orr stood with his arms crossed.

'The Middleton Male Peace Choir is touring Northern Ireland,' Fatty said, 'singing voluntarily in schools and halls, in yet another attempt to promote peace and reconciliation.'

Maeve'd already seen the choir. They'd been on telly earlier that week in some community hall up the Falls Road, belting out 'From a Distance'. The BBC had interviewed the choir master, a beardy bloke who'd explained that after the little kids were killed in the Warrington bombs, his choir had felt they just couldn't stand idly by for a minute longer, doing nothing. So they'd decided to put their own lives at risk by touring Northern Ireland to sing songs of peace.

'Dick,' Maeve's mam had said, a word Maeve did not know she knew until that moment.

Something twanged inside Maeve as a baldy fella strummed the opening chords of a song she knew she'd never love again, and twenty-five overweight English blokes started singing the Eurovision classic 'A Little Peace'.

When they finished, most of the teachers clapped, but the pupils were wise to the situation now. They crossed their arms like Mr Orr, leaving it to lick-arses like Dermie Crockett to clap.

The guitar player stepped back to the mic and cleared his throat. 'Your headmistress, she tells me you lot know this next song. So this time we'd like you all to sing along, yeah?' He gestured at a bloke on the piano, who started playing the opening of 'Imagine'.

They got as far as 'hell' before Maeve stood up. McVey gestured at her to sit the *FUCK* back down. But Maeve picked her way across a tangle of trainers and ankle boots and stalked out of the assembly hall. She slammed through the front doors of the school and came to a stop in the yard. A coach was parked at the school gates, sandwiched between four armoured RUC cars and two Brit jeeps. Maeve stood still, at a loss for something to do.

Then the doors opened behind her.

She turned around with her jaw out and arms crossed, ready to face McVey or Fatty Dolan or whoever. But Joanne McGlinchey from sixth form came bulling out, with Paddy the Muck from seventh year tearing up behind her.

'Fuck them. Who do they think they are? Fucken, fucken *singing* at us?'

More and more students came pouring out into the car park. Mr Orr came out, grinning for the first time ever. He started singing 'The Fields of Athenry', and everyone joined in, belting the song out at the bus, at the RUC, and the English choir left standing in the assembly hall.

Deirdre'd walked up to Maeve, one eyebrow raised. 'Nice one.'

Maeve had glowed with pride.

'But you know you're dead meat, right?'

Deirdre wasn't wrong. Ten minutes later, Maeve was summoned to Fatty Dolan's office. She'd marched in, defiant as Roddy McCorley stepping up to the gallows on the bridge of Toome, but when she saw the beardy choir master bloke sitting there she knew what was coming her way was going to be way worse than being hung, drawn and quartered by Fatty Dolan. She turned on her heel and tried to scoot back out of the door, but Fatty barred the way. 'Sit DOWN, Maeve Murray,' she said.

Maeve slunk over to the empty seat beside the English bloke. He was looking at her with concern – an expression she'd never witnessed on an English face in the flesh. She sat down, crossed her arms and looked straight ahead.

'So, Maeve, Mr Smith here wants to speak to you,' Fatty said, staring hard at Maeve. Something in Fatty's eyes told Maeve that this confrontation hadn't been her idea and that she wanted Maeve to do whatever was necessary to make these men go away as quickly and quietly as possible. Ideally before the press arrived.

'My-eve.'

Maeve winced at the beardy bloke's pronunciation of her name.

'I just wanted to say that we're here to show our hope for a brighter future. We're here to . . .'

Inside, Maeve screamed *Please don't say build bridges and tear down walls!*

'. . . build bridges and tear down the walls of hatred that have been built up here in Northern Ireland.' Mr Smith used his hands to demonstrate the act of wrenching down walls.

Maeve tried to swallow her emotions. She could tell by the twitch on Fatty Dolan's face that she was going through a similar struggle. Maeve knew that this eejit wasn't to blame for all the shit they had to shovel. She knew all she had to do was let him burble on so he'd head out the door eventually, feeling like he'd Made a Difference. She sat in silence until he eventually quit talking.

Fatty took a deep breath and laid her hands, palms down, on her desk. 'We appreciate your gesture, Mr Smith.' Then she turned to Maeve. 'Now, Maeve. Do you want to say something to Mr Smith?'

Maeve shook her head. Fatty stared wide-eyed at her. She stared slit-eyed right back at her. Then Mr Smith laid his big English paw on her shoulder. 'Look, My-eve, I'm Aye-rish too,' he said. 'My mum's from Leitrim. My dad's from Kerry.'

Leitrim and Kerry. The sort of ungodly union that only ever happens in an Irish dance hall over in London.

'Mr Smith, don't kid yerself you're Irish,' Maeve said, shrugging his hand off her shoulder.

'Maeve Murray!'

She ignored Fatty. Something had burst inside her. She wasn't fit to stop. 'You can talk shite about your Irish blood but ah'll tell ye for free, you're sure as fuck not Irish.'

'Language, Miss Murray!'

'What you don't get is I'm not even Irish – not proper Irish. I just want tae be. But all I am to the Free Staters is a dirty Northerner. I'm as pathetic as the Prods trying to be British when your lot think they're just a pack of Paddies. You don't want them. Them down south don't want us. Everyone just wants us to crawl away and die some place dark where they don't have to listen to us squealing for attention.'

Of course Maeve went and ruined her speech by bursting into tears. At which point Fatty marched her out of the door and locked her in the caretaker's storeroom. Maeve sat picking at her nails under the naked lightbulb, surrounded by bleach, scourers and mop buckets, wondering if she'd ever be able to scrub her feelings away.

'You know, they only wanted to sing a few songs,' Caroline said, scraping the last of her tikka masala out of the heel of a foil box. 'They were trying tae cheer us up. They'd good intentions.'

'But it's all these good intentions that's killing me,' Maeve said. 'Everyone's always asking us to paint pictures or write poems. Ye've artists sculpting doves. Teachers sucking the fucken lifeblood outtay us by asking us tae sing "Imagine" – like, no harm, but is that not showing a total *lack* of imagination?'

'Aye,' Fidelma said. 'Nobody's tackling the hard stuff.'

'Like what?' Caroline asked.

'Like taking religion clean out of schools,' Maeve said. 'Leaving it in on the altar where it belongs.'

'Aye,' said Fidelma again. 'They should integrate the schools so we get to know each other before we have to work side by side.'

'Definitely,' Maeve agreed. 'You'd be less likely to shoot someone you've been tae school with.'

'Ah dunno if ah'd go that far,' Fidelma said, darkly.

Maeve and Caroline exchanged a quick did-she-really-say-that? look.

'Well, if we were doing stuff right,' Caroline said, 'we'd build some decent new housing estates. Shared wans. With playgrounds for the weans. And benches for the likes of Nana Jackson.'

'Ah'd like tae get me teeth into the police,' Fidelma said. 'Thin out the Prods. Recruit more Taigs. Get more women in. Maybe some of the Asians ye see up in Belfast.'

They all chewed ferociously on their takeaways for a few moments. Then Maeve swallowed and put her box down. 'Ach, listen tae us talk shite. All this is hard work. It's far easier to up sticks and leave.'

'Is it, though?' Caroline asked. 'I'm feared leaving'll be the hardest thing any of us ever do.'

'Fuck's sake, Caroline,' Maeve said. 'It's Derry you're going tae, not the moon!'

Fidelma sat back and let a rift out of her. 'Sure, whether it's London or Derry, ye can always get yerself back home if ye're needed or if ye want. Not like my sister over beyond in Australia. Haven't spoken tae her this three years.'

'Three years!' Caroline said, putting her hand on her chest. 'That's wild.'

'But ah've a plan tae get her on the phone wan of these days,' Fidelma said, with satisfaction.

Maeve didn't want to admit how pleased she was to see Aoife standing at her ironing board first thing Thursday morning. 'Missed you!' she'd said, making Aoife go all pink-cheeked.

But as the morning wore on, she realised that something had changed between them. For years she'd believed that if only she had something that Aoife craved – like the Nirvana *Out-cesticide* bootleg – things would be easier between them. But now she'd earned the results that Aoife'd needed, the gap between them hadn't narrowed. It had cracked wide open.

That gap was the reason Maeve found herself going slow at the shirts, letting Aoife get way ahead her. The gap was the reason she tried to make herself smaller and quieter, less pleased with herself, so she wouldn't upset Aoife.

She slipped her iron over a shirt collar, wondering if that's what it'd been like for Aoife for years. That maybe Aoife'd never really enjoyed her house and clothes and music and books and soft carpets and parents with Maeve hanging around with her dead sister and shabby shoes and the hungry look in her eyes.

Maeve realised Aoife needed friends who were like her. And Trinity College Dublin would be crawling with folk like Aoife.

Maeve's guts sank as she realised it was her who'd end up being the fish out of water at university, not Aoife.

After lunch, Mary emerged from her office and huffed up the stairs to Andy's office. It wasn't like her to leave her office on a Thursday, when she was flat out with the pay cheques. Five minutes later, they both came down the stairs and stood grim-faced at the top of the floor.

'Oh ho,' Mabel Moore crowed. 'I told youse now. I told youse! Be some craic now.'

Maeve grabbed Aoife's arm and pulled her down the back of the factory, out of the firing line.

'I know you lot have been busting a gut for me these past few weeks,' Andy said. 'This McAllister's contract is a big deal for us. And you haven't put a foot wrong. Great work. Great shirts. You are doing a fantastic job. Absolutely fantastic.'

Andy looked around the factory, as if waiting for approval. But Mabel Moore pounced: 'Aye, Andy. We know we're fucken wonderful. But spit out what's troubling ye.'

Andy cleared his throat, then stared over the top of everyone's heads. 'Mary has learned from the administrator in McAllister's that our cheque won't clear until next week.'

Mary dropped her head as the factory floor erupted in fury.

'Well, Andrew Strawbridge,' Marilyn Spears snarled, 'that's your problem, not ours. We get paid the morrow and that's that.'

Andy folded his arms, staring at everyone like he was Sir Sidney Ruff-Diamond in *Carry on up the Khyber* and his workers were a laughable rabble of marauding natives. 'I'm here to ask a favour of you.'

'Favours are something ye do for friends, Andy Strawbridge,' Fidelma said. 'You're no friend of anyone in this factory.'

'I was relying on the McAllister's cheque to pay the wages this week,' Andy said.

'We don't rely on McAllister's,' Mickey McCanny shouted. 'We rely on you!'

'The McAllister's cheque will clear next Thursday,' Andy said, as though Mickey hadn't spoken a word, 'on which day, I will pay you for two weeks' work.'

'Like fuck ye will!'

'Ye think we're thick?'

'And how d'ye think we'll feed our weans this week coming?'

'Look,' Andy said. 'I haven't drawn pay at all this past month. Have I, Mary?'

Mary pulled her lips to the side and shook her head.

'It's one week,' he continued. 'I'm not pretending it's going to be easy. I know what it's like to have bills to pay.'

'It's not an XJS Jag we're paying off,' Mabel said. 'We're trying to put food on the fucken table.'

'You can't get blood from a stone,' Andy said, like it was a done deal. 'So it's your choice. You can walk now, and pick up a single week's pay next week. Or you can work now, and pick up double next week.'

'You're a real fucker, Andy Strawbridge!' Marilyn Spears shouted, stomping up the factory floor. 'I've got weans to feed! And a mortgage to pay! How am ah supposed tae trust a snake like you?' She stopped and glared at the other machinists. 'Ah'm walking!' she shouted. 'Ah'm fucken walking and getting work some other road.'

A few other Prods pushed back their chairs and joined her. But most people sat where they were, sunk into their chairs, stunned.

'If enough of you walk,' Andy said. 'I'll walk too.'

Marilyn Spears had a head of steam worked up so she kept going. But Mabel Moore and Sharon Rogers hesitated at the door. And Billy wasn't in the thick of things for once. He was standing quietly by the cutting machine.

'I'll shut these factory doors and I won't open them again,' Andy said. 'I've plenty of other options.'

Maeve didn't believe that Andy'd plenty of other options. But he had some. Most of them didn't have any other options.

'Think it over,' he said, before walking up the stairs to his office.

Fidelma Hegarty slammed her foot into her trolley of shirts, sending it flying against the wall. She eyed it like she was considering teaching it a lesson it wouldn't forget, before letting a big sigh out of her. She turned around. 'Anyone for a smoke?'

'Me,' Maeve said. Caroline and Aoife nodded, and they all followed Fidelma out of the side door. The factory gates yawned at the edge of the car park. Paddy Quinn was standing nearby, speaking to a small group of machinists. Everything felt unreal to Maeve, the way it had during Deirdre's funeral. She felt like she was an actress in a soap opera, waiting for someone else to write her next scene, to tell her where to stand, how to look, and when to scream.

'I think we need to quit,' Aoife said. 'He's not going to pay us what we're owed. Not when he's defrauding the place.'

Fidelma Hegarty squinted at Aoife with one eye. 'What are you shiting on about?'

'Me and my daddy had a look into this place. We analysed our pay. The number of shirts we do. The grants he gets. It doesn't add up.'

'So he's screwing us.' Fidelma shrugged. 'Big grants in. Skinny wages out. His pockets lined with gold. And not a scrap of evidence to prove a thing.'

Maeve thought of the fake payroll burning in Ciarán Friel's grate. 'I don't think it's just Andy who's lining his pockets,' she said, quietly.

'What d'ye mean?' Fidelma snapped.

'It's just something Mary said to me ages ago,' Maeve said, staring at the ground. 'About how Andy manages the factory. But someone else runs it. And I heard Ciarán Friel say that Andy pays his community dues.'

'Protection money?' Aoife said.

Maeve nodded, wondering how things would've gone if she'd taken the payroll to Aoife.

'Then shouldn't we explain to Ciarán that Andy's not paid us?'

Fidelma looked at Aoife the way Maeve's mam used to look at her during a time she believed in moving statues. 'Ah think the wisest thing for all of us tae do is tae steer clear of Ciarán Friel. He probably knew about the McAllister's cheque before Mary did.'

Maeve's stomach turned. She didn't feel like admitting what she'd done to anyone, let alone Fidelma.

'So we should walk, like Aoife's saying,' Caroline said, shoving her hands deep in her pockets. 'I mean, we need this week's money, but we could do without being screwed for another week.'

'Youse uns have no weans, no mortgages,' Fidelma said. 'Ye could fire JP a week's notice on the flat and move back

262

home. If I were youse ah'd spend the rest of me summer in front of the telly. Or fuck away aff tae England early.'

'She's not wrong,' Caroline said. 'Auntie Joan'd put you up, no bother, Maeve. Ye could get a job over in London. Get yer feet on the ground.'

Maeve stared at the tarmac. She could be in London by the weekend.

'Or we could go to France for a few weeks.'

Everyone turned and gawped at Aoife.

'We could stay in our villa,' she said. 'It'd only cost us the price of a ferry and rail tickets. Barely a week's wages.'

'Is that an open invitation, Miss O'Neill?' Fidelma said. 'These dolls and me?'

'Of course, Fidelma . . . I mean, if you'd like to join us, we could . . .'

'Ah'm ripping the piss,' Fidelma said, laughing from deep in her chest. Then she got serious. 'Ah've a notion to head tae England meself. Fucken sick of the same oul shite here.'

'Would ye leave the town, Fidelma?' Caroline said, big-eyed. 'Would ye?'

'Ah would,' Fidelma said, defiantly.

'And what would ye do over in England?' Maeve asked.

'Ah've me own notions about that.' Fidelma shut her mouth tight and crossed her arms. Maeve tried to imagine how Fidelma'd do over in England. Probably no worse than her, if she was honest. But she wasn't convinced that running to London early was the right answer.

'Where's Mary?' Fidelma asked, peering in the door.

'She's out at the front door there with Mabel Moore and Marilyn,' Aoife said.

'Right, Maeve. Ah need you tae go and keep an eye on her. Try and keep her occupied. And gimme a shout when she's heading back inside.'

'What are you gonna do, Fidelma?' Maeve asked, her heart pounding. 'Are ye going to go looking for evidence of fraud?'

'Fuck naw,' Fidelma said, sauntering indoors. 'What would ah do with evidence? Ah'm away tae Mary's office tae ring me sister in Australia. Been far too friggen long.'

Later that evening, Caroline and Maeve were watching *Top of the Pops*. Liam Gallagher was droning 'Live Forever' over the heads of some seriously stokey English dolls. Maeve had a fear on her that she'd have to dress like that to pass as English, which she supposed might be less embarrassing than ending up like Auntie Joan.

'So, are we gonna get up Monday morning and head into the factory to work for no wages for another week instead of sailing to France tomorrow?' Saying it out loud, Maeve realised they were mad to stay in the factory. That they should pack their bags and go someplace hot, foreign and sexy for the first time in their lives.

'Och, France is just silliness. It'd cost a pile of money and there's a load of travelling. It's a wild lot of work for a few days away in the sun, d'ye not think?'

Caroline didn't often spit the dummy. Maeve took a few seconds to gather her thoughts.

'We'd be far better off in France than here. It's not like a break in Bundoran.'

'But my French is shite.'

'You don't need to speak the lingo. Aoife'd be dying to do a bit of ooh lah lahing.'

'It's Nana Jackson's birthday soon. I've never missed her birthday.'

'Och, Caroline, there's plenty more ahead of her! Go on. I'll go if you go. It'll be an adventure.'

'I don't want tae go without Martin.'

Maeve felt a big, fat bubble burst in her gut.

'Youse two can go on your own,' Caroline said, softly. 'You and Aoife always have fun.'

'Me and Aoife do not always have fun. *We* have fun. The three of us.'

Caroline shook her head, gentle but firm.

Maeve sagged into her chair. 'So we'd need to think about giving notice on this place. I'm heading to London the second week of September. When are you starting Magee?'

Caroline's face took on an odd stubborn cast that Maeve rarely saw on a Jackson. 'Ah'm not.'

'Eh? What do you mean you're not?'

'Ah'm not going tae university. Ah'm going tae stay here. Ah can't face more school.'

'What? But ye got three Bs! You could do anything with three Bs! You could be a– a fucking *dentist* if ye wanted!'

'And what I want tae do,' Caroline said, folding her arms, 'is stay here.'

'And how are you gonna afford the flat?'

'Me and Martin've talked about keeping it on. We're going tae look at jobs outside the town.'

'You and Martin living in sin, Caroline? What'll your mam and dad say? What'll Nana Jackson think?'

Caroline took a reddener. 'Martin reckons they'll get used tae us living together. It's different times, so it is. And he says they'll be happy having me near home. Magee's wild far away.'

'It's only forty-five minutes up the road.'

'Forty-five minutes in a car, Maeve. It's two hours on the bus. And they can't be dragging Nana on the bus, or leaving her on her own.'

Maeve remembered what her mam'd said at the start of the summer: 'She's a Jackson, and Jacksons sit tight.'

No France for Maeve. No university for Caroline. Still, there was an upside.

'That spare room's mine come Christmas.'

'Ah'll put a wee stocking out for you,' Caroline said, with a smile.

Monday, 22 August 1994

9 days before the flight of the girls

Everyone slunk back to work on Monday. Everyone except for Aoife.

'Daddy said to steer clear,' she'd said to Maeve. 'I've got to start swotting up on my Irish.'

The factory'd never felt so grim. There was no craic. No singing along to the radio. No banter at the break. But Maeve had a fair idea that if she didn't turn up for work that week, she'd have no hope of getting her wages for the week before.

Every morning a truck pulled up to deliver the McAllister's material. Billy sliced it into pieces before the machinists stitched them together.

As Maeve ironed, not knowing if she'd get a penny for her work, she pictured the shirts sweat-stained and beer-spattered, filled with English meat, being worn in English towns with names like Upper Bucklebury or Thrumpton.

Mary was living on her nerves, chain-smoking fags, barely taking time to have a sup of tea. She wasn't seen at the biccies all week.

Andy spent more time than usual on the factory floor, pacing around like oul Fatty Dolan on the corridors during a school inspection. Maeve watched him for clues as to whether or not he was shitting them. She wanted to believe that he was telling the truth about the McAllister's contract, even if he was screwing Invest NI, and that she'd get paid alongside all those non-existent workers on Andy's list. But if McAllister's weren't colluding with Andy, they were probably fucking him over. And even if McAllister's were honest, someone above them would be fucking them over in turn. It was the factory workers – both Prods and Taigs – who were at the bottom of a very long and merciless food chain.

One evening that week, Maeve stood beside Fidelma, watching Paddy and Billy carry the boxed shirts out of the door.

'The only stuff left in this place overnight is what's nailed to the floor,' Fidelma said.

She was right. The machines, tables, radiators and toilets were screwed in place. And though Maeve didn't feel nailed to the floor, she'd the impression Andy had an invisible collar and chain around her neck, tying her to the factory.

As Maeve watched telly in the evenings after work, she kept an eye on Andy's office window. When his blinds clipped shut, she moved to the window to watch him leave the premises. She wasn't the only one watching. A knot of lads from her side sat on the lip of the window outside the shop, eyeballing Andy as Billy locked the factory doors. They nodded at him as his car stopped at the gate, as though at a checkpoint. Then they watched him roar off up the road while Paddy Quinn locked the gates. After Paddy pocketed the padlock key, he'd nod at Billy, then raise his hand at the lads, who'd disperse without saying another word.

That Thursday, Mary'd been tucked away in her office for most of the day, her door and blinds closed. She didn't come into the canteen for the second tea break.

Mabel Moore, who was at the head of the queue, began lamenting. 'No biccies? No biccies, is it? Well, let me tell youse now, there's a bad oul smell about this place,' she said, hobbling to her table. She sat down, shaking her head over her tea. 'No biccies indeed.'

The machinists rummaged in their handbags in search of emergency KitKats and Twixes. They broke the chocolate bars into bits and shared them out like Jesus and the disciples had shared the loaves and fish.

But Mabel wasn't consoled by a finger of KitKat. She kept up her dirge. 'If there's not even a dry Rich Tea biccie for my cuppa, ah can't see there being tuppence in the bank.'

Mabel hadn't done a stitch all week. She'd clocked in on time every morning, but then squatted in front of her sewing machine doing fuck fanny all. Whenever she fancied a change of scenery, she'd hobbled out to the emergency exit, hitched her skirt up over her knees, and spread her legs, saying, 'Well, at least the sun's for free, any roads.' She did a few rounds of the sewing machines from time to time, gossiping, but she didn't once lift a finger to help with production.

'Well, there's no point in droning on about biccies, Mabel,' Fidelma said, rolling her eyes. 'If we're fucked, we're fucked.'

'How can you look at the empty biccie tin and not see what that Andy buck's telling us? That frigger won't even dip intil his own pocket for a fiver for a few biccies!'

Mabel's words lodged in Maeve's spine. She didn't see the point in mouthing off – it only made things worse. Quitting now'd be like giving up on a novena on the ninth day. And Maeve knew she wasn't the only person who dreaded not working, who feared the weight of empty hours that pressed you deeper and deeper into everything you wanted to run screaming from.

When the bell rang, they trudged back onto the factory floor. Andy was pacing at the top of the factory floor, his arms folded, a frown eating into his forehead.

'Och, now, what's this, eh?' Mabel asked. 'What's this buck at now?'

Andy didn't look at them as they filed into place. He cleared his throat before speaking. 'I was in the bank earlier ascertaining the status of the McAllister's cheque.'

'Try again Andy, this time in English,' Marilyn said.

Andy tightened his lips and took a deep breath. 'The McAllister's cheque has cleared. There's money in the bank.'

A cheer burst out – the loudest and longest Maeve had heard all summer. Andy stood with a big smug head on him, waiting for the noise to die down. 'Mary's in her office,' he said, 'preparing your wage packets. She'll have them ready for you lot to take home this evening. The bank will be closed, but I've been assured that you may cash them first thing tomorrow.'

'How in God's name will Mary calculate the bonuses for the week?' Mabel asked.

'Ah'm sure figuring your bonus out'll not fry Mary's brains,' Fidelma jeered.

'Mary has already calculated your basics and bonuses from last week,' Andy said. 'She'll add that to your basic for this week. You'll get that cheque today. This week's bonuses will be added to next week's pay. Then we'll be back to normal.' Andy looked around, obviously pleased with himself. 'Any questions?'

'Are ye gonna backdate the biccies?' Mabel asked.

Andy laughed, then turned and climbed the stairs to his office.

'Ah was serious about the friggen biscuits,' Mabel said, firing a dirty look at his back.

Just before the final bell rang, Mary emerged from her office clutching a bundle of envelopes. She went to the front door and stood there doling out cheques. Mickey McCanny muttered 'Thanks,' at Mary, before crumpling his cheque into his back pocket. Maeve took her cheque without a word, tucked it into her jeans pocket and left the factory.

Mabel was leaning beside the gates, puffing on a fag.

'Are you right there, Mabel? Heading down the town fer a drink?'

'I am not,' Mabel said, shaking her head. 'We've cashed nothin yet. Them cheques is only bits of paper. Ah'll not rest til ah see Queen Elizabeth – God bless her – resting in mah hand.'

She dropped her fag end on the ground and hobbled off home.

Maeve pushed the living room window wide open when she woke the next morning. The day had the smell of a scorcher getting going, the sun burning over the wet hills, the factory standing grey and dusty under clear blue skies. Maeve loved the dregs of summer, when you had to suck the goodness from each sunny hour, for fear it'd be the last of the heat for the year. She'd just sat down with a cup of tea when she heard a disturbance on the street below. She got up and looked out of the window.

Marilyn Spears and a few Prods were banging on the factory door. Mabel Moore was standing to the side, grim-faced, her arms folded over her chest. A sick feeling rolled up from Maeve's stomach to her throat. She ran to Caroline's door and battered it. 'Caroline! Get up! There's ructions down at the factory.'

Maeve rushed back to the window. 'C'mon! There's a crowd of Prods trying to bate the door down.'

Caroline staggered into the living room, blinking in the daylight.

Outside, a few folk from their side of the town were storming up the road to join the mob of Prods at the factory doors.

'What time is it?' Caroline asked.

Maeve glanced at her watch. 'Quarter past nine.'

'So the cheques have bounced,' Caroline said, folding her arms.

Maeve sat down heavily in her chair and squeezed her eyes shut.

'That's not going to help,' Caroline said. 'Get yer clothes on so we can go and see what the craic is.'

Maeve and Caroline crossed the road and joined the edge of the crowd without a notion what they were going to do. Maeve pictured herself with a camera crew reporting live from the scene as Marilyn Spears battered at the factory door. 'So what happened?' she asked Mickey McCanny.

'We were down the bank first thing,' Mickey replied, shaking his head. 'They wouldn't entertain us. Said Andy hasn't lodged a penny this past month.' He popped a cigarette between his lips, then offered Maeve the packet. She took a fag and rolled it between her fingers, thinking of the fat Invest NI cheque Andy had received, big enough to cover a month or more of factory wages. She wondered which bank had cashed that for him.

'So what's the craic now?'

'They reckon Mary's in there,' Mickey said. 'The gates were open when we came up.'

'And no sign of that Andy Strawbridge bucko, I bet,' Caroline said, jerking her head back.

'None. Ah'd say we've seen the last of that fucker.' Mickey hawked some snotters out of his throat, then spat on the ground.

'So we're all in the same boat.'

'Aye. Floating up Shit Creek without a paddle.'

Maeve wasn't fit to light her fag. She put it between her lips and tipped her chin in Mickey's direction. He struck his lighter and held it out. She'd just taken her first puff when there was a commotion at the door. Mary shouted something from inside the factory and Baldy Magee roared at everyone to get back. But nobody moved until Billy Stone guldered, 'Back fuck yeez anyway,' like he was addressing a trample of hungry cattle. Everyone retreated and came to a standstill, listening to the scrape of the deadlock being pulled back inside the factory.

Mary pushed the door open.

'Where's our money?'

'Pack of thieving cunts.'

'How am ah gonna feed mah weans?'

'Ah've a mortgage tae pay.'

'Where the fuck is he? Where is the cunt?'

Mary wilted under the barrage of abuse. Mabel Moore shoved her way to the front of the crowd and put herself between Mary and the mob. 'Take her easy, will youse? No point in roaring Mary down! If youse calm yerselves we might get some answers!'

Mary pulled her cardigan tight around her diddies as the dogs in the parks started to bark. Maeve turned around. Something inside her warmed at the sight of Fidelma Hegarty bulling down Barrack Street past a Brit patrol.

'Why didn't ye warn us, Mary?' Mabel said. 'Wan week of being fooled was bad enough. But ye let us go two.'

'Ah'm wild sorry,' Mary said, tugging the hair on the nape of her neck. 'He had me fooled and all. Ah saw the cheques coming in, and him going down to lodge them. Ah thought he was playing us fair.'

'Thon fucker play fair?'

'Could ye not've checked up on him?'

Mary shoved her glasses back up her nose, but kept her eyes on the ground. 'Ah thought he was playing us fair.'

'Ach, Mary, since when've the English ever played us fair?' Fidelma Hegarty said.

Maeve picked up the drone of a helicopter coming from the direction of the army base. It was really fucking annoying how quickly the Brits could scramble to this sort of scene, though it'd take them hours to turn up to an alleyway where a lone Catholic was getting his head kicked in by a crowd of Prods.

Marilyn Spears barged towards Mary, bristling with fury. 'Well, ah'm gonna take a machine fer what's owed til me.' She pushed past Mary and entered the factory. A surge of people carried Maeve towards the door as a helicopter thumped in and hung low over their heads. Maeve tucked her chin down to avoid the camera lens above. Then three army jeeps screeched to a halt. The back doors flung open and a dose of Brits trained their guns on the crowd. It thinned out and a sullen, explosive silence settled in the yard. Everyone kept an eye on the guns, which were harder to evade than the overhead cameras.

'No surprise whose side those fuckers are on,' Mickey McCanny grunted.

A fleet of armoured police cars pulled up. Two cops climbed out of the first car and took a long, slow look around. Sweat trickled down the face of the biggest fella, who'd the intractable look of a man reared by a Bible and a bowler hat. He walked towards Mary. 'Everything alright here?'

Mary shrugged. The cop took another look around and tried again. 'Having a bit of bother, are ye?'

Mary stared at the ground.

'There was cheques bounced this morning,' Mabel Moore said. 'Two weeks this factory owes us. Two weeks' money.'

The big policeman nodded. 'And where's the proprietor?'

'Frig knows.'

'And who's responsible for the factory in the proprietor's absence?'

Mary croaked 'Me,' then pulled her cardigan even tighter around her.

'I think the best course of action right now would be for us to help you secure these premises,' the big policeman said to Mary, before nodding at his colleagues, who were resting half in, half out of their vehicles, nursing their guns. They stood up and moved in closer.

'I suggest you follow up with the proprietor next week, during normal working hours.'

Mary glanced at Billy Stone, who frowned at Paddy Quinn. Paddy moved his head so slightly it could've been a twitch. Then Mary nodded at the policeman.

'Right then. Let's get this place closed up for now. And I'm afraid the rest of you will have to move on.'

But nobody moved. The police were used to Maeve's side disobeying orders, but she could tell by the wee glances they were firing at the Prods that this was a new dynamic for them.

'I said, you'll all have to move on. This is an industrial matter, best settled by negotiations between your union representative and management.'

As another two police officers slowly stepped in behind the two cops, Fidelma and Mabel eyed each other.

'There's no union in this factory.'

The big policeman tilted his head back into his neck to look at Fidelma. 'No union?'

'Naw,' Mabel said. 'So we've tae speak for ourselves.'

Paddy Quinn frowned and glanced at Billy Stone. Maeve wondered if it was the spectacle of women standing up to the so-called security forces that was getting their dander up.

The smaller cop came to the front, shifting his gun as if checking it was a TV prop. 'Without the management on site, or the proprietor here,' he said, 'I don't believe a meaningful dialogue can take place.'

'And I don't believe a "meaningful dialogue" can take place even if the proprietor was here,' Fidelma said.

A murmur of agreement rumbled through the crowd, which drew tighter together.

Maeve saw a Brit bark something into a walkie talkie before one of the Land Rovers emptied out. The soldiers took up positions in the car park, surrounding them.

'So that's the craic, is it?' Fidelma said.

Maeve moved deeper into the heart of the crowd. Never in her life had she wanted to be so close to a pack of Prods.

'I'd like to ask youse – again – to leave these premises,' the burly wee policeman said. 'Or we may have to consider booking you for trespass.'

The crowd felt skittish, like sheep shoaling against a wild dog.

'Right,' Fidelma said. 'C'mon, youse uns. We'll tackle Andy another time.'

'Aye,' Mabel concurred. 'No point in wasting these good officers' time. They've work tae do. Hunting criminals, tackling terrorists and the like.'

Voices spat and crackled on the security force radios as the soldiers watched the crowd retreat outside the gates. For a few minutes they milled around together, everyone grumbling, while Paddy and Billy locked the factory doors and chained the gates under police supervision. Then it started to lash rain.

'What'll we do now?' Mabel Moore asked Fidelma.

Fidelma shrugged. 'There's nowhere we can take this lot for a chat. At least no place neutral.'

As Mickey McCanny kicked the wire factory fence, Maeve suddenly remembered the only time in her life she'd bounced in synchrony with a Prod. 'We could all head tae the leisure centre!' she said.

Mabel hunched over against the rain. 'Ah think I'm a bit past playing five-a-side. Ah'm away home for a cuppa tay.'

Mabel shambled off up the road with Marilyn Spears, and everyone else dispersed. Maeve climbed the stairs to the flat, wondering where Andy'd slunk off to, and if they'd ever see him again.

Saturday, 27 August 1994

4 days before the flight of the girls

The sun had already sunk behind the Donegal hills, even though it was only half eight. There was the bite of autumn about the evening. Caroline and Martin were over minding Nana Jackson so that Mrs Jackson could get out to clean the chapel. Maeve had asked Aoife and James to come over for a few drinks.

'I suppose you'll be away to England by the time I'm back from France,' James said.

Maeve raised her eyebrows and nodded. She hadn't counted on the goodbyes starting this early.

'That summer flew by,' Aoife said, staring out of the window at the factory.

'It did, aye,' Maeve said. 'Kind of feels like we should have our shoes polished and our new uniforms ready for going back to school next week.'

'No more uniforms for you now, Maeve!' Fidelma said.

'Not unless I end up in McDonald's.'

Fidelma'd ambushed them with a bag of cider just after Aoife had opened a bottle of wine. She didn't seem one bit annoyed to be drinking with the O'Neills. The discomfort was all Maeve's.

'When are you leaving?' James asked.

Maeve shrugged. She hadn't changed her ticket yet.

'Sure, ye could head any minute, for there's no factory tae go back to,' Fidelma said.

'Could we not talk about something else other than getting out of town?' Maeve asked.

'Jesus, what's ateing you?' Fidelma demanded. 'Sure, getting the fuck out of this place is all you've whinged about all summer.'

'Aye. Well. Maybe I want tae enjoy my last couple of weeks here,' Maeve said, as if she had something other than the Brits to occupy her.

'Who's that?' Aoife asked, frowning out of the window.

Maeve stood up and stared down at the street below. Someone was fiddling with the lock on the factory gates. 'Not sure. Fidelma, come see.'

Fidelma went over and they watched the intruder open the gate, slip through, then shut it and rearrange the chain so it looked closed. When he started walking towards the factory, Maeve recognised the strut.

'Andy Strawbridge,' Fidelma said, sounding both surprised and pleased.

James jumped up and came to the window as Andy let himself into the factory and closed the door behind him.

'What on earth's he up to?' Aoife asked.

'No idea,' Fidelma said. Then she sank her can, sat down and began lacing up her trainers.

'Where're you going?' Maeve asked, rather pointlessly.

'Tae do a bittay overtime,' Fidelma said, standing up. 'Here, gimme yer spare keys.'

'They're on the mantelpiece,' Maeve said.

Fidelma picked up the keys, lifted a couple of cans of cider, said, 'See yeez later,' and dandered out the door.

Maeve grabbed her trainers and turned to Aoife and James. They hadn't moved. 'Well? Are youse coming?'

James glanced at Aoife, who shook her head.

Maeve looked out of the window again. Down below, Fidelma pushed the factory gates wide open, then she walked towards the gloomy brick building, leaving the gates gaping behind her. Maeve looked back at Aoife and James. 'Well?' she said.

The O'Neills said nothing.

'We can't let Fidelma head over there alone!'

James glanced at Aoife, then rubbed the back of his neck. 'She's trespassing,' he said.

'She's what?'

'I know it seems like a bit of craic,' Aoife said. 'But, technically, Fidelma's trespassing. If I get caught down there and get a record, I won't be able to practise law. My career would be over before it started.'

Maeve sat down. 'But it's not right, us leaving Fidelma to face him alone.'

'Maeve,' James said, softly, 'a criminal prosecution won't make much of a difference to Fidelma's life. But it'd mess things up for you worse than you can imagine.' He sat on the rickety wee coffee table, which creaked weakly in protest. Aoife took a big glug from her wine glass.

Maeve placed her trainers on the floor, then took up her tin of cider and emptied it down her throat. 'I could live with a criminal prosecution,' she said, wiping her mouth with the back of her hand. 'But I can't live with letting a friend down.' She pushed her feet into her trainers, then got up and lurched down the stairs.

The factory floor glowed orange under the gleam of the street-lamps. Maeve walked to the bottom of the stairs and stopped to listen. Andy's voice rumbled from behind his office door, Fidelma growling almost as low in response. Maeve took a deep breath and started to climb the stairs. When she opened the office door, both Fidelma and Andy looked around sharply.

'Ms Murray. I have to say I'm surprised to see you trespassing, as well.'

'Ach, sure, Maeve's no more trespassing than I am myself. Sure, we're here for the overtime.'

Fidelma gazed at Andy in high good humour, her eyes twinkling as if she were Terry Wogan with a particularly interesting guest on her couch. Andy, for once, didn't look like he was pleased to be where he was.

'I hope you closed the gates and door after you, Ms Murray, as your friend Fidelma had the good sense to do.'

Fidelma's eyebrow flicked up at Maeve.

'Aye, surely,' Maeve said. 'We wouldn't want any gate-crashers at your leaving party.'

'So it's just the three of us here, Mr Strawbridge, sir,' Fidelma said. 'And, sure, we can help ye finish off whatever it was ye left undone.'

Andy sighed irritably, slung his jacket on his chair and sat down. 'Frankly, Fidelma, it's none of your business.'

'Ach now, Andy,' Fidelma said, sitting on Andy's desk. 'That's not very friendly.' She stared down at the forms and books littering the surface. 'D'ye want a can, Maeve? Andy here says he doesn't drink and drive.'

'Good to know he's got some standards,' Maeve said, taking a tin. She nearly licked the hiss of it opening, her mouth was that dry.

'So, where are ye parked, Andy? I couldn't see yer Jag out there,' Fidelma asked.

'It doesn't matter where I parked,' Andy said, checking his watch. 'I'd like to suggest that you two ladies jog on.'

'Are ye expecting someone?' Maeve asked, conscious of the sting in her voice.

'As a matter of fact, I am, Ms Murray. And trust me, you'd be better off not getting in any deeper with these chaps.'

Maeve remembered her conversation with Ciarán Friel. She glanced at Fidelma, no longer cocky. Then something clattered on the factory floor below. Voices rang out and someone cackled.

Andy frowned and got to his feet. 'Did you tell anyone you were coming here?'

Fidelma opened her eyes wide and shook her head. 'Didn't say a word tae no one.'

Andy opened the office door and stepped quietly onto the mezzanine.

'Keep him occupied,' Fidelma said, shoving Maeve out of the door towards Andy. She crept out behind him, clutching her cider. On the floor below, figures moved between the tables. Someone switched on a torch and flashed a beam of light over the factory floor, illuminating slices of people, machines and chairs.

'Fuck,' Andy said, quietly.

'Not who you were expecting?' Maeve asked.

Andy turned around, furious. 'This is not a game.'

She shrank back from him. 'I never said it was, Andy.'

He strode towards her and Maeve retreated, realising too late that she'd backed herself into the dead end of the mezzanine.

Then the door to his office opened and Fidelma strolled out. 'Ach, Maeve. It's time you left Mr Strawbridge to get on with his work.'

Andy glared at Fidelma, who squared up to him almost gently, drawing herself to her full height. Andy snorted and turned to the factory floor as Maeve slid towards Fidelma.

'You OK?' Fidelma asked, as they started down the stairs.

'Ah'm grand,' Maeve said, trying to forget the look in Andy's eyes when he'd moved in on her.

They were halfway down the stairs when the lights flickered on. Maeve froze and shielded her eyes as the light juddered across the factory. Mickey McCanny put his hands in the air, looking around for the Brits. Mabel Moore scowled up the stairs, her face scrunched up against the light. Marilyn Spears frowned up at Maeve, one arm wrapped around herself, as if she was cold, the other deflecting the light.

Andy gazed at them from over the balcony. Maeve held her breath, waiting for someone to move, for somebody to grab an iron bar and charge up the stairs and give Andy the hiding they'd talked about.

But only Mabel Moore moved. She sat down with a sigh. 'Scuttling back off tae wherever it is ye crawled outtay, eh, Andy?' she said, wearily.

'At least I have somewhere to go,' he said smirking.

Then the factory door swung open and Billy Stone and Paddy Quinn walked in. They stopped at the sight of their former colleagues.

Maeve wanted Billy to charge up the stairs and take a swing at Andy. For Paddy Quinn to fell him. For Mabel to spit in his face. For Fidelma to batter him good looking.

'Gentlemen,' Andy said. 'Should we conclude our business?'

Billy Stone nodded, then glanced at Paddy Quinn, who jerked his head as if to say, 'After you, my good fellow.' Maeve gawped as they walked across the factory floor towards Andy.

'So that's how Equal Opportunities works is it?' Fidelma said. 'Him up there charming the knickers off Invest NI for grants, and the pair of youse down here shafting us behind our backs? Great to see that all the investment in community relations has paid off.'

Paddy Quinn paused at the bottom of the stairs, his face dark with bad temper. 'Yeez didn't do too badly out of the set-up. Yeez all got paid for long enough. More money than youse would've seen on the dole.'

'No harm, but ah'm still short a couple of weeks,' Fidelma said. 'Is that what you're here tae sort out? What's owed tae us?'

'Ah suggest ye take a look around,' Billy said. 'See if there's anything that'd compensate ye for your pains.'

They climbed the stairs and disappeared into the office with Andy. When the door snapped closed, the factory floor erupted into activity. Maeve saw Marilyn Spears on her hands and knees, unscrewing her sewing table from the floor. Mabel Moore was puffing on a fag and swiping armloads of sewing thread into a bin bag. Mickey McCanny was gathering shirts and piling them into a trolley, while Baldy Magee was tackling the screws on a radiator.

Maeve took a big swallow of cider and considered what she should rob.

'Get down them stairs now and follow me,' Fidelma said, prodding Maeve in the ribs.

As she passed the repairs table, Fidelma lifted a pair of scissors and passed another pair to Maeve.

'Souvenirs,' she said, grinning. Then she ducked out of the front door.

Maeve followed her out and up the road. 'Where are ye going, Fidelma?'

'Ah'm after his car.'

'Eh?'

'Andy's Jag. Ah want tae find where he's parked.'

Then it clicked with Maeve. Fidelma was going to hit Andy where it hurt. 'I think I know where he might've left it,' she said, turning down the road towards the garages in their park. And, sure enough, Andy's car was pulled neatly into the shadows beside the garages where strangers parked, next to Martin's Vauxhall Astra.

'Lovely machine, eh?' Fidelma said, fondly.

Maeve's hand tightened around the scissors in her pocket. She looked around. There wasn't a being about.

'Won't be so lovely after we're done,' she said, raising the scissors above the bonnet.

'What the fuck are ye at, Maeve Murray?' Fidelma hissed, grabbing her hand.

Maeve looked at Fidelma, confused. 'What?'

'We're not here tae wreck the car,' Fidelma said, reaching into her pocket. 'Ah've got the keys!'

Maeve stared as Fidelma clicked a button and the car winked awake. She climbed inside, then pushed the key in the ignition and lowered the passenger side window.

'C'mere and get a whiff of this. Great smell altogether. Leather,' she said, taking a good sniff. 'And there's a bit of that nice Andy smell too.'

'What the fuck are *you* at, Fidelma Hegarty?'

Fidelma clamped her can of cider between her thighs. 'Ye heard Billy yerself. He said tae look around for something tae compensate us for our trouble.'

'Ah think he was chatting about a sewing machine, not a friggen Jaguar!' Maeve said, as Fidelma started the engine.

'Och, now. Listen tae the rub of that.'

Maeve tried to open the passenger door, but it was locked. 'Fuck. Open it, will ye?'

Fidelma looked over at Maeve, shaking her head as if to say, 'Ach, God help your innocent wit.'

'Maeve, you're not coming with me. Ye don't want tae be caught in a stolen car. Not when ye've a future ahead of ye. Get yerself away over home and put yerself tae bed.' Fidelma pressed a button and the window hummed closed. Then she put the car into gear and drove off up the border road.

Maeve heard the twang of Garth Brooks from inside the flat even before she got to the top of the stairs: Caroline and Martin were back, but otherwise occupied. She grabbed the left-over cider, then shut herself inside her bedroom. She tore the MURDER LATEST NEWS AND PICTURES newspaper off the window, then sat with the lights off, smoking and drinking, watching her former colleagues stagger out of the factory loaded with sewing machines, radiators, tables and chairs. Mickey McCanny ran out the door holding an ironing board, looking as if he was heading for a surf. Eventually Andy left the factory, flanked by Paddy and Billy.

Maeve knew the shit was about to hit the fan. She slipped away from the window and climbed into bed. She hoped Fidelma was miles away. And she hoped she'd have the good sense never to come back.

The next morning, Fidelma dandered into Maeve's living room as if she'd just gotten in from Sunday morning mass. 'Hiya!'

she said, before sitting down on the sofa and firing the spare key for the flat on the coffee table.

'And where the fuck've you been?' Maeve asked, sounding way too like her mam.

'Ah took a spin over the border tae see family,' Fidelma said, grinning. 'Does my heart good seeing family.'

'In Andy's car?'

'Ah wouldn't know what you're talking about, Maeve Murray.'

'Och, Fidelma, what'd ye do tae it?'

Fidelma looked at Maeve, then reached inside her denim jacket and threw a wad of cash on the coffee table. Maeve raised her eyebrows and crammed a fist against her mouth. 'Oh, fuck. *Fuck*. You're dead meat, Fidelma!'

'Ach. There's no law against winning money on a lottery ticket, is there?'

Maeve burst out laughing. 'Jesus, Fidelma. What are ye going tae do with all that cash?'

'That's only the half of it. Ah dropped in tae Mabel Moore earlier today. Told her tae divvy up the other half among her lot.'

'Ye did not.'

'Ah did too.' Fidelma picked up the wad of cash and peeled some notes off. 'And here ye go. Yer severance package from Strawbridge & Associates Shit Factory.' She placed the notes on the table.

Maeve picked them up and swiftly counted them. 'Fidelma. That's a whole lot more than two weeks' pay.'

'As ah said. It's not just yer pay. It's a severance package. What a union woulda negotiated for ye if we'd been allowed wan.'

Maeve sat and looked at the notes in her hand for a long time. Then she crammed the money into her pocket and laughed. 'But c'mere and tell me this, Fidelma – how'd you swing all this?'

'My mother's wee brother, over the border there, is a big man at the cars,' she said, getting to her feet. 'He's the fella what taught me to drive. But you keep that til yerself.' She peeled a few more notes from the wad of cash and put them on the coffee table. 'Make sure Caroline gets her share, will ye?' Maeve nodded as Fidelma tucked the wad down her top. 'Can't hang about,' she said, getting to her feet. 'Ah've a few more homes tae visit. Then ah'm gonna lie low for a bit.'

Before Maeve could say another word, Fidelma was up and out of the door. Maeve sat running her fingernail through the notes. Fidelma was right to lie low after pulling a stunt like that, for she'd have more than the police on her tail.

On Tuesday morning, Maeve was lying half-asleep in her bed when the doorbell rang. She'd kept a low profile since Fidelma's visit, sticking to the flat. So she lay on, leaving Caroline to answer the door. Her stomach flipped when she recognised her mam's voice – she was only a slightly less frightening visitor than Ciarán Friel.

'Right so. Ah'll go in tae her.'

Her mam didn't knock. She opened the bedroom door and stepped over Maeve's make-up, books, belts and shoes towards the bed. Maeve clenched her eyes shut and wrapped the sleeping bag tight around her, ready to resist her mam's attempt to drag her out of bed. But nothing happened. Maeve heard the rustle of a cigarette pack, the click of a lighter, a long smoky sigh. As she puffed on her fag, Maeve thought about the week Deirdre had taken to her bed. She'd only got up to use the toilet, and just ate whatever Maeve smuggled up to her room after their mam had banned Deirdre from carrying food upstairs. On Sunday, her mam'd filled a jug with cold water, walked into Deirdre's room, opened the curtains, and fired the water over her. Deirdre didn't even flinch as the water hit her. And she didn't get up for mass. She'd just lain on in her wet bed for the rest of the day.

Maeve wanted the storm of her mam's anger to break over her, for her to drag Maeve from the bed by her hair, like she'd done so many times before with Deirdre, as if she was trying to wrestle a sheep out of a flooded ditch. But all she heard was her mam fiddling with the catch on the window.

285

'We could do with a breath of fresh air in here.'

Maeve threw the sleeping bag off. 'We could do with a breath of fresh air in this fucken town.'

Her mam sat down on the end of Maeve's bed. An odd calm pooled in the room, crept like floodwater around them. 'Ciarán Friel called in to see me yesterday.'

Maeve suddenly wished her head was back under her sleeping bag. 'Did he now?'

'Aye. He says he heard you were up to no good in that factory.'

Maeve opened her eyes wide to say, 'Who, me?' and her mam narrowed her eyes to say, 'Aye, you.'

'There was more than me up to no good in there,' Maeve said, all sulky.

'And he said something about a stolen car.'

Maeve stared at the floor. 'The only thing I stole was a pair of scissors.'

'Look. Ah'll cut a long story short. He says you're not welcome here, not now, not never. You've got twenty-four hours tae get out. After that there'll be *consequences*.'

Something wicked grabbed a hold of Maeve's heart and squeezed.

'Do you understand what's going on, Maeve Murray?' her mam growled. 'Do you get what's happening?'

Maeve nodded. She knew what being run out of town meant. She'd not be allowed home to put up a stocking in the flat or flowers on Deirdre's grave come Christmas. There'd be no trips back for Easter eggs or weddings. No paying her respects at wakes or funerals, unless she crawled over broken glass on her hands and knees to beg Ciarán Friel's forgiveness.

'And d'ye know how lucky ye are? Tae get the chance tae walk away? Manys another didn't get away so lightly for getting up to less.'

Maeve sighed. Again with the luck. This particularly shitty brand of Six Counties luck.

'Ah called Ulsterbus,' her mam said with a sigh. 'They said ye can change yer tickets. And ah've had Donal in the shop hold on tae any sterling that came into the till this past while so you'd have English notes fer over beyond.' Her mam placed Deirdre's old purse on the bed. 'Ah'll take ye as far as Omagh on the ten o'clock bus the morrow.' She looked at Maeve as if she'd more to say. 'Ashtray?'

Later that evening, Maeve went up to the caravan park to see what the craic with Fidelma was. But she wasn't in and nobody knew where she'd gone. So she'd come home, stuck on some Placebo and gone pure mad with the matches. She'd lit every smelly candle in the fireplace and used up all the tea lights. Pale flames flickered in the late summer light on the mantel-piece, in saucers on the coffee table, and on the windowsill. Maeve was now sitting on the sofa, striking one match after another, watching each one burn to her nail before blowing the flame out.

'Sure it's like Diwali in here now,' Caroline said.

When she was wee, Maeve'd loved the idea of Diwali – the victory of light over darkness, hope over despair. But her bones knew the weight of a wake.

'More like my London wake. And only you tae mourn me.'

'Och, now, Maeve, Martin would've come y'know, only he thought—'

'I've a feeling I'll see enough of Martin tae do me in the years to come,' Maeve said, rolling her eyes.

Caroline went pink with anticipation.

'Ah wonder where Fidelma is,' Maeve said.

'Aye,' Caroline said, frowning. 'Ah was kinda expecting her tae drop in tae say goodbye.'

'Ah hope she's OK.' Maeve nodded.

'She'll be grand. Fidelma can take care of herself.'

'She's a boxer, not a bullet-proof tank,' Maeve said.

'She'll be grand. And so will you,' Caroline said.

Maeve looked at the mantelpiece where her ticket to London sat.

'Och, Caroline,' she burst out, 'I dunno what I'm gonna do over beyond without you.'

'You'll be fine. You'll get on fine,' Caroline said. 'You always do.'

'In a country full of Brits?'

'They won't all be wearing uniforms.'

'Huh. Too bad for me that that's the only way I like my Brits. Ah've no time for the undercover bastards.'

'You never know. Maybe you'll meet somebody nice.'

'Hard enough to find a nice man, let alone a nice Brit.'

'There's nice fellas about, ye know. Martin's decent. And James was always good to you.'

Maeve shot Caroline a don't-you-fucken-start look.

'Awww, Maeve I still think you should drop over. He heads tae France tomorrow. And you're away tae London. Ah just think a goodbye wouldn't kill ye.'

'Ah've enough goodbyes tae say.'

Maeve looked at her bags piled up in the hallway. She'd always dreamed of getting the fuck out of the town, but she'd never imagined not being allowed back. It was one thing to leave the shithole; it was a whole other thing to never be allowed to come home and turn your nose up at it, to never be able to show off your fancy new clothes and shoes, to revitalise your accent and, most important of all, to have your wings clipped so you didn't turn into a total dose.

Wednesday, 31 August 1994

The flight of the girls

Maeve stood beside her bags at the bus stop in Omagh. Cars were lapping the town, blaring horns, with men and boys hanging out of the windows, roaring, for the IRA had announced a ceasefire.

Maeve hoped the cessation of hostilities hadn't come too late for Fidelma.

The Belfast bus pulled in and the driver jumped out and opened the luggage hold. Maeve's mam stood silently watching the stampede for the bus. She'd not spoken to Maeve all morning. She lifted one of Maeve's bags and hefted it into the hold like she was dumping a body in a river. Maeve helped her heave the bags on board, wondering if her mam would cease her hostilities. When they were finished, her mam turned around, red-faced. 'Well. Ah suppose this is you.'

Maeve nodded. It had started to drizzle. The queue beside her had dwindled to a few studenty-looking types.

Suddenly Maeve's mam grabbed her tight. 'Just so ye know,' she said in her ear, 'ah went in tae Ciarán Friel this morning. Ah went in and ah said to him you're going and ye'll not be back. Ah said ye'll never be back to thon shithole. That's what ah said to him. As if you'd be bothered with the place.'

The driver blasted the horn and shouted out the door. 'Are youse coming or are youse going?'

Maeve's mam let go and rubbed tears from her eyes before roaring back at him. 'She's coming, and you'll houl yer horses if ye know what's good fer ye.' The driver shrank back in his seat as Maeve's mam turned back to her. 'Wan last thing,' she said, wiping her nose on her sleeve. 'You're not named after yer grandmother, ye know.'

Maeve remembered little of Granny Murray. A smell of mints, the flick of her watery grey eyes out the window, the thin ash stick she kept by her chair for swatting her dogs and grandchildren when they got on her nerves.

'She was a sour oul bitch. Happiest day of my life was when we buried her,' her mam said, grimacing. Maeve's heart clenched as she realised her mam was trying to smile. 'I named you for Queen Maeve. Warrior Queen of Connacht. You look her up. She gave Ulster hell in her time. They buried her standing up, on a hill, facing her enemies.'

Swallows flicked above their heads, scooping air from the sky, days away from migration.

Then her mam turned on her heel and walked away.

Maeve wiped her nose on her coat and boarded the bus. The driver grumbled as he nipped her ticket, no longer cowed now that her mam was gone. Maeve stumbled down the aisle and collapsed into an empty seat. The doors closed and an alarm sounded as the bus began to back out of the parking space. Maeve gazed at the tearful families waving outside. Her mam was smoking a fag over by the river wall, staring into the water. Maeve slid down in her seat and tucked her face into her fleece, her heart breaking.

Suddenly there was a loud batter on the door. The driver braked hard. 'What the fuck?'

There was another, more insistent batter on the door. The driver hit a button and it opened. 'D'ye have a ticket?'

The front of the bus dipped to the left with the weight of someone climbing on board.

'Maeve Murray. Where are ye?'

Maeve sat up and put her hand in the air like she was back in school. Fidelma Hegarty nodded at her, thrust her ticket at the bus driver, then shoved her way down the aisle. She dropped a single bag beside Maeve's feet and sat down with a puff. Maeve caught the reek of cider off her breath. 'Ah ran in tae Marty No-Pegs in the Clock bar there. Nearly forgot meself.'

'Where are you going?'

Fidelma eyed Maeve with her is-it-pure-stupid-you-are? face on her. 'Ah'm headed to London, just the same as you. Fed up of this place, so ah am.' Then she leaned in close to Maeve and whispered, 'Ah'm away tae join the police.'

Maeve wiped some cider-sweet slabbers off her ear and laughed. 'That is fucken deadly, Fidelma. No better woman.'

'Tell me this. Do they have toilets on this frigger?'

'They do. Down the back.'

'Grand job.' Fidelma bent down and opened her sports bag and took out two tins of scrumpy. Maeve accepted a tin, which hissed in relief when she cracked it open. She held it out towards Fidelma and said, 'Sláinte.'

'Ach. Fuck that oul shite, Maeve. It's cheers from here on in.'

They clashed tins, then guzzled the warm cider as the bus carried the pair of them closer and closer to the grimy pavements of London.

Acknowledgements

I am forever grateful to:

The Arts Council of Ireland, without whose backing I would not have finished this book.

Mehdi, Rónán and Cillian, who gave me time to write and rewrite and space to think and rethink.

Super-agent Marianne Gunn O'Connor and my amazing editors Betsy Gleick and Becky Walsh, whose feedback and wisdom helped me whittle a sprawling manuscript into the book you're holding today.

The wonderful teams at John Murray Press and Algonquin Books, especially Sara Marafini, Alice Herbert, Grace Brown, Mae Zhang McCauley, Stephanie Rene Mendoza, Lauren Moseley and Fiona McDonnell.

Charlie and Mary, Úna, Christine, Mickey, Deci and Pauline for more than I can say.

Tina and Cinta for training me up and calming me down the summer of '95.

Brideen, Julie-Anne, Karen, Carey, Fleur, Clare, Russell, Anja, Sorsh, Roni, Tom and Brendan for the moral support on WhatsApp and IRL throughout several lockdowns.

Declan Gallen, Fiona O'Rourke, Marianne Lee, Julie-Anne Graham, Fabi Santiago and Graeme McNabb for reading extracts and/or the entire manuscript and providing critical feedback.

Fellow misfits – Charlene, Fiona, Marianne, Lisa, Olivia and Sheila – for inspiration and motivation via Zoom and text.

The staff of St Patrick's Primary School and St Eugene's

High School, especially Maureen Kelly for putting stars in my eyes, Danny Glackin for keeping things chill and Colette Rush for art and colour during even the dullest, wettest school week.

Early champions Maria McManus and Patsy Horton (who have continued to provide support and advice long after their Arts Council funding ran out), and the Irish Writers Centre and Anthony Glavin for kickstarting my publishing career at the Irish Novel Fair.

Michelle Sally-Lower for informal legal advice.

Dolly Parton for reminding me we've got dreams they'll never take away.